CURSES AND CRIMES

KATE SPARKES

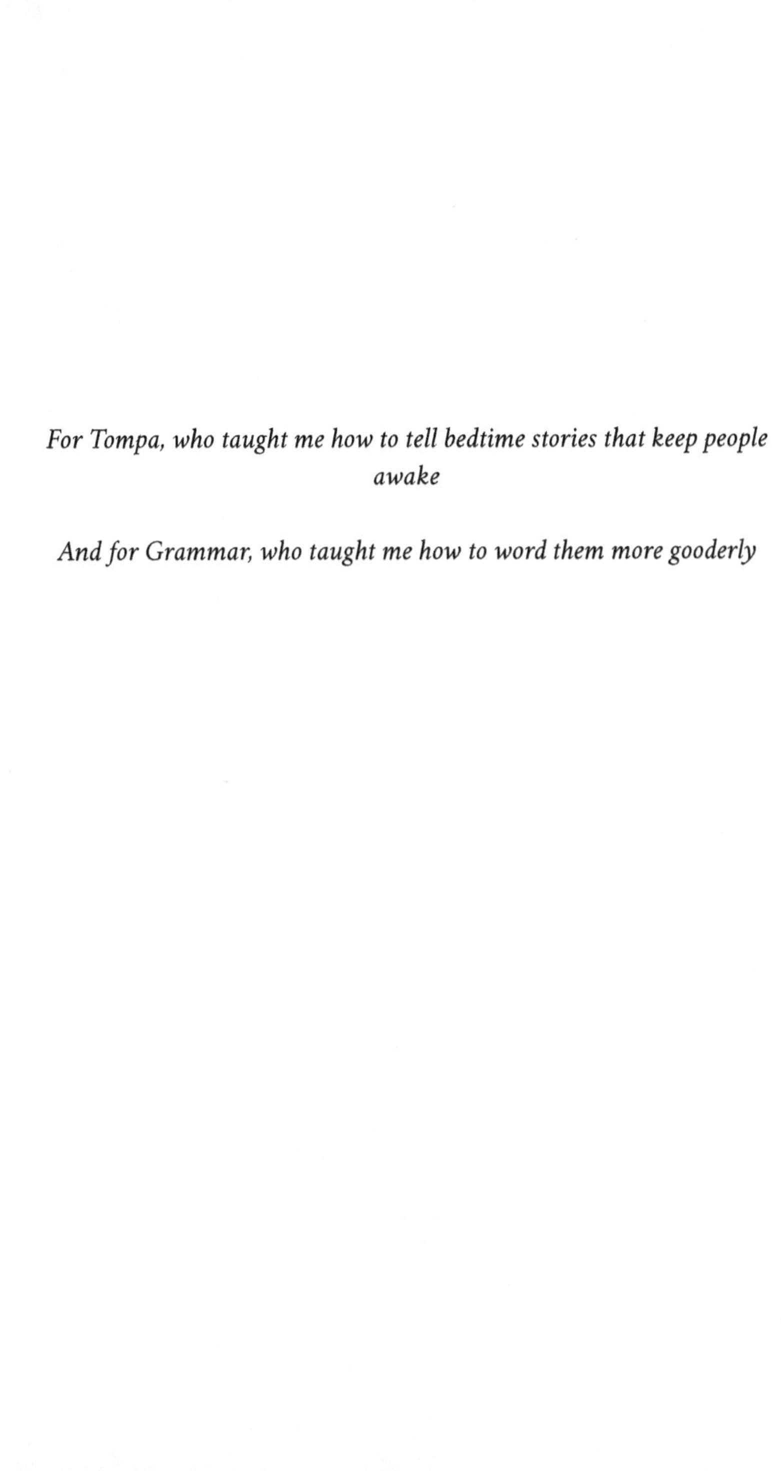

For Tompa, who taught me how to tell bedtime stories that keep people awake

And for Grammar, who taught me how to word them more gooderly

AN ADEQUATE MAP OF
ANDONIA
NORTHERN MOUNTAINS
GRENALIS
EMBERCLIFFE
CHAIN LAKES
QUEEN'S RUN
BLISS GROVE
WESTERN MOUNTAINS
GREENHAVEN
KARDAV
N
W
E
S

PROLOGUE

TEN YEARS AGO

THE WORLD RETURNED to life with every step Gale put between herself and the dead witch's cabin.

Two years of blight and famine had left her village and the mountain forests that surrounded it starving. Dying. Now the curse was broken, and as she and her brother Hawk had walked home, ferns had sprouted around their feet, leaves had burst forth on the trees, and the woods had filled with birdsong that had been absent for too long.

But Gale walked with her head down, focusing on the squish of newly fertile soil beneath her too-large boots as she and her big brother crossed Mister Coldstream's wheat field.

Almost home. Mama. Papa. Home.

Home.

It was all her seven-year-old mind could handle, so it was all she allowed herself to think. Even questioning why her heart didn't leap at the thought of seeing her parents again was too much.

Hawk took her hand and pulled her forward. "Almost there, little bird. We're going to be heroes for killing that witch, you know."

Gale glanced up at him. He was still skeleton-thin and too pale, just as he'd been when Father had taken them into the woods and left them there. Though Gale had been just as gaunt when they'd left home, she'd gained back every stolen ounce as she'd eaten at the witch's table, and her skin glowed tan and healthy from long days in a bountiful garden that hadn't been touched by the curse.

A flash of laughing eyes came into Gale's mind.

Don't think of her.

She focused instead on Hawk's words and tried to make the word *hero* in her mouth, just to try it on and see how it fit her.

It tasted bad.

Hawk deserved to be called a hero. Not her.

The shocking green of the fields, the riot of life and noise and God-given goodness that had sprouted around them since the witch's death were all the proof Gale needed that he'd been right to want to kill the witch.

And Gale had been wrong to trust her. To eat at her table. To embrace her as a guardian after their own parents had placed the siblings in God's hands when there was no food left for them at home.

Her throat closed at the thought, choking her.

I'm glad to go home, she told herself, desperate to believe it. *Mother and Father will be pleased.*

The curse is broken. God's will has been done. We are heroes.

Bright Hollow would be in view soon, past these sprawling fields, cradled in its sheltered space on the mountainside.

It had been a sour, dull place when they'd left. No snow forts this past winter, no dances, no candies and songs, no candles in the windows to chase the darkness away on the longest night of the year. But maybe now, if enough folks had survived, it would be like before. Classes in the big schoolhouse. Harvest festivals. Friends playing in the streets.

Gale's chin trembled as she forced herself to take in everything around her, to make it all fit what she remembered from before the curse.

For Gale, the world had changed. Her time with the witch, with magic, had made it different. Where once she'd seen and heard and felt and tasted and smelled, now there was something else she experienced beyond those natural senses.

Magic. Not everywhere. Not here. But it had been present in patches of the land as she and Hawk walked home, in the new forest plants and the animals that fed on them. She was glad to find there wasn't any magic near Bright Hollow, though its loss made her feel strangely empty. In the woods near the witch's home it had sung, called, teased, beckoned.

Sinful. Corrupting. Vile. The words Hawk had whispered to her when they lay in the loft of the witch's cabin echoed in her mind. He'd tried to warn her. She hadn't listened.

It hurt to remember magic flowing through her body, a river of warmth and light.

It hurt to think something so lovely could be so bad.

She cursed the land and Bright Hollow. The curse ended when she died. I was wrong. Wrong.

Someone shouted—a man's voice, high and reedy. Across the field a thin figure in a grey shirt and bib overalls ran toward them, waving his straw hat in one hand. Mister Coldstream. One of Bright Hollow's farmers.

Someone had survived. There would be others. Mother and Father, if God had willed that they live out the curse. The Luminary, surely, waiting to hear the story of their victory over evil.

Gale fought the urge to turn and run away. It wasn't sensible, and Mister Coldstream would think it odd if she was afraid to go home.

Besides, there was nowhere to run back to anymore, even if she'd wanted to go. The witch was dead, the cabin burned.

Hawk slowed and turned her to face him. "We need to get our story straight. I swear I won't tell anyone what you did." He crouched slightly, placing his eyes at her level. "I'll protect you, Nightingale. No one needs to know."

Gale scrunched up her face to keep tears back as Hawk's words broke through the dam she'd built around her memories.

The sleeping potion, perfectly made. Madrigal would have been so pleased to know how her student had used proper magic, but it had to be a secret.

Madrigal collapsing to the floor, her golden curls spread out around her as the potion subdued her magical protections enough to make her fall asleep.

Hawk's knife, hidden in his belt, then pressed to her throat.

Madrigal's eyes opening, meeting Gale's. Widening. Understanding.

Gale's breath hitched, and she pinched herself to call her mind back to the present.

She tried to answer Hawk, but words wouldn't come no matter how badly she wanted to speak.

Hawk nodded. "Probably better if you let me talk for the both of us. I'll say we worked together, that we both defeated the witch and ended the curse, that it was *our* plan. The two of us, all along."

Gale wanted to ask what would happen if anyone found out about her sin, but it didn't matter. Hawk knew best. He'd proved it, and he'd keep his word. All she had to do now was follow him back to town, learn how to be a better girl, and forget.

The garden. The cabin. The warm fire. Secret lessons. Fresh rosemary bread.

The knife. The blood pooling on the floor, staining it the colour of death.

"Ready to go home, little bird?" Hawk asked, raising an arm to wave back to Mister Coldstream.

The farmer continued toward them, calling their names.

Gale's legs trembled. She sank to her knees and sobbed as though she would never stop, telling herself it was because she was so happy to be home.

CHAPTER ONE

GALE CREPT THROUGH THE HOUSE, avoiding every creaky board in the well-worn floors, and took her warmest coat from its hook by the door. She'd left a reed basket packed with glass jars on the floor there last night, and collecting it without making too much noise was a simple operation.

She had the door halfway open before her mother's voice stopped her.

"Nightingale, where in God's world are you going?"

Gale winced and turned back toward the kitchen doorway, where her mother stood with a steaming cup of tea in her hands. One of Gale's blends, no doubt, made from dried herbs she'd grown in the garden or collected from the woods. Mother's greying chestnut hair was still tied up in rags, and she wore her old, cream-coloured robe over her nightdress.

Gale held up her basket and smiled. "Thought you were still in bed, didn't want to wake you. I came up with an idea last night and wanted to collect a few things."

Her mother raised a dark eyebrow. "Now?"

"Has to be early in the day if I'm to get what I want. Don't worry, I'll be back in plenty of time."

Her mother crossed the little sitting room and ran her fingers through Gale's tangled hair. "Better be sure it is plenty. You've got some cleaning up to do before the ceremony."

"I know. I will."

She pulled away from her mother's touch, and the lines around the older woman's eyes deepened as she held back whatever she felt about it.

"Did you say your morning prayers?"

Gale's smile faltered. "Of course."

"Good."

They stood awkwardly for a few moments, Gale shifting from one foot to the other, her mother standing with the calm grace trained into every acolyte who walked the Path.

"I should go."

Her mother offered a serene smile. "May God go with you and guide your steps. You have your watch?"

"Of course." Gale slipped a hand into the pocket of her heavy skirt to double-check. The simple pocket watch had been a gift for her seventeenth birthday, a sign of her new adulthood and the responsibilities that would soon come with it.

Gale ducked out the door, closed it tight behind her, and descended the wooden steps to the street.

The sun had barely begun to show its face over the eastern horizon, and much of Bright Hollow still lay in shadow, awaiting its light and warmth. It would be a lovely day. Spring had come early this year, and the old trees that grew between the brightly painted wooden houses and shops already bore fully grown leaves in a dozen shades of green that waved in the gentle breeze. But nights always grew cold on the mountainside. Smoke rose from the fieldstone chimneys on most of the houses in town, rising over their sharply pitched slate roofs and warming the homes' inhabitants. Gale pulled her coat tighter against the frosty chill that lingered in the air and wished she were still in her cozy bed under the open rafters of her room.

As she walked over the flat stones of the road that curved toward the forest, she muttered the prayers she'd skipped that morning in her hurry to get out of the house. She preferred praying through her activities, anyway. Sincere, but informal. Speaking to a friend instead of following a formula.

"God grant me safety and success, if it be your will. God grant me strength to see your will done." She paused. "And God, please let everything go well later, and—"

"Good morning, dear!"

Gale turned toward the cheerful voice. Marigold Hallowtree leaned out the window she'd opened at the bakery, and Gale stepped closer without meaning to, drawn by the scents of fresh pastry, cherry preserves, and the mouth-watering sweetness that wafted out.

"Good morning to you, Marigold. You're up and about early today."

"I was going to say the same to you." Marigold beamed down at her. She wore her multitude of long braids tied back beneath a brightly patterned scarf, and her umber skin shone from the heat of her ovens. "Big day. I'd have expected you to be busy dressing before you meet up with the others."

"I will be soon enough." Gale held up the reed basket she had slung over one arm. The glass jars inside clanked together. "Just going out to gather a few things for River."

Part of the appeal of going out early to do her gathering was avoiding questions like these, but not every day was a lucky one.

Marigold clucked her tongue. "For little Alder, I suppose?"

Gale's smile tightened. She wasn't surprised that Marigold had heard about Storm bringing her toddler son to the clinic about a strange rash on his chest last week, or River being unable to find a treatment in any of his books or in the depths of his experienced healer's mind even as the condition worsened.

Everyone knew everyone else's business in Bright Hollow. They shepherded each other, kept their brothers and sisters walking the Path in the light of God's will. Darkness hid secrets. Sin. The fact that Gale kept her own secrets cloaked in shadow only showed how deeply her time with the witch had scarred her.

"For Alder," she agreed. "Best be on my way."

Marigold's brow creased. Gale supposed she'd been hoping for more details, but the disappointment vanished quickly.

"Wait!" Marigold ducked away from the window and returned with a tart cradled in a white cotton handkerchief. "Take this. It'll fortify you for your journey, and for the ceremony later." She grinned at Gale, eyes shining. "Hard to believe our smallest hero is a grown woman already. I suppose you'll be declaring for medicine?"

And there, the expectant, wide-eyed look. Waiting for information she'd no doubt pass along to someone else as soon as the next batch of tarts was out of the oven. Anyone else Gale met would have done the same, though most without offering such a pleasant gift in return.

Gale accepted the treat, which steamed in the cool morning air and warmed her fingers. The smell was downright intoxicating, and her mouth watered. "I am, and thank you."

No one was required to speak publicly about what they'd declare their intentions to be at the placing ceremony, but in her case it was hardly a secret. Gale had finished her schooling and done her rotation through a number of jobs in town, seeking God's will for her life, but she'd known as soon as she'd mixed her first medicine where her future would lie. She'd kept on at the clinic even as she completed her other jobs, unable to stay away from what called to her, and had already taken the healer's oath.

She'd had doubts about many things in her life, but never about what she would declare as her place on the Path. It was God's will. All that was left was for the Luminary to confirm it at the ceremony.

Gale waved goodbye and continued up the street, leaving

Marigold to her tarts and breads. She had declared her intention to become a baker back when Gale was too young to understand such things—before the blight and the famine, before all of it. And like the hundreds of other adults in Bright Hollow she seemed perfectly contented with her life.

River was the perfect healer, calm and wise and comforting. Her parents had both become acolytes before they decided to marry, following their passion for knowledge and deciphering God's will. Folks became parents when God willed it, either by nature or by making the dreaded trip to Queen's Run to adopt children and save them from the outside world. Every person fit into the quiet little community like a piece in a puzzle. The same had been true for Hawk when he'd become a hunter, and Gale's heart raced at the thought that she'd find peace and certainty in her God-given purpose.

Bright fingers of sunlight cut through the leaves of the big elm on the corner as Gale passed, eating the scrumptious cherry tart in four bites as she walked. She'd thought the old tree was doomed during the blight that had stolen the life from field and forest alike, but it had come back just as surely as everything else had.

What had been broken had been made new. At least, much of it had. So many good people had died of hunger and the sicknesses that came with it. Elders first, often under circumstances that made folks wonder whether they'd sacrificed themselves to leave more food for others. Then children and those already ill had started dying, and even healthy adults. Large families became small, either because of death or because, like Gale and Hawk, the children were abandoned on the mountainside, set into God's hands when their parents and community could no longer care for them.

The curse had hit hard and fast, sparing no one.

No wonder the town had called her and Hawk heroes for ending it by killing the witch responsible. The title was quite grand, as long as Gale didn't think too much on how little she felt she deserved it.

She continued through town, past the clinic and into the forest, kicking up leaves once she left the neatly tended streets of Bright Hollow. Over the past few years, she'd worn a path up the side of the mountain here, and it pleased her. It marked the way to her land, chosen by her and granted by the Luminary and the town as thanks for her heroism. She already had a fine cabin and a massive garden full of vegetables and medicinal herbs laid out there in her mind.

Not like hers, though, she thought. *Not enchanted, no "candies" on the walls.*

She brushed the thought away as soon as it surfaced. It was habit now—think something good of that time with the witch, then crush the thought back down to nothing before she could feel something other than anger toward her. For years after she and Hawk had broken the curse, she'd pinched her arms to punish herself for remembering the warmth, the kindness, the garden... Double or triple pinches for feeling sad about what they'd done in the end. She'd long since abandoned the pinching, having gained enough self-control to school her thoughts toward more proper things.

It was good to hate the witch for her lies and her dreadful curse. It was better not to think of her at all.

But today she'd need to open the door on that closed room in her mind and remember the witch's teachings. Learning magic from her had been wrong, but conventional methods weren't working. The medicine itself wouldn't require magic to prepare it, only knowledge of how natural things might react if prepared in unconventional ways. Surely God wouldn't object to using wisdom from a corrupted source to do some good, as long as Gale didn't corrupt own soul in the process.

For little Alder's sake, she reminded herself. She didn't know if the medicine she was planning would work, but it would be a sin to not try.

"Curious creatures," Gale said aloud, her voice echoing the strong cadence of the witch's. Hazel eyes rimmed in thick lashes flashed through her mind, bright with pleasure as her young student listened eagerly to her teachings. "During the day, they hide deep in holes they make in the oak tree, but if you can catch them before the sun's chased them away…"

"Enough," she said, answering her own voice, shutting away the memory.

Every kindness had been a lie, and every lesson had led Gale toward magic that had scarred her soul. Remembering more of that morning in the woods, of the witch praising her for understanding the lesson, of the temptation to learn more, could only tempt her to anger now.

The old oak stood on Gale's land, its heavily leafed branches reaching wide around it, shading the ground and creating a clearing around its roots. Gale pulled a glass jar from her basket, then dug her fingers into a crevice in the tree's rough bark and tugged, revealing the living wood beneath.

Half a dozen whitelings froze in alarm, round bodies like banded ivory shields hiding the dozens of tiny legs beneath, antennae pressed to the wood. Each of the bugs was as large as a copper coin. Before they could scurry for shelter Gale slipped a finger beneath one and popped it free of its moorings, flicking it into the jar. Another followed, then a third, before the others realized they'd be better off running for cover.

Gale watched the trio scuttling around the bottom of the jar for a moment before closing it and setting it back in her basket.

"We must be mindful of what and why we kill," the witch's voice continued, rising like a ghost from the depths of Gale's memory. "It must be with purpose, whether we take plant or animal. Death is a part of life, sacrifice made for benefit. Never shy away from it, but never take it lightly."

And how many lives did you take with your curse, Gale asked the memory, *even as you were offering me that lesson?*

No answer came, but the witch's voice fell silent, and that was enough.

But the lesson itself had been a good one. These little creatures would die so their bodies could become medicine. Not what they would have chosen for themselves, surely, but a necessary action. Gale would have to come up with an explanation for where the idea had come from, though. It wouldn't do to tell River or anyone else exactly how much or how enthusiastically she'd learned about potions and magic during her time with the witch if she didn't want them to shun her for that long-ago sin.

Hawk had kept the promise he'd made her when they returned home all those years ago. Not one person in Bright Hollow knew that Gale had befriended their enemy, and no one knew she'd taken magic into herself to make the potion that had put the witch to sleep and dulled her power, leaving her defenceless against Hawk's blade.

And if God was willing, they never would.

A change in the air caught Gale's attention. She froze like a deer that had spotted a wild dog in the woods. The shift wasn't in a sound, sight, or smell, but something else.

There.

It was that feeling, the one she'd grown so accustomed to during their month at the witch's house but had rarely felt since Hawk had set the body aflame. Something like distant music that she felt rather than heard, that echoed through her at a level deeper than her body or her mind.

It brought the familiar temptation to take into herself power that wasn't meant for humans. There had been a time when Gale had known only what the Teachings said about magic, and as a young child the thought of blackened, rotting souls had given her nightmares. Now that she'd experienced the true nature of magic, it beckoned to her, still terrifying, but unspeakably beautiful.

Gale knew she should turn away and shut the feeling out just as she did her memories of the witch, but surely it would be better to discover its source.

A hare emerged from the underbrush, apparently unaware of her presence. It was a rangy old thing, thin after the long winter, brown as a spring hare should be but with eyes like glass marbles, their brown traced through with shimmering gold and green. The feeling grew stronger as the hare approached.

Gale's breath came quick and shallow as everything but the hint of magic the animal carried faded from her perception. She tried to shut it out, but the magic drew her in. Her body ached for it, her skin itched, her mouth went dry.

The hare moved closer, still oblivious to her presence.

The animal had lived a long life on the side of the mountain, probably feeding on plants that carried the energy Gale felt faintly on her own land. Gale wondered what the witch would have thought of this, whether she'd have taken the hare's eyes to create a potion to feed her own power or—

A low whistle interrupted her thoughts, and the hare fell dead, an arrow lodged in its chest. Gale squeezed her eyes closed, willing herself to un-know the call of magic. Letting Hawk see her desire for it would expose something dark and shameful that she'd long since convinced him she'd left behind.

"Morning, Hawk."

Her brother emerged from a dense patch of undergrowth, grinning bright as the sun as he brushed his thick hair back from his face.

Facing him was always like looking into a distorted mirror. So much had changed since their childhood. Hawk was a man of twenty-one now, already with a wife and an infant son. But the physical similarity that had made folks call them off-twins as children hadn't changed—the earth-brown hair that he wore short and she long, the thick brows, the upward curve of their lips and the pale blue of the eyes they'd both inherited from their mother. And beyond the physical, they shared much in experience and memory that no one else could ever understand. Their terrible adventure as children had made them more like halves of a whole than a sister and brother.

At least, most of the time. As long as they avoided speaking of magic, murder, and corruption, it was easy to pretend everything was as perfect and sweet as one of Marigold's pies.

"Morning, Gale." Hawk slung his bow over his shoulder and grinned. He was dressed for the hunt in leather trousers to protect him from prickling brush, with knives hanging from his belt and boots that covered him to his knees. "What brings you out so early?"

"Same as you, I suppose. Different sort of hunt." She fished the jar out of her basket and held it out for Hawk to examine.

He held the jar close to his face, squinting, and handed it back. "My prey will taste better in a stew."

"No doubt." Gale looked down at the hare, which stared blankly up at the forest canopy, the light gone from its marbled eyes. If Hawk noticed the oddity, he didn't comment on it as he snatched the body up.

Gale considered asking for the eyes.

The longer she thought about it, the more she wanted them. Her heart pounded and her fingers curved into hooks, ready to snatch the hare away from Hawk and run. She wouldn't use the magic. Couldn't. But she could keep the body close, letting the perfection of its lingering power flow through her like—

No. Never again.

She'd met magic like this in the woods before and had never given in to the temptation to claim it for herself. Surprises like this one only made her stronger, and for that she was grateful to the hare, and to God for allowing its presence.

"Gale? All well?"

Gale forced her hands to relax and smiled up at Hawk. "All well. How's Frost? How's Fox?"

"Oh, fine. She's tired, he never wants to sleep." Hawk picked up the hare's limp body and slung it from his belt. "She said to thank you for that balm you prepared. She said, and I quote, *that girl's got a gift, my nipples feel as though there's never been a precious little monster gnawing at them.*"

Gale laughed. "Tell her to talk to me when he starts teething, we might need to find something stronger."

"I will." His eyes shone with laughter, too, and perhaps relief. He hid it well, but Gale knew how he worried about every little thing when it came to his wife and son. "Big day today. Are you ready?"

Gale rolled her eyes. "No, dear brother, I'd completely forgotten about deciding how I want to spend the rest of my life."

Hawk grinned and reached out to ruffle her hair. Gale ducked away, and they turned to walk back toward town. She paused along the way to gather curled fern heads, false binberry leaves, and the buds of a wild rose. None would be useful for Alder, but she'd dry them to add to a blemish treatment for herself and a salve for her mother's arthritic fingers.

"You're certain about your choice?" Hawk spoke casually, but it would have been impossible to ignore the weight of the meaning behind his words.

Gale pressed her lips together and silently prayed for forbearance. "Certain as I've been since I first tested the job. Why?"

Hawk placed a hand on her arm, and Gale turned to him, her heart speeding up as she realized where the conversation was headed.

Let him say it and then it's done.

"I'm concerned," he said.

"Don't be. Hawk, I need to go." She started walking again, knowing he'd fall silent when they got back to town. He wouldn't so much as whisper her secrets where anyone might hear.

He fell in beside her, the hare swinging against his leg. "This isn't the right job for you. I know you're passionate, I know you're talented. But given your history—"

"Given my history, it might be perfect," she replied. Rude to cut him off, but it was a conversation that deserved to be abbreviated where possible. "I'm good at medicine. The witch lied to us about many things, but she was right about my potential."

Hawk's lips narrowed at the mention of the witch, but Gale pressed on.

"I know things even River doesn't, and my mind is quick to learn what he has to teach. I'll serve the town well as his apprentice and as a healer."

Hawk cleared his throat softly and nodded. "I know. And it would be a loss to us all if you chose a different position. But healing, working with plants and medicines and such? Gale, it's a gateway back to all you left behind when we escaped. The draw you felt toward magic there, the temptations you suffered…"

"Are behind me, thanks much." They'd reached the road by the clinic. Gale brushed a stray patch of last autumn's leaves aside with her toe, revealing the pattern of flat stones that interlocked like the lives of everyone in Bright Hollow. "I know in my heart what my place is. I respect your opinions, but this is between me and the Luminary."

"I know it." Hawk's voice had gone low. "I only ask because I care. The best way to resist temptation is to keep it out of one's sight, isn't it?"

Gale shrugged. "Maybe."

Hawk had voiced this concern before, but not recently, and not so forcefully. It was the wedge that pushed them apart when other aspects of their history pulled them together. She wanted to speak to him about her plans for her life—not only her job but the home she planned to build here in the woods, close enough to be of service but far enough from town that she wouldn't feel as trapped as she did beneath their parents' roof, careful with every word and every step not to let her soul-deep scars show.

She often imagined her little cottage with a thriving garden and big windows where she could watch the seasons change, and enjoyed secret dreams of a beautiful huntress coming upon the cabin and stopping in for a meal only to fall madly in love with the local healer. She wished she could share all of it with the only person who had truly known her for the past ten years—the one who kept her secrets, who protected her from the consequences of her mistakes.

But what would Hawk make of those dreams? Of her wanting to create a pale, permissible version of the place he'd seen as their prison and she had thought of as her home, or of her need to live outside of Bright Hollow's pleasant confines just so she felt like she could breathe?

He'd say she'd gone mad for sure. That the witch's enchantments were still on her, that her ongoing sin was making her shy away from the openness and accountability of their community.

It will be fine, she told herself. *As soon as I have the Luminary's blessing, he'll see that I'm strong enough, that I can do the work that speaks to my soul without straying from the Path.*

"I don't want to see you in trouble again," Hawk said. He spoke carefully, as he might to a spooked animal.

"I know." Gale made herself smile, though her patience was wearing as thin as it had ever been with him. "And I know you're only keeping the promise you made me when we came home, when you said you'd keep me safe."

He'd spared her a lifetime of loving restrictions and observation, let her join him in being nothing but a hero, the stain on her soul hidden. No matter how annoying his concern for her became, she'd always be grateful for that.

"But?" he asked.

"But I've lived with this for a decade. I've grown up and learned to keep myself within the bounds of what's right and good. I can take care of myself now."

She thought again of the hare's eyes, and with the thought felt their seductive power reaching for her. She ignored them and their magic, as she would any other temptation that came across her path.

I am strong enough, she reminded herself. *I am scarred, but not broken.*

In the distance, the first bells of the morning rang out from the clock in the centre of town. Gale checked her watch. "I'd best be getting home."

Hawk nodded, but he still looked troubled. "I'll see you at the ceremony." Then, as she stepped away, he spoke again. "Gale?"

"Hawk, I really need to go."

"I know." He cleared his throat. "I—never mind. Go on. I'll see you at the ceremony."

Gale let out a huff of breath and took off running. On a less important day, she'd have pried, asked why he was being so strange, so unlike his usual forward, open self. But today there wasn't time.

It wouldn't do to be late for the first official day of her adult life.

CHAPTER TWO

GALE LEFT her house at noon and hurried toward the nearby public well, her bare feet slapping against the sun-warmed road and her long white skirt gathered in one hand. Willow and Buttercup were already waiting in the shade of the trees, their pale clothing stark against the shadows. Willow had dressed impeccably, as Gale had expected, in a perfectly tailored dress with a puffed skirt and her dark hair intricately braided at the back of her graceful neck. Buttercup, like Gale, seemed to be wearing clothes passed down from someone else, but his cream-coloured shirt and trousers were light enough to have the proper effect.

Clean. Pure. Blank canvases for God to paint their lives onto.

"Good of you to join us." A long piece of spring grass twitched between Buttercup's teeth as he crossed his arms over his broad chest and grinned at Gale.

Gale resisted the urge to stick her tongue out at him. She, Buttercup, and Willow were adults today, or would be the moment the Luminary confirmed their callings. Starting off the day by acting like children seemed wrong. She punched him in the arm instead, and he winced dramatically.

"I was out gathering medical supplies," she said. "I'm here, aren't I? Dressed and everything." She held the skirt of her plain dress out to one side. It had been in the family for three generations, though it had needed to be let out to accommodate her curves after being fitted to her mother's more slender frame.

Buttercup had pumped a bucket of water from the old well, and Gale took a quick drink from her cupped hands. "Thanks for waiting."

Willow stepped behind her and pulled her fingers through Gale's hair, arranging the heavy mass into something that pleased her critical eye. Willow was the prettiest, most elegant girl in town—Gale had thought so ever since she'd first looked into her black-brown eyes on the first day of school. She was more a princess than the sort of person who belonged in an isolated mountain town, and Gale had always considered herself lucky to be friends with her.

"Let me fix this," Willow said, a smile in her voice. "Can't have you looking wind-blown on such a special day."

Gale shot a beleaguered eyeroll at Buttercup. "Did she fix you already?"

He spat out the grass stem and shrugged. "Didn't need fixing. I'm perfect as I am."

"Or a lost cause," Willow muttered, and Gale pinched back a laugh.

The sky above was a blanket of deep, cloudless blue. The Teachings advised against reading omens, but Gale couldn't help thinking it a good sign for all of them.

Not that any such sign was needed, of course. It was nearly unheard of for the Luminary to deny a blessing for a person who had chosen a career or marriage that would allow them to seek God's will and perform God's work.

"Ready?" Buttercup asked.

"Ready, B," Gale and Willow answered. He'd be called by his full name in the ceremony, but no one his own age had called him

Buttercup to his face since he'd flattened Coyote on the third day of school for laughing at it.

It was a stupid thing to make fun of a person for, anyway. A child was named after whatever element of God's world spoke to its mother after the birth, and Buttercup's mother's labour had come quickly when she was out walking in the meadows. He'd been born on a bed of the bright, hardy flowers.

At least it made for a good story. Gale's own, of being born under the new moon and a nightingale singing out of the darkness as she opened her eyes for the first time was fine, but Buttercup's was far more exciting.

Coyote had been an irritating and occasionally cruel child, but a lump still formed in Gale's throat at the thought of him. It only worsened as she and Willow arranged themselves behind Buttercup, leaving gaping spaces between them as they walked barefoot toward the Great Hall.

Alphabetical order by given name. Buttercup first, then empty spaces left for Coyote, Ivy, and Jay. Gale maintained the distance carefully, just as Willow would for Oak's empty space before she brought up the rear. Their places had been established when they started school, before the famine. It only seemed right to leave room for the imagined ghosts of those who had been sent out into God's hands and never returned.

Buttercup walked with his back straight as a fencepost, his hands clenched at his sides, the skin on the back of his neck flushed. Gale understood his anger. He'd been sent out, as she and Hawk had, but he'd already been well trained by his father as a woodsman. He'd celebrated his birthday alone, and someone had found the scrappy eight-year-old after the famine in a little lean-to he'd built, living off frozen roots and the starving rabbits he trapped.

Few others had been as lucky. More than a dozen sets of parents had chosen to follow the old traditions, sending their offspring out in the belief that it would be God's will to spare them in the wilds when there was nothing left for them at home. Of the fifteen children sent away with the clothes on their backs and the prayers of their families to cover them, only Gale, Hawk, and Buttercup had come home.

Gale imagined the line continuing behind Willow. Younger children who'd had no chance, whose parents had been unable to bear the idea of watching them slowly starve and had instead chosen to leave them to the wolves.

Uncharitable, she thought, and almost pinched herself for it.

The curse had only ended because she and Hawk had been sent out and God had led them to the witch's cabin. Maybe Buttercup would have starved if he'd stayed here at home, along with his parents and his baby sister, who, thanks to his absence, had managed to make it through to better times. Gale could imagine this much being God's will, even if it had taken years for Buttercup to lose the haunted look in his eyes.

But what of those empty spaces in the line? She glanced at the folks they passed as they made their way past shops that had just opened for the day—the tailor, the grocer, the toymaker. Bright smiles at the expected procession of young folks faded as they understood the meaning of the spaces in their line. Several turned away. The barber glared at them red-faced, as though the lost had no place in their hearts anymore. But many smiled sadly, and Blackbird and Wasp Underhill, who had lost Ivy and Oak, each placed a hand over their hearts and lowered their gazes.

There were parents, especially those of the older children who had failed to return, who insisted that their missing children had found new homes and great adventures on the path God set for them. Gale had never known whether Blackbird and Wasp were that sort, but she guessed now that they weren't. They probably still suffered nightmares about what might have ended their children's lives in the woods.

Tears burned her eyes, and when she looked back, she found Willow letting hers flow freely.

If I lived because God saved me, they died because God didn't.

Marigold's cherry tart threatened to come up all over the street, but she held it down.

The Luminary always had an explanation. The famine and the curse were not God's will, so neither were the deaths. God mourned the losses more deeply than human hearts could possibly fathom.

Good thoughts. Comforting ones to some, and enough for most days. But not today. Not when this ceremony should have been twice as long as it would be.

The Great Hall stood at the far end of town, giving folks plenty of time to observe the procession. A few bowed respectfully to Gale. The same had happened when Hawk had passed through on his blessing day.

Most folks treated the siblings as regular citizens these days, but every so often—on the anniversary of their return and the miraculous harvest that had followed the breaking of the curse, or on days like these—an odd sort of remembering came over people. The triumph, but also the loss. The sweet and the bitter. It was always that way, heroism and tragedy, honey mixed with vinegar. The smiles, the eyes shining with tears.

Even as a child, Gale had preferred the days when she was just the acolytes' daughter with leaves in her hair and scabs on her knees. If she was a hero, she'd become one reluctantly, and only after much convincing from Hawk.

But I will be a hero, she reminded herself. *I will save lives. I will become what they think I am.*

The Hall came into view as they rounded the corner past the General Goods store. Volunteers had finished the Hall's annual repainting, and the white wood panels stood out in stark contrast to the U-shaped roof of black slate. Two massive oak trees that had been there longer than the town itself stood at the sides of the building, their inner branches growing through the walls, reaching into the space within and up through the opening in the roof. A pair of tall doors forming an arch stood open beneath a round stained-glass window, and more townsfolk stood at the bottom of the steps to greet them as they passed.

Violet and Sparrow Goodwin, four-year-old twins, looked shyly up at the big kids and handed them freshly picked daisies. Gale crossed her eyes at them as she took her flower and tucked it behind her ear. The twins giggled.

A hard lump formed in Gale's throat as she looked at the people—her community, which felt more like an extended family most days. They had their squabbles and their differences from time to time, but there was too much love here for real darkness ever to take root. Each of these folks fit into their places in Bright Hollow, and now Gale and her friends would take theirs among them.

Buttercup reached the bottom of the five steps and led the way up and through the open doors. Warm sunlight streamed down through the open rooftop, lighting the interior of the Hall and illuminating dust motes that danced through the air in spite of the acolytes' care in preparing for the event. The dark wooden floor and bare plank walls gleamed, and the scents of herbal cleaning solutions and bouquets of fresh flowers filled the air.

Hawk stood inside the doors and shot Gale a pleading look. She kept her eyes ahead.

His concerns would become irrelevant soon enough.

The chairs that so often stood in neat rows in the hall had been removed, leaving only standing room for most of those invited to witness the ceremony. Buttercup's and Willow's families stood to one side near Hawk, and the adults who waited to welcome them to their new careers had arranged themselves on the other, leaving an open aisle down the middle of the big, open room.

The trio of supplicants kept their eyes on the raised dais where the Luminary sat, her long white robes flowing before the legs of her plain wooden chair like the churning waters of the river in spring, her uncut, silver-streaked hair pulled forward over one shoulder.

Buttercup bowed and took his place to the left. Gale followed, bowed, and stood to the right. Willow took the middle spot, standing in order according to their family names.

The Luminary, God's chosen voice to guide God's people and interpret the past Teachings of those following the Path, smiled at them, the gentle care lines around her eyes deepening. Pairs of acolytes in dove-grey ceremonial robes sat on either side of her. Gale glanced at her parents, who both sat to the Luminary's left. Her father beamed at her with pride. Her mother winked.

Gale's heart swelled. The dangers of the past wouldn't be forgotten today. The imagined ghosts of the lost were here and welcome. But there was cause for joy, and she would embrace that as well.

"Welcome," the Luminary said, her voice soft, strong, and resonant. She rose and stepped forward, hands raised in a graceful gesture of blessing. "You enter as children and will leave as adults, ready to continue your journey on the Path with new responsibilities, ready to gain wisdom and knowledge of God's will for your lives and the world. Buttercup Wilder, how do you declare?"

Buttercup stepped forward and knelt on one knee, his head and shoulders covered in the light from the window above as though it were God's own approval shining down upon him. "My desire is to walk the Path as a smith, using the strength of my body to serve the people of Bright Hollow."

The Luminary looked past him. Colt Dearstone, who was both the local blacksmith and Buttercup's uncle, stepped forward. "I accept Buttercup as my apprentice. He showed great promise during his trial visits and has continued with his education in his own time with great passion. I have no doubt this choice falls within the scope of God's will."

The Luminary nodded. "And I agree wholeheartedly. Buttercup, may you be blessed as you step forward as our apprentice blacksmith."

Someone let out a whoop from the back of the room, and Buttercup turned, grinning, before stepping back into his place.

"Willow Redfern, how do you declare?"

Willow stepped forward and knelt, her full skirt pooling around her like a puff of whipped cream. Suitable enough, given what Gale knew of her intentions.

"My desire is to follow in my aunt's footsteps and work in the bakery, nourishing the folks of Bright Hollow."

Marigold, now dressed in a pale blue dress and lacking her usual white apron, stepped forward and accepted in many of the same words as Colt had accepted Buttercup. It was all as expected and as tradition dictated. But happy though she was for her friend, Gale found herself unable to concentrate on what Marigold was saying. The words she herself would speak as she made her declaration were running circles through her mind, distracting her from her friend's special moment.

The Luminary spoke again. "Willow, may you be blessed as you step forward and follow the Path as a baker." She turned to Gale, and her smile faltered. Gale's heart skipped. "Nightingale Goodweather. Have you fully considered and prayed over the manner in which you choose to walk the path, giving thought to your strengths and challenges as well as the needs of your community?"

The wrong words. A break with tradition.

Gale stepped forward, her legs suddenly trembling, and knelt. A soft whisper passed through those gathered behind her who had obviously noticed the deviation.

"I have." At least her voice wasn't shaking.

"And how do you declare?"

Gale's mouth went dry as she thought back over the morning and Hawk's objections. *This isn't the right job for you. I don't want to see you in trouble again.*

"My desire is to continue my studies as a healer and to serve Bright Hollow by using my mind and my hands to ease pain and cure disease."

No one moved or spoke. To Gale's ears it seemed they weren't even breathing.

The Luminary looked down at Gale with what might have been pain, regret, or pity, and didn't look up as River Dellwick stepped forward.

"I accept Nightingale as my apprentice," the healer said. He'd dressed well today, shunning his usual work pants and white cotton shirt in favour of a grey suit, and he'd tamed his thinning strawberry hair. "She's shown incredible promise—a quick mind, an eagerness to learn, and an ability to see past what's been done before to find new ways to help. She's been a dedicated student even during her turns at other jobs. She's taken her oath to heal where it's within her power, without judgement or hesitation." He cleared his throat. "And as you and God are both aware, we're going to need someone to replace me one of these days."

More than he needed to say, but not one word of it would do any good. The Luminary had known her answer before Gale had knelt within the flood of sunlight that suddenly felt colder than it should.

The Luminary's hands tightened around the heavy folds of her robe.

"I'm sorry, Nightingale," she said. "Your declaration does not reflect God's will."

CHAPTER THREE

SILENCE FILLED THE GREAT HALL, heavy and oppressive enough that Gale felt it might crush her. She closed her eyes in the habit of prayer, asking—demanding—that the past few seconds had been a dream. But when she opened them again, she found the Luminary looking down on her with an expression of serenity, the storm-defying calm she was always meant to embody. Gale was no more successful in reading her parents' expressions when she looked to them, schooled as their faces were into placid passivity befitting those who should most perfectly obey the flow of God's will, no matter how unexpected.

Seconds passed, feeling like days, before anyone spoke.

"Your Brilliance," River said, daring to step forward to stand beside Gale. She turned and found him with his hat clutched tight in his hands. "If I was unclear—"

The Luminary held up one hand to silence him. "I understand your acceptance. But the desires and plans of humans must not supersede the true will of God, and it is not God's plan for Nightingale to pursue healing as she walks the Path."

Gale rose to her feet, trying to ignore her pulse pounding and the heat that burned her cheeks. "Perhaps God would be so kind as to enlighten me, then, on what I am meant to do?"

Her parents' mask-like expressions cracked into shock from her mother and a warning look from her father. She ignored them. She'd keep her temper in check but couldn't stay silent. "I've tried every job in this town, every trail I might follow along the Path, and this is the only one that feels right for me."

There was so much more—the way she forgot herself when she was working on a new problem, how her heart swelled when someone she'd helped left the clinic healed or cured, the way overcoming challenges made her feel free in a way she hadn't since she'd been pulled down by secrets and...

Secrets.

Gale's blood cooled within her as she understood what must have happened, and her useless arguments died on her lips.

The Luminary shouldn't know what had really happened during her time with the witch. Hawk had protected her all these years, allowing her the freedom to be seen as a normal child instead of one stained by magic.

Their parents didn't know. There was nothing in the official report.

Until now.

He told.

Gale spun on her heel and searched the shadows until she spotted Hawk standing beside the door. He watched, still as a statue, giving nothing away.

"You may all go," the Luminary said. "I wish to speak to Nightingale alone."

Hawk was the first one out the door. Gale itched to race after him and tackle him from behind, bloodying his nose in the dust outside, demanding answers. But it wouldn't do to disobey. She turned back to the Luminary as the rest of the guests filed out of the Hall.

The acolytes retreated to the back rooms without so much as

a final glance over their shoulders, leaving Gale alone with the Luminary beneath the branches of the oak trees.

"Do you have another option?" the Luminary asked. Her voice was as soft and soothing as Gale had ever heard it, but she found no comfort there.

"None." Gale cleared the lump from her throat. "Healing is the only thing that speaks to me." She considered several other choices—working at the dairy farm, teaching children, tending to a shop—and each idea only made her feel as though the bars of an invisible cage were closing in around her.

It's not because of the magic. Medicine calls me for its own sake.

She'd told herself so many times. True, medicine would allow her to sinlessly work with plants that carried magic in them, as long as she never tried to take it into herself. She'd occasionally felt its faint call as she gathered plants in the forest, and some of those she'd chosen to work with had carried weak magic that made for better medicine.

But God, I won't destroy my soul with it. I promise. Please tell her.

The Luminary's lips tightened.

"Can you tell me why you've denied me my choice?" Gale asked, her voice tight.

"It is not God's will. Do you need more than that?"

I do, Gale thought, but didn't say. It was clear enough. The Luminary knew the truth and considered it too much of a temptation for Gale—and therefore too much danger for the community—for her to get close to magic that would threaten to corrupt not only Gale, but the entire village.

Bright Hollow had trained folks to hunt down witches who dared try to take up residence on their mountain, and Gale knew all too well what had happened the last time they failed to drive one off. They would never risk harbouring anyone who worked magic in their community.

"I accept your judgement," she said, trying to hide the anger that threatened to explode out of her and make everything worse.

What else was there to say? There was no way to argue against the divine being's will as delivered through the Luminary, and no point venting her feelings when it would do as much good as screaming at a wall. "I will consider my other options."

"Good. I will await your decision."

Gale turned to leave.

"Nightingale?"

She turned back and tried not to show her anger. "Yes, Your Brilliance?"

The Luminary tilted her head gently to one side. "It will do no good to carry rage in your heart, against God or anyone else. Understand that it is God's will for you to remain safe and untainted and find your right place on the Path. Choose a future that allows you to do so with ease instead of struggle."

Gale wished her skirt had pockets so she could hide the way her fingers tried to clench into fists. "I will. Thank you."

She bolted from the hall and raced toward the river, to the spot where she and Hawk used to meet to talk when they didn't want their parents to overhear.

She'd do her best not to stay angry at God, but there was someone else who had some answering to do.

CHAPTER FOUR

HAWK STOOD by the shallows at the edge of the river, his back to Bright Hollow. Had she not known him so well, Gale might have thought he was unaware of her approach. But Hawk was, above all things, a hunter—he'd applied himself to improving his tracking skills soon after their return from the witch's house, clearly stung by his failure to find their way home.

Perhaps it had been God's will at the time that they both be unprepared so they could become lost in the forest, find the witch, and end the curse, but Hawk had since taken his life and his skills into his own hands. He didn't miss a sight, sound, or smell when he was hunting, whether it be a fox or a dove or a trespassing witch. Gale had no reason to suspect he was less than completely alert to her approach.

She stalked toward him, fists balled at her sides, her body pulsing with every wave of embarrassment and anger that had been building since the Luminary's denial. She didn't slow before she planted her hands against his back and shoved him hard enough that the river wet the toes of his boots as he stepped forward.

"What did you do?" She tried to keep her voice low but didn't quite manage it.

Hawk turned slowly, his eyes downcast in an apology Gale wasn't prepared to accept. "She needed to know, Gale. The Luminary communicates God's will, but she can't do that properly without all the information."

"You swore you'd never tell." Gale trembled, fighting the urge to shove him again.

Hawk's expression hardened and his voice dropped low. "I only did what you couldn't do for yourself. You know as well as I do that you're still drawn to magic, but you insist on exposing yourself to temptation. You persisted in following a dangerous course, so I did what I had to."

Gale spoke through gritted teeth. "I can take care of myself."

"Can you?" Hawk stepped forward, hands resting on his hips. "I saw how you looked at that hare this morning when you felt the magic in it. I've seen it a dozen other times when you thought I wasn't paying attention. You're acting like a child who can't keep herself from playing with fire."

Gale stepped higher on the riverbank, placing herself closer to eye level and putting space between them. "Fire is a tool," she said, nearly whispering. She wasn't ashamed of her anger, but this part of the discussion had to be private. "I'm smart enough to not get burned."

Hawk shook his head. "You don't even feel the heat of it, do you? I'll tell you what will happen if you pursue medicine as your career. You'll start out fine, controlling your urges, just warming yourself on those flames. Then you'll be tempted to move closer. It will get too hot, but the witch did something to you that makes the fire call to you. You won't realize you're burning until it's too late."

"You're wrong."

"The Luminary agrees with me, so that's that. The only safe course, the only way to ensure you can resist temptation, is to avoid it completely. You should be thankful she was too kind to shame you by saying it in front of everyone."

Tears burned in Gale's eyes, and she blinked furiously to hold them back.

He was right. Not about magic, but about the Luminary. Her decision was as good as final. She could only change her mind if circumstances changed and with them her perception of God's will, and the scars on Gale's soul weren't going to disappear.

Gale had been so close to finding something that offered her a taste of what she craved without letting her be consumed by it, and now that door had been slammed in her face.

And all because Hawk had decided she was still a child, too weak to know what was best for her. All because he'd opened his big mouth and spilled the one secret he'd sworn he'd keep forever.

Then there were no more thoughts. There was only hot rage mixed with the chill of doubt as something deep within her whispered that perhaps he was right—perhaps she was fooling herself into thinking she was strong enough to ignore magic's call forever. That doubt only fuelled her anger. She leapt at him again, shoving him back toward the water, fists flying as she hit his chest and arms.

They'd fought frequently when they were children, tumbling in the yard like puppies, throwing punches over real and imagined injustices. Hawk had always been bigger, and Gale had realized as she grew up that their parents had instructed him to go easy on her. Still, she knew she'd won some of those fights fair and square. Hawk had been a skinny scrap of a boy, and Gale had always had her temper to propel her fists. She'd given up on fighting after he'd become her protector, but any goodwill he'd earned for that had vanished.

"Stop," Hawk ordered.

She didn't. She barely heard him.

"I'm trying to help you." He held his hands up to defend

himself but didn't hit back. Gale wished he would. A tussle like they'd had as children would clear the air. "You refuse to see reason, so I had to step in to protect you. Again."

"You're not our father!" she grunted, still throwing punches that seemed to fall without any effect at all.

He moved more quickly than she could react, grabbing her by the wrists and halting the flurry of punches. She pulled back, but he held tight until she looked into his eyes.

"I'm better than our father," he said. "I'm the only one who knows enough to save you from yourself, who's done it before and isn't afraid to do it again. I could've told the Luminary how bad it really is—how just this morning I saw you catching magic on the wind like a hound scenting a hare, how it lights you up like nothing else I've seen even as it makes me want to run."

A chill passed over Gale's skin, cooling her anger. Her arms fell slack, but Hawk didn't let go. "You can feel it, too?"

He glared down at her. "I can. It's like nettles pressing into my skin."

"That's how you found that last witch so easily."

Gale had nearly put the incident out of her mind—not the witch they'd killed together so long ago, but the last one who had dared settle on the mountainside. The witch had intended to make use of the magic that flowed strongly in so many spots there, not knowing he'd chosen to make his home near a town full of people who followed the Path. Hawk was the youngest of the hunters but had led the group that went out to drive the witch away.

"It is," Hawk said. "I began to feel it after a few weeks at the witch's cabin, but I never told anyone. I didn't want them to know either of us was tainted by it."

Gale gave another tug, but Hawk held tight.

"Are you still angry?" he asked. "Or do I need to dunk you in the river to cool you off?"

Gale bared her teeth at him. "You wouldn't dare."

Hawk's mouth twitched at one corner, and a second later he'd adjusted his grip and hauled her around so her back was to the water. She struggled, kicking her bare feet and scratching with her fingers. He released her arms to catch her around her waist, and despite her efforts she found herself sailing through the air toward the deepest part of the river.

The water, shockingly cold from the snowmelt still flowing down from the peak of the mountain, sucked the breath from her. She kicked, cursing the flowing skirt she wore, and surfaced. By the time she stepped back into the warmer shallows with as much dignity as she could muster, she was shaking but in better control of herself.

Hawk watched as she wrung the water from her hair and skirt and tugged at the clinging fabric that covered her torso, which pulled away with a wet slurp.

"You dared me," he said. Not an apology by any means. Not that Gale would have accepted it if it had been. "Don't pick fights you can't win."

Gale snorted out a bitter laugh. "Of course you'd win this one. You've been allowed to take your scars and turn them into strengths." She glared at him, an ache spreading through her chest. "You felt trapped and hunted by the witch, and you've been allowed to become a hunter in return. You felt weak and have used that to become strong. You found your talents and developed them."

He frowned. "Should I not have?"

Gale stepped onto a patch of grass and wiped the mud from her feet. "Of course you should have. All I wanted was a chance to do the same. I'm good at medicine, Hawk."

"I know." His voice was thick now, heavy with genuine sorrow. "And if the witch hadn't put that enchantment on you, I have no doubt you'd have become a great healer. But I love you too much to see you tempted into the corruption of your soul."

A wailing cry rang out from the direction of the town square and Hawk's gaze sharpened as he scrambled up the river bank, Gale following close behind.

Storm Ashgrove ran through the streets with her red hair flowing like a banner behind her, a large cloth bundle clutched tight to her chest.

Gale's stomach clenched. *Alder.*

"Storm!" she called, running after the distraught woman. Storm turned. It took her a moment, but her eyes widened as she recognized Gale. She hurried over.

"Help me," she begged. Her eyes were bloodshot, her hair wild as tangleweed. "It's Alder. His rash. He went to bed without a fuss last night, but it's spread and now he won't wake up, and—" Her voice caught in her throat as she held the bundle out to Gale.

Gale exchanged a glance with Hawk, who watched intently. For all the anger she still felt, it was good to have him with her. She pulled the blanket back and held in a gasp.

Little Alder, who had been toddling around the clinic hollering at the top of his lungs a week ago, lay pale and silent in his mother's arms. The purple, flaking rash had crept over his throat and chest, leaving weeping abscesses and rotting flesh in its wake, and vein-like purple streaks vining out across his skin.

He wasn't breathing.

Gale closed the blanket and looked to Storm.

"Go to the clinic," she said, forcing herself to speak more confidently than she felt should be possible. "River needs to see to him."

Storm took off running again as though there might be anything a healer could do for her child.

"He's dead, isn't he?" Hawk asked.

"He is." Gale's voice broke. "I couldn't be the one to tell her God had called her boy home. Not out here. River will tell her in private."

Hawk sucked in a hard breath, and Gale wondered whether

he was thinking of his own babe at home. "What was wrong with him?"

"I don't know," Gale said, all thoughts of the morning's events vanishing from her mind as she hoisted her wet skirt up to her knees and started towards the clinic.

They'd seen five cases of the rash since Alder, all of them following a similar course.

If this was the outcome, it didn't matter whether it was God's will for Gale to keep working in the clinic. If God wanted to stop her, God would have to come down and personally bar the doors.

CHAPTER FIVE

THE CLINIC STANK OF SWEAT, excrement, and the putrefaction of flesh. Gale supposed a person could become used to it after a while, but though she'd seen more than fifty cases of the strange rash in the weeks since Alder Ashgrove's death, it had not, by any means, been long enough for Gale.

Young, old, healthy or sick, the strange disease seemed inclined to spare no one. It progressed differently in each body, some quickly and some slowly, but the progression was always the same. Spreading rash, flaking skin, infection, abscess, pain, numbness, fever, delirium.

And thus far, for those in whom the disease had progressed to its end, death. Those with a slower progression were the lucky ones, if having more time to suffer could be considered fortunate.

Gale herself hadn't been affected yet, nor had anyone in her immediate family. It had struck just as deep, though, when Willow had shown up three days past with the tell-tale red rash creeping up her leg.

"How are you feeling?" Gale asked as she sat on the edge of Willow's bed. Her friend's dark hair stood out against the white sheets and skin that appeared deathly pale in the flickering flame of the few lamps that lit the clinic each night.

"You tell me." Willow gave her a shaky smile as Gale wiped the sweat from her brow. It was too early for the fever, but her skin was warm.

Gale swallowed back the lump in her throat. "You're going to be fine. You just need rest and the medicine River and I are working on."

"Just like everyone else has been fine, right?" Willow took a shaky breath.

Gale squeezed her hand. "Hold on. We'll have you back to baking cakes in no time."

"I'll make you the biggest one ever if you make this go away." Willow closed her eyes and looked away. "Go on. You've got lots of people to see to, and I'm not going anywhere."

Gale fixed the blankets and left Willow to rest, pausing to scrub her hands with harsh soap. The sickness didn't seem to spread by touch or by breath, but she, River, and the others volunteering to care for the sick were taking every precaution.

She dragged her stool toward the next bed and pressed a cold, wet cloth to Cotton Highgrove's wrinkled forehead. His eyes rolled, showing the whites all around, and he grabbed her with one bandaged hand. Gale fought the instinctive urge to pull away.

"Tend to the younger ones," he breathed.

"I am," she promised, smiling as reassuringly as she could. "But we're not ready to let you go just yet either."

He grunted and closed his eyes. Gale wasn't sure whether he was sleeping or had slipped into unconsciousness. He was breathing, though, and for now that had to be enough.

She unwound the bandages that covered the lower portion of his left leg and gritted her teeth to keep from gagging. Skin and liquefied fat pulled away with the bandages, leaving exposed muscle beneath. She'd tended to injuries that left such tissues open to the air before, but that had been nothing like this—healthy tissue should be red and angry about its exposure.

Healthy muscle should bleed.

The insides of Cotton's leg were dead, wet and black and carrying the stench of the grave. The rash had appeared on his right foot, too, though it hadn't eaten in as badly there.

River peered over her shoulder and sighed.

"It has to come off, hasn't it?" Gale asked without looking up at him. She already knew what she'd see in the healer's eyes—the exhaustion, the resignation, the determination to save as much of a citizen as he could.

"Looks like," he whispered. "Let him rest for now. Take a break. I need to speak with you."

Gale covered the wounds with the old bandages. A few citizens had been brave enough to volunteer to care for their sick family members and had stayed on after their deaths, changing bandages and applying whatever new salves River and Gale wanted to try. They'd take care of him.

Gale shut out the groans of the sick as she walked through the clinic. The long, open room that had once held four examination beds surrounded by privacy curtains was now stuffed with twenty cots crowded in next to each other against the wood-panel walls, with space left only around River's office door and the wood stove in the corner. The beds, most of which had been hastily built or brought from the homes of generous citizens, were reserved for the most serious cases. If River managed to slow the rate of death but not the number of new infections, they'd have to start bedding folks down in the storage room and on the back porch.

The only people who had recovered were those who'd consented to having the offending limbs lopped off along with a good portion of healthy flesh to make sure all the danger had been removed. And as two of today's new cases had proved, the disease was happy to return once they'd left the clinic and returned to their homes.

People were falling ill in every part of Bright Hollow. At first there seemed to be a pattern with it moving through families, so measures were taken to protect those who came into contact with the sick from becoming infected. But it didn't help, and the pattern soon proved false. Folks who worked together might or might not share the illness, and one member of a family might die while others remained entirely unaffected. River, who lived at the clinic and spent every moment among the sick, hadn't succumbed no matter how often he was exposed, and the volunteers who never left the bedsides of the sick were mostly fine.

Not spread by breath. Not by touch.

While the healers and volunteers worked at the clinic, other folks investigated possible causes—something carried by rats, a bad batch of wheat. A few days ago, they'd covered the open wells and publicly accessible water pumps in town when they realized the rash showed up in people who drank regularly from them. Only time would tell whether it slowed the disease's spread.

Disease. That was what most folks called it when they spoke of it aloud. Disease felt like something that could be managed, even cured. But another suspicion hung over the town like invisible fog, ever present, rarely spoken inside the clinic.

Another curse, more direct and deadly than the last.

A cool breeze brushed against Gale's skin as she stepped into the darkness outside the clinic. She wiped the sweat from her brow with the sleeve of her cotton blouse and breathed deeply. The air smelled of spring flowers and ground still wet from the thunderstorm she'd barely noticed as it swept over the town earlier in the day, and she welcomed its chill after the close, pressing warmth inside.

It was beautiful. Even the buzz of biting smallflies couldn't mar the atmosphere.

"I don't suppose you brought me out here to tell me the Luminary's changed her mind about my placement," Gale said when River joined her.

He let out a derisive snort as he sat on a narrow wooden bench and leaned back against the wall. "No, though one could imagine that an emergency of this nature might broaden the scope of God's will."

Gale sighed and sat beside him. "You'd think."

Almost three weeks into this plague and the Luminary's position hadn't shifted in the slightest, save for her allowing Gale to continue her work in the clinic. If it were God's will that everyone did their utmost to save their fellow townsfolk, then it was God's will for Gale to use her skills there.

But only temporarily.

Gale supposed she could look at the hell she was walking through in the clinic as motivation to leave this profession behind her, but as she experimented with ingredients, testing for harmless magical properties and choosing those that would best react to create something new, all she felt was a sense of peace in the midst of the storm that had descended on Bright Hollow. It was the closest she'd come to working true magic in a decade, and it felt more right than she cared to admit, even to herself.

"Salve sixteen is showing promise," River said.

Gale sat up straighter. "In what sense?"

"No regression of the rash," River said, cutting off her hopes before they'd grown too unruly. "The patients we're testing it on are as bad as they were two days ago. But three of the four have shown no further progression, and the one who did might have been beyond help anyway."

Gale stretched her legs out in front of her, relieving the pressure on her feet. They'd ache in bed tonight, as they did every night, but it wouldn't keep her from being back at work before sunrise.

"I'll teach Honey and Marigold the formulation," she said, already considering how she'd also need to teach them exactly where to gather the merriweather leaves and corrieroot to ensure maximum efficacy. "If they can keep producing it I can work on something more like an actual treatment."

River nodded and closed his eyes. "Thank you. I'm growing tired of surgery. Have you got any ideas?"

Gale drew her next breath slowly, thinking carefully about how she'd spend it.

The Teachings were funny about magic, and especially about magical plants used for food or medicine. There was no sin in a plant growing where the wind had blown its seeds, and if magic in the land made it a more potent ingredient, so be it. It was a person taking magic into herself, using the raw power to create spells that changed natural reactions, that was the danger. Control gave a witch the ability to subvert God's will and the workings of the natural world in ways the deity had never intended.

Such power was what led to soul-deep corruption. To curses.

But as Gale worked, she had ideas. The witch she'd learned from had possessed a golden, glittering potion of pure magic that had amplified and changed the reactions of ingredients, even when a person didn't step off the Path to take that power into herself. It could be the key to manipulating natural ingredients into a more effective medicine.

The trouble was, Gale couldn't produce that pure magic potion without using existing magic to do it. And even if she could, she didn't know the recipe. That knowledge was forbidden, and she'd helped kill the only person who'd ever tried to teach it to her.

But then, times were desperate, and there might be a way. Sometimes it took a controlled fire in the woods to prevent a larger one later. And if this were a curse, if only magic might fight it, the person who discovered the right medicine would be a true hero.

As long as she didn't corrupt herself in the process.

"I do have a few ideas," she said, speaking slowly and carefully as brushed away a smallfly that had landed on her cheek. "Did the Luminary tell you why it isn't God's will for me to work here?"

River didn't open his eyes as he shook his head. "Officially? No. But I'll confess I've been thinking a lot about a day when two brave children came to my office to give a report, and I've wondered whether this might not have something to do with all the things that little girl was too scared to speak of."

Gale's cheeks warmed. "You suspected something?"

He shrugged. "Nothing I put in my report. Seemed to me it was your business, and I guess I was right. You've grown into a fine citizen."

"I appreciate that. And you were right. It was no one's business at the time."

River opened one eye and glanced at her. "And now?"

Gale settled back against the wall. Might as well find physical comfort while she pried a small piece of her carefully guarded secrets out and exposed it to the light.

"I think Hawk told you that I learned enough about magical herbs and such to make a draught that put the witch to sleep so he could slit her throat."

"He did. But he only admitted it after some careful questioning, if I recall correctly."

Gale's chest tightened. Fear's claws prickled the skin on the back of her neck as Hawk's stern eyes appeared in her mind, frowning, warning her to stay silent for her own good.

"The truth is, I had to learn more than natural potions. The witch was powerful. She had enchantments placed on herself and her home to protect her. For me to make a potion that was strong enough to knock her out for the few seconds he needed, I..." Gale cleared her throat. "I had to do more than work with what nature gave me."

She didn't dare look at River, but she watched from the

corner of her eye as he sat up straighter and turned to her. "She taught you true magic."

Gale nodded. "Hawk told the truth—I was a good student, and the witch loved teaching me and testing what I could do after never having any exposure to magic. It pleased her, I think."

Her throat tightened as she remembered the witch, her loose golden curls tied up in braids with flowers woven through, her bright eyes shining as her pupil willingly drank a pre-made potion and let magic flow through her for the first time.

"She was a good teacher. It's just that I learned more than Hawk let on."

The craving gripped her, twisting through her gut, telling her to run into the woods and find a spot where the power was strong so she could bask in its shallows. She clasped her hands in her lap and ordered her mind to be still.

"Too good a teacher for her own health," River said. "And since then, have you—"

"No," Gale said, a little too quickly. "I did what I had to, no more. I drank a potion that let pure magic flow through my body, but it didn't remain in me. I've been free of it since our return. But I confess I'm still attuned to it. And with everything that's been going on, the salves I've tested, I can't help that my thoughts turn toward magic as I try to find new ideas for cures. Real cures, not just these natural remedies that buy us time. The witch had plants in her garden we don't have here, ones that might allow us to create a cure without stepping from God's light."

Her breath caught in her throat, and she held it there, waiting for River to speak again.

He nodded slowly. "I knew there was more to it. Explains a lot about you, Nightingale. I've had some good students come through the clinic on their trial rotations—several of them are hard at work in there right now, and I don't know what I'd do without any one of them. But for you to have such a facility with medicines at such a young age and so naturally... well, it only makes sense."

Gale exhaled and relaxed a little. At least he wasn't yelling. "Do you think the Luminary is right to deny me this?"

"Tricky question." He thought for several moments. "Perhaps, but not as you might think. The Luminary sees this connection to magic as a danger, and maybe she's right. You've been exposed, and I assume this means you could be tempted. You could pursue it, become the very thing that brought the last curse on use."

"I haven't."

River waved her off. "Anyone can tell by looking at you that you're no witch, and even if this is another curse, it's not your doing. But it could happen, and maybe avoiding temptation is the easiest way to not be consumed by it. That means the Luminary is right."

Gale's heart skipped. "But?"

"But maybe she's also wrong." River leaned back again and folded his hands over his stomach like he was relaxing on a fine summer afternoon, not speaking of things Gale barely dared to whisper to herself in the dark. "Let's say the bit of magic you worked did scar you in a way—made you sensitive to magic, made you crave it like Cotton Highgrove has been craving his pipe since we took it from him. But what you've got is something that could be used for good if you can be strong enough to resist the bad that comes with it."

Gale frowned at him. "I'm sure you're not suggesting I should work magic."

River kissed his palm and held his hand up to the sky in a warding gesture. "God be praised, no. What I'm saying is your scar left you with a talent, and it's one that could save a lot of lives if you were allowed to use it within the bounds of God's light. You should never take magic into yourself, never allow your soul to be corrupted with witchery. But I believe God's in the business of pulling treasure out of shit-piles, if you'll pardon my language."

"I will." Gale spoke at a whisper, not trusting her voice not to tremble.

"Magic getting its hooks into you is a steaming heap for sure. But what you're doing here to help folks? That's diamonds." River patted her knee and stood. "Go home and get some sleep. Dream up a cure. Turn your curse into a blessing and maybe it'll change things for all of us."

He opened the door and stepped into the clinic, letting a wave of warm air out that carried the sighs of the sick and the somehow audible silence of the voices that had gone missing.

The back of Gale's right forearm itched. She scratched absently at it, brushing away whatever insect might have landed there, then stood and stepped into the light of the moon, which cast its cold light over the forest beyond the clinic.

"There has to be a way," she whispered. "God grant me the strength to be the one to find it."

CHAPTER SIX

THE NEXT MORNING, Gale hunched over the kitchen basin and shovelled oat porridge with cream into her mouth, caring more about speed than the mess she was making.

"Sit down, darling," her mother admonished, looking up from the book of Teachings she'd been reading from for her morning studies. "There's nothing that can't wait another minute."

"Don't need to sit." Gale swallowed the last of her meal and pumped cold water into the bowl that she'd wash later.

Well, someone would wash it. She hadn't been home enough recently to appreciate the nightly miracle that saw the table tidied and the dishes done after her parents returned from their duties at the Hall.

Her mother clucked her tongue. "You're going to wear the soles of your feet down to the bone. Your body needs rest, Nightingale."

"I know. I got five hours last night." Gale swished peppermint-infused water around in her mouth and spat it into the basin, which drained into the yard behind the house.

"Restful sleep?"

Gale considered this. "No. But productive. Will you be at this morning's meeting?"

Her mother cupped a mug of tea between her hands but didn't drink. "As always. Why? Do you have an idea to present to the Luminary?"

Gale's heart warmed toward her mother. Things had never gone back to what they were before her parents had sent her and Hawk out in God's hands. Before that, she'd trusted her parents fully to be her guides and protectors, but that balance had shifted irrevocably when they'd abandoned their children to the forest. Though it had all worked out for God's purposes in the end, something had broken that could never be mended.

But times like this, when her mother asked a question with genuine interest and none of the wariness and implied prejudgement she'd have received from Hawk if he'd asked the same question, she wished things were different. That they were closer, that she could feel this pleasant, liquid ache more often.

"I just might have something." Gale's fingers twitched at her sides, releasing some of the pent-up energy she'd awakened with, which came along with the plan she'd settled on as she'd lain awake long past midnight. Once she'd fully opened the door, the witch's teachings on magical potions had come back with frightening clarity, and she was almost certain they were the answer the town needed. "I'm not sure what the Luminary will say about my plan, though."

Her mother sipped her tea and smiled serenely. "Don't tell me, then. She wants all ideas, no matter how outlandish. I'd hate to make you second-guess anything truly wild."

Gale's smile faltered. Wild was one thing. Potentially sinful was quite another. But if it might save everyone and maybe reopen the discussion about her own future, it was worth the risk.

"We'll see," was all she said.

"Shall we walk up together?" Her mother drained the last of

her tea and rinsed the mug. "It's a lovely day, and I've hardly seen you since all of this began."

"I—I'd love to, but I need to go over some things first." That was a lie. Gale's proposal was ridiculously simple. But something in her still balked at the idea of strolling through town with her mother as though all had been forgiven, and needing time was as good an excuse as any. She had learned to stand on her own, and it wouldn't do for anyone to think she was leaning on her parents now that bad times had come again. "I'll see you there?"

"Of course." Her mother swallowed hard, but the serenity of her expression didn't change at Gale's rejection. Even in their private lives, the acolytes were held to a high standard. Those who studied the Teachings were presumed to be steeped in God's will, and therefore expected to be content with whatever came.

This meant her parents hadn't yet asked direct questions about the Luminary's refusal of her declaration, and Gale was immensely thankful for that small mercy.

"Your father's at the Hall already. I'm sure he'll look forward to hearing your idea."

Gale leaned in and kissed her mother on the cheek. She smelled of rose water and white soap, just as she had when a younger Gale had cuddled in her lap before everything changed.

Gale excused herself and dashed up the stairs to finish dressing. Looking presentable wouldn't change God's will or the Luminary's mind, but it definitely couldn't hurt.

THE LUMINARY SAT on the dais, flanked by three acolytes. She had eight in total who rotated in and out of their duties as needed. Currently two were searching deep in the Teachings and past interpretations for guidance, one had fallen ill, and two were caring for sick loved ones at home. It was strange to see an empty chair, a gap in the Luminary's enlightened team. But Gale's mother and father sat to the Luminary's right, which meant there was still some stability in their little world.

And yet, cracks were showing.

The Luminary had not spoken of falling ill herself, but the pallor of her skin was clear in the morning light that shone through the roof, and the sheen of sweat on her brow hinted at fever. Gale's stomach sank.

Bright Hollow could carry on after the loss of nearly any citizen, but the death of the Luminary would cut the beating heart out of the community.

Maybe she'll be more open to strange ideas if she's ill, though, Gale thought. *Maybe she'll give me a chance to prove myself.*

She turned the idea aside. Selfish thoughts had no place in her mind today. If she were to propose this plan—using magic to fight magic, within the constraints of the Teachings—it had to be about the community, not her own future or becoming the hero everyone already thought she was.

There were plenty of empty chairs on the floor, too. A dozen had been set up last week to accommodate everyone who came in with ideas about the illness, but when it had been decreed that repeat ideas would not be heard, and as the well of inspiration ran dry, fewer people had been coming.

River entered a minute after Gale and sat in the chair beside her in the front row. He was always needed at the clinic but had agreed to consult on ideas regarding the treatment of the illness, and the meetings gave him a chance to get away for a while each morning.

Gale thought he'd be better off getting a little more sleep, but today she was glad of his presence. He, of all people, would back her up.

She leaned toward him. "Do you think the Luminary looks—"

He placed a hand on her arm to silence her. "It's progressing as slowly as we can hope for. She doesn't want to cause panic, but I doubt the news will stay hidden for much longer."

Gale smoothed her skirt and tried not to stare. She'd worn one of her better dresses, the dark blue one with a full skirt and high lace collar, and had carefully brushed her hair before she left the house, aiming to look as respectable and trustworthy as possible.

It seemed at first that she and River were the only folks coming. The old clock in the square chimed, and the Luminary stood. "I suppose this will be brief," she said, smiling gently.

The doors opened again, letting in a breeze that ruffled Gale's hair. She looked over her shoulder and watched as Hawk strode in, dressed in his hunting leathers from boots to gloves, bow and quiver strapped on his back.

She turned back to the Luminary and folded her hands in her lap without greeting her brother, even when he stood in the aisle beside her. They weren't fighting now, exactly, but they also hadn't had time to make amends since the day of Gale's disastrous declaration. She thanked God every morning and night that he, Frost, and Fox had thus far been spared from the illness, but she was as irritated by his presence now as she was pleased by River's.

Hawk was the last person she needed here when she made her proposal.

"Well." The Luminary's brow creased, then smoothed as she smiled down at them. "Our young heroes have come to save us again."

Hawk shot Gale a questioning look that she ignored.

"Who will speak first?" the Luminary asked.

Gale nodded at Hawk. "He seems to be in a hurry. Best let him say his piece."

Hawk bowed slightly toward her. "Much obliged. Luminary, I think it's time for us to properly address the idea that this may be another curse."

"Indeed." The Luminary leaned forward. "It has been suggested that the witch we most recently ejected from our territory might have cursed us for our actions, but I believe you your-self said it was impossible."

The hairs on the back of Gale's neck stood on end. It *could* be a curse. It seemed likely. But she hadn't felt magic in the town or in the bodies of those who'd fallen ill.

If it was a curse, whoever had created it hadn't meant for it to be found out easily.

Hawk nodded solemnly. "That is so, Your Brilliance. The witch we ran off was nowhere near powerful enough to have done anything like this. Based on that and the fact that we had no knowledge of other witches in the area, we assumed this must be a disease of more natural origins. But with the way this is spreading and the way it's killing perfectly healthy folks, the inef-fectiveness of prayer and natural cures, I believe we need to hunt down that last witch and question him about it. He may have learned new tricks since he left."

Gale's blood turned to ice.

True witches were rare. Even in the rest of Andonia, a wild and sinful place where folks no longer cared about God's will, magic was legally reserved strictly for use by the king's mages.

But other witches existed, as she and Hawk knew all too well.

It wasn't impossible that one of them might have set these events in motion, either by cursing Bright Hollow or simply by corrupting the land with their presence. But how many could there be who were powerful enough to do a thing like this?

"If it is a curse," Hawk continued, "the only answer is to find the witch who placed it and force them to revoke it. And if that's not possible..." He lowered his head. "We all saw how quickly the last curse ended when the witch passed from this world."

The Luminary leaned one elbow on the chair's armrest and rested her chin on her hand, doing a poor job of hiding the tremble in her arm. "I suppose this means you're volunteering for the hunt?"

"I am." Hawk placed a hand over his heart. He hadn't removed his gloves—a minor breach of etiquette, but such things were forgivable these days. "I've seen magic, felt its horrors. It's made me better able to find those who would wield it for their own purposes, as I proved when we drove the last one away. I'm better at tracking game than anyone else in Bright Hollow, and I can do the same with a witch."

Better at tracking and at killing, Gale thought, remembering the blood and fire that had been her nightmares for years after their return to Bright Hollow.

"Where will you begin your search?" the Luminary asked.

"Queen's Run." Hawk said the words as though they tasted bad. "I've asked Thunder to search the immediate area for other witches who may be causing the trouble, but I think the city is the most reasonable place to hunt for the one we ran off. Plenty of people there to hide among but close enough if he wanted to return to harm us."

The Luminary's brow furrowed. "Be careful. Our ancestors had good reason for drawing away from the world. The people of the city follow every god who crosses their path instead of devoting themselves to the greatest God and seeking God's will for their lives. They live carelessly, thoughtlessly, living for themselves instead of the good of others. It is a dangerous place."

Hawk lowered his gaze. "I know. I've heard the stories from those who have ventured out before. I won't stay longer than I need to."

"Very well," the Luminary said. "If your wife and child are safe and unaffected, if they'll not suffer in your absence, I grant you and Thunder permission to hunt whatever witch may be corrupting our land. Should you find it, I grant you absolution for whatever actions become necessary to end these horrors."

She spoke as though Hawk might need to give someone a stern talking to or a boot to the arse to get them out the door, not as though she was giving him license to murder. Gale understood. It would be one life to prevent dozens of deaths, if not more. Not an insect's life given to heal illness, but the same concept on a far larger scale.

And if it made her flesh crawl, if she doubted once again that she herself would be brave enough to kill to break a curse, that was more reason to be glad he hadn't asked her to go along with him.

She'd hoped Hawk would leave after he got the permissions he wanted, but instead he took a seat and looked expectantly at Gale.

She sighed and stood, smoothing her skirt again to keep her hands busy. She wished she'd dressed more like Hawk, ready to begin her proposed task the second she stepped out the door. Urgent. Capable.

She cleared her throat and straightened her shoulders.

"Hawk may be right," she said. "But we still need to treat those who are already sick, and the ingredients we're currently working with aren't enough."

The Luminary looked to River, who nodded.

"We're slowing the progress," the healer said, "but people are still dying. There have been no reversals in anyone who hasn't undergone an amputation. Even if we see no new cases, it seems likely that many more of those good folk already affected will die."

Gale glanced at Hawk, who sat with his arms crossed, eyes firmly on the Luminary.

She waited for the Luminary to look at her again before she continued.

"I believe we need stronger ingredients and better techniques. There is nothing growing naturally on the mountainside that can help, but I've seen a place where there were different plants. Better medicinal herbs." She paused, then pressed on. Either her idea would permanently close the door on her hopes of working in medicine or it would change everything for the better. No risk, no gain. "I've also seen books with knowledge the likes of which we've never had here. Assuming that those books haven't been destroyed by fire or weather, there may be a place I can find the information that will allow us to save lives."

Hawk turned slowly toward her. "You can't be serious."

Gale did her best to reflect the mask-like calm of the Luminary and her acolytes. "I am entirely serious. I learned only a little from the witch during our captivity, but I have reason to believe there may still be plants growing in her garden that would help us. There was a flower she called *alluminius* that—well, I believe I might find something that will work."

There was more to it. In her wildest hopes, Gale imagined finding one last bottle of what the witch had called *lucistra*, the potion apprentice witches used to take magic into themselves and mature witches used to increase the magic they carried as a part of themselves. It was the potion that had allowed Gale to create the deadly sleeping draught. She wouldn't drink it again, but the idea that it might be the key ingredient to a true cure had burrowed into her mind and refused to leave.

But that would be too much to confess here. To stumble on a bottle of the stuff accidentally would make it clear it had been God's will for her to find it. To deliberately seek out such temptation...

Hawk stood and stepped forward. "With respect, Luminary, if I'm successful and break the curse, we won't need a cure. As we saw with the last one, everything went back to normal once the witch was dead."

Gale glared at him. "That doesn't mean all curses end so cleanly. People are dying, and this might save them." She thought of Willow, of how time was running out.

Hawk's jaw clenched, but he didn't answer.

Gale turned back to the Luminary. "Ignoring the chance to find a proper cure is foolish. And anyway, there's no guarantee Hawk will find the source of the curse, or even that it *is* a curse." She glanced at her brother. "No offense intended. You're an excellent hunter, the best choice for the task. But we should be prepared for anything. Time is running out, Your Brilliance."

The Luminary looked away.

Her illness is worse than she or River are letting on, then. Gale took a deep breath and waited.

"You may be right, Nightingale," the Luminary said. "But there are concerns related to sending you back to that terrible place. I wonder whether it might not be better to send River instead."

Hawk nodded sagely. Gale resisted the urge to punch him for it.

"Gale has explained your concerns to me," River said. Gale ignored the wounded look that flashed across her mother's features before she schooled herself back into indifference. "But the fact is she's the only one with the knowledge to find exactly what we need." River stood and stepped closer to the Luminary. "She's the one who has created the medicines that are working so far, holding the illness at bay. But what she's able to do here isn't enough. That witch's garden might be our best shot, and Gale's the one to do it. Besides, I'm needed here. I don't have a trained apprentice who can take an arm without costing a life. I know Nightingale as well as anyone here in town does. You can trust her to resist temptation, to bring back what we need to create a potent, natural cure."

The Luminary met Gale's eyes. Gale looked back, unashamed and unafraid.

I am strong enough, she thought, willing her eyes to convey the message. *I've already resisted temptation. I can prove myself. I can save us all.*

"Very well," the Luminary said. "A natural cure, nothing that will risk corruption. I won't sacrifice your soul for any number of lives."

Gale clenched her jaw and nodded. It was hard to ignore the double standard—Hawk being given permission to murder to save the town, her being denied the choice to use magic to do the same. Two sins, but not equal in God's eyes.

Or at least in the Luminary's. It was supposed to be the same thing, but there were moments when it was hard not to question the idea.

The Luminary looked to Hawk, including him in her commissioning. "Remember the Teachings. Do not stray from the Path."

"It will be done by God's grace," Gale and Hawk said together.

"Then you are dismissed. May you return safely. May you save us again."

The three acolytes rose and pressed hands to their chests, then filed into the rooms behind the meeting space to return to their work.

"A word, River?" the Luminary asked, and the healer nodded.

He patted Gale on the arm as she turned to leave. "God's grace be with you along the Path," he murmured.

Gale left, with Hawk trailing behind her. She waited for him at the bottom of the steps. Better to get his ranting over with.

"Sent out into God's hands again," she said.

He smiled ruefully. "At least it's our choice this time."

She waited for more, but he just stood with his face turned to the morning sun, eyes closed. Praying, maybe.

"No lecture?" she asked.

He shrugged and looked down at her. "It's not my choice. The Luminary knows the risks and has judged this step allowable if it restores God's will. It's all in our hands now. I pray we're both strong enough to do our parts."

"I'll be fine."

"I know. And I truly don't want to cause trouble for you. It's only because of love that I worry." Hawk frowned and rubbed a gloved hand over the back of his neck. "But this is bigger than you or me. May we both be the tools God requires."

"Agreed."

She still felt tension coming off him, either doubt or fear, but at least he was trying. Something loosened in her chest, and the anger she'd felt earlier flowed out of her.

"This is awkward," Gale said, and Hawk laughed.

"It is. It shouldn't be. Not between us." He paused. "I'm going home for one last meal before I leave. Do you have time to join us for lunch?"

Gale smiled. This, finally, felt a bit like normal life. "I wouldn't miss it."

"Good." Hawk's brow creased. "Good."

He left, and Gale started her journey to the clinic to leave instructions and recipes for the volunteers.

I'll prove myself, she decided as she hurried through town. *I will find the cure and be back before it's too late to save Willow and the Luminary. God will see what I can do without succumbing to temptation, Hawk will see that I don't need his meddling and protection.*

Bright Hollow will be saved, and the life I want will be mine after all.

CHAPTER SEVEN

AT PRECISELY NOON, Gale approached Hawk's home with a bottle of last autumn's cranberry cordial in one hand and a fluttering feeling in her stomach. But when she opened the front door and stepped into the fire-warmed light of the white cottage on the edge of town it was like crossing into a tiny island of normality in the midst of the chaos outside.

The house wasn't large, just an open room where most of the living took place and a bedroom set to one side, plus the neat-as-a-pin outhouse in the yard out back. Since Hawk had married and moved out two years ago Gale had spent many pleasant evenings playing card games at the table or sipping cold mint tea on the wide front porch, and it had become her second home.

A welcoming fire blazed in the hearth in spite of the spring weather outside, crackling pleasantly under the sounds of Hawk and Frost's muted conversation in the kitchen area at the back of the house. Frost stood over the black cast iron stove stirring what smelled like deer stew, her dark curls pulled back in a messy bun at her neck, baby Fox in the cloth sling she wore across her chest. She turned to Gale and offered a welcoming smile, and Hawk motioned for Gale to come closer.

"Dinner's almost ready," Frost said.

Gale slipped her boots off and left them by the door. "Need any help?"

"Not today. Our kit is finally taking long enough naps that I can get things done."

Hawk leaned in and kissed Frost on the head. "One of these days maybe you'll take a chance to nap, too."

As Gale moved toward the kitchen she noted the dark circles under her kin-sister's eyes.

Frost smiled sadly. "I'll sleep when Fox does after you've gone, love."

Gale doubted sleep would come easy if Frost had to worry about the danger Hawk might be placing himself in. Hunting could be a dangerous job, but Hawk was clever and careful and knew his limits... at least when it came to animals. Gale couldn't help wondering how much further he might push himself now, though, and how much more dangerous and unpredictable a witch might be than a stag or a mountain lion.

And the city itself would be another kind of monster entirely.

The wood-plank table had been set with the young couple's plain, practical dishes, and a milky white pitcher filled with wildflowers sat in the middle. Gale passed the table and stepped closer to the stove, and Frost turned so she could peer into the sling.

"Hey, Foxy-man," she whispered. The baby yawned and let out a gentle burp, and Gale smiled. She had no plans of raising children herself, but Fox brightened her heart in a way she hadn't expected before his birth. She already had plans for taking him out to explore the woods when he was old enough. With Hawk to teach him about animals, Frost to instruct him in the creation of useful items at the carpentry shop where she worked, and Gale to share the quiet wonders of living plants, this little one would have a fine education before he ever started school.

Everything would be perfect once this curse was gone.

"Wash up," Frost ordered. She'd been speaking more like a mother these past few months, and it suited her. "Everything's ready."

Hawk sliced a loaf of bread as Gale washed her hands in the kitchen basin. She frowned. He'd removed his hunting gloves but now wore plain leather ones more appropriate for a ride through the forest than dinner at home. She caught his eye and raised an eyebrow, and he sighed.

"Might as well show her," Frost said softly as she ladled stew into white bowls. "Better to know whether it is or it isn't."

As Frost set the food on the table, Hawk led Gale into the cottage's single bedroom and sat on the pure white quilt that covered the bed. "It's probably nothing," he said. "Can't be too careful, though."

Gale's heart stilled as he pulled his gloves off and held his left hand out to her. A red, flaking rash covered the lowest segment of his index finger. Gale reached for his hand to examine it, but he pulled back.

"It doesn't spread by touch," she said. "Whatever you think about the source of my abilities, I know what I'm doing. Let me see."

He let her take his callused hand in hers. "I know you do," he said, speaking quietly. "God's my witness, Gale, I have nothing but faith in your natural talents."

Gale focused on the rash, prodding with her fingers, willing it to be a reaction to a poisonous plant, a bit of irritation from the new clothes Willow's father had shipped in from outside to sell at the store—anything but what it so obviously was. In that moment, she didn't care about their fight or the distance between them. All she knew was that this was her brother, her oldest friend and most irritating adversary, who in a few weeks might be lying in the clinic with his body rotting around him. Everything else was insignificant when compared to that.

She straightened her shoulders and adopted her most professional tone. Crying would only make it worse for both of them.

"Been drinking from anywhere but your own well?" she asked. "Eating anything out of the ordinary?"

Hawk's face paled. "Before they decided to try shutting down the public wells, sure. I always filled up on my way out into the woods, at the pump near the square."

The pump had been shut down just yesterday, but it was one that Gale herself had taken drinks from before she'd confined herself to water from the clinic and her parents' home, neither of which seemed to be affected.

The spot on her forearm that had itched last night tingled again, the crawling sensation growing deeper and hotter, but she didn't dare scratch it. If Hawk had any reason to suspect it was more than an ordinary itch or a bug bite, which it surely was, he'd only worry.

"It's not bad yet," she said. "You've got time."

"God, Gale."

She released his hand. There was no point offering false comfort, saying *it will be fine* or *nothing to worry about* when they both knew better. "You'd best see River before you set out."

Hawk shook his head and slipped his gloves back on, though Frost would likely make him remove them at the table. "No one can know. If the Luminary finds out I'm infected, she might insist I stay here. You've noticed she hasn't sent for help from any other community?"

Gale nodded. Aside from a little trade and occasional adoptions Bright Hollow kept to itself. Admitting they needed help from the ungodly people on the outside would open them to judgement and ridicule.

"But maybe she'd be right to want you to stay," she said. "Exertion will only make things worse. What good will it do us if you die out there?"

"What good will it do us if I die here? If I go, maybe I can stop this thing before it gets its claws into everyone in town. Before it gets Frost or Fox." Hawk's voice became thick and heavy. "Please don't tattle to River or the Luminary. Or to mother and father. I've already said my goodbyes. They don't know anything is wrong."

Gale sighed. "Fine. Not like we haven't kept each other's secrets before." *And I'll actually keep yours,* she added to herself, though without anger. "At least let me get you a jar of my latest formula from the clinic before you go. No guarantees of how well it will work if you refuse to take bed rest and let your body heal, though."

"It will be something. Thank you."

He stood, and Gale wrapped her arms around him, embracing a body that felt strong and terribly vulnerable at the same time. They weren't usually the sort of siblings who did such things, but it felt right. The fights, the challenges, the secrets they'd kept—all of it was from and for the kind of bond that could never be broken.

They'd kept each other alive, once. She'd do everything in her power to do it again.

The meal passed with delicious food and pleasant conversation, and Gale wished it could stretch out forever so she could pretend for a while longer that the world wasn't crumbling around them. But when Fox cried and Frost excused herself to feed and change him, Gale knew from the resigned look on Hawk's face that it was time to return to reality.

"You'll be all right?" he asked.

"Of course. I've spent nights in the woods on my own before. I've got the knife you gave me and the skills you taught me. I know how to look for danger."

Hawk looked down as he smiled without saying anything else. If he wanted to ask again whether she could resist temptation or warn her of the special dangers she would face, he kept it to himself. She hoped it meant the Luminary's blessing had erased his doubts.

It would have been nicer if he'd admit he was wrong. She'd always enjoyed seeing her brother humbled. But this would do.

"Shall we?" he asked, standing and reaching for the packed knapsack in the corner that Gale had been trying to ignore as she'd pretended all was well.

"Sure."

Frost emerged from the bedroom and enveloped Gale in a bone-crushing hug. "Be careful out there," she whispered. "Find a cure for our Hawk and the others."

Gale squeezed back. "I'll do my best, I swear."

Frost yawned. "When do you leave?"

"Just need to change and finish packing my things."

Frost looked like she wanted to say something else, but offered only a forced smile before she turned away, wiping at her eyes.

Gale and Hawk didn't speak much on the way to the clinic nor as she walked him to the edge of town afterward, a jar of salve in his bag. There wasn't much to say, really, until it was time to part ways.

"Swear you'll be careful," she said. "If that witch thinks you might be coming for him, he'll be wary."

"I will. You be careful, too."

He didn't need to say why. Gale just nodded. He wasn't trying to stop her, and she did need to be cautious. Now wasn't the time for defensiveness or needless irritation.

No matter their differences, and even if Hawk's efforts were sometimes wrong-headed, they'd always done their best to protect each other. And now, once again, it was time for them to protect everyone else.

❧

GALE HAD FINISHED PACKING, changed into her travel clothes—sturdy cotton skirt, warm sweater over a cotton blouse, and hooded jacket—and was buckling the straps on her knapsack when her mother knocked on the doorframe and poked her head into the bedroom.

"Might we speak for a moment?"

Gale moved the heavy bag to the floor and gestured to the spot next to her on the bed. "I didn't realize you were home."

"I wasn't. I'm needed back at the Hall, but I wanted to be here to see you off. I wish I could have seen your brother one more time before he left."

Gale smiled sadly. "He knows your prayers go with him. I walked with him to the crossroads myself. He seemed confident. Prepared."

She didn't add, "You have nothing to worry about," though it seemed like the most comforting thing to say. It would have been untrue, and they'd both have known it.

"What of yourself?"

Gale nudged the bag with her foot. "Prepared as well, though less certain of what I'm looking for. I've got some food and equipment packed, and the forest will see to the rest of my needs, God willing. I'm prepared to sleep outdoors, to gather water even when I've left the river behind, to make shelter if it rains."

The words came out strange and formal, as though she were still presenting her argument to the Luminary.

Her mother nodded. "I had no doubt you'd be prepared to face the physical dangers of the journey."

Gale clenched her jaw tight and took a long, slow breath. "You have other fears?"

"Should I?"

A small part of Gale wanted to finally let all of her secrets pour out, to shed light on every scrap of darkness she'd carried inside her since she and Hawk had escaped from the witch. She'd been trapped by them for so long, and the weight often felt unbearable.

But to speak of those things would bring another kind of consequence. If she revealed all of it now, that would be the end of it. Her mother would tell the Luminary, and Gale would be forbidden from leaving Bright Hollow to pursue even the barest hint of magic.

It was wrong to lie, but the truth would cost too many lives when there was no one else to find a way to heal them. Gale wished she saw God's will as clearly as the Luminary did, but in the absence of such wisdom a person sometimes had to guess.

"You should have faith that you've raised your daughter well," Gale said, taking her mother's hand in her own. "And that God will watch over me until I find a way to save God's people."

Her mother's lips tightened, but she nodded as she looked down at her hands—one in Gale's, the other clenched in her lap. "It's hard to remember you're not a little girl anymore."

Not like I was the first time we ended a curse, Gale thought. A long-buried memory surfaced—her small hand in her father's large one, her legs sore as he escorted her and Hawk deep into the woods. Father leaving them with a little food and water, saying he'd be right back. Heavy eyelids, sleep, and suddenly feeling smaller than ever when she'd wakened to find herself and Hawk alone in dark and unfamiliar woods.

"No," she said, and cleared away the thickness from her throat. "I'm not little. I can take care of myself this time."

Her mother flinched at those last words but nodded. "You always could. Here." She opened her other hand and Gale gasped as sunlight sparkled off the bright amethyst set into an ornate gold ring.

"Grandmother's," Gale whispered, and her fingers itched to touch it just as they had when she was a child and had been told it wasn't hers to wear. Acolytes didn't wear jewelry or do anything else to draw attention to themselves or their appearance, and it was rare for Gale to see the beautiful ring.

Her mother's eyes filled with tears as she took Gale's hand and slipped the ring onto the first finger of her right hand.

"I should have given it to you weeks ago," she said. "I had planned to after the ceremony, to welcome you to your place on the Path."

Gale's breath trembled as she turned her hand to let the purple stone catch the light again.

"I was wrong to wait," her mother continued. "I see that now. The Luminary's denial doesn't mean you're unprepared to take your place in Bright Hollow, only that your trail along the Path isn't lit as clearly as most." She turned, resting one knee on the bed, and squeezed Gale's hands tight in hers. "I believe God has great plans for you, Nightingale. God has used you once, and will again, so long you seek God's will with every step. Wear this ring and remember us here at home, where you came from and where you will return."

"Thank you," Gale whispered. "I'll make you proud."

Her father poked his head into the room. He'd aged more than her mother had over the past decade, and his hair had gone completely white. In the sunlight, it formed a sort of halo around his head. "The Luminary needs us, dear." He looked to Gale with a faltering smile. "You'll be careful?"

"Of course."

There was so much more to say. Her parents had never asked for forgiveness for abandoning their children in the woods, and they never would—not when it had so clearly been God's will. That meant Gale was never required to offer forgiveness, though she sometimes wondered whether doing so would have healed things between them.

"Good. God be with you, Nightingale."

"And with you, Father."

He nodded solemnly and stepped out of the room.

Gale's arm itched again, deep and burning. She tried not to scratch, but it was too much. She rubbed her arm against her sweater as subtly as she could.

Her mother frowned. "Everything all right?"

"Got bitten by a smallfly a few nights ago." Gale smiled. "I've got something for it in my bag."

"You really are prepared, aren't you?" They both stood, and Gale's mother pulled her into a tight embrace. "Save us," she whispered, her breath tickling Gale's ear. "I know this is too much to ask of you, but I believe you will succeed."

Gale stiffened and pulled away.

It's always been too much, but that never mattered before.

"I will," she said. "God willing."

"God willing," her mother echoed, and brushed away a tear as she turned to leave. She closed the door behind her.

Had she cried the last time they'd said a hard goodbye? Gale had never asked. Father had seemed so strange that day as he'd led them into the woods, but Gale had been too happy about going on an adventure with him to be bothered by it. Even when the hunger that had plagued them for so long had made her weak, she'd only been glad when her father carried her onward.

Into God's hands. Off the beaten path. Not knowing whether he'd ever see his children again.

Her mother must have wept. She was an acolyte following the Teachings, but she was also a parent.

Gale took another moment to admire the ring, feeling the weight of what it represented—adulthood, responsibility, her place on the Path and in her family. Then she took a deep breath and rolled up the sleeve of her sweater.

She stared at the irritated patch of flaking skin on her arm, willing it to not be there.

It had been hard to tell this morning whether it might only be a fly bite, the spot had been so small. But it was larger now and turning an angry red. A strange numbness came over her as she thought back over the disease's progression in others.

"Early stages," she said, and pulled out the jar of healing salve from her bag. She'd taken one for herself when she'd stopped by with Hawk, just in case.

She'd expected to feel more of something. Fear. Anger at whoever had placed this curse on her town. But there was nothing except a wave of calm washing over her as she applied the salve to her skin and packed an extra roll of bandages for later.

The idea of her falling ill and dying seemed ridiculous. Impossible.

And anyway, I'll have more and better medicine soon enough.

All she needed to do was find it before she became too weak to travel and too delirious with fever to think. In some folks, it took weeks. In others, especially those who wouldn't rest, it went faster.

So hurry up and move.

She tied her rolled bedding to the bottom of her bag and slung it onto her back, then stepped out of her bedroom.

Her parents had already left, and the house was empty when Gale pulled the front door closed behind her and set out to retrace her steps across the mountainside—alone this time, headed toward a place she'd hoped never to visit again.

CHAPTER EIGHT

THE TRAIL LEADING to the witch's cabin was ten years old, so cold not even Hawk could have followed it. Gale paused in the forest clearing where their father had left her and Hawk, surrounded by bird song that hadn't been there the first time she'd made the trip, straining to recall where to go next.

Getting this far had been simple. She'd been to the woods many times over the past few years to gather herbs and had often found her feet carrying her toward this place, called like a migrating bird drawn to its nesting grounds.

But this was the first time she'd actually visited it, or desired to go farther.

The little clearing was more overgrown than it had been years ago, but she remembered the cluster of stunted pines growing on the bare rock outcropping that had sheltered her and Hawk for two days before they realized Father wasn't coming back. The remains of their campfire were long gone, the carefully placed stones scattered by animals or covered by leaves.

She sat and closed her eyes, letting herself remember what she'd tried so hard to forget and forgive.

The cold. The hunger that gnawed at her belly until she could barely feel it anymore. The waiting, the worry that something had happened to their father, and the decision to try to find their way home.

Gale opened her eyes, but for a moment she was still living entirely in her memory. The trees were larger and more forbidding in her mind, the ground bare of anything fresh or edible, Hawk's hand too thin and too cold as he took hers and led her across the gentle slope of the mountain, trying to take her home.

She stood and walked, half in the past and half in the present.

They'd gone the wrong way. Hawk hadn't been trained as well back then as he was now and hadn't kept track of what direction they'd walked on the journey up and across the mountain. He didn't know how to guess directions when the sun was hidden behind clouds, and he certainly couldn't tell one unfamiliar stream from another.

Gale stopped when she reached a trickling brook and looked for anything familiar. She'd been so frightened then, too hungry to think, not focused on making memories. But she'd been searching then, too, and had noted the smooth stone of the opening in the mountain where the water bubbled up. This, at least, hadn't changed.

She turned and followed the stream, holding her skirt up and keeping her boots clear of the water. They'd thought this stream would lead them home. It hadn't taken them to their familiar river but on toward wider streams and eventually to an unfamiliar hollow on the side of the mountain.

The sun shone warm on her back, and Gale carried her jacket in her arms as she walked along what had been the wrong path then, but that she prayed was the right one now.

SHE WALKED FOR SEVERAL DAYS, gathering roots and eggs and whatever else the forest provided, boiling water in her little tin pot for drinking, applying salve to her rash every morning and night. The redness spread in spite of her efforts, and in the quiet of the woods it was hard not to imagine she could feel it eating deeper into her flesh.

When the stream joined a river, she stopped to bathe, change clothes, and wash what was dirty from her travels. She tried to rest while her things dried, though everything in her screamed that she had to keep moving.

Her spare socks and underthings were still damp when she packed them up and moved on, following the course of the river through the heavy forest that covered the mountainside.

This was a different world from the one she and Hawk had travelled through before. During their first journey, the forest had been devoid of life, silent and still. Now she had the company of birds, rabbits, and an orange fox that she caught watching her when she woke one morning, its pointed face tilted to one side, its dark eyes curious.

Then she moved, and it vanished as though it had been a dream.

Late in the afternoon of the third day the river made a sharp turn, no longer flowing down the mountain, but sideways across its surface and climbing back up before resuming its natural course.

Wrong. Unnatural.

Magic.

Gale's heart skipped. She hadn't remembered to watch for this landmark, but now it came back to her—a bit of strangeness that had been buried under everything that had come after, waiting to be remembered. She was getting close now.

Magic existed in pockets all through the mountains, and presumably through the rest of Andonia, imperceptible to any who hadn't been touched by it.

The power grew more noticeable as she approached the place where the river bent to flow upward. The hairs on her arms and the back of her neck stood on end, and her skin tingled with it. She hadn't felt magic this strong since the journey home.

What had Hawk said? That he feared it, that it pained him?

Gale wished she could say the same, but it wasn't so. This was the thrill of being infatuated with someone and seeing her across the square, a quick jolt of something that was joy and desire and a little fear, anticipation and longing and possibility all wrapped into one moment, twisted and tangled and beautiful even as she knew it would lead to nothing.

Her hands trembled as the feeling grew stronger.

She forced herself to cross to the other side of the river, away from that raw power.

It was enough to know it was there, to have felt it and prepared herself for what she'd find when she reached the plot of land the witch had chosen for just such energies.

The sensation eased as Gale walked away and continued downstream. She didn't stop to make camp until she was no longer worried temptation would creep into her dreams.

Rain came later the next day, and Gale walked on with the deep hood of her jacket pulled up to shelter her face. The weather brought her closer to herself as a child—cold, tired, and wet, if not nearly as miserable as she'd been on their first journey all those years ago. Back then, it had taken them twice as long, at least, to cover this much ground. They'd been so hungry, unable to walk far without stopping to rest.

The river met up with another broad stream, and they joined to course down the mountainside as one.

Almost there. Gale's steps quickened, but she forced herself to slow and walk at the pace she had so long ago, up a promising little path away from the river that was now unused, overgrown, and nearly invisible.

Her stomach had ached then, and her toes had been numb.

She followed the path and let herself fall deeper into memory.

~

GALE'S BREATH caught as she and Hawk stepped out of the forest. She blinked and rubbed her eyes, sure that the scene ahead of her was a dream. Or maybe her life had ended after only seven years, and this was paradise.

Her stomach grumbled, informing her that she was still alive. Not paradise. Not a dream.

A cozy log cabin with a squat stone chimney stood in a clearing, the sun shining down on it like the rays that flooded in through the roof of the Hall back home. Someone had painted white circles around the door, each with a bright pattern inside. It reminded Gale of the houses made of gingerbread sticks and candies that Mister Dearwood set in his shop window to brighten the town's spirits in winter, and the memory made her heart ache for home. Moss grew in little patches on the roof, and vines climbed the walls, making the building feel like a living part of the garden that surrounded it.

And what a garden it was. Gale stepped closer, her mouth already watering at the sight of trees weighed down by fruit.

Hawk grabbed her arm. "Wait."

Gale wanted to punch him until he let go, but mother always said words solved problems better. "There's food."

"I see it." Hunger had made Hawk's face thin and sharp, aging him beyond his eleven years. He nodded at the garden. "What kind of place has an autumn harvest in early spring?"

Gale stopped pulling. "One that God sent to save us?"

Hawk pressed his lips together and shook his head. "It's like the grown-ups have been saying. The land is cursed, and a witch who could do that could sure spare their own little patch, couldn't they? And have harvests whenever they wanted?"

Gale's eyes prickled, but she was too tired to cry. "You don't know for sure."

"You explain it, then."

Gale thought, but she couldn't come up with another idea. "Guess *you're right," she said. "But we've been praying for God to guide our steps, and this is where we ended up. Maybe it is a witch's garden, but there's no law that says we can't sneak in and steal a bite, is there?"*

It was a genuine question. Gale wasn't old enough to have begun serious lessons in the Teachings. Hawk was. He'd only been at it a few years, but compared to her, he was an expert.

Hawk chewed on his lower lip as he thought, his eyes fixed on the bough of an apple tree that reached over the wooden fence a few paces from the edge of the clearing.

"I guess there's no sin in taking what a witch is hoarding for itself," he said slowly. "An apple is an apple, no matter how it's grown."

"And hungry is hungry," Gale added.

The long grass outside the fence, brown as it had been everywhere else for the past few years, brushed against Gale's skirt as she hurried toward the fence, which was made up of nothing more than posts and a few cross-pieces—more the idea of a fence than anything meant to keep something in or out.

Hawk crouched beneath the low bough and picked an apple. "Better let me taste first," he whispered. "If I turn into a frog or something, you run away as fast as you can."

Gale nodded solemnly, though she thought maybe she'd take a second to catch him and stuff him in her pocket first. It would be the sisterly thing to do.

Hawk sank his teeth into the bright red apple, which looked bigger and juicier than anything grown back home. Gale held her breath and waited, but nothing happened to him as he chewed and swallowed.

As she waited, a faint breeze blew through the clearing, carrying the scent of baking bread. Gale's stomach groaned.

"Come on, gimme," she whispered, grabbing for the apple. She pulled it from Hawk's hands and bit into it.

It was like tasting autumn. Crisp and sweet and crunchy, but it went beyond that. With that first bite, Gale was transported to hayrides and cider pressings and leaves crunching under her feet—things that used to seem so regular, that now she'd have given anything to have back.

The apple was gone before she knew it, and Hawk had polished off another. Her stomach still felt like a gnawing hole, but there was no more fruit within reach.

"We could sneak in," Gale said, already knowing Hawk would say no.

But he stood and surveyed the garden with one hand raised to his brow. Gale looked, too, and saw nothing but fruit trees and flowers and a vegetable patch overflowing with green lettuce and orange pumpkins and things Gale had never seen before. A few hens pecked around for bugs and a goat watched them from near the cabin, but there was no sign of any people about.

"Wait here," Hawk said, and slipped under the fence.

Gale counted to ten before she followed, further muddying her already filthy dress in the soil beneath the fence.

Hawk looked back and glared. She stuck her tongue out at him.

He slowed and waited for her, then motioned toward the little orchard. "See that?"

Gale looked. At first, all she saw was fruit—apples and pears and cherries and some pale orange things with soft, fuzzy skin. It looked like a fine harvest to her. Then she frowned.

"There's more kinds of fruits than there are trees."

Hawk nodded. "Cherries and apples on the same tree. I told you, it's witchery."

Still, they ate. Whatever magic had grown these strange trees and caused them to bear fruit in the spring had left them with plenty to choose from, and now that they'd tasted one, they couldn't help wanting to try them all.

Gale was reaching for one of the furry fruits when she froze at the sound of soft, padding footsteps approaching from the direction of the house.

Hawk spun and picked up a club-like length of fallen branch. "Don't you come any closer. We know what you are."

Gale squeezed her eyes shut, not wanting to turn and look. She'd heard stories of what magic did to a person, turning their skin to patches of purple and green, leaving them with lumpish noses, bent bodies, twisted fingers and croaking voices and—

"Peace, children."

A woman's voice, but soft and gentle and musical. She sounded young and... happy. Gale turned slowly.

The woman who stood before them couldn't be a witch. She was younger than their mother, her face unlined but her brow furrowed with concern. Hair of deep gold swirled down over her shoulder, tied into a loose braid with curls falling free around sharp eyes and faintly flushed cheeks. Her brown dress was smeared with flour, and she held a dish towel in her hands as if she'd just stepped out of the kitchen.

"Where did you come from?" she asked.

Hawk's makeshift weapon trembled until he steadied his hand. "We got lost in the woods."

Gale bit her tongue, which wanted to tell this lady that lost was maybe not the word for it, that she and Hawk had argued themselves half to death over whether their father had left them on purpose and why.

The woman's lips pressed together, just for a second. "You're from Bright Hollow, aren't you?"

"Sure are," Hawk said.

"Hmm." The woman turned to Gale. "Do you speak, little one?"

"I do, ma'am," Gale said. Hawk glared at her, but she saw no sense in being impolite. Witch or not, they'd just been caught stealing from this person's garden. "Are you going to eat us? Ma'am?"

The witch smiled sadly. "Certainly not. But since you mentioned food..." She gestured back toward the log cabin, where the door stood open. "I just baked some fresh bread and was considering roasting a chicken for supper. You look tired and hungry. Would you like to come in?"

"Not on your life," Hawk said. "We'll be leaving now."

The woman tilted her head to one side. "Where will you go? You're days from home. At least take some food with you, and I could spare a blanket or two. But look. See those dark clouds beyond the trees?"

Gale turned to see over the orchard. A solid bank of charcoal grey thunderheads had built up on the horizon while they were busy sneaking and filling their bellies, and the peculiar heavy feel of oncoming thunder hung in the air.

"I'd be a terrible neighbour if I left you to be caught up in that storm," the witch said. "You're welcome to weather it under my roof."

Hawk's nostrils flared. "You can't fool us, witch. We won't trust you."

She closed her eyes and took a deep breath. It looked to Gale like she might be praying, but that wasn't a thing a witch would do. "My name isn't witch. *It's Madrigal. I know you've been taught that I'm corrupted, that I eat children, that I'm a monster. None of it is true."*

Thunder rumbled in the distance. The hairs on Gale's arms stood like the back fur on a frightened cat.

Madrigal stepped a little closer. "I can offer shelter and a place to sleep." She looked around the garden. "With the help of a few more hands this place could feed us all until things look brighter and you can go home. What do you say?"

Gale looked around. She'd always loved gardens and wondered whether her future might lie in farming or tending to the flowers in the town square. This place was like nothing she'd ever seen, wild and unruly, less orderly and constrained than anything back home. The idea of staying was certainly more appealing than going back into the woods, being drenched by the rain, and either starving or freezing to death.

The sky overhead was darkening, the half-sun-half-cloud combination casting a weird yellow light over everything.

Neither Gale nor Hawk spoke.

Madrigal sighed and ran her right hand down her cheek. The index finger was completely missing. "Your choice."

She walked back to the house and closed the door, leaving them alone and free to escape.

"She's nice," Gale said.

"That's what she wants us to think. She's trying to tempt us to leave the Path."

Gale chewed the inside of her cheek, praying for an answer, but nothing came to her. She stepped forward.

Hawk grabbed her arm again.

This time Gale shook him off. "We're going to die if we go back to the woods."

"And we'll die if we go in there and she eats us," Hawk added, scowling at the cabin.

Gale lifted one shoulder in a half shrug. "Sure. But maybe she won't. And even if she is bad, maybe we'll at least die with warm bread in our bellies."

She ran for the house, breathing in humid air that smelled of lilacs and lavender and good, rich soil.

And just as she'd known he would, Hawk followed.

CHAPTER NINE

GALE WAS DRAWN back to the present as she stepped out of the forest and into the clearing. The rain had grown heavy and fell on her hood in fat drops that dripped onto her nose, but she hardly noticed. She was too busy taking in the destruction she and Hawk had caused when they left this place.

The cabin hadn't burned to the ground as Hawk had hoped, but its peaked roof, which had once been so proud and straight, had collapsed in the middle, leaving a gaping hole with beams protruding into the empty space like grasping, broken fingers. The fence had fallen in a few places, and within its borders the garden ran riot—bright flowers growing like weeds in the vegetable patch, fruit trees reaching out as though to pluck pumpkins from the ground, the wide paths overgrown with anything that could take root there. It was encouraging in a way —the loss of the witch's presence hadn't kept anything from blooming or fruiting year-round, which meant her spells were still in place.

Enchantments, not spells. Gale had spent years trying not to think about the mechanics of magic, but the knowledge bubbled easily to the surface of her mind as she stepped past the broken gate and felt the magic of the land wash over her.

Spells are for immediate and temporary direction of magic, sending energy to do a witch's bidding.

Enchantments create a more permanent effect, are applied to a physical object, and may outlive the witch herself.

The lessons came to her in the witch's voice. She'd spoken them only in the little garden shed out back, never in the cabin where Hawk might hear from his perch in the loft.

But the books Gale needed now were kept safe in the cabin. She remembered them well. The witch had allowed her to pore over the pages, tracing the unfamiliar script with her fingers, memorizing drawings of strange and wonderful plants and creatures. She'd learned to recognize a few words in that old language and had devoured other notes written in pretty but too-fancy modern Andonian script. The witch had been so proud of her student.

"She should have been afraid," Gale whispered to herself. The witch's books had betrayed her in the end, giving over enough of their secrets to allow a little girl to put her to sleep in the hopes that she and her brother might slip away without her noticing.

Lightning flashed and thunder rumbled after it, bringing a fresh torrent of rain. Gale dashed toward the cabin and wrenched the door open.

Wind must have blown it closed. Gale stepped inside and shook the rain off. *Hawk made me leave it open—said air would feed the flames.*

Her heart hammered as her eyes adjusted to the dim light provided by the overcast sky.

"Please, God," she prayed. "Let me find the books, if it be Your will. Let there be enough notes in a language I understand for me to work out what we need and let me find the cure without corrupting myself with magic."

The first thing she didn't see was the witch's body. That, at least, was a relief. Hawk had done a thorough job of making sure she was truly dead, and the flames had burned bright over her body when they'd left—there was no chance she'd got up and wandered out. More likely an animal had come in and dragged her charred bones away.

Gale's stomach turned at the thought, but it was better than having empty eye sockets watching her as she searched.

But the rest of the cabin was less encouraging by far.

The remains of the collapsed section of roof occupied the middle of the room, standing at sharp angles where they'd broken over the heavy wooden table where Gale had taken meals with the witch. She'd always felt guilty leaving Hawk alone in the loft, but he'd been so surly, hunching over his bowl as he ate his soup, grimacing like it was poison, leaving most of it in the bowl every time. And the witch had been so interesting, even when her smiles seemed strained as she glanced toward the hostile stranger in her loft.

Gale had told Hawk she was only trying to win the witch over, not actually becoming her friend and student. She'd never been sure of whether he'd believed her.

The loft itself still stood, but several rungs in the ladder leading up to it were missing. The roof sheltered that end of the cabin, covering the loft and the witch's cozy sleeping area beneath it, which seemed to have been untouched by the flames before the rain had come in to ruin everything with dampness and rot.

For a second Gale imagined she could smell the cabin as it was the first time she'd climbed that ladder to the loft—baking bread, dried herbs hanging from the beams, the heavy, warm scent of the wool blankets she and Hawk had pulled from the chest in the loft to make beds for themselves.

But only for that moment. The odours of now were too strong for memory to hold much sway.

Rotting wood.

Damp earth beneath floorboards with gaps wide enough to let the rainwater drain as soon as it poured through the hole in the roof.

Moss and musty blankets and mouse droppings.

The iron stove still stood in its place, though the witch would have been horrified to see the rust that had accumulated on it. The cupboards all stood open, canisters knocked onto the counters and emptied, butter dish overturned on the floor, mildew spreading in patches over everything.

And scattered across the floor, piled in the corner or lying in damp clumps, the pages of books.

Gale set her jaw and crossed to the area beneath the loft. The witch's bed was made but sunken in the middle. And the shelf beside it, where she'd kept her books full of notes and recipes, was empty.

One book lay on the floor, peeking out from under the bed, and Gale snatched it up to page through it. The binding fell apart in her hands, and though the pages were dry, they were terribly warped, and the ink had bled into illegibility.

Gale squeezed her eyes closed and willed herself not to cry as she dropped the ruined book to the floor.

Hawk would say the world was better off without those recipes, that knowledge of dark things could never bring light to the world. He'd hoped the books, herbs, and everything else would burn with the witch. He didn't understand that there could be good there as well, that God's will might be to sort it out from the bad.

But there was still the garden, still Gale's own scarred soul drawing her toward magic in all its forms. It would be impossible to sense what effects a given plant might have in a medicine, but returning to the cabin had already brought back so many memories. There had to be at least a chance she'd remember something the witch had taught her all those years ago that would help.

If this was where the answers waited, surely it would be God's will that she find them.

The cloudburst had let up as Gale explored, and the downpour that had washed through the hole in the roof turned to light rain and then a faint drizzle. The room lightened as the cloud cover thinned, revealing the extent of the filth on the few windows that hadn't broken over years of neglect.

Gale set her bag on the floor at the end of the witch's bed and headed back outside, raising her hood before she stepped out.

At least I can gather samples to take back. River might recognize things I don't.

And if I can find enough dry wood in the forest, I can certainly have a hot supper.

As she moved through the garden it was as though there were two versions of it present—the one she remembered, which had at first seemed so wild and unruly but possessed its own kind of natural logic, and the small jungle she now faced.

She let the memories come, hoping there would be answers in them somewhere.

~

*"*NOT THAT ONE, GIRL.*" Madrigal's sharp tone stung Gale, and she pulled her hand back from the blossom she'd been reaching for.*

The witch sighed. "I'm not going to hit you. I only want you to do better."

"Sorry, Madrigal."

Hawk still called her the witch, and Gale did, too, when she spoke to him. But in her mind, she was Madrigal—a witch, certainly, but more than that. She was a person, and one who knew all sorts of wonderful things that Gale had never been taught in school. She'd promised to teach Gale all about her garden and the things that lived in it, and now, after nearly a month, she'd agreed to share some of the secret things she knew about them.

Gale loved secrets, and she'd promised not to share these ones with Hawk.

She figured he wouldn't care for them, anyway.

"Remember what I told you," Madrigal said, more gently.

Gale let her hand hover over a flower, eyes squinted, nose scrunched with the effort of feeling something from it. A dozen galariel flowers stood before her, their pink, lacy blossoms nodding in the warm breeze. They all looked the same, smelled the same, and would feel the same if she touched them. Gale was supposed to sense something different in one of them.

"Don't try so hard," Madrigal said. It sounded like she was trying not to laugh, but when Gale looked back at the witch her expression showed nothing. "Just let it come."

I shouldn't, though, *Gale thought.* Hawk would tell her it was bad, that she was stepping from the Path by even wanting to feel magic. Mother and Father would certainly not approve.

But they're not here, are they? They sent us out, and Madrigal saved us. Magic saved us, so how is that not God's will?

Something came to her then—not a feeling of warmth or tingling or happiness, though in a strange way it was all of those things. Every one of the flowers gave it off, but it was strongest in one blossom in the middle.

Gale pointed to it. "There. The little one." She looked back at Madrigal, who smiled down at her. "Is it always the little ones?"

"No. But small things often have unimaginable potential." She laid a hand on Gale's head and smoothed her hair down. "Go ahead. Take it."

The flower's stalk snapped beneath Gale's fingers.

"Good. Now come, I'll show you how we dry them."

"Galariel," Gale murmured, reaching out to touch a pink blossom. It felt like greeting an old friend, one she hadn't seen for so long she'd nearly forgotten about them. Magic waited in this bloom and all the others—in everything that grew on this plot of land.

And all of it would be useless if she couldn't call later lessons to mind. It was time to remember even the things she'd tried so hard to forget.

"She was kind," she told the flowers, speaking quietly and feeling a little foolish. "You wouldn't remember, but your great-great-grandflowers would. She was a hard teacher, wouldn't stand for inattention or carelessness, but..."

Warmth trailed down Gale's cheek. She brushed away a tear and scowled at the wetness on her finger.

"This is going to be more dangerous than I thought."

She wouldn't admit Hawk was right, but she also hadn't expected to have mixed feelings. She'd accepted her brother's version of the truth for so long—that the witch had been an evil curse-caster, that she and Hawk had saved everyone by killing her—that she hadn't realized what it would mean to remember all the things that had made Gale love her.

All lies, she reminded herself, and massaged away the tightness in her throat. *I'll be fine as long as I don't get swallowed up by the past.*

She headed toward the orchard, noting plants along the way and willing her mind to remember something useful, when the hairs on the back of her neck suddenly stood up as though someone was watching her.

"Well, well." Madrigal's voice spoke not in Gale's mind, but aloud, ringing through the garden. "Look who dared to return."

CHAPTER TEN

GALE TURNED SLOWLY, prepared to see the scarred form of the witch she and Hawk had left dead on the ground a decade ago reaching for her with burned and twisted hands.

Instead, her heart hammered as she stood face to face with the witch as she remembered her the morning before she died—hair like waves of flowing honey braided over one shoulder, her old-fashioned green dress with its confining bodice and flowing skirt, her feet bare.

Bare, and hovering a hand's breadth above the ground.

But Gale had never seen the witch so angry before, not even when she'd wakened at the slitting of her throat and so obviously realized how Gale had betrayed her. Nor had she been so thin before. Not in form, but in presence. She was like a pale, coloured glass window. Every part of her down to her missing index finger and the narrow scar on her left collarbone stood out clearly when Gale focused on it, but everything beyond her—the cabin, the collapsed shed where the pig had once lived—was visible through her.

The witch's eyes widened as Gale stared at her, and her lips parted as though to speak again.

Gale's breath caught in her chest as she turned and ran, her boots slapping against the flat stones between the weeds, racing back toward the cabin to grab her bag. She'd almost reached the door when the witch appeared in front of her, her teeth bared and hands reaching. Gale's boots slipped in a patch of mud, and she wheeled her arms as she fell backward, twisting and landing on one hip.

She was back on her feet a moment later, pushing off from the ground, stumbling away from the cabin and the witch.

The ghost.

In Gale's panic, there was only that word echoing in her mind. That and the desperate desire to get as far away from it as she could.

She raced toward the gate, leaning forward in her eagerness to be gone. With every step, she expected icy fingers to close around her neck or grasp at the trailing hem of her skirt, but a moment later she was beyond the fence. She kept running, not slowing until a knife-like stitch set in beneath her ribs and she fell.

It was only then that she realized she'd been screaming.

She turned to look for the witch, searching the path behind her, the dark woods, and the sky above, but there was nothing. Gale climbed to her feet, though her legs trembled so hard she felt she might collapse again.

"It wasn't a ghost," she told herself, sounding more convinced than she felt. "There's no such thing."

The Teachings were clear. A soul corrupted by magic would vanish at its death, having chosen to live out its glory in the power and pleasures of this world instead of the paradise that came in the lands beyond. And those who were faithful, who did live beyond death, were taken away to enjoy their rewards.

There was no room in the Teachings for ghosts.

She made herself take a step down the path toward the cabin.

"Probably an enchantment," she said aloud. It felt better to have someone to talk to, even if it was only herself. It felt more rational. More real. "It makes sense, doesn't it? If she left behind enchantments to keep the garden alive, then of course she would have left other things."

It sounded good. A witch who had trapped and magnified the magic on her little plot of land would certainly be jealous enough to guard it even after death.

But with every step, Gale felt like she was forcing herself to walk into a fire.

She froze at the edge of the woods.

It's not real.

The apparition hovered at the gate, hands on its hips in an all-too-familiar pose, brow furrowed and jaw set.

Gale stepped closer and saw tears in its eyes, and her chest tightened.

If it's an illusion, it's an awfully good one.

"How dare you?" the witch asked. She spoke in her familiar voice, but in a way Gale had never heard before—broken, trembling, hard and unspeakably vulnerable at the same time. "How dare you return, Nightingale Goodweather, after what you did to me?"

Gale sucked in a hard breath at her name. No illusion could have been set to know how the witch had died. Not when she'd trusted Gale so thoroughly.

Gale lifted her chin and tried to look down her nose. "I don't owe you an explanation, whatever you are. How dare you demand answers from me? You're dead, you have no more business being here than I do."

The ghost's jaw dropped, then she scowled. "I see your manners haven't improved in your time away."

"My manners were fine when I lived here."

The witch's eyes narrowed to bright slits. "You murdered your host in cold blood. I'd call that a pretty poor show of etiquette."

Gale's cheeks warmed. "Let me by. I'm here on important

business. Just... just go back to wherever you came from. I command it. In God's name."

The ghost let out a hard laugh. "Oh, in God's name? Then by all means, let me pack my things and be off." She patted the pockets of her dress and looked at the ground around her. "Pardon me, I seem to have no things. And I also seem to be lacking any intention of leaving my land. You and your God can stay outside and rot for all I care."

They glared at each other over the remains of the gate.

Help me, God, Gale prayed. *I need whatever it is she's protecting.*

She stepped forward. The ghost didn't move, but her expression softened from anger to uncertainty.

"Stop me, then," Gale dared her. "If you're not just an illusion, that is." She stepped closer again, now within arm's reach.

The ghost's lip curled in a silent snarl and she lashed out, open-palmed, to strike Gale's cheek.

Her hand passed through, leaving nothing but a feeling like a cold draught blowing through Gale's body where she'd touched her.

She is real, then. It didn't hurt, but that cold was undeniable evidence that something had made contact. The Teachings said it couldn't be so, but the evidence of her senses was impossible to ignore.

It was magic. Witchery. Something that defied God's will and could surely be explained.

Gale stalked forward, boots landing heavy on the stones, bracing herself for the cold as she passed through the ghost. But it stepped aside, letting her pass.

The witch kept pace beside her. "Have you come to finish what you started, then? Come to destroy my garden as you destroyed my body and my home?"

"What?" Gale's steps slowed. "No, not at all. There's an illness in my town that requires medicine we don't have. I thought this place might provide something our own gardens and forests couldn't."

She decided not to mention hoping to find the books and being disappointed. That would only please the witch.

"So you're here to steal from me again."

Gale spun to face her. "And what about what you stole from me?"

The witch's jaw dropped. "I offered you and your ungrateful brother everything, even if he didn't want most of it. Food, shelter, chores to keep your hands busy and lessons to occupy your mind." Her voice cracked. "Affection, as well as I knew how to offer it."

"And what did you take in return?" Gale's eyes prickled with tears, but she burned with anger, not sadness. "You led me from the Path, away from God's will and into your own. You exposed me to knowledge and power not meant for humans, and you scarred my soul."

The ghost's cheeks, which had appeared pink and lifelike, turned ashen. She hovered before Gale, her face a shifting spectrum of emotion—furrowed brow, lower lip sucked slightly into her mouth, narrowing eyes.

Then she laughed, but without humour.

"They got you back, though, didn't they? I offered you so much, but you were too afraid to take what should have been yours. It was foolish of me to try to free you." Everything about her hardened—her eyes turned to ice, her jaw to stone. "Know this, Nightingale. No matter how prettily you sing for them from your cage, no matter how well you've lied to your people and to yourself about the nasty old witch corrupting a poor child, you cannot lie to me. I was there, just as you were."

Gale licked her lips, which had gone dry even in the humid garden. "I—"

The ghost flashed her a pained smile. "I remember the girl

who came to me, who offered to help with the chores. I pitied her, but I admired her bravery for defying her horrid brother and giving me a chance. I remember her questions about magic, how I tried to respect her by not revealing any of it. How she pressed and prodded, how her bright little mind grabbed onto everything I did tell her until it became clear that this was her path..." She paused for a breath, though it seemed to Gale that it should be unnecessary for a dead person. "I thought you were different."

Something strange welled up in Gale. Not anger, which she should have felt at such accusations. It was more nauseating, more fearsome. More like shame.

"You were wrong." Gale's voice trembled, and she hated herself for it.

"I was. And I paid dearly for it, didn't I?"

With that, the ghost vanished. There was no puff of smoke, no sound as she went to wherever she'd been before Gale's arrival.

"Good riddance," Gale muttered, and stalked toward the garden to resume her search for medicines and a bit of supper.

Her throat tightened and her eyes burned. She told herself it was anger. The ghost was lying again. She'd tempted her, drawn her into magic. Gale had been a fool to fall for it, but she hadn't wanted to—

Her left toes knocked against something in the long grass that went skittering away over the stones, and Gale's thoughts fell still as she reached down to pick up the bent and broken form of a bird fashioned from tin and half-rotted leather.

MADRIGAL HELD her hands with their palms facing each other, her fingers tented to form a little cage. Gale set down the trowel she'd been using to dig potatoes and stood attentively with her hands folded before her. It had been two weeks since she and Hawk had arrived at the cabin,

and though she'd grown comfortable with calling the witch by her name and had begun helping with cooking and chores, it still seemed right to keep as much formality to their interactions as she could.

Mother and Father were waiting for them at home. It wouldn't do to grow close to another grown-up, especially one who Hawk kept reminding her was bad, bad, bad.

Madrigal smiled uncertainly and crouched, hands held out before her.

"You've been working so hard, Gale, and I'm grateful for it. I wonder, though, whether you might not miss your toys?"

Gale's gaze was fixed on the caged fingers. Something was moving inside.

"I've been fine," she said.

"Well anyway, I made you this as a little gift," Madrigal said. "Something to keep you company until Hawk decides to come down from his perch in the rafters."

Madrigal lifted the hand on top and Gale gasped as a little mechanical bird tilted its head to look up at her. Its head and body were made from bright, shiny tin, its joints held together with thin leather that allowed it to lift its wings to flutter them.

"Can it fly?" Gale asked, whispering so as not to frighten the strange little creature.

"No. But it can sing if you ask. Say, 'sing little friend,' and—"

A stream of warbling trills poured from the bird's open beak, silencing Madrigal. Gale clapped her hands together and laughed.

"It's a wee nightingale!"

"Naturally." Madrigal set the little bird in Gale's hands. "Keep her in your pocket or set her on the ground, and remember the words to speak to make her sing."

Gale swallowed hard and looked down at the bird. "Is that a spell? I'm not meant to—"

Madrigal's eyes widened. "Oh, my dear, no! I know you're not supposed to use magic. The magic is all in the bird, I promise. It's enchanted to move, and to sing when it hears the right words. That's all."

That was fine, Gale decided. Not harmful at all.

"Is your name a kind of bird, too?" she asked. She'd wanted to before, but it had seemed too personal. Too friendly. Now it somehow seemed all right. "Did you have a toy madrigal when you were a girl?"

"Not a bird," Madrigal said. "It's a sort of music. Voices coming together in a special kind of song. That's strange to you, I suppose—to be named after a human creation."

Gale turned to take in the garden, the cabin, and the witch herself. "It is. But I like it."

The little bird twisted its neck to rub its cold tin face against Gale's hand, and she laughed. It was the most wonderful toy she'd ever seen, and it had been made just for her. True, it was made with magic, but also with great care and skill. She couldn't help wondering what it must be like to be Madrigal, to be able to create such enchanted wonders.

Gale raised the little bird to her face and placed a gentle kiss on its head. "I love her. Thank you, Madrigal."

Madrigal's smile relaxed and she stood, shaking the dirt from the hem of her dress. "Good. But don't show Hawk right away. He might not like it."

Gale nodded solemnly and placed a protective hand over the bird. "I won't. Thank you."

But a week later, Hawk ventured out into the garden while Gale weeded the pumpkins—weeds took root here as readily as the seeds Madrigal planted, and the witch seemed disinclined to enchant them away.

Madrigal had gone into the woods to collect wild herbs. Hawk only ever came out when she was gone.

He snatched the little bird up from the nest Gale had made for it in the shade beneath a pumpkin leaf and scowled as he examined it.

"Please, Hawk," Gale said. "It's just a toy."

"It's magic, isn't it?"

He didn't wait for an answer. His fist closed tight around the strug-

gling creature, and he pulled one flapping wing loose, so it hung limp beside the body.

Gale cried out and tried to take it back, but he pushed her away.

"It's for your own good," he said. The bird's tweets fell silent as he crushed its fragile form between his hands and tossed it into a bed of rambling flowers. "Magic is poison for the soul, little bird. Makes people think they're like God. You're a good girl. Not like her."

"But—"

Hawk rested a hand on her shoulder. "You're only little. You don't know better. But I do, and I promise I'll protect you."

He walked away, leaving Gale to her tears.

She reached out, opening herself to the gentle atmosphere of the garden. She'd begun to take comfort in it, and needed it now that the bird's magic was gone.

I could bring it back, *she thought.* I could make another... if only I knew how.

~

GALE CRADLED the broken little body to her chest. The tin still shone bright, even if the leather had largely rotted away.

She'd worked so hard to make herself forget, to believe what would allow her to live with less shame and guilt, but Madrigal was right. Maybe the witch had corrupted a child by introducing her to magic. Maybe she had led her from the Path and changed her in ways that could never be undone. But...

"But I wanted this. I asked her for it."

She'd questioned, prodded, nearly begged until Madrigal had agreed to share a few of her secrets. It had been wrong to do so. She'd forgotten her parents and the Teachings so quickly even as Hawk clung to them. In a child's mind, what fascination could dusty old books hold in the face of the wonder of magic?

"It means nothing," she told herself, and made herself set the bird down on the ground. "I was wrong then. God forgives, and I know better now."

But she covered the nightingale in dirt and leaves, burying it like a beloved pet.

Right or wrong, a friend deserved as much.

CHAPTER ELEVEN

GALE SMEARED a thick layer of freshly brewed salve on her arm and covered it in cotton bandages, then left it to do its work while she cleaned her knife, mortar, and pestle.

Madrigal's tools, really. She'd found them in the garden shed and felt no shame about using any of them.

She stepped outside, into the warm orange light of sunset, and leaned against the log wall where faded symbols she couldn't hope to read were still carved deep into the wood, even long after the paint had faded.

The rash on her arm itched terribly, but she resisted the urge to scratch. She had high hopes for this new salve, which she'd based on her last formula but improved with new ingredients. She'd added a root that she remembered Madrigal saying had potent cleansing effects for use on wounds, and every common herb and flower she'd gathered had been humming with magic unlike anything she'd ever found at home.

Every piece of the medicine, though, came from a natural source, even if magic infused it. The Luminary would allow it to be used, those who had survived for this long would be saved, and God's will for Gale to work as a healer would be clear.

If the salve was going to work, it would happen soon. She just had to be patient.

The witch appeared next to her, legs crossed as though she were sitting on the ground but floating high enough to meet Gale's eyes.

"What are you doing, anyway?" she asked.

Gale raised an eyebrow at her. "Have you not been watching?"

"As though I don't have better things to do with my time."

"Then go do them."

The witch sighed. "I'm not going to sabotage you. I can't. I could haunt your dreams, rob you of sleep as I have any who dared to make camp on my land since I died, but I can't foul things up worse than you undoubtedly already have."

"There's still not much point talking about it if you won't help me."

"It does seem unlikely that I would, doesn't it?"

Gale glared at her. "Then why are you here, witch?"

"I'm hardly going to ignore it when one of my murderers shows up, am I?"

Arms crossed, Gale slumped against the wall. "Have those other intruders had the pleasure of your company while they were awake?"

"No. They couldn't see or hear me."

"Then why must I?"

The witch shrugged. "Maybe your God is punishing you. Or both of us." She laughed. "For so long I wanted to see the two of you again. The idea of revenge does get stale after some time, though, even if the bitterness continues to grow." She looked into Gale's eyes. "Honestly, it's dull being dead."

"You said you had other things to do." Gale tried not to sound interested.

"I lied. I'm bored." The ghost frowned. "It would be different if I could pop off to anywhere in the world, but I can't. Not much happens here, and the borderlands are dull as dry toast. You're clearly on a mission, though, and that's interesting."

"The bor—never mind." Curious as she was, Gale decided not to give the witch the satisfaction of denying her knowledge of what lay beyond death. She rolled up her sleeve, but left her bandages in place. "Bright Hollow is suffering a terrible illness that causes infection, pain, spreading rot of the flesh, madness, and death. You'll be pleased to know I haven't been spared. I'm here to search for a treatment." She tugged on her sleeve, covering the bandages again. "Some folks think it's another curse. At least we know it wasn't you this time."

The witch's lips tightened. "Right. But the last one was me, was it? Is that why you look at me now as your brother did every day the two of you lived under my roof? You used to see me as Madrigal, or at least I thought you did. Now I'm 'witch' again."

"Should I see you as a friend after what you did to us? After you cursed us to starve?"

The witch leaned forward, her eyes sharp and searching. "Oh, yes. Me, the nasty old monster who cursed your poor town when all you'd done is judge and persecute people like me for generations." She shook her head. "I didn't, even if you'd have deserved it. Couldn't have. You'd have known that if you'd asked instead of letting your brother's lies fester in the darkness of your heart."

"As if you'd have confessed."

The muscles in the witch's jaw flexed as she clenched her teeth. "Did you know the curse was larger than your little village? That it encompassed all of Andonia, that it caused not only famine but plagues and infestations and madness in other towns?"

"I—yes."

In truth, Gale had heard only a little of this. She'd known that traders had stopped coming to Bright Hollow during the famine, and when they'd returned, they'd said the trouble was greater than they'd realized. But she hadn't known it was so widespread, so varied.

The witch watched her expectantly, then let out a huff of breath when Gale didn't say anything more. "You're telling me that you believe I was strong enough to destroy all of Andonia, but not to defend myself against the children who happened to drop by to murder me?"

Gale shut out memories of blood and flames, focusing instead on what she'd accepted since she and Hawk had been embraced as heroes. "The curse ended when you died. That's all the proof I need."

The witch closed her eyes and nodded. "Bad timing for me, eh?" She uncrossed her legs and stood in front of Gale. "My death didn't end that curse. If it had, its magic wouldn't still be affecting you and every other living soul in this land."

Gale frowned at her. The sun had disappeared behind the mountain peaks to the west, but the ghost was as visible as ever in the fading light of dusk. "What do you mean? It's all over—the blights, the droughts, whatever else you claim was going on. The curse vanished."

"Did it?" The witch nodded to the north, to the rounded peaks of the mountains. "What lies beyond the northern mountain range?"

"What do you mean?"

"What's on the other side?"

Gale opened her mouth to answer, but nothing came out. "There's... what other side?"

"Think logically. I know you're capable of it." The witch's eyes brightened, as though she were willing Gale to understand something. "The world doesn't end at any of those peaks or passes, so what lies beyond?"

Gale struggled to remember. Surely something about it had come up in class. She could point out Queen's Run on a map, or

Embercliffe, or a few other places she had no intention of visiting. But to the north...

"It's just the top of the map. Or blank space. It's..." Her heart pounded as she found herself unable to think. *I should know something.* "What is it?"

"The forgotten lands. Magic." The witch smiled sadly. "Whoever cursed this land all those years ago withdrew the worst of it. But their magic lingers, blinding living minds to even the idea that there's anything to the north of Andonia. People once knew there was something there, even if it's only wilderness or a sea or a vast crevasse that swallows everything... but now only the dead know it exists at all. So tell me how I was ever powerful enough to still be doing that after my untimely demise."

Gale's arm itched again, and this time she scratched it, too troubled to stop herself. The pain sharpened, distracting her.

"How you did what?" she asked, feeling stupid. Even her lips and tongue had grown heavy and dull.

The witch's hands balled into fists. "How I made the lands to the north disappear."

Gale frowned. A thick fog had rolled through her mind, and she'd lost the trail of the conversation within it. "There are no lands to the..." She paused. "We've spoken about this already, haven't we?"

"Never mind, then." The ghost faded slightly, as though discouraged. Gale couldn't quite remember why. "The point is, I didn't curse your people. Whoever did is far more powerful than I and chose to withdraw the curse for reasons I can't know. My death was the result of me being too trusting, of ignoring instincts that said I should turn away anyone who hated me as much as your people do. I thought I was helping you by letting you see the truth about magic—its beauty, the good you might do with it if you let yourself learn. I even thought I might win over your brother in time. I was a fool, not a villain."

Blood rushed to Gale's cheeks, warming them. "Hawk and I are heroes."

The witch's jaw tightened visibly. "Believe what you will, then." She reached out, and before Gale could pull away, her hand passed through Gale's afflicted arm, leaving echoes of deathly cold. "Your salve will do no good. A curse has taken root in your flesh, and fighting it will take far stronger magic than you'll ever concoct on your own. It's hidden itself well, but that's blood magic—the source of nearly all curses and, incidentally, a form of magic I myself could never work." She offered a grim smile full of dark pleasure. "Best of luck to you, dear."

"I don't need it. This is God's will."

The witch shrugged and vanished.

Gale gave her head a hard shake to clear the cobwebs that had gathered there.

"She's lying again," she told herself. Hawk had convinced her of it as they'd walked home after they'd broken the curse, watching the world come back to life around them, celebrating God's victory. The Luminary had confirmed it and had praised Gale's bravery for winning the witch's trust so they could break the curse and escape.

She could believe it, too, if she ignored what the witch had said about the true scope of the curse and something else she'd said that Gale had already forgotten. And as for that blood magic thing, something about how she could never create such a curse...

"That was probably a lie, too."

Because it couldn't be true that someone else had cursed Andonia. If it were, that would mean Hawk and Gale weren't heroes but murderers.

It would mean the Luminary had been wrong about the curse and how it ended, and that idea felt dangerously close to doubting God.

Like stepping off the Path, into dark woods where beasts waited to feast on unwary souls.

But if the Teachings are wrong about ghosts, then what if...

Gale twisted her grandmother's ring on her finger, bringing herself back to home and truth and light. "I won't stray. I won't doubt. God, forgive me."

She hoped what the witch had said about the salve was a lie as well. But when she unwrapped the bandages, her rash was as red and angry as ever.

The witch was right about that, then. The answers might lie in this garden, but the books that had held the answers were gone, leaving the ghost herself as the only chance Gale had of learning anything useful. She needed help from the only soul in Andonia who would delight in not giving it to her.

Gale crouched against the wall, rested her face in her hands, and screamed her frustration into the coming night.

GALE LAID out her blankets on the sheltered wood floor under the loft, expecting to find her dreams invaded by the witch, by her taunts and lies, by nightmares of her own death. But though her sleep was ruined, it wasn't by dreams.

The rash was troubling her, though the salve dulled some of the pain, but that wasn't the worst of it.

She just couldn't stop thinking.

The witch had said Gale would never find the answers on her own, but maybe she'd been lying to discourage her. Maybe Gale *could* find the cure if she kept at it.

A comforting thought, but useless. The burning itch burrowing deeper into her arm was a constant reminder that she didn't have time to experiment blindly or to try formula after formula to see how the curse reacted. She needed help, and she needed it immediately if she was going to save herself or anyone else.

And there was only one person around who might be able to offer that help.

It's not so unthinkable, she decided. *I came here wanting her books and her knowledge... working with her is simply going directly to the source.*

As long as she wasn't drawn in and tempted to stray from God's will, there was no more harm in questioning the witch than in looking through pages of notes. Consorting with such people went against the Teachings, but she saw no way that it was a sin on the scale of letting dozens of people die if she could prevent such a tragedy.

Fight fire with fire, fight magic with magic—a little now, carefully controlled, to prevent destruction by a lot of it running wild.

The idea still felt right, but her belly cramped at the thought of the hate in the ghost's eyes.

The night grew cold, and she wished she'd slept outside where she could build a fire, or that she'd thought to find a way up to the loft to see whether Hawk had stored their blankets away in the old wooden chest the day they'd left.

She managed a little sleep once she'd burrowed under the blanket she'd brought from home, but woke before dawn with her thoughts still firmly on their course. She lay on her back, staring up at the underside of the loft where she had slept and Hawk had kept himself prisoner, and listened to a nightingale trilling its babbling brook of a melody outside the cabin.

The question was how to get the witch—the woman she'd helped murder—to help her when she had every reason to want to see Gale, Hawk, and everyone else in Bright Hollow removed from this world.

She wouldn't do it out of the goodness of her heart. Not when that sort of thing had ended so badly last time.

If she ever meant well, Gale reminded herself. *It was all lies, deliberate temptation and corruption...*

She sighed and watched her foggy breath rise into the darkness.

Over the course of a decade, she'd constructed a fortress of certainty in her mind, built on the Teachings and beliefs that served her well in Bright Hollow and allowed her to live peacefully among the people she loved. But those thoughts she'd clung to so firmly rang hollow now that she'd come back to the cabin. The memories were too real here to be silenced.

The enchanted mechanical nightingale that the witch had never asked about after it disappeared.

The witch's repeated overtures toward Hawk, hiding her magic and giving him his space, offering to make his favourite foods, which he invariably left nearly untouched on his plate.

The connection Gale had felt to magic, the witch's stern corrections when she recited a lesson wrong or messed up the preparation of ingredients for one of the witch's potions, the swelling sense of achievement when she got it right.

That's what I've been chasing in the clinic, she realized. *Not only a connection to magic, but the joy I felt in learning something that had rooted deep in my heart.*

Wherever it takes me, this is where I found my calling.

She got up and lit a fire in the rusty stove to boil water for tea. There was no point trying to sleep any longer when there were plans to be made.

The truth was, it didn't matter what was true or not true—at least, not in this moment. In the grander scheme of things, it mattered quite a lot whether she and Hawk were killers or heroes or both, whether they had ended the curse or coincidentally murdered an innocent woman, and whether their parents sending them into the woods in God's hands had really resulted in the completion of God's will or simply set off a sequence of events that had happened to save their lives and end someone else's.

But in the moment, and in the absence of evidence either way, those questions were useless.

All that mattered was the cure and how to get the witch to help her.

Start by thinking of her as Madrigal, maybe, instead of as "the witch." The ghost didn't seem able to read her mind, but she'd always been perceptive, and obviously understood Gale's current opinion of her. Changing her thoughts in that small way would make the conversations go more smoothly.

It seemed an apology was in order. Gale would get nowhere without one, even if she didn't truly mean it.

Gale carried her tin cup of brewed herbs outside and stepped into the pure gold light of the sun rising over the low curve of mountain to the east. She sipped and closed her eyes to enjoy the way the drink chased the chill from her bones, and when she opened them again, Madrigal floated beside her, dressed as she'd been the day before. Her presence was less startling today, but still unnerving as Gale considered how strange it was to stand as an adult next to this shade of a young woman who hadn't changed or aged since the day she died.

I'm catching up, she thought, and tried not to let the idea trouble her.

"Good morning," Gale said, soft and calm.

Madrigal snorted. "Is it, now? Have we had a change of heart overnight?"

Gale let the sharpness of Madrigal's voice roll off her. "A change of mind, anyway." She kept her eyes on the forest, unwilling to look into the witch's ghostly eyes. "I didn't see you in my dreams."

"I left you your privacy. Some of us still have manners."

Gale nodded and sipped her tea again. "I appreciate that. And I've decided I owe you an apology."

Madrigal let out a cackling laugh—the most witch-like Gale had ever heard from her. "Oh, well, if you've decided, by all means."

Gale pressed her lips together and reminded herself to keep her temper in check no matter how Madrigal baited her. "I've *realized* I owe you one, then. What we did was wrong. Not only what Hawk did when he killed you, but what I did when I took what you'd taught me and turned it against you. I thought we meant to escape and leave you sleeping, but that's no excuse. Willing or not, I played my part. And I'm…" She paused and drew a deep breath, trying to make her tone match the words. "I'm sorry."

Gale looked to Madrigal. Loose tendrils of the witch's hair moved as though blown by a breeze Gale couldn't feel.

"Apology not accepted."

Irritation flared through Gale's body, warming her face and tempting her to lash out.

"Why?" She schooled her tone into curiosity, not the demand that wanted to burst past her lips.

"Because that's a thin, provisional apology if ever I heard one." Madrigal cast a withering glare in her direction, then turned her attention toward the garden. "Even if you are sorry for your part of what you did, you're not sorry for the results as you perceive them."

Gale squeezed her cup tighter between her hands. "I'm not sorry the curse ended, if that's what you mean."

Madrigal nodded. "You think that my death ended it, and that if I'd lived, more people would have died. Therefore, you're not sorry for what your brother did, or for your own part that allowed him to do it."

"Fine, you're right. But know this." Tears stung Gale's eyes as hurts she'd buried long ago rose to the surface, and she didn't blink them away as she waited for Madrigal to face her again. "Your death was the worst moment of my life—worse than nearly starving at home or in the woods, worse than realizing my parents had left us to the mercy of God and the mountain." She paused for a breath, already regretting the depth of the truth she was about to speak but unable to hold it back now that she'd started. "I thought you were a godsend. You made me think we might be wrong about witches, and I'd have followed you away from God's light and into the darkness if only you'd kept showing me wonders and sharing your secrets. And then you died. We walked home and saw the forests coming back to life, the trees blooming and bearing all the fruit they'd denied us for years, the birds flying overhead when they'd been absent for so long, and that was the second-worst moment of my life because I realized my heart had led me astray and I'd loved a monster like a mother."

She looked away, facing the forest and the sunrise but not seeing either. "So there's the truth of my apology. I don't know what I'm sorry for, but I know what I regret. I've believed for ten years that we did the right thing, but I've felt like a fraud because I did it against my will. I *am* sorry we killed you, even if I shouldn't be." She sniffled and wiped her nose on her sleeve. "And more than anything, I'm sorry Hawk was right about you."

None of it made sense. None of the pieces fit, though it had all been so blessedly clear back in Bright Hollow.

"If that's your apology, here's mine," Madrigal said, her voice trembling. "I'm sorry I gave you what you wanted. I'm sorry I thought you were clever and sincere enough to open your mind to something outside of what you all think is your God's will. I'm sorry I underestimated how your brother could poison your mind with his misguided faith." Her nostrils flared, her tone hardened. "And above all, I'm sorry I didn't turn you away the night you arrived. It would have haunted me for the rest of my life, but at least I'd have lived."

Gale stared down into her empty cup, only realizing now that the mixture she'd brought from home—tea leaves, dried apple, honey crystals, and horrice weed stalks—was one that Madrigal had taught her.

"Sorry means two different things, I guess," she said. "Regret isn't an apology."

"Not in our case, anyway."

They watched in silence as the sun continued its climb,

bathing the garden in its light. Gale tried to sort out what she felt now and couldn't. Her anger had faded, but the pain lingered, reflected in and deepened by Madrigal's own in ways that made no sense. They were enemies. If anything, she should have enjoyed the witch's suffering. The Teachings said she deserved it.

But she couldn't, just as she couldn't ignore the irritating, gnawing guilt that ate away at her stomach when she'd let herself wonder *what if*.

"I need your help," she said, more sincerely than she'd felt when she offered her first attempt at an apology. "You were right. If this can be done at all, I can't do it alone. I apologized to you because I thought you might forgive me and want to help, but I also didn't want to lie about my feelings, so I couldn't say…" She sighed. "It was a foolish idea."

"It was."

"I'm still asking you to help me."

Madrigal walked deeper into the garden, and Gale followed.

"I have no reason to help you," Madrigal said, touching a rose blossom that didn't move beneath her fingers.

"You cared for me once."

"But no longer. This was my land. My garden. It was so beautiful—so useful, full of intent and purpose and magic. Now the magic lingers because it was here before me, and because I left enchantments that were built to last even when I travelled. But the rest… There's nothing I can do now. My presence is strong here because I can tether myself to this world through magic, but I can't *use* it. I couldn't haunt you in your magic-forsaken town, much as I wanted to. I can't pull weeds. Can't—" Madrigal turned to glare at Gale. "I had plans, you know."

"I know."

"Plans that had nothing to do with cursing all of Andonia or taking revenge against those who would drive me from this land. I wanted to live. To learn. To experiment. To pass my knowledge on to the next generation of witches, to keep magic in the hands of those who would use it well." Her breath caught. "I thought I had time."

Gale turned this over in her mind. "If that's true, then I am sorry we took it from you."

"Still provisional, isn't it? *If* you weren't a monster, *if* we were wrong."

They'd reached the orchard. Gale paused to admire a branch of mixed cherry blossoms and fruit, then plucked a handful of pink flowers and held them out to Madrigal. "Can you smell these?"

Madrigal nodded. "Less clearly than I see or hear, but a little— like an echo of what it used to be. Taste is beyond me, and you've seen how well I can touch anything. Even the earth supports me only because I decide it does." She sank into the ground until it swallowed her to the knees, then rose again until she appeared to be standing on it. "I can sense warmth or cold, but those are hollow. Not true reflections of what I knew in life."

"Then why stay?" Gale asked.

Madrigal glared at her, and she took a step back.

"What I mean is... well, clearly your soul wasn't destroyed when you died. Is there not anything for you to go on to?"

Madrigal hesitated, then shook her head. "There is something, on the other side of a veil beyond a bridge I cannot cross. I travel between this world and the borderlands that divide life from death, and I see others there—the newly dead. Lord Death comes to collect them, wearing his dark robes, never revealing his face. Those folks willingly take his hand... usually. Those few who fight him have truly stained souls, and I don't care to know what they did in life. Whether they go with excitement or fear, he takes them all. But not me. He doesn't look at me. Doesn't speak to me." She shot a sharp look at Gale. "And it's not because I'm a witch, so don't put on righteous airs about that. Witches are taken same as anyone else, and with as much gratitude."

Gale tucked this away to think about later. It contradicted the

Teachings and was likely a lie, but for now it was better to accept Madrigal's words if she wanted the conversation to move forward. "So why not you?"

Madrigal shrugged. "I've had time to speak to a few wise souls as they passed through the borderlands. Most folks aren't worth talking to, but some are, and I'm grateful for them—they're the only excitement I get most days. They've given me the idea that it's because I cling to purpose here."

"But you'd choose to move on if you could? Past the bridge and all that?"

"Without hesitation." Madrigal frowned, now more discouraged than angry. "My purpose here will never be fulfilled, and all I'm left with is regret, hate, and boredom. You're the only person who seems able to see or hear me. I'm not likely to find an apprentice now, am I? I'd move on if Lord Death would let me."

Gale thought on it. The answer was clear. And dangerous.

And necessary.

"Very well." She straightened her shoulders and turned toward the witch, looking directly into her eyes. "There's our deal. If you help me with my medicine, I will help you with your unfinished business. I will hear what you meant to teach me when you lived, therefore fulfilling your purpose."

Madrigal made a choking noise in the back of her throat as she stared at Gale. "Are you mad?"

"What other options do you have for finishing things up here and moving on?"

Madrigal floated away and back, hands flexing at her sides. "It's ridiculous. I thought once that you were exactly what I'd always hoped for—a blank slate, drawn to magic and desiring to become my apprentice, in time to become greater than I. But look at you now. Even if all those lost years weren't an issue, which I assure you they are, you can barely say the words *witch* or *magic* without gagging on them." She drifted closer and pointed a finger at Gale's face. "You say I'd have corrupted you if you'd stayed, but I say your people have done worse. They've caged you, Nightingale, and broken your wings. You despise what should have made you free. Teaching you now would do me no good. My knowledge is to be cherished, not tolerated."

"I thought it was to be used." Gale swatted at Madrigal's hand and tried not to flinch at the chill. "You say your plans were never to hurt people. Now your knowledge could help them. You say you didn't create a curse, and now you could heal the effects of one."

Madrigal raised herself higher off the ground so she could look down on Gale, her lip curling into a sneer. "I owe you nothing."

"No. But if we work together—if you teach me what I need to know to save my people—maybe Lord Death will walk you across that bridge." Gale held the witch's gaze. "That's what matters, isn't it? Or is revenge more important than your last chance to find peace?"

Deep furrows formed between Madrigal's brows as she thought it over. "Here are my terms, then," she said after a long silence, "and I'll not negotiate. You won't just *hear* what I meant to teach you. You'll learn it properly, as you would have back then. You'll need to, anyway, if you want your cure. Magic accepts no half-measures, as I'm sure I told you once before."

Gale set her jaw and nodded. "More than once."

"Good. You will truly become my apprentice. You will walk as far along my path as your God allows." Her eyes softened, now searching Gale's. "If you believe it's God's will for you to save yourself or anyone else, you'll have to follow where I lead. I don't want to corrupt you or make you a witch. In fact, I no longer believe you deserve to become one, even if magic would accept your sacrifice."

Gale glanced down at Madrigal's missing right index finger. Magic demanded a painful physical sacrifice before it would inhabit a person, and Gale had lain awake for a whole night with terrible visions in her mind after she'd learned that Madrigal had cut her own finger off as the final step in becoming a witch. She'd said she felt it gave her an edge in enchantments, offering a piece of her hand to gain strength in creation.

Gale moved her hands behind her back and touched her ring, a reminder of faith and home and family, which sat on the same finger the witch had lost for the sake of power.

"But you will listen," Madrigal said. "You will obey. You will understand. You will work what magic is necessary. And then you'll be free to return home an actual hero."

Gale's breath trembled, but she nodded.

Heroism isn't meant to be easy, and nothing worth having comes without risk, she told herself. *I will prove myself capable and faithful. I will not stray, no matter how far I must wander into these dark woods.*

She held out her right hand, and Madrigal rested hers against it, turning Gale's palm to ice.

"We have a deal, then?" Madrigal asked.

"We do."

"Good." The ghost wiped her hand against her skirt and gestured toward the house. "Your first task as my apprentice is to clean up the mess you made so we have somewhere to work."

Gale gaped at the cabin with its collapsed roof, remembering the mess inside. "I may not have made it clear, but I don't have much time. A week before I'm useless, if not dead. Surely we could use the shed, or—"

"You agreed to do what was necessary." Madrigal's eyes sparkled with amusement. "Go. We'll review your old lessons while you work."

Gale closed her eyes, prayed for strength, and stalked toward the cabin.

CHAPTER THIRTEEN

"ABSOLUTELY NOT." Gale stood in the mostly clean cabin with a tattered old broom in one hand, staring down a ghost. "That's going too far."

Madrigal sat on a chair Gale had pulled out for her and shrugged. "Then you might as well go home. You can't work magic without taking it into yourself."

"I can, though." Gale set her free hand on her hip. "You showed me potions that only required the addition of *lucistra* to make special reactions happen."

Madrigal waved her hand near her face as though batting away invisible flies, or perhaps the dust that floated through the fading late-afternoon light. "Child's work. You can cure a headache with that, not a curse. And that's what's needed here. Treat only the symptoms and they'll come back. Knock out the curse and balance will be restored, allowing healing that would be impossible under normal circumstances. You're not going to do that without real magic."

Gale's head had begun to ache from the onslaught of information.

"You must remember some of your lessons," Madrigal said, obviously irritated. "What is *lucistra*? How does it work?"

The memories came so easily that it felt like a betrayal of everything Gale had done to bury them. "It's one of a number of recipes used by witches to capture magic in a usable form. Specific ingredients are chosen, spells are spoken. The finished potions aren't pure magic, but they're the closest you can get to physically capturing it."

And it's so good, she thought, but decided not to say it aloud.

Madrigal drummed her fingers silently on the tabletop. "And why don't we just consume the ingredients instead of making those potions?"

"The potions contain more and purer magic than you can get from those elements alone," Gale said quickly, not trying to hide her impatience. "I'm dying, what's your point?"

Madrigal's lips narrowed. "My point is that your stubbornness makes it clear you don't remember your lessons as well as I'd hoped. Why did you have to take magic into yourself to make the potion that allowed your brother to kill me?"

Gale's stomach sank as she remembered. "If I'd added *lucistra* to the mix it would have amplified some reactions, but I couldn't have directed them without using a spell."

"And for that you needed magic in you," Madrigal said, "which could only come from consuming my lovely little potion. I'm proof of how well you learned that lesson, and how well you did on your first solo attempt."

"Thank you."

"That wasn't a compliment." Madrigal glared at her. "My point is that what I'm asking now is no worse than what you did before, and it's every bit as necessary. I see no harm in you doing it again."

Gale gripped the broom tighter. "No harm? I consumed magic here and I walked away permanently changed."

"Corrupted?" Madrigal asked, now more interested than challenging.

"I don't know. Scarred, at least. I can feel magic more clearly than before. And it's not just feeling it. I'm drawn to it."

"You crave it. Of course you do." Madrigal smiled. "It's wonderful. And, despite what you may believe, harmless. Harm comes from how it might be used, but the power itself is benign, even good. It energizes, revitalizes, lifts the spirits even without a spell to ask it to do so."

Gale held back a groan. She didn't have time to argue. She'd wasted an entire day cleaning the cabin when she'd hoped to have a new salve by now, but she couldn't help herself. "At what cost, though? I live in a community. I have interests outside of magic. I'd like to marry some day. Magic seems to have left you utterly isolated until Hawk and I showed up, just as it has every witch our people have chased from the mountain."

Madrigal continued her silent finger tapping. "True. Magic was my calling. I loved it more than I ever could have loved a flawed and fallible human, and I pursued it with all my passion. Magic welcomes us, but it demands much if we're truly to master its secrets. There are witches with families, but they're usually weak and useless. Or dead, when their connections make it easier for them to be found out and executed by the king's mages."

"You don't regret your choice, then?"

Madrigal stretched backward, passing through the hard back of the chair with her arms outstretched, then sat up straight and leaned on the table as though she were just as solid as the wood beneath her elbows. "Not in the least. And if you have any memory of what magic felt like as it flowed through you, you'll understand why."

"It was amazing." Gale placed the broom in the corner near Madrigal's bed and crossed her arms. "I still feel echoes of it when I'm near magic. When it calls me. It's like a hint, though, or a promise, or... All I know is that I had it here and it made me want more, always. And the more I let it in, the harder it will be to let it go." She crossed toward the kitchen area, skirting a soft spot in the floorboards where the fallen roof beams had lain. "I swore before I left home that I'd never do it again. I came here hoping to find *lucistra* and use it as a catalyst. Drinking it goes against the Teachings."

"What's worth more, your honour or your life?"

Gale glared at the witch and didn't answer.

Madrigal shrugged. "Your choice. If you want an effective medicine, you'll drink that little potion again and let magic flow through you so you can work spells. There's no other way."

Gale thought it over as she polished a freshly filled oil lamp that was already as clean as it was going to get.

Risk it or die. Not a pleasant decision to have to make, but surely it would turn out all right in the end. It had to be if God wanted to see this curse cured. The Path was still in sight, and she'd worry later about getting through whatever consequences came.

She'd only need to use magic once to make the medicine, and then it would be over.

"Fine." Gale spread her arms and gestured around the cabin. "It's not going to get much cleaner without me patching the roof, and that's beyond my skills. Show me what's next."

"It's not fully clean," Madrigal said. "You didn't take the rugs out to shake them."

"I took this one out." Gale nodded at the bare space beneath the table. "There's no point beating it when it's ruined, though. It'll rot just as well in the woods as it will here."

Madrigal moved toward the area below the loft, where things were a little less damaged. "This one. By the bed."

Gale gritted her teeth and prayed for strength. "I'm running out of time, you know."

"So get on with it."

The ghost pointed with one toe at the remains of a wool

carpet that had once been blue and yellow but was now a uniform, faded brown.

Gale tried not to wince as she grabbed the dirt-crusted fabric and heaved it out of the way. Beneath it lay a trapdoor with a rusty ring handle. Her heart leapt as she realized she might have been wrong when she thought all was lost here in the cabin.

Madrigal's smile faltered.

"What?"

The witch shook her head. "I still don't like it. Still don't trust you. But what good is any of this to me now? Go ahead."

She spoke the last words with confidence but wrapped her arms protectively around her torso. Gale wondered whether ghosts got stomach aches or whether it was an old habit from life.

So many questions. So few of them as urgent as the spreading rash on her arm.

She worked her fingers under the stiff metal ring and hauled upward. The door stuck at first, then came free all at once and crashed to the floor when Gale released it, leaving an empty square leading to a space beneath the cabin. The scents of damp earth and moss rose from the darkness.

"Well?" Madrigal asked. "Go on. I'll be right behind you."

Gale lit the lamp and held it over the opening but saw nothing but darkness. "What's down there?"

"Things I'd have wanted to protect if another witch had ever darkened my doorstep seeking to use my power to increase her own." She paused. "And my vessel. I don't know how much magic it holds after all this time, but it may be of use."

Something awakened in Gale, a beast she'd kept sleeping for a decade that now opened its eyes and flexed its fearsome claws. It was made of the memory of magic flowing through her, the bottomless craving she'd so often fought, and a surge of desire and curiosity that came with the mention of a witch's vessel, which was said to hold more power than any potion ever could.

Gale let herself feel the magic of the garden, which made the hair on her arms stand on end and her heart tremble when she focused on it. But there was nothing of that from down below as she descended the ladder into a bare dirt cellar.

The magic is protected, she thought as she reached the bottom and found only deep shadows that the dim lamplight barely penetrated.

Or it's not here at all. Maybe Madrigal had only been pretending to have no effect on the physical world. Maybe she'd find the strength to close the hatch after Gale went down, trapping her there until she starved.

The witch would surely feel it served her right.

"I don't see anything," Gale called, reaching for the ladder. "I'm coming back up."

"Have a little faith, girl." Madrigal's voice came from right behind her, and Gale jumped.

"Don't do that." She shone the lamp around and stepped forward, turning to illuminate the darkness. A thin layer of mud squelched under her boots.

The light picked out a large but sparsely furnished cellar. The few shelves were empty of the canned goods she'd have expected back home. But then, what need did the witch have to preserve food when her garden offered fresh produce year-round?

For a moment she allowed herself to consider what a life of magic would mean to a certain kind of person—the kind of thing she hadn't allowed herself to think about since she and Hawk left this place. Madrigal had said the learning was hard and the sacrifice great, that it was a lonely life spent in pursuit of knowledge, a path that made one strange to others and an outcast from society.

But it could mean healing those folks brave enough to ask for cures—or, depending on the witch's inclinations, wealthy enough to pay. It would mean never fearing famine. Protection from enemies, if not from people she invited willingly into her home.

Answers to all the fears that had plagued Gale since the day her father had left her and Hawk in the woods.

And all it would cost was her family, her community, and her soul.

Some prices were too high to pay, no matter how she longed for the benefits. That was what she hadn't understood as a child.

Madrigal gestured to a cupboard in the corner. Gale knelt and opened the doors, finding nothing within but dust.

"Someone's been here," she said, ignoring the disappointment that pressed against her chest and made it hard to breathe.

Madrigal swept around behind her and crouched. "Close it and speak the word I give you."

Gale tensed, and Madrigal sighed.

"It's only the password for an enchantment. You wouldn't be able to manage a spell even if you wanted to."

Gale's face warmed. "I knew that."

Madrigal whispered the word. The ghost had no breath, but the word itself tickled her ear, and Gale's tongue tingled as she thought of saying it.

She closed the doors. "*Elhalmadra.*"

The word rolled off her tongue. Nothing happened.

"Open it again."

Gale did and gasped. The empty cupboard now held a dozen thick books on a shelf, all leather-bound and in fine condition. Beneath the shelf sat a few boxes, and from a small black one radiated—

"Pure magic," Gale whispered. She turned to Madrigal. The witch's eyes were closed. "You can feel it?"

"As well as I see you," Madrigal said, speaking softly. Her eyes shone in the light of the lamp. "Take the third book in the row, and the fifth. That one with the reddish cover, and the dark one on the end. That's all you should need for your purposes."

Gale scrambled to keep up.

"Take the black box, too."

Gale did as she was instructed, taking the surprisingly heavy little wooden box and balancing it on the stack of books in her arms, then closed the cupboard. "Shall I take them upstairs?"

"I suppose." Madrigal didn't sound pleased. "The lamp oil will only last so long down here. No sense wasting it."

Before she left, Gale peeked into the cabinet again.

Nothing but dust.

She told herself she'd do well to forget, that only temptation lay behind those doors now. She had everything she needed for her current purposes, and that was the only way she'd ever allow herself to use magic.

Still, the key to that forbidden knowledge echoed through her mind as she climbed the ladder, carrying the books, the lamp, and the box in two trips.

Elhalmadra.

Elhalmadra.

CHAPTER FOURTEEN

MADRIGAL'S neat script covered every page from top to bottom and margin to margin—legible but utterly overwhelming, and most of it written in that strange language Gale couldn't begin to comprehend. There were few headings, leaving the illustrations that dotted the text as the only signposts. She looked up at Madrigal, who nodded.

"You'll need me to guide you," she said. She stood over Gale's shoulder and traced her fingers over the words on the page. "Even if you knew the language, you'd never make it through this on your own before that curse consumed you."

There was no pleasure in her voice. If anything, she sounded sad.

"You should have known all of this by now," she added, speaking as though to herself. "Should've been working all these years to learn magic's language so deeply it became a part of you. Creating your first external vessel within a year of arriving here, working magic and opening channels within yourself so *you* could become a vessel for magic..." She trailed off and her gaze sharpened as she turned it on Gale. "And what have you been doing instead?"

Preserving my soul, Gale thought. *Hiding my scars.*

"I've been walking the Path," she said. "Learning from my elders, as I would have been if I'd never come here."

"Letting them cage you," Madrigal added.

"Letting them protect me."

"From what, exactly?"

"From my desires," Gale said. "From magic."

"Your natural desires, yes." Madrigal shook her head sadly. "You took to magic like a fledgeling to the skies. Faltering at first, but eager. That's not something I did to you."

"But it's still dangerous."

The witch snorted. "Of course it's dangerous. Anything that's worth having is. But if you'd been brave enough to fly... well, you'd be in a far better position to help your people now."

Heat welled up in Gale's chest, and she slammed her fist on the table, surprising herself. "I wouldn't have my people if I'd stayed here. Even if you're telling the truth about the old curse not being your fault, even if it had ended on its own and they'd all survived, they'd never have taken me back if I'd learned what you wanted to teach me."

"What you wanted to learn," Madrigal replied, and Gale had no answer for that. It had been easy to lie to herself when no one else had known the truth, to believe she'd been lied to and tempted.

Now she had no defense, and she was beginning to realize how exhausting the effort had been.

"Have you ever seen a caged nightingale?" Madrigal asked, as though this were a perfectly logical progression of the conversation.

"No." Gale frowned. "We don't keep animals that don't do work for us."

Madrigal chewed her lower lip, deep in thought. "I've never seen one captive, but I heard once of a merchant who thought there'd be a market for them among the upper class and nobility.

Kept as pets, you know, to sing their beautiful songs in their mistresses' drawing rooms."

"Let me guess," Gale said, resting her chin on her hand. "The birds were placed in cages and refused to sing. They lost their spirit and became nothing more than drab little brown birds. Are you saying that's what walking the Path has done to me?"

Madrigal smiled sadly. "Not at all. The birds sang their songs within their cages. They ate, they messed their papers, they did all the things pretty little pets do."

Gale rubbed her aching forehead. "Then what's the point of this story?"

"The point, Nightingale, is that they still carried the wild in their hearts. No matter how happy they pretended to be in their cages, it called to them. And when the change of seasons came and told them to fly to their southern wintering grounds, every one of those pretty little birds threw themselves against the bars of their gilded cages, breaking their wings, killing themselves as they attempted to do what it was in their natures to do."

Gale sat up straight, her heart suddenly galloping. "I'm not like that. I know what I want, and it's all back in Bright Hollow. It's on the Path, following God's will. I'm only here to learn what I must to cure this disease and appease your desire to pass on your knowledge, not to follow some mad voice off into the dangers of the wild."

And the world *was* dangerous. Even when one wasn't walking with witches, Andonia was peopled with folks who didn't know or acknowledge God's will, who chose selfishness and greed over the hard but rewarding ways of the Path.

"You had so much potential." Madrigal sighed and looked away. "But very well. Turn to the middle of the book. Back a few pages…"

Gale followed her instructions and jotted notes as Madrigal translated. The recipes for healing medicines were simple enough, but the notes went into detail explaining how the magical reactions occurred so a witch could guide them by her knowledge and her will.

The wheels in Gale's mind turned like a great watch that had been wound after years locked away in a drawer, shifting bits of information around, hoping for answers to questions she'd never dared to let herself ask before, wishing she could read the words for herself.

She frowned as Madrigal dictated the end of the recipe. "You need magic to create this."

"That's where the box comes in. Open it."

Gale reached for the box, a lovely little thing with twisting vines carved into the surface of its dark wooden lid. Inside lay a small vial made of black glass, large enough to hold a few spoonfuls of liquid. Beside it rested a silver brooch inlaid with mother of pearl carved into the image of a hummingbird.

"Your vessel?" she asked as she carefully removed the brooch. She cupped it in her hands, letting herself feel its power.

"It was. What do you remember about them?"

Gale didn't try to resist the knowledge that freely returned to her. "Vessels hold far more power than a potion ever could. A person, even if not a true witch, can create one and access its power. Apprentice witches use them for their magic stores until they make their bodily sacrifice and become vessels themselves."

"Hmm." Madrigal didn't sound impressed, but Gale was pleased that she didn't offer any correction. "And why create a vessel instead of carrying an abundance of *lucistra* or some other magical potion made from other ingredients?"

"Because..." Gale frowned, searching deeper in her memory. "A vessel amplifies the power. Natural ingredients hold magic that is increased when the proper spells are used to make a potion, but a vessel does more. A witch could take ingredients with only a little magic, make an excellent potion, drink that and use it to fill her vessel, and when she drew it back out, it would be far more powerful than what went in."

"Quality as well as quantity, but you are correct," Madrigal said, a little grudgingly. "I never had much need of mine when I lived here, but it would have come in handy if I'd ever drained myself and needed to replenish quickly. But that's irrelevant to you. Do you feel anything from my vessel?"

"I can, though not as much as I'd have expected." Gale held it tighter, feeling the magic moving within it like a living thing. "It's lovely."

"It is. And it's not for you." Madrigal's fingers flexed as though to snatch the brooch away from her. "It's depleted after all these years in the cellar. Even if it weren't, it would take a powerful and talented witch to access the magic contained in another's vessel. Try the vial instead."

Gale took the dark glass container in her hand and opened the stopper. A familiar scent rose from it that made her chest ache with longing—sweet and light, smelling somehow of sunshine. The liquid within, if she poured it out, would no doubt be thick and golden, shimmering with magic.

"Still good." Her fingers trembled as she closed the stopper. The temptation to place just a drop on her tongue to see if it was as good as she remembered was nearly unbearable.

"Of course it is. Now, are you prepared to use it?"

Gale shivered. She told herself it was fear and not excitement. "If I must. May I go out and gather the ingredients for the medicine now?"

Madrigal shook her head. "Curses are tricky. We'll need to experiment, which means you'll need a stock of strong *lucistra* to work with. Use what's in the vial to make more, if you can manage it."

"And if I can't?" Gale's fingers tightened protectively around the vial. "If I mess it up and lose the magic entirely when this is gone?"

"Then I suppose you and yours are doomed." Madrigal didn't seem upset by the notion. "Write down the ingredients I give you. We'll see how well you remember your old botany lessons."

The sun had sunk low in the sky while they'd been reading. Glimmer beetles flitted through the air, flashing messages to each other and giving the garden a warm, languid glow that Gale associated with deep summer nights.

She moved quickly through the garden and collected the items from her list. The rose petals held magic unlike anything in the ones back home, but they were nothing compared to a flower called incardium that Gale had never seen outside this garden. The iris roots would help release that power into a usable form, as would a scrap from the living bark of a gnarled tree in a corner of the garden. A dozen ingredients in total, each holding the potential for great power if only a person had the knowledge and the power to guide them.

Madrigal floated behind her, humming her approval when Gale selected an excellent piece, *tsk*-ing when she didn't approve. She peered into Gale's basket. "That'll do. Let's get back inside."

They returned to the cabin, and, without prompting, Gale gathered the freshly washed instruments she'd gathered from the cabin and the shed—bowls, cauldron, knife, spoons, jars, mortar and pestle. She set the black vial beside them, her hand shaking.

It was such a small amount. One chance to get it right. Two at most.

And then either failure and death, or more steps away from God's light as she let temptation in again and again.

It still felt as though it must be God's will that she cure the disease, and at the same time it seemed terribly wrong. But there was no one here to ask for permission or advice—not the Luminary, not her parents, not even Hawk.

One step at a time. See if this one works at all, then worry about the next.

That was a big *if*. She'd succeeded in making a magical sleep draught once, but that had been when she'd been exposed to magic and learning about it every day, not denying it with each thought and breath for a decade.

She mixed the ingredients carefully, crushing roots to release their juices, adding water from the rain barrel, watching as thin strips of bark dissolved when they touched the mixture.

"It's time," Madrigal said, and pointed to the open page of her book. "You can read the spell?"

"I think so." Gale read the words out loud, feeling guilty speaking them even when they were harmless without magic. Madrigal corrected her pronunciation and nodded.

"Go ahead. Use what's in the vial, make more *lucistra*, and we'll see whether you have any chance of making this work."

Gale reached for the black vial and hesitated. The potion within called to her with a voice she felt rather than heard, promising a return to the heady heights she'd experienced so briefly as a child. And that desire came from the mere presence of magic. Taking it into herself would be consummation of sorts, a satisfaction of all the longing and temptation she'd resisted for so long.

Nothing so tempting could lead to good. But when not giving in would lead to so much worse...

Before she could hesitate again, Gale opened the stopper and drank.

CHAPTER FIFTEEN

It was as she remembered and more.

Gale had forgotten how magic opened her, made her larger and more diffuse, a greater part of the world and yet somehow more separate from it. She drifted on a sea of pure power, warm and bright, feeling that magic held her within it even as she held it within herself. It coursed through her body, awakening her, stealing her breath. It was everything she'd felt from magic in the years since she'd left this place magnified a thousandfold.

The world changed around her, revealing new colours and smells. The gears in her mind spun faster than ever before, and it became clear that anything most folks considered impossible was merely the result of a lack of insight and imagination.

She wanted to lose herself in it, but her heart stilled in a burst of panic as she felt the magic slipping away as quickly as it had come. She wasn't a vessel formed to contain magic, and the power would pass through her and be lost unless she could return to herself and finish what she'd started.

The potion wouldn't form until she spoke the spell and willed the power to move from her into the bowl on the table. She tried to make her lips form the words, but her mouth had gone dry with fear for her soul.

But it was necessary. It would be forgiven.

"Hercalae voldanu re'ardiun." Her voice echoed within her expanded mind, a softened *h* and gently rolled *rs*, and she watched as the ingredients in the bowl shifted and changed on a level far below what the eye could perceive, drawing out the essence from the incardium petals and infusing the thickening liquid with magic that glowed as bright and golden as the power that filled her.

Or had filled her. It flowed from her body, draining up from her toes and down from her head, exiting through her fingers as the spoken spell carried it into the potion. The urge to clench her fists and keep some of it for herself was overwhelming, and she fought to hold her trembling hands open above the bowl until all the magic was gone.

She leaned against the table's edge, breathing hard, eyes closed. She felt like she'd run leagues across a flowery meadow, swum the length of the sea. Like she'd flown.

It felt incredible, even with the magic gone.

"Not a bad result," Madrigal said, peering over Gale's shoulder and passing a hand through the liquid in the bowl. "For your level of experience, I mean."

"I did it?"

"It could be far stronger, but it'll do for your purposes."

"I can do it again," Gale said, speaking in a breathless rush, without any thought of honour or sin, only of what she'd just seen and felt. "I'll use this lot to make a stronger batch, and that to make one that—"

Madrigal's knowing smile cut her off. "That sort of aspiration is for those who pursue magic with passion and purpose," she said softly. "For witches-to-be. It's not for caged nightingales who stand with one foot on the Path for fear of what roams the woods beyond."

Gale shuddered as an echo of magic passed through her. "Of course." She cleared her throat. "I misspoke."

"No. You spoke truly." Madrigal leaned in closer, looking deep into Gale's eyes. "If you believe otherwise, you're lying to yourself."

Gale gave the mixture another stir and watched as tiny pinpricks of light shifted and shimmered within the *lucistra* she'd created. The tiny amount of magic she'd used in the spell had changed the ingredients to make so much more.

I did that. It's mine.

"I did speak truly in the moment. I was caught up in the excitement." Gale laughed, sounding to her own ears a little mad. "I understand why someone would wish to pursue magic no matter the cost. To have that within oneself all the time would be..." Another shudder passed through her. No hint of magic this time, though. Just the echo of a memory that made her want to drink the whole bowl in one gulp in the hopes of feeling the universe within her.

She turned and walked away. It was better when she wasn't looking at the potion.

"I'm strong enough to resist," she said, speaking more to herself than to Madrigal. "To use it only to find the cure. Maybe in extraordinary circumstances in the future if it's God's will, but..." She took a long breath. The air smelled musty and unpleasant, not as it had under the influence of magic, where even the mildew she'd missed scrubbing out of the corners seemed to sing with potential.

"Next recipe, then," Madrigal said, as though nothing unusual had happened.

Gale carried the lantern back to the garden and gathered the medicinal ingredients Madrigal instructed, more than a dozen of them. With each item Madrigal muttered to herself, "If it's a dorsaline enchantment..." or, "They might've cursed the well itself and not just the water, which would mean..." or, "But then, blood magic can be unpredictable..."

Gale listened and obeyed. The garden echoed back its magic more strongly than it had before, and she had no trouble picking out the strongest samples of whatever Madrigal turned her attention toward.

Back inside the cabin she mixed and shredded and pounded ingredients, focusing on them hard enough that Madrigal's voice behind her shoulder became a part of her own thoughts. Then came the creation—the selection of different combinations of ingredients, the ingestion of *lucistra*, the flow of magic through her and the heartache brought on when she released it to do its work outside of her.

"You can't hold onto it," Madrigal said, observing the way Gale's fingers curved in an attempt to do just that. "It will pass out of you no matter what. Better to direct it to work your intentions than to waste it."

Potion after potion, long into the night. Gale made eight of them and tested none on her rash, as Madrigal rejected all of them after she'd observed the reactions during creation. Magic and magic and magic, waves passing through her, carrying her and being guided by her. The initial effect was less now that she was using her own *lucistra* instead of Madrigal's more potent stuff, but still real and present.

Between attempts, she tried to find the words to describe magic to herself, and she failed. Not like the feeling when she explored her body beneath the bedsheets at night, but the same kind of exhilarating rush. It was the cool of the stream against bare skin on a hot summer day, the warmth of a fire on a cold winter night, the embrace of a mother, a dream of flight...

In the end, there was no other experience that compared to everything magic was.

One thing she could firmly state was that it was utterly exhausting. Magic filled her with energy, but every time it drained away it took more of herself with it. Her eyelids grew heavier with each attempt. As the night wore on, she sat at the table preparing the mixtures, standing only to speak the spells Madrigal gave her and to let the magic pass through her.

Midnight had passed and they were deep into the hours before sunrise when Gale sank into one of the chairs, another medicinal potion completed. She didn't gaze in wonder into the bowl to see what she'd created, only rested her head on her arms and closed her eyes.

"It's good."

Gale snapped to attention, ignoring the sharp pain from a crick in her neck. "It's what?"

Madrigal passed her hand through the bowl and the thick mixture within and nodded. "Given the way the curse has affected your body and the possibility of blood magic, this is as good as it's going to get with the magic and plants we have here."

Gale didn't like the caution in the witch's tone, but it would have to do. She unwrapped her bandages, revealing a rash that had spread toward her wrist and become deeper, eating into the flesh beneath her skin and weeping pale pus. Accustomed as she'd grown to seeing such wounds on others, it still turned her stomach to see it on her own arm. She used her bare fingers to scoop up the thick, cream-coloured salve and smooth it over the angry, itching, aching mess.

The sensation was immediately cooling and soothing, far better than the salve she'd brought from home.

"Not so much," Madrigal cautioned. "We'll want to observe the effects. I can't see a damned thing if you lay it on so thick."

Gale scraped the excess off and rested her arm on the table.

And they watched.

"Nothing is happening," Gale whispered.

"And the medicines you were making at home worked in an instant?"

"Faster than you might think."

"Give it time, girl."

The cooling sensation worked deeper into the muscle, but nothing changed on the surface.

Gale slumped back in the chair. "Might I ask a question while we're waiting?"

"I suppose." Madrigal answered without moving her focus from the rash.

"What's blood magic? You've mentioned it several times in relation to curses."

Madrigal narrowed her eyes as she looked Gale over, considering something. Gale had decided she wasn't going to get an answer when Madrigal finally spoke.

"It's the only form of magic that most of us consider purely dark," she said. "Those who practice it claim otherwise, of course. It's a powerful form of magic, and one that can be used not only to influence nature but to change it entirely. Other magic can do harm through spells or poisons or dangerous enchantments, but blood magic is something else, able to cause the kind of far-reaching damage your community is experiencing. A true curse."

"And that's why it's dark?"

"It's considered dark because it requires the unwilling sacrifice of a human life." Madrigal's brow furrowed. "Most witches draw on the magic that exists in the world and its living creations, holding it in ourselves. Practitioners of blood magic draw it from pain, blood, and the very life force—the soul, perhaps—of what they consider lesser humans."

A chill crept up Gale's spine. "That's..."

"Unthinkable? Yes. Tempting to those who crave more power, but repugnant to any moral being. The corruption your people speak of is a true thing with blood magic." Madrigal paled. "A witch who uses it is no longer a vessel. The darkness destroys their ability to hold magic within them."

Gale's mouth went dry.

Madrigal had magic in her when we met, which means she didn't use blood magic.

No blood magic means no curse.

No curse means her death wasn't what ended the famine.

Which means...

She gave her head a quick shake to chase away the thoughts.

She could be lying about blood magic. Or the nature of curses. Or how widespread the one that brought us here was.

But those excuses felt paper-thin—weak, reflexive defenses to protect the story she'd told herself for so long. She set the idea aside, if only until she found some way to prove one way or another whether Madrigal was telling the truth about any of it.

"If they can't hold magic, then how—" Gale glanced at the brooch that still lay on the table and answered her own unfinished question. "They use external vessels for blood magic."

Madrigal nodded. "Very good. One taste of blood magic and that's all we're left with." Madrigal held up a hand to hold off any further questions. "Look!"

She didn't need to say it. Gale felt a strange tingling on the surface of her wound.

"It's working," she breathed, as though afraid of frightening the magic away.

Madrigal said nothing.

The redness at the edges turned pink, then to the warm, natural tones of new skin. Gale's heart pounded as the wound became shallower and the skin began to heal.

The words "we've done it" were on the tip of her tongue when a sharp pain cut through the centre of the rash, burrowing into the muscle and spreading to the edges. Gale gritted her teeth against it as blood spots diffused into the salve, turning it pink as the skin opened up, and once again the edges of the rash bloomed out into the surrounding area, sending out vining purple lines over its surface. Gale held back a frustrated scream.

"The curse is fighting back," she said, her voice still quiet.

Again, Madrigal didn't answer. She only grunted her agreement.

"What should I do?"

The witch pursed her lips and watched as the effects ended, leaving little changed from before. "Cover it. Keep it clean. If nothing else you've gotten rid of the infection that was brewing there. Don't let it come back."

"What happened?"

Madrigal let out a long breath and pinched the bridge of her nose, and Gale wondered whether a ghost could get a headache. "What happened is that this curse is stronger than I thought. And your best wasn't good enough."

Gale tried not to let her disappointment overcome her as she wrapped her forearm in fresh bandages. "There must be something else. What if we—"

Madrigal shook her head and sat on the counter by the stove, staring off behind Gale's shoulder. "We have more information now than we had before, and that's something. Your attempts at medicine back home weren't enough to trouble the curse, but now that we're really attacking it, it's showing its true nature."

"Very helpful," Gale grumbled, cradling her arm against her chest.

"Don't be childish." Madrigal spoke in the same distant, thoughtful tone she'd used to speak of the curse. "We don't have time to indulge your hurt feelings. Not if you want to live."

"Then what do we do?"

Madrigal turned her head slightly, focusing on Gale. "That depends on you. And how far you're willing to go to be a true hero."

"Very well," Gale said, setting her hands in her lap. "What do you propose?"

"A journey to Queen's Run."

Gale laughed. "You're joking. You said you can't leave this place."

"I said I need magic to anchor myself. If you carry my vessel, I believe I can go with you as long as I stick close when I'm in this world. And I think it's familiar enough that I'll find my way back to it from the borderlands if I leave you. All we can do is try." Madrigal stood and drifted about the room in circles, pacing without taking a step. "It's the only plan that makes sense given what we know. This garden, much as I hate to say it, is a dead end —for your purposes, at least. We need information and ingredients you can only get from another witch, and the place to search for them is in the city."

"Why? Is there magic there like in the mountains?"

Madrigal wrinkled her nose. "Not at all. But cities provide other things—goods from distant lands, plenty of false witches and fortune tellers plying their trade on the right side of the law to provide cover for legitimate work, and wealthy merchants and nobles who are willing to pay for the real thing. True witches won't be easy to find thanks to the way the king's mages hunt them, but there must be a few in the city."

"Maybe one will know about the curse on Bright Hollow," Gale added. "Hawk thought another witch who recently left the mountain might have gone there."

Madrigal nodded cautiously. "Perhaps. But offering too many details about that could cause more trouble than it eases if you're not careful." She met Gale's eyes and seemed to hold back a smile. "What's more important is that you'll need to learn the enchantment and create your own vessel."

Gale's blood cooled. She sat down hard on one of the chairs, suddenly light-headed.

"No."

"Why?"

"It's too far."

That wasn't exactly what she meant. The truth was that it was too tempting, that possessing a source of easily accessible magic seemed like a wonderful idea, but she'd grow accustomed to it. It would hurt too much to lose it when she went home. It would make her want more.

It would be everything she'd taught herself to hate, everything she'd promised the Luminary she wouldn't pursue, and she wouldn't admit her desire out loud to herself or this witch.

She cleared her throat, which had grown thick with want. "It's one thing to mix medicines using magical ingredients. Taking magic into myself was another step, one God would surely forbid under more ordinary circumstances, but that I..." She paused, noticing how Madrigal's eyes shone with laughter. "What?"

"You're a ridiculous child," the witch said, shaking her head. "You'd rather be good than honest. Worse, you'd rather be *seen* as good than follow the true goodness that's in you." She sobered quickly. "Even with the right ingredients, you cannot hope to defeat this curse without taking this too-far step. Do you understand that? There's only so far a potion can take you. You need more magic. Better magic. More personal magic."

Gale frowned. "It's a commitment, isn't it? Creating a vessel. It's a step toward becoming a witch."

"It doesn't make you one," Madrigal said bitterly. "But yes. If you believe the path I walk is against God's will, it's a step along it. You'll have to decide what your God and your conscience make of that."

But I'd have the true Path in my sight if I looked back over my shoulder. It was forbidden but still forgivable. She could repent later. Give it all up. It wouldn't be easy, but surely if she were doing it for the good of her people...

"I'll consider it, if it becomes necessary."

Madrigal gazed evenly at her. "Do you think I'd suggest it if it weren't?"

Gale rested her face in her hands. "You think I could really create a vessel?"

"If you have me to guide you through it, though it will be

difficult," Madrigal said, sounding mildly disgusted. "You could use that pretty ring as a vessel, if you'd like."

Gale hid her hands in the folds of her skirt. "No. If I create a vessel, I'll need to destroy it before I go home. This ring was my grandmother's and my mother's. It has to return with me."

"Then you'll choose something else, something more disposable." Madrigal's voice dripped with ice. "There's a false bottom in the box you brought upstairs. Press down at the front to open it."

Gale did so, and the bottom of the box lifted neatly out, revealing a nest of gold, silver, and copper coins, along with several bills of the sort she'd only seen in books.

"For the journey. And, I suppose, your vessel."

Gale sorted through the coins. They weren't often used in Bright Hollow, where trade and barter were as valid a form of commerce as hard cash, but things would be different in Queen's Run. No one would let her open an account in their shop, and she had nothing to trade.

"Thank you," she whispered. "I really do appreciate all of this. It's just that if I go home with magic in my pocket, they'll know. Hawk will feel it, and he'll report me. I can't lose my place in the community."

Madrigal drifted closer, her expression softening, if only slightly. "It's hard, I know. Choosing magic will always mean choosing to separate yourself from the rest of humanity, even if you hope it will be temporary in your case. Find your cure, and surely all will be forgiven."

Gale fetched her bag and slipped the coins into a little pouch that had held food on her journey.

"Can I sleep before we go?" she asked. "I can barely see straight, let alone walk all day."

"Fine." Madrigal glanced up at the night sky through the hole in the roof. "You have four hours. We'll want to reach the crossroads before tomorrow evening, and you'll need to collect some things from the garden before we go."

Madrigal went on, muttering about the frailty of mortal bodies, but Gale barely heard her as she crawled into her makeshift bed on the floor.

CHAPTER SIXTEEN

G ALE'S FEET ached by the time Madrigal suggested it was time to make camp the next day.

"Crossroads ahead," she said, drifting a little in front of Gale on the winding forest road at the base of the mountain. She passed over a set of railroad tracks, then waited for Gale to look and listen for trains before following.

The brooch Gale now wore contained enough magic for Madrigal to anchor herself to it and remain with her, but she couldn't go far. She hadn't been out of sight or earshot since they'd left the cabin, as she vanished into the borderlands when she strayed too far from her vessel and had to find her way back using its familiar magic. Even at the farthest reach of her magical tether, she couldn't have walked out the front door of Gale's house in Bright Hollow if Gale had been standing at the back.

She'd had the decency to disappear when Gale needed to stop in the woods to relieve herself, but always returned quickly, and observed each time Gale reapplied salve to her arm. The new medicine was doing a better job of holding the curse at bay than the old one had, but Gale knew the curse would win out if she didn't start getting more rest.

"Why the crossroads?" Gale asked. It didn't really matter. She'd have happily spread her blankets in a reeking swamp if it got her off her tired legs for a few hours.

"There's a large campsite. Trees felled and cut back for visibility, pits for cooking fires. Merchants stop there to sleep and share news. You'll be safer with them than alone."

Gale frowned. Sleeping near other people hardly seemed safer. At home she wouldn't have questioned it, but these were outsiders. Not people of the Path, but those raised and living outside the light of God's will. They were likely to be monsters. Liars. Thieves.

She slipped her mother's ring from her finger and tucked it into her knapsack, next to the ingredients and tools for making the *lucistra* she'd need to create and fill her vessel. It wasn't much, but it was all the garden had provided. One more thing for folks to steal from her.

On the other hand, they'd be people she could practice speaking to, a way to make sure she didn't sound too sheltered and vulnerable when she reached the city. She could see how they behaved, and merchants might have food she could buy for a few coins.

And being around people would mean Madrigal couldn't expect her to answer questions as she'd been doing for the entire journey, reviewing lessons she'd learned as a child and having unfamiliar magical theory about potions and vessels poured into her ears. It had gone on all day, until Gale's brain overflowed and went numb.

The worst part was that no matter how she tried to hold her interest at bay, the beast that had awakened in her sunk its claws deeper, pulling her close and promising wonders if only she'd forget the Teachings and give herself over to magic.

The sun hadn't yet set, but there were already two large wooden carts parked in a wide, dusty circle of land shielded from the road by a thin wall of young birches and alders. The horses were enjoying a no doubt well-deserved supper, and a man with copper skin and a shining black beard was perched on the boards along the side of one of the carts, removing something from beneath the canvas that covered its contents.

Gale wanted to ask Madrigal what she should do—whether it was proper to introduce herself or pretend this fellow traveller didn't exist—but it was too late. He spotted her, dropped to the ground, and strode toward her, adjusting the suspenders he wore over his cream-coloured shirt and brushing the dust from his trousers.

Madrigal hovered close, watching him. The stranger didn't react to her, or even seem to sense that anything was amiss.

She'd told the truth about that much, then. No one but Gale could see her.

"Greetings," he said.

"To you as well," Gale replied. "Is this the place where folks camp along the road?"

"It is, indeed." The stranger held out a hand, and Gale shook it. "Name's Basim. Where's the rest of your party?"

"I am my party. Just need somewhere to sleep for the night. I won't be a bother."

"No worries about that."

Another man approached from the woods, this one broad-shouldered and strong, with sunburnt cheeks and wild red hair that he'd tied behind his neck. As he walked, he dried his beard on the hem of his shirt. A big dog with a white-salted brown coat walked beside him, head down and tongue lolling.

"Please join me for supper, if you'd like," Basim said, raising his voice loud enough for the other fellow to hear. "One does get bored of seeing the same tired, ugly faces every time one stops here."

The big man came closer, laughing. "As if you aren't thrilled by the tales I tell of my adventures." He spoke with a thick accent

Gale had never heard before, the *r*s held back in his throat, his inflections odd.

"Maybe the first twenty times you repeated them." Basim winked at Gale. He, too, spoke with a faint accent, crisp and precise. "Stranger, this is Olivier, travelling merchant from Durond and teller of tall tales. His friend there is called Brigid." The dog let out a quick bark, and Basim smiled. "I myself am a cartographer, born in Kardav and currently employed by King Ranthorn of Andonia."

Olivier rolled his eyes dramatically and thumped Basim on the shoulder. "He never forgets to add that royal detail."

They both looked expectantly at Gale.

"Introduce yourself," Madrigal said. She spoke at normal volume, but neither man reacted.

"Oh, sorry. I'm Nightingale. Gale, that is. Originally from Bright Hollow, and currently... from Bright Hollow."

Olivier let out another laugh. "You certainly are. This your first time out in the real world?"

Gale smiled uncertainly and held her hand out for the dog to sniff. "You know of my town?"

"I was there once or twice in my youth, before more lucrative trade opportunities presented themselves." He sobered, his expression becoming gentle and serious. "I hadn't heard anything for a while. Glad to see any of you survived the curse."

It took a moment for Gale to understand he was speaking of the old curse, not the new.

"Thank you." She swallowed hard and forced a smile. "I'm glad you did, as well. It was..." She wasn't sure how to ask without sounding foolish, but she had to know whether Madrigal had also spoken the truth about this. "It was bad everywhere, was it?"

Olivier and Basim exchanged a look Gale couldn't read.

"It was devastating," Olivier said, his voice heavy. "I regretted ever coming to Andonia, and I suppose Basim here did, too. I lost my wife in the wasting sickness that took hold in our town. And

Basim—" He glanced to him for confirmation. "Crop failure, was it?"

Basim nodded. "Locusts, in fact, that darkened the sky and consumed everything, and no food to be had from anywhere else for months. I'd only just arrived and wanted to return to the familiar dangers of the desert, but there were no ships to be had by the time I reached a port city. And the people there..." He shook his head.

Pain like a knife's blade twisted in Gale's heart.

Madrigal hadn't lied—not about this part, anyway. It hadn't just been Bright Hollow and the areas around it. All of Andonia had been touched, and the curse had been unimaginably destructive.

Unless Madrigal had been hiding impossible power when she lived, and unless Gale took her for a liar even though everything else she'd said had been proven true, if it could be proved at all...

We killed an innocent woman.

It wasn't that she had never suspected it. It had taken years to force herself to truly believe Madrigal a villain.

Tears burned her eyes. She glanced at Madrigal, who looked away.

But Olivier and Basim seemed to take it as sorrow for the harm and losses they'd all suffered. Olivier rested a massive hand on her shoulder, and Gale rested hers on top of it for a moment, accepting the comfort even if was offered for the wrong reason.

"We all had losses," he said, speaking gently. "We all choose whether to shut the pain away or share the burden, don't we?"

Gale nodded and brushed her sleeve across her eyes. "Thank you. Where should I set up my bedroll?"

"Anywhere you'd like, really," Basim said. "There's lots of room. Trouble is, there will likely be others joining us, and you don't want to get trampled. You're welcome to set up here."

Gale did as he suggested, laying out her blankets on the ground a short distance from a pair of small, triangular tents that had been hidden from view by the carts. It only took a few minutes, but it gave her a moment alone when the two men went to start a fire in a nearby pit.

"What do you think?" she murmured.

"I think your social skills need work," Madrigal said. "But about them? I don't know. They seem nice and helpful, which I suppose means you think they're out to harm you."

"Should I trust them, then?"

"No, don't be foolish. You were wrong to doubt me, but that doesn't mean you should let your guard down around them. It'd be good if more folks came. The odds of them all being out to rob you are slim."

Gale meant to ask more, but Olivier returned to his tent and she didn't want to risk being heard.

No one else arrived, and it was only the three of them—four, counting Madrigal—and the dog who sat around the campfire that night.

Supper was a thick, reheated stew of rabbit and barley provided by Olivier, with the addition of the carrots, potatoes, and spices Basim had been digging out of his cart when Gale arrived. She had left the campsite for long enough to gather mushrooms to add to it, not wanting to feel as though she owed the strangers anything they might try to take back later.

She'd kept her bag with her, though it would have been more convenient to leave it behind.

There was no conversation while they ate, as the men seemed as hungry as Gale herself was after a day on the road. But once Brigid had licked the bowls and Olivier had returned from washing them in the stream, there was little to do but talk.

Gale tried to think of something to ask to keep the focus off herself, but Olivier spoke first. "Did you walk all the way down the mountain, Gale?"

She nodded. "Didn't have a horse. Can't say I'm a good rider, anyway, even if I'd had one."

Basim smiled kindly. "Your feet must be sore. I hope you don't have much farther to go."

"Careful," Madrigal warned.

"I don't know," Gale said. "How far is it to the city?"

"To Queen's Run?" Basim asked. "On foot... You'll be on the road until midday if you get an early start."

Gale sighed. "I suppose I'd better get some sleep, then. How does this work? Do we take turns keeping watch?"

Olivier scratched Brigid between her large ears, and the dog yawned. "We'll do most of the watching," he said. "This old girl sleeps like a stone these days, but I don't sleep deep on the road."

"I'll keep watch better than anyone," Madrigal said. Gale wanted to thank her but didn't want the travellers to think her odd.

She wished them a good night and lay in her thin bed of blankets on the hard ground, using her arm as a pillow, her back to the light of the fire. Madrigal sat next to her, watching and listening as Basim and Olivier spoke and laughed quietly next to the dwindling flames.

"It'll be a boring night for you," Gale whispered, and yawned.

Madrigal chuckled. "I haven't spent time away from the borderlands or my ruined cottage since I died. Won't be any trouble for me to enjoy it."

Waves of sleep engulfed Gale, making her thoughts drift, but she fought them off.

"Madrigal?"

"I'm here, girl."

Gale hesitated, then gave up on trying to pry the right words free from the tangle of regret, grief, and fear that tied her mind into knots.

Speak the truth, even if it hurts. She deserves it.

"I believe you about the old curse being larger than anything you could have managed. And I believe you when you say you're not the sort of person who would have done that. I'm sorry I thought you were a liar, and that all the good things you did were tricks." Her throat grew tight and her eyes burned. "I was right about you the first time, when I trusted you. I'm sorry I wasn't smart or strong enough to fight back when Hawk convinced me we needed to escape, and..." Gale swallowed back a sob, not wishing for more sympathy from the others. "We were wrong, and I've been wrong ever since, and I'm sorry."

"All right, then." Madrigal said, her voice as heavy as Gale's heart. She was silent for long enough that Gale had to look to make sure she hadn't vanished. "You were a child who grew up only allowed to see the world one way, who had been taught to fear me. I thought I could free you, but... Well. Here we are. And has this revelation about me changed your mind about anything else? Magic? Your future?"

"No. I mean, not practically."

She didn't say the rest of it—that if the Teachings could be wrong about ghosts, perhaps they could be wrong about why magic was dangerous, but that she understood better now than ever that it *was* dangerous. Tempting. Alluring. A thing that could call a person away from the Path.

That all that mattered in the end was that she be able to go home. She might have been questioning her memories and even the Teachings, at least on minor matters, but it didn't change anything.

Madrigal sighed and looked away. "We'll see what happens."

She said something else, but Gale didn't catch it as she drifted off.

SHE WAS DREAMING of gardens and magic when Madrigal appeared before her, as solid and real as if she'd been alive.

Gale stared in disbelief as the dream world shattered around her. "You said you wouldn't invade my—"

Madrigal didn't wait for her to finish. "You need to wake up. Now."

Gale's eyes flew open, and she found herself lying on her back, staring up at the stars. She looked around, expecting to see Olivier or Basim trying to steal her bag, but she could make out Basim in his bedroll on the other side of the fire, his tent unused. Olivier sat with his back against one of the carts, snoring loud enough that Gale couldn't believe she'd slept through it.

Brigid lay next to him. And just above the dog's head, the white feathers at the end of an arrow stuck out from the side of the cart, still trembling from the impact.

Gale shrieked and rolled out of her bed. An arrow whispered through the air and buried its head in the ground where she'd lain, barely missing her.

She ran toward the fire pit with Madrigal close behind. Basim was already stirring, but she had to shake Olivier. He snorted and swatted at her.

"Help!" she yelled, as Brigid let out a half-hearted growl and got to her feet.

Olivier' eyes flew open and he sat upright, glaring at her. "What in the world—"

Brigid yelped. Another arrow had landed in her thigh.

"Someone's here," Gale said. "Attacking. *Move.*"

Gale left them and ran to where Basim was crouched between the carts. Olivier joined them a moment later, carrying Brigid in both arms. The dog whined as Olivier set her on the ground.

"My poor girl," he whispered. "I never would've let myself sleep if I'd thought…"

"You can apologize to her and to us later," Basim said, his voice gentle. "Now hush."

Gale held her pack tight to her chest and waited. Her fingers twitched, and though the thought was a sin she longed for the power that had flowed through her the night before—and for the ability to wield it against their attacker. She'd never seen

Madrigal use magic for anything defensive or violent, as she'd never had the need until it was too late. But surely it could be done, and they'd all be safer for it.

Madrigal drifted beyond the carts, then back.

"I can't see anything," she said. "Can't get far enough from that vessel to do any good."

Gale wanted to assure her she'd done enough already, but she couldn't risk speaking.

Brigid made up for her silence. She struggled to her feet and let out a volley of barks that echoed through the forest, sounding far stronger and more dangerous than the old dog looked.

They waited a minute. Then another.

Olivier stood and took a few steps closer to the woods, as though daring anyone to take another shot at him or his dog. "They're gone, the cowards," he said, and sat next to Brigid. "Hush, now. Let me get that out of you, eh?"

Gale looked away as he pulled the arrow free. The dog yelped, but when Gale turned back, she was resting with her head on the ground.

"Poor thing," Madrigal said, then looked to Gale.

"May I?" Gale asked, gesturing to the wound.

Olivier nodded and held Brigid's head in his lap.

"You know medicine?" Basim asked.

"Only for humans, but it might be helpful." Now that she had a job to do, Gale's panic calmed. She felt more like herself, more like she belonged here. "I don't suppose you have any farrow among your things? Forest plant with blue flowers, leaves sting if you touch them?"

Olivier brightened. "I saw some by the creek. How much do you want?" Then, before Gale could answer, he set Brigid's head gently on the ground and stood. "I'll bring it all. Anything else?"

"I'll need boiled water."

"Done," Basim said, and reached into his tent for a glass flask.

"That's all."

Olivier darted into the woods.

"Brave of him," Gale said, and bent to examine the wound. By moonlight it didn't look too terrible.

Basim stood over the fire and prodded the embers with a long stick. "If no one has pressed the attack by now, it was a lone thief. They tried to put the dog down hoping to sneak in unnoticed and steal from the carts, maybe slit our throats on the way. Probably fled as soon as you woke."

Soon the fire was blazing and Gale had placed what was left of the healing salve she'd brought from home into a copper pot with farrow leaves crushed and added to it. Not a perfect solution, but the best she could do without better ingredients.

Madrigal hung back and said nothing, and that was fine. Gale had done this many times at home and had no intention of trying anything remotely connected to magic in front of strangers.

"This will keep it from festering," she told Olivier as she applied the cooled ointment to the wound. "This spot is too awkward to bandage, so just keep it clean."

"Not bad," Madrigal said. "For a plain-as-dirt medicine, that is." There was no sting to the half-hearted insult, though, and Gale sensed that she was pleased.

The sky had lightened as she worked, and the sun broke over the horizon to the east as she left Olivier and the dog. She hauled her bed closer to the fire and sat to rest, though she supposed there was no more time to sleep. Basim sat cross-legged on his bed and fed bits of wood into the fire.

"When Olivier's nerves recover enough for him to remember his manners, he'll wish to thank you," he said, sounding as exhausted as Gale felt.

"No need," she said. "Back home we help where we can. Not for thanks, but because it's what we do."

"Hmm." Basim reached into a stiff leather satchel inside his tent and pulled out a thin sheet of paper, a feather quill pen, and a bottle of night-black ink. "Well, then, allow me to do what I do in the hopes that it will help you in return. I owe you this much for waking us, never mind what my friend owes you for the dog. You said you're going to Queen's Run?"

"I did."

Gale noticed that Madrigal didn't jump in to tell her to be careful this time.

"Anywhere specific? I know the city well enough to draw you a map."

"Not exactly," Gale admitted.

"I can get you around," Madrigal said.

"I can get around," Gale repeated. "I know someone in the city who will guide me."

"I see." Basim's moustache twitched as he smiled and set the paper flat on the ground. His quill moved over it, and as though by magic, the coastline of Andonia appeared, followed by Kardav below and the islands on the eastern coast. Mountains followed, and rivers, and finally a few dots marking cities.

"You've seen this before?" Basim asked, still working.

"A little." Gale said, speaking quietly so as not to break his concentration. "We didn't study much geography at home. Never expected to go anywhere past Queen's Run, if we even had to go there, so there wasn't much point talking about it." In truth, she'd seen a map of all of Andonia only once or twice and heard stories from a few far-off cities.

"But look at you now," Basim said. He added the word *Andonia* inside a box that looked like a broad, flowing bit of ribbon, then handed the map to Gale. "You could go anywhere. This isn't my best work, but it's adequate. You can add to it as you see and hear about more of the world. Maybe some day we'll meet again and you'll show me your adventures."

Gale watched as the wet ink dried by the heat of the fire. "It's beautiful. Thank you."

Olivier looked over her shoulder, then sat down. "Take care of yourself, Gale. There are good people in this world. There are terrible ones, too. You'll find plenty of both in the city." He tossed the arrow he'd pulled from Brigid into the fire. "Do you have to leave right away? I feel like breakfast, if you want some."

Gale looked to Madrigal.

The witch smiled. "Just don't be too long about it. Time is short."

Gale smiled back at her. Now that the excitement had died down, the sun was up, and the world felt safe again, the enormity of what had happened weighed on her mind. It had been a bad night, but not *all* bad, and suddenly she didn't mind having a ghost by her side.

She could have let me die. She could have had her revenge, but she saved me.

An accomplice to murder and her victim. A witch and her unwilling apprentice.

They made an odd pair, to be sure, but for the first time Gale truly believed that maybe this was exactly where she was meant to be.

CHAPTER SEVENTEEN

FOLLOWERS of the Path had little use for notions of damnation. After death, a soul would be rewarded or destroyed, not tortured. But others believed in a sort of eternal punishment for the wicked, and Gale's arrival in Queen's Run was a perfect reflection of what she imagined that mythical place of eternal torment would be like.

The city wasn't a world of flames and open torture, but bleak and filthy and teeming with people who walked with their eyes cast toward the ground. It was the kind of place that would wear down a person's spirit so gradually they didn't even notice until there was nothing left. She reached under her jacket to grasp Madrigal's brooch tightly in her fingers, a protective talisman against the slow, sucking greyness of her surroundings.

"Stop that," Madrigal murmured. "If some clever-fingered wretch catches on to the fact that you're guarding valuables, you'll lose more than a bit of jewellery."

Gale forced her fingers to open and shoved her hands into her pockets.

Madrigal didn't have to keep her voice down, but Gale appreciated it nonetheless. She wanted to keep her eyes and ears open, and an extra voice would be more than she could process if it were too loud to tune out. Madrigal floated next to her, easily visible if Gale turned to reassure herself that her guide hadn't vanished.

"Stop looking around like a wide-eyed doe," Madrigal ordered, and Gale forced her eyes forward. "Look like an outsider and you'll become a target."

Queen's Run was as it had been described in the stories of townsfolk who had reluctantly visited for business or to adopt children, yet nothing like what Gale had imagined. It was at once more human and more alien, not just a larger, busier, and dirtier version of Bright Hollow but something all its own. A street back home was a wide thoroughfare of packed dirt or flat stones, with plenty of space for everyone to pass by or to stop and chat as they went about their business. It was a place to bask in the sun or run through puddles in the rain, to build a snow fort in the square with the other children.

Here, buildings pressed in on all sides, looming dark and sooty over the streets, which were as wide as those in Bright Hollow but so crowded and contained that they felt oppressively small. Gale suspected that anyone who took up too much space or moved too slowly here would be immediately trampled.

And the people... She tried not to stare, but couldn't help it. The place was a wild mix of folks of all stripes. Gale was accustomed to a variety of skin tones and hair colours—the ancestors of folks in Bright Hollow had been as varied in their origins as anywhere else in Andonia. But the range of clothing styles, the scents of unfamiliar spices drifting from food wagons, and the symphony of languages being hollered across alleys were strange to her. It might have been fascinating and lovely if everything else hadn't been so overwhelming.

Dirty children ran barefoot through the streets. A man lay in an alley, reeking of something sharp and unpleasant, a puddle of vomit under his head. Gale stepped closer to make sure he was all right, but Madrigal shooed her on. When Gale glanced back, the children were picking through his pockets, giggling.

"Close your eyes to it," Madrigal said, "or it'll break your sheltered little heart. The cities aren't like what you're used to."

"No, they're not," Gale murmured, and pulled her jacket tighter.

There was so much life. So much potential. But corruption and sin hung in the air like the smoke that spewed from the factories that loomed to the west. Surely there were good people here, as Olivier had said—Gale had to believe most were good, if perhaps misguided. But someone had strayed from God's will for this to have happened. The Luminary would say it wasn't God's punishment but the natural consequences of greed or neglect of fellow-folk or...

A man stumbled out of an establishment on the corner that smelled like the fellow in the alley and leered at Gale as he passed. She pressed herself against a wall until he was gone.

I want to go home.

She longed for the welcoming smiles of her parents, for a snuggle with little Fox while Frost took a well-needed rest, for cherry pies left untended on windowsills without thought of them being stolen, for moonlit dances in the square and the faint magic of the mountain that was, save for the vessel she wore pinned to her blouse and what she could still feel from the wilting plants she carried in her bag, completely absent here.

They'd entered the city through the merchants' gate and were now passing vast, open shipping yards full of boxes, crates, and animals. Chickens screamed in tiny cages, dogs watched warily from under wagons, and great draught horses stood with their heads down, hitched to their carts even as they tried to rest. Gale watched workers with dirty clothes and callused hands loading and unloading great wooden crates from carts and wagons. Goods brought upriver would travel to other cities in northern Andonia, and those from local factories would be loaded onto riverboats bound for the open sea and lands beyond. The workers who loaded the boxes would likely never see those lands—no more than they'd see a fair portion of the profits.

Madrigal explained it all as they walked. The workers, the merchants who came to collect the goods, and the overseers in their red hats ignored Gale, and soon she was past the yards and back onto streets that cut between stables and factories and run-down shops. She couldn't say whether it was more like being caught up in a great, impersonal machine or a river that swept her along in its current.

Someone bumped into Gale from behind. She checked her pockets and her bag. Both her purses were still there—the little pouch she'd put a few coins in so as not to flash her small wealth to every soul on the street when she stopped to buy lunch and the larger one that held the rest of what Madrigal had provided. And her ring was still in her pocket, where she'd moved it before she started the day's journey. Gale slipped it onto her finger and pulled her sleeve down to hide it.

It felt safer there, and it felt right to wear that reminder of home and the people she needed to save no matter how tired she felt or how deeply the curse's pain gnawed at her.

The sizzle and heady scent of spit-roasted meat drifted towards her from a shop on the corner. Its front wall had been cut away, giving the space within the feel of an outdoor market without letting the rainfall in. The food didn't smell like anything she'd ever tried at home. The spices burned her nose as she walked closer, and her mouth watered. The women who worked inside, one at the spit and one handing out meat wrapped in flat bread and taking payments, spoke in a foreign language of clipped syllables and lilting notes. Gale slowed, then lingered near the opening in the wall.

"Pithini food," Madrigal told her. "Probably lamb."

"Is it good?"

Madrigal's shoulders slumped. "I don't know whether you'd

like it. I suppose the most flavourful thing they allow in your town is cinnamon. I'd die all over again for a taste, though." She sighed. "Come on. Once we get to the market you'll find plainer breads, maybe some roast chicken."

The woman at the counter, who wore a bright red dress and a matching scarf to hold her hair off her face, smiled at Gale. "You hungry, friend?"

Gale cast a sidelong glance at Madrigal and pulled her coins from her pocket. "How much?"

Ten minutes later she was seated on a bench outside, licking the last of the juices from her fingers. The meat had burned her tongue with its heat and its spice, and all she wanted was to go back for more.

Madrigal sat beside her, chin resting in her hand, watching with clear envy. "We should move on," she said. "Time's passing."

"I know." Gale reached into her sleeve to make sure her bandages were secure. The wound was becoming more painful, and though the city had distracted her from it she'd need to stop to tend to it soon. At the same time, she didn't want to look.

Gale followed as the ghost drifted onward and was thinking that perhaps the great cities of Andonia weren't all bad if they had food like that when she caught the roar of a crowd up ahead.

"What's that?"

Madrigal paled. "Nothing we need to worry about."

Gale's steps slowed. The noise was strange—a combination of excited shouts, jeers, and horrified wails. She followed it to a small square packed with people, all of them jostling and pushing to see something.

Gale stayed back and climbed onto a parked carriage, clinging to the side, leaning out to see.

"It doesn't concern you," Madrigal warned again, but Gale didn't listen.

She wished she had.

A man in dark grey robes stood on a wooden platform, hood

pulled up to shield his face from the crowd, a bloodied axe in one hand. Three men in black uniforms—they'd be police, Gale supposed—stood at the corners, keeping an eye on the crowd.

And in the middle of the platform, the headless body of a woman with her hands bound behind her back, her head mercifully hidden in the basket that had caught it.

Gale dropped from the carriage and hurried away, fighting the urge to close her eyes, swallowing back the meal that rose in her throat.

She stepped into an alley, out of the path of people who walked more calmly away from the scene, and crouched with her head between her knees until a wave of dizziness passed. When she looked up, Madrigal had taken up the same position across from her.

"She was a witch, wasn't she?"

Madrigal nodded. "No other executions are public. No one else is so humiliated, and no one else warrants a visit from the king's mages to take care of that dirty bit of business." She spat on the ground. "They're no different from witches, you know, except that their magic is legal because the king controls it. They only call themselves mages to separate themselves from us common criminals."

Gale's limbs shook, and she didn't dare try to stand. "Was she a bad one? One who would do blood magic and curses and such?"

"She certainly didn't have to be. That mage would have taken my head as readily as he took hers, and I never harmed a soul with my magic."

"I see." Gale wiped her sleeve across her eyes. "So the wider world really does hate you as much as we do in Bright Hollow."

"No." Madrigal looked into Gale's eyes, studying her. "Your people hate us because you believe us to be monsters who defy God's will. Some of this crowd might have cheered the execution from pure blood lust, but they didn't hate that woman more than they'd have hated a thief or a swindler. She probably did good for some of them. It's laws that hurt us here, not Teachings. It's about keeping power in the hands of those the king trusts with it, not about good and evil."

Gale nodded toward Madrigal's ghostly form as a pang of regret swept through her. "Doesn't make much difference in the end, does it? Hate is hate."

She pushed to her feet and left the alley on trembling legs, not wishing to talk more about it. If the Teachings were right, she should be glad another witch was gone. But she couldn't be. All she could think was that this might have been another Madrigal, clever and kind, and that magic had nothing to do with it. Executing a person for being a witch was wrong.

But it was all the more reason to be glad she'd be leaving magic behind when this was over.

The rash burned and itched under her bandages, reminding her that she had more urgent things to worry about than any witch's fate.

"Where are we supposed to find magic in a place like this?" she asked. It seemed impossible now that she'd seen the consequences of practicing it openly.

"Take a left here. We'll try the market. Back in my day witches would sometimes set up shop there, acting as mere herbalists or even selling true magic disguised as fakes."

Gale followed directions that took her up a steep slope. The air cleared, if only slightly, and now it was plodding cabs and coal-black carriages that pushed pedestrians off the street instead of carts full of goods. Gale stopped to buy a loaf of bread, a bit of cheese, and a few pears for later, then followed Madrigal farther into the market.

Madrigal flickered beside her and vanished for a moment, and Gale's heart stopped as she imagined herself truly alone in the city. The ghost reappeared, but she looked even less substantial than before.

"You all right?" Gale asked. She spoke softly, but a young man in a crisply tailored coat and a grey top hat gave her a quizzical look before stepping away to give her more room.

"Fine," Madrigal said, though she didn't sound it. "But the sooner you create a properly filled vessel for me to anchor myself to, the better off we'll be."

Beyond a pair of pubs bookending the street, much finer than the ones they'd passed earlier, the way opened into a large square packed with market stalls. Tables beneath colourful fabric coverings were laid out with goods—vegetables, fresh and salted fish, bolts of cloth, spices, and bread, a bounty of variety Gale had never imagined. It was as though the world had been laid out before her in bite-sized pieces, all of it available if she had the coin.

"You've never tasted apples like these!" called a child, no more than six years old, waving a bruised yellow piece of fruit toward Gale.

"Should they not be in school?" she asked, speaking just above a whisper.

"Many are," Madrigal answered. "The wealthiest board their children or supply them with tutors. Others are in more common schools. But these unfortunates? They're making runs outside the city's gates to pick from the gardens and orchards before sunrise so they can earn some coin here. Those are the lucky ones."

"And the others?"

Madrigal nodded back toward the factories.

Gale's stomach turned. "Surely no one is cruel enough to make them work in there."

"This way," Madrigal said, and led Gale through the winding pathways between stalls.

Gale was tempted to stop and look, to run her hands over turquoise silk laid out like a running river, but she kept pace with the ghostly form that led her through the centre of the square, where a statue of a beautiful woman in flowing robes, four times life-sized, carved from granite and wearing a worn-down stone crown, stood watch over the bustling populace below her.

"Come along," Madrigal said again, drawing Gale's attention back to her. "Dead queens are no help to us, today or any day."

Gale felt a chill as she turned her back on the statue. It was Linnea, she was sure. Queen's Run was named for her unsuccessful attempt to flee her own coronation, so it seemed natural that they'd honour her. But Linnea had always been a suspicious figure in the history lessons of Gale's childhood. She was said to be descended from the ancient faeries who had once walked this land, to have possessed naturally the kind of magic that witches could only dream of claiming for themselves. The question of whether it could be God's will that one with such power should rule over humanity had been a factor for those who followed the Path in deciding to leave the rest of Andonia behind. Even her untimely death and the passing of the monarchy to human caretakers hadn't changed their minds about the state of the world. Linnea was said to have been hauntingly beautiful, able to enchant with a word or a smile, and to have spoken in a voice as sweet as honey.

The skin on the back of Gale's neck tingled, and she glanced back. The statue had not turned to watch her, though she'd almost felt it had.

Linnea hadn't wanted to be queen, but even those who'd opposed her because of her magic had found little fault in her actions once she'd taken the throne.

Linnea used magic for good, Gale reminded herself. *She wasn't a monster any more than I am.*

She didn't let herself consider the rumour that Linnea's body still lay beneath the palace in Embercliffe, untouched by decay and as lifelike as could be save for the eyes and the heart that had been stolen by her killers.

That story had given her nightmares as a child.

They reached a corner of the market shadowed by the tall

buildings surrounding the square. Fewer customers roamed here, and those who did tended to walk with their collars turned up or their shawls guarding their faces, casting suspicious glances at Gale as she passed. The stalls themselves were decorated in purple, black, and midnight-blue fabrics, several with candles burning on or behind the tables, which were covered in an odd assortment of objects, from rabbit's feet to small mirrors and bottles of brightly coloured liquids.

At a nearby stall, a young woman in an expensive-looking pink dress made up of layers of silk and lace picked up a gold pendant on a long chain. "What's this one?"

Gale paused to listen.

The vendor, an old woman with a deeply lined face and fingers as thin and quick as a spider's legs, looked Gale over before turning back to the woman in pink, who clearly had more money to spend.

"Ah. Miss has a fine eye for enchantment." The merchant's gaze dropped to her customer's fingers, which were bare of rings. "This one is a fine piece. If you slip it under your pillow, you'll dream of your future love."

The young woman wrinkled her nose. "I already have some thoughts about that."

The seller's gaze sharpened. "Not only that, my dear—a trinket that only brought a nighttime vision would come cheap, and this does not. During the day you wear it close to your heart, and it draws your love to you like a moth to a flame."

Madrigal snorted. "Come along. There's no one worth speaking to here."

But Gale didn't follow, and there was only so far the ghost could go without her. If someone was being swindled, it was the duty of any good person who knew better to step in.

The Teachings and God's will were mercifully clear on that point, at least.

She waited for the seller to end her speech, which finished with a request for a ridiculous sum of money.

The young woman laughed nervously. "You're joking."

The merchant shrugged. "You see these other tables, these other sellers? Junk, all of it. They'll sell to you for a fraction of this cost, but all you'll get is gold that will turn your skin green. You want true magic, you pay for it."

A fair enough proposal if it were true. Gale stepped forward and cupped the pendant in one hand, startling the buyer, who pulled it away and held it to her chest.

"Don't," Madrigal said, louder than she'd spoken all day.

"This one's mine," the young woman said, and reached into her pocket for her purse.

"Your choice," Gale said. She closed her eyes and felt as she did in the forest when she was searching for the best ingredients, trying to catch a hint of magic in the stall. "But she's right. Everything in this market is junk. Even this." She gestured to the necklace. "You're wasting your money."

"How do you know?"

"She doesn't," the merchant snapped, glaring at Gale. "She's probably trying to lure you away to buy something worthless. Ignore her."

The young woman looked uncertainly from the merchant to Gale and back again, then put the necklace back on the table. "I think I'll figure things out for myself without magic, thank you."

She left, and the merchant turned on Gale, suddenly looking far less meek and accommodating than she had a moment ago. "How dare you?" she demanded. "That was three weeks' bread for my family. Are you working for that hussy on Deermont Street who's claiming to sell magic? Trying to send my customers her way for sad scraps of enchantment?"

Gale took a step back. "You lied to that woman."

"She had coin enough to spare!" The old woman picked up the

necklace and shook it in Gale's face. "You'll buy it right now for twice what I asked of her."

"Or what?"

A bulky shape appeared from the shadows at the back of the stall, a fellow with a roughly shaved head, rubbing sleep from his eyes. "What's going on, Ma?"

"Troublemaker, Harry," the merchant said.

Harry cracked his knuckles.

"I told you not to get involved," Madrigal sighed. "You're not in Bright Hollow now. This world plays by different rules."

"What do I do?" Gale asked her.

"Do?" the merchant said. "You give me my gold and Harry here doesn't break your fingers. It's that simple."

"That's one option," Gale said. She pretended to reach into her bag, then turned on her heel and fled.

CHAPTER EIGHTEEN

HARRY, as it turned out, wasn't hard to lose among the crowds in the market, especially with two sets of eyes watching for him. But Madrigal didn't have to tell Gale they shouldn't stick around—not only because of the risk of broken bones, but because they weren't going to find what they were looking for.

"If not at the market," Gale asked as they followed a broad street away from the colourful tables, "then where do we find a —" She caught a lady in voluminous blue skirts watching her curiously and dropped her voice to a whisper. "A real witch?"

Madrigal drifted beside her now. "There must be a few left in the city. But they're in hiding, as they always must be."

Gale shivered and rubbed her throat. "What did that woman say? Something about scraps of enchantment. Is that anything?"

"Probably not, but we could see. Deermont Street is this way." Madrigal turned left at the next intersection. "Nicer area than this. We won't find a witch openly running a shop, but if someone is selling second-hand magic, they might know where to find one."

Gale's steps dragged, and her mind was growing sluggish. She told herself it was only because of how little sleep she'd been getting the past few nights. "Second-hand?"

"Sure." Madrigal glowered, though at nothing in particular. "No potions or spells on offer, but if someone happens to possess an enchanted object, it's not *technically* illegal to sell it, or for others to buy it. Only to make it. Wouldn't want a witch to benefit from their own work, would we?"

They reached a cross street and waited for a traffic officer to halt the flow of carriage traffic. Gale's heart thumped wildly as she thought of the hooded executioner standing over a headless body and of the small magic she wore pinned to her sweater.

"Calm yourself," Madrigal said. "Most folks don't feel it like you do, remember?"

The officer didn't even look at Gale as she passed. Still, she held her breath until he was out of sight.

"How does anyone live like this?" she murmured.

"Some of us are wise enough to leave the cities behind," Madrigal answered. "A few may find it's worth the risk to be here. They might even have the cops in their pockets if not under the occasional enchantment. Here, I think this is Deermont."

They walked until they came to a large park bordered by streets. On the opposite sides of the roads, tall brick buildings with copper roofs turned green with age crowded together, looking down at the park. Gale stepped up to the park's wrought iron fence and peered through, admiring the willow trees gazing down at their reflections in a duck-filled pond, the low, grassy hills where a few well-dressed children sat reading under the watchful eye of a young woman, and the gravel path that wove toward a massive gazebo in the centre of the space.

The entire concept of the park was a strange thing to Gale. Bright Hollow was a town surrounded by true wilderness, but here the city was so large it had swallowed up far tamer imitations of the natural world. Gale wondered how often the people who enjoyed this park got outside the city and into the real thing.

She trailed her fingers along the fence and turned to take in the buildings across the street. The bottom level of each featured a pretty shop front, all advertising some specialty. Hats here, dresses next door, a candy shop, then fine suits for men and yet another separate shop advertising clothing for children. It made Gale's feet ache to think of travelling to so many different places to do the shopping she could manage at the general store back home.

A shop near the corner caught her eye, and she squinted to read the curling gold letters painted on the plate glass window next to the recessed door.

"Bellawick's Curiosity Shop," she read aloud. "What do they sell there?"

Madrigal shrugged. "I suppose that's what you're meant to be curious about." She drifted a short way out into the road, not trying to avoid the carriage that passed through her. The horse pulling it reared, and the driver had a hard time quieting it before they went on. Madrigal leaned toward the shop, but couldn't move closer.

"Looks like used goods," she said. "Furniture, jewellery, that sort of thing. Could be worth a look."

A familiar figure appeared on the opposite side of the park, and Gale held back a gasp. Hawk still wore his hunting leathers and looked entirely out of place among the suits and dresses in the park. His beard had grown in a little over the past few days, leaving him looking rough and wild. A few folks turned to stare at him, but he didn't seem to notice.

Gale's heart fluttered, and she fought the irrational instinct that told her to run.

She and Hawk were fighting for the same goal. She should be glad to see him.

And yet I'm keeping company with the spirit of the witch we killed, she answered herself. *And she's tied to me by magic. And given what I'm considering doing next...*

She stepped closer to the fence and crouched, pretending to admire a tulip that had nodded its way between the bars, but kept a close eye on Hawk as he walked away.

"What's wrong?" Madrigal asked.

"Hawk."

Madrigal drifted through the fence for a better look, and Gale fought the urge to draw attention to herself by calling the ghost back.

"Got big, didn't he?" Madrigal glared after him. "What's he doing here?"

Gale turned her back to her brother and crossed the street, trying to blend in with the strangers who surrounded her. "Still trying to find whoever cursed our town. I suppose his search has led him in the same direction as ours. Maybe that means we're on the right track for finding a witch."

"Not going to say hello, then?" Madrigal asked as they reached the opposite corner. "Tell him what you're up to?"

Gale pressed her lips into a thin line. "Better to ask forgiveness when I have the cure in hand," she said, "rather than permission to find it. He won't understand. Not yet."

Madrigal raised an eyebrow. "Fair enough."

Gale forced her steps to slow and peered through a few windows as she passed, watching the reflection for any sign that Hawk had spotted her and was following, but he'd disappeared.

She paused at the window of the curiosity shop, taking in the window display. There was a standing mirror with an ornate gold frame and a ridiculous price tag, and a dressing table beside it similarly marked. On top of the table rested a box filled with sparkling jewellery. Costume, surely. No one would be so mad as to put anything but glass and imitation pearls on display so close to the door.

She pushed the door open. A bell tinkled pleasantly.

"I suppose you could find your vessel here, if nothing else,"

Madrigal said. She leaned in close to look at the jewellery. "Something cheap and meaningless?"

Gale shrugged. "It's your gold," she said, keeping her voice to the barest whisper. "I'm not going to waste it on something I can't keep." She paused. "Do you feel something?"

A faint hint of magic imbued the shop, barely noticeable, humming at a slightly different tone from what Madrigal's vessel contained.

Several hints, in fact, each feeling different from the others in a way Gale couldn't begin to define.

Madrigal drifted ahead. "Indeed, I do. Now I truly am curious."

Gale peered out the window one more time to make sure Hawk wasn't following her, then walked deeper into the shop, past more furniture. A wild variety of items were displayed in tall glass cases and on open shelves, many of them with neatly printed descriptions on vellum tags but few prices to go with them. Toys and books, glassware in a perfectly displayed rainbow that caught the light from the window, hunting trophies and hairpins and polished candlesticks... a person could spend days in the shop and not see everything. It was almost enough to distract her from her arm, where the itch was becoming a throbbing burn that wouldn't allow her to ignore it for much longer.

Madrigal wandered off on her own and examined the items on a tall display case made from a wood frame with glass shelves.

A young woman dressed in a fitted jacket and full skirt seemed to materialize from the shadows behind a massive oak desk, startling Gale. She was pretty. Striking, really, with light brown skin, dark hair falling in shining waves over one shoulder, a firm jaw, and full, doll-like lips. Her smile seemed intended to set a customer at ease, but there was something about her eyes that drew a second glance. Gale thought at first that it was their sharp, intelligent look. And perhaps that was part of it, but she found it became difficult not to stare when she realized one of those eyes was a deep chestnut colour and the other a rich, golden green.

Unusual, and entrancing. But there was nothing magical in them, or in their owner.

"Good morning," the young woman said, her voice as soothing as her smile. "My name's Delian Carraway, owner of this shop. Is there something I can help you find?"

"I—I'm not sure," Gale stammered. "That is, your store seemed interesting. I thought I'd look around, if it's all right."

"Of course." Delian tilted her head slightly, taking Gale in with one quick glance. "I only asked because you entered with such purpose." She leaned in closer, smiling. "Thought for a second you might be avoiding someone."

Gale felt the blood drain from her cheeks.

"She's reading you," Madrigal said. She was examining a display of glass marbles in a spectacular array of colours. "Pull yourself together. And keep an eye on that one. She's sharper than a shopkeeper has any right to be. There's more to her. And if that's her real name, I'll eat my boots. In fact..."

Madrigal drifted through the ceiling, leaving Gale with nothing but that warning.

Gale looked away, focusing on the ancient-looking books displayed on a wooden bookcase that stretched from the floor to the shop's ceiling. Staring for too long at anyone with such presence unnerved her, and a girl needed all the nerve she could muster in the city.

"Is everything in here old, Miss Carraway?"

"Old and valuable, mostly. What's your name, friend?"

"Gale."

"And what brings you to Queen's Run, Gale?"

Gale was about to ask how Delian knew she wasn't a local, but supposed it wasn't hard to see what she was—drab travel clothes, a bag slung over her shoulder, dirt from the road clinging to her skirt.

"Searching for an old friend of my family's." Gale brushed a finger over the spines of the books, none of which bore a title she recognized, then turned back to the shopkeeper. "It's a long story, and probably leads to a dead end."

"Might as well enjoy the city where you can, then," Delian said. "Would you like to set your bag down? I can keep it behind the desk."

Gale gripped the straps tight, then forced her fingers to relax. She didn't need Madrigal to explain this one. Bellawick's welcomed browsers, but the owner didn't wish to be robbed blind. Fair enough. Her ring was safe on her finger. Madrigal's brooch and coin purse were the only other things of value she carried, and those were in her pockets, not the knapsack.

It would seem suspicious to refuse.

"Thank you," she said, and handed it over.

"Please call out if you have questions," Delian said, and made her way back into the shadows.

With her gone, Gale allowed herself to relax and focus on the magic of the place. She didn't dare call out for Madrigal now that she was sure someone was listening, so she couldn't ask where the magic was coming from, but she approached the display the ghost had been examining.

The case held items on several shelves, but it was the ones at eye level that caught Gale's attention. The label accompanying a bowl of colourful glass orbs read, *marbles 10h each*. These undeniably beautiful items could be picked up and held to the light. Three others, slightly larger, were locked inside glass boxes, visible but inaccessible. Placed in front of these was a tag: *Enchanted! 60f.*

An unthinkable price jump, a little copper to a fair chunk of silver, far more than the woman in the market had dared to ask for a fake enchantment.

But there was real magic here, if terribly faint. The horrible woman in the market hadn't lied about this shop's existence.

These scraps of enchantment might not be useful on their own, but could be if they led to more.

"Delian?" she called, and the shopkeeper appeared. "Are these truly enchanted?"

Delian smiled. "That's the story." She pulled a keyring from her pocket and unlocked the three glass cubes in quick succession, plucking the black, green, and tiger's eye marbles up in her long fingers and cradling them in one hand. "We have plenty of toys in here, mostly acquired from nobles, factory owners, and wealthy merchants who bought them for children who quickly grew tired of them. Even the few enchanted ones." Palming the other two, she held the tiger's eye between her thumb and forefinger. "Story on this one, though, is that it belonged to a prince."

Gale smiled. "The story doesn't cost extra?"

"It's not worth anything extra," offered a low voice from the back of the shop. Gale glanced up and found a young man in a grey suit leaning against the desk. He moved closer, holding his hands behind his back. A handsome enough fellow, though the scar on his chin and mischievous glint in his eyes gave him a bit of a roguish look. "The only difference between a prince with a trick marble and a merchant's child with one is that the prince's friends will be too afraid to quit playing with him after they figure out that his can't miss."

Delian's eyes softened, bringing amused sincerity to her professional smile. "The stories are free, anyway," she said. "And I can't legally offer guarantees on the enchantments. But you can test them out if you'd like."

Gale took the tiger's eye and held it up to the light. The swirls of amber and green moved within like they were caught in a gentle current. "Fascinating," she whispered. And there was no trick to it but magic—she felt it as clearly as she had ever felt magic in anything. The *how* of it was unimaginable to her, both in the appearance of the thing and in how one would make it always find its mark, but she had no doubt it was more real than anything the sellers in the market had called magic.

She wondered what it was like to create such a thing, whether it had been made on demand or whether the enchanter had let her creative spirit form its beauty.

Delian handed her the black one next. It felt magical, but she was disappointed to find none of the visual evidence of magic she'd seen in the other. But she couldn't help thinking there should be more to it, and it only took a moment to realize why.

If she herself had enchanted it, she'd have wanted to show off a little. Not that she'd ever do such a thing.

"Is there a word to activate this?" Gale asked, thinking of how her mechanical nightingale had slept until she awakened it with her voice.

Delian arched a thick eyebrow and glanced over her shoulder. "Cas?"

The young man—Gale judged him to be in his early twenties, old enough that he'd be married and have children back home but wearing no ring on his finger—moved behind the desk in a few graceful steps and paged quickly through a massive book.

"Try..." He squinted down at the page. "Universalum?"

Gale spoke the word as he had, with the emphasis on *ver*. Nothing happened.

"Univer*sal*um," Gale said, better echoing the natural cadence of the language of magic. The marble changed so suddenly that she nearly dropped it, lighting up with thousands of tiny points of light. She brought it closer to her eyes and drew a sharp breath. It was like holding the night sky in the palm of her hand.

Delian let out a low whistle. "Good to know," she said. The fellow she'd called Cas scratched a note in the book, muttering "univer*sal*um" under his breath.

Gale took the green marble and reluctantly handed the black one back, watching as the stars faded. The green one sparkled prettily in the light from the window, casting white, gold, and green shards onto the walls, but there was nothing more there.

"This one's a fake," she said, almost apologetically, and handed it back. "No magic to it."

Delian narrowed her strange eyes, and for a moment Gale feared she was about to throw her out of the shop. But she only nodded and put it back in the display with the others, apparently with no intention of changing its price or its label. "How did you know?"

Gale shrugged. "I get a feel for things, that's all." She wouldn't tell them more, but knowledge of magic was certainly no less legal than selling it, and she'd have to start somewhere if she wanted to ask these strangers whether they could direct her toward any witches. She crossed to a pair of long, spiralling horns labelled *unicorn, 10,000f each—slices 500f.* "Not one of these is real," she said.

Delian was unfazed. "Of course not. They come from a whale that lives in the northern seas. I don't think unicorns are real, to be honest. But those who do believe in them want a piece."

Gale frowned. "You charge enough for the lie."

Too bold, she told herself. Her exhaustion and the pain in her arm were making her irritable, but she couldn't afford to make these people hate her.

But Delian didn't seem bothered. "The price gives truth to the lie, and that truth makes the customer happy. Sometimes my job is to sell an enchantment, sometimes it's to sell an illusion."

Gale caught a hint of magic and followed it, but it took her behind the desk. "What's back here?"

Delian and Cas exchanged a glance, and Cas pulled a rough wooden box from a shelf on the back wall. "I suppose the lady is looking for this," he said, and dug a smaller, lacquered box out from a nest of paper scraps inside and handed it to Gale.

It was black, covered in a pattern of pink flowers painted in lifelike detail, and stood on four short, delicate legs. A tiny white key stuck out from the back. The magic in the box was stronger than what she had felt in the marbles, but she couldn't guess its purpose. Gale turned the key and nothing happened. When she touched the lid, Delian and Cas both held their hands to their ears.

As soon as the hinged lid was fully open a wretched screeching noise filled the shop. Gale just had time to see that the box's white interior was empty save for a pattern of flowers roughly sketched in black paint before her vision turned blurry and the room started to spin. She clapped the lid shut, cutting off the sound, then set the box down and pressed the heel of her hand to her forehead. Her brain felt like it had been infested by a nest of buzzing bees.

"You might have warned me," she said when the vibrations had subsided.

Delian grinned. "What fun would that be?"

Gale wondered whether she played with all her customers like this and decided that no, it was likely just the ones who didn't seem ready to drop a bank's worth of coin on false unicorn bits.

"What's the story?"

"Unknown," Cas said. "The box was here when Delian bought the shop. No notes, no instructions. Her appraiser knew as much as you seem to—that there's magic in it—but has given up on figuring out its purpose."

Appraiser. That would have to be someone who knew magic, who recognized it as she did.

Maybe a witch. These two would certainly never reveal such a connection to her, but it made sense. Gale's stomach twisted with excitement.

A lead. Finally.

"Your appraiser... is she local?" Gale asked, ignoring the unnerving sight of Madrigal floating down through the ceiling, feet-first.

Delian crossed her arms and leaned against the desk. "Could be. But he isn't keen on having his name passed freely about. He's no witch, but anyone associated with magic needs to be careful. I'm sure you understand."

"Of course." Gale took a deep breath. "What if I needed to find someone who could maybe direct me to a true witch, and it would help save many lives?"

Delian lowered her chin and smiled. "And what if a dozen undercover coppers had been through my shop in the past year with similar tales of woe, assuming I had such connections?" She shook her head. "My appraiser's just a fellow with a keen eye and a bit of training, that's all."

"Then why's he hiding?"

Delian didn't answer, but she also didn't suggest Gale should leave.

Madrigal moved closer. "People like these don't deal in sob stories," she said, looking Delian over. "I didn't find much upstairs in her apartment. No sign of what they're up to. Her name's not Delian, though. It's Jes, if the note that boy left upstairs about a meeting late tonight is accurate. If she's hiding her identity from the public, there's more going on, and I doubt it's good."

But they're our only connection to magic.

Folks in the city might not help anyone out of the goodness of their hearts, but gold or silver might do the trick. Gale mentally calculated the coins in her purse and held the sum against the numbers on the price tags. Not nearly enough.

"What if I could prove that I myself am in possession of magic, and therefore would have no reason to be working with the authorities?"

The shopkeeper bit back a smile. "Oh, I'd love to see that."

Gale squared her shoulders. "Your name's not Delian. It's Jes."

Delian—or rather, Jes—narrowed her eyes.

"Stupid." Madrigal stood behind Jes. "She'll think you've been spying, not that you have magical insight."

Gale's mind went blank for a moment. "That is... I can show you another way, I swear. What if I figure out that screeching box so you can actually sell it? If I did, would it prove I'm connected to magic, and therefore not a... a copper?"

Jes still looked displeased, but the tilt of her head revealed a hint of curiosity. "If you offered me something like that, and if it turned out to add value to something I can't sell otherwise, I suppose it might buy you a message to my appraiser. It'd be up to him to decide whether he wanted to meet."

"Excellent." Gale took the box and sat cross-legged on the floor with it. "You'll want to cover your ears again," she said.

Jes and Cas moved toward the front of the store. They were still watching, but they wouldn't be able to hear her speaking. Gale turned her back to them, hiding the movement of her lips.

"You'll need to help me," she told Madrigal. "Does the sound affect you?"

"I can tune it out." Madrigal sat next to her. "Let's examine it closed, first."

The tone of her voice, calm and firm, took Gale back to her childhood, to the garden where Madrigal had spoken in the same voice, urging her to guess the magical potential in each plant. The memory came back with the force of a flood, pulling at her heart as she thought of what might have been.

She examined the underside of the box, then studied the patterns of the flowers, and found nothing.

"Open it and set it down," Madrigal instructed.

Gale did, and covered her ears. The noise was still irritating, but less shocking when muffled. Madrigal leaned closer to examine the painted flowers within, then turned back to Gale. "Close it," she shouted, and Gale snapped the box shut.

"The enchantment is written inside," Madrigal said, "hidden in the petals."

Gale glanced behind her and found that the others still had their ears covered, then repeated the words Madrigal gave her—not a spell, but another spoken key: "Away and goodnight."

Then she wound the physical key, braced herself, and opened the box again.

This time there was no harsh noise. Music flowed out instead, a rich and haunting melody. The sound was impossible to identify, seeming to be a thousand tiny bells, the wind whispering through reeds beside a lake, and the sound of distant voices lifted in joyful song all at the same time. Gale's tensed shoulders relaxed, and every ache and pain she'd collected on her travels drained out of her. In that moment, her troubles, too, vanished, and she couldn't quite remember why she'd come to the city. Nothing outside the shop seemed to matter. There was only the music.

Jes and Cas wandered over and sat on the floor with her, leaning over the box.

"Gods," Jes whispered.

"You don't believe in such things," Cas said absently.

"I'll allow myself to pretend for a moment."

Madrigal floated a few laps around them, observing. Gale barely noticed her until she leaned in and said, "Close it."

"I don't want to," Gale said. Neither Jes nor Cas questioned why, seeming lost in their own experience of the music.

"Now," Madrigal said, more firmly.

Gale reluctantly lifted a heavy hand and closed the music box. The beautiful sound cut off, but it left behind its sense of serenity even as she remembered her mission and the pain crept back into her arm and her aching muscles.

"What was that?" Jes asked, blinking hard.

Gale waited for Madrigal to answer, then repeated her words. "The purpose seems obvious," she said. "It's a music box meant to calm fears and induce a peaceful state. Probably used to help an anxious person sleep, or maybe a child. It requires a simple phrase to work it—the speaker wouldn't need magic to use this any more than they would the marble, but if you don't know the words, you're out of luck."

"Imagine the dreams with that playing," Cas said, and smiled sheepishly.

"And what did you say to it?" Jes asked.

Gale smiled. "I'll let you know after you've set up that meeting."

Jes laughed under her breath. She looked down at the box again, and Gale could almost see the gold coins dancing behind her eyes. "Go ahead, Cas. I think he'll want to meet this one."

He left through a door at the back of the shop. Jes and Gale got to their feet and brushed off their skirts.

"That was impressive," Jes said. "You have more experience with magic than you let on. Anything else here that might interest you?"

Gale glanced around the shop. Her gaze was drawn back to the marble that held the stars in it.

Madrigal shook her head. "You need a vessel. You can't use an enchanted object for that, and you can't afford it anyway. You need coin left over for when we find someone who can sell us the ingredients we need for your medicine."

Gale sighed. She was right, of course. It would be lovely to carry the night sky in her pocket, but it was a waste of money, especially when she'd have to give up on magic when she went home.

"I'm actually considering something fairly mundane," she said.

Her feet dragged a little as she moved toward the window display. The costume jewellery was still nice, but less so than it had been before she'd seen the enchanted objects. She dug through and found a teardrop-shaped pendant, a red stone set in gold. It flashed prettily in the light from outside but held no magic.

"That would do," Madrigal said.

"How much?" Gale asked.

Jes pursed her lips. "That's a real stone. Garnet, not ruby, but the gold is real as well. You have a decent eye. I'll let you have it for twenty forins."

Gale reached for her coin purse, but paused. "That's close to what you're charging for magic, and this doesn't even have the promise of it."

Jes shrugged. "Magic isn't the only thing in here with value. I could show you something cheaper." She glanced down at Gale's hand. "Or I could trade you for that pretty ring."

Gale hid the ring behind her back. "It's not for sale."

She looked again at the jewel in the pendant. It was quite pretty, shining like a crystallized drop of cherry cordial. She could imagine a fine lady wearing it close to her heart. And though she knew she should pick something cheaper for her vessel, something it would be easy to dispose of before she returned to Bright Hollow, her magic might like a nice home. Perhaps something beautiful would show magic she respected it even if she had no intention of keeping it forever.

"I'll give you ten," she said.

"Fifteen and I'll throw in a chain," Jes replied, smiling like this was a game.

"Twelve."

"Done."

CHAPTER NINETEEN

SUNSET WAS SHINING in bright ribbons between the buildings of Queen's Run before Gale set out with Cas to find the mysterious contact. She followed close behind him as he strode through the streets, unwilling to lose him in the crowd.

Losing him soon ceased to be an issue. They left the streets of nice shops with apartments above and headed west. Soon they were passing buildings with tattered awnings and dirty windows, and Cas began to stand out among the working class in their plain, faded clothes. Madrigal walked a handbreadth above the ground to keep her bare feet out of puddles that couldn't possibly dampen her.

"Aren't you afraid of being robbed?" Gale asked.

Cas glanced back, eyebrows raised, and looked around. "Here? No." He lowered his voice so only she could hear. "There are worse places. Here they might spit on the ground after I pass, but that's not my business. Do stay close, though."

Gale frowned, but followed his advice, walking by his side instead of behind him. He held his chin up and offered nods to the people they passed, but his eyes never stopped moving, taking in the shadows of alleys and noting every soul on the street save for the one he couldn't see.

"I still don't trust him," Madrigal said. She kept pace with them, only occasionally winking out into the borderlands before returning to the magic of her vessel.

Gale couldn't answer, couldn't even nod, but she agreed. Cas seemed nice—friendlier than Jes, offering a reassuring smile as they turned down a long alley between two buildings, shadowed and empty of people. But Gale had no doubt there was more to him than being the—*Beau? Friend?*—of a shopkeeper who charged too much for magic both real and fake. Madrigal was right. Using a false name didn't prove anything about anyone except that they had reason to hide from their past, but it seemed best to keep her guard up.

It was too easy to imagine a knife in her back, her gold stolen, and her jewellery ending up with hefty price tags in that shop window.

Cas slowed and smiled again as though reading her thoughts.

"Not the nicest locale, I know," he said, following her gaze up the soot-darkened brick walls. He stepped—flowed, really, light as a ghost—around a cloth bag of rubbish that leaked something dark onto the ground and looked suspiciously the size of a human body. "Our contact has far more to be afraid of than you have. This is where he felt safest, where he can be sure no one followed you."

"So you're here to protect him?"

"To protect both of you. If all goes well, it will be a mutually beneficial meeting. I'll stand guard at the door to make sure no one disturbs you."

"Good of him to do that," Madrigal said, suspicion heavy in her voice.

"Good of you to do that," Gale repeated, feeling the ghost had a place in the conversation.

Cas's steps slowed. "Jes sees something in you that interests her. Thinks you're worth protecting, which means she hopes your business with her isn't entirely concluded."

"Self-serving, then," Madrigal muttered. "As I thought."

"And you always do what she says?" Gale asked Cas, deciding that in this case Madrigal's interjection might not be productive.

His eyes shone in the dim alley. "She has good instincts, honestly earned and sharply honed, and I'm happy to follow them even when they lead us to strange places. I owe her a lot. My life is far more interesting now than before we met."

Gale wondered about that—about the true nature of their relationship and what his life had been before if lurking around in a curiosity shop and guiding wayward travellers through dangerous neighbourhoods was a step up.

"May I ask you a question?" Cas turned and walked backward as he spoke, still neatly avoiding a stone on the ground that might have turned his ankle.

"Say no," Madrigal told her. "He'll want to know your business, probably because his mistress ordered him to ask."

Cas's expression, which had hardly been dull before, brightened. "That, right there. That's what I'm curious about."

Gale narrowed her eyes and slowed to put space between them. "What?"

"That look, like you're listening to something I can't hear." He stopped walking. "You did it before you came up with answers in the shop. And you spoke to yourself, or to something invisible. Is it magic?"

Gale stuck her hands in her pockets. "You wouldn't believe me if I told you."

Cas laughed. "And you wouldn't believe what I've had to believe in the past year or so." He sobered, if only slightly. "Try me."

Gale glanced at Madrigal, but the witch only waited to see what her student would do.

"It's not magic," Gale said. "As I said before, I have a feel for it, but I'm no witch."

"But you're learning," he said. "You have some connection to it, or you wouldn't be able to sniff it out so easily. So what is it?"

He'll never believe it, anyway, she decided. He'd have to be mad, or genuinely more interesting than he'd let on thus far.

"What if I told you I had a ghost whispering in my ear?"

"Fool," Madrigal grumbled.

Cas's brow furrowed. "My first thought would be that you believe it to be true, but it can't be. But then I'd remember that... Well. Anything's possible, isn't it? Something strange around every turn in this world."

They squeezed past several stacks of old crates and a tall wooden ladder at the end of the alley. Cas led the way out, checking above, behind, and to both sides before crossing the street and striding toward a blackened single-storey building with a sign reading FABRICS AND ADORNMENTS, NEW AND USED in front. The roof was somewhere in the process of slow collapse, sinking in at the middle and dotted with holes, but the building had fared better than the place next door, which had fallen at some point into a pile of burnt rubble.

"Fire," Cas explained, somewhat unnecessarily. "About five years ago. As I've heard it, there was some mix-up with ownership or insurance. In any case, no one has managed to rebuild. Not that most would want to in this neighbourhood. Come around back."

Gale followed him down another alley, narrower and darker than any street they'd walked before it. A rat scurried across her path, and she held back a startled cry. Cas knocked three times on a heavy wooden door.

The door cracked open. "You're sure about this?" asked a man's voice, thin and reedy.

"Of course," Cas said. "I'll be out here if you need me." He turned to Gale. "If either of you do."

The door opened farther, revealing a tall fellow in a well-cut suit that nearly matched the sooty walls outside. Gale glanced down. His shoes were practical and a little dirty but in good condition, and his thin moustache had been oiled and curled in what Gale supposed might be the fashion here in the city.

The only truly strange thing was the fact that his left ear was almost entirely missing. He'd grown his hair a little long to hide it, but the scarred bump on the side of his head was hard to miss.

"Not a witch, my arse," Madrigal said, and drifted through the wall to get a look at the man from behind. He shivered and glanced over his shoulder, but apparently didn't see her.

Gale wondered whether there was any significance to his choice of sacrifice.

"It's rude to stare," the man said.

"Sorry," Gale muttered, and looked away.

"Alec, this is Gale," Cas said.

Alec sniffled and looked down his long nose at her. "Come in, then. I only have a few minutes to spare."

Gale stepped inside and the door swung closed behind her with a bang. An oil lamp on a spindle-legged wooden table in the corner cast shadows over the nearly bare interior of the shop's back room, which had been set up as a sitting area. A pair of mismatched, threadbare armchairs sat near the table, and a battered carpet bag rested the far corner. The walls, made of vertical wood slats, were largely undamaged, and after five years there was no smell of smoke.

It was a nice enough spot, and surprising given the state of the outside of the building. Gale glanced up and found the roof perfectly intact from the inside.

"Illusion," Madrigal said, not sounding particularly impressed. "He keeps the outside looking abandoned so no one disturbs him. This is no random meeting place."

Alec looked at her, arms crossed, eyebrows raised. Waiting.

"I know what you are," Gale said.

Alec sniffled again. "I'm not sure what you mean."

Gale stepped closer. "You're a witch. Your ear was your sacrifice when you called magic in and took it into yourself forever."

His lips tightened. "And who are you then?"

"I'm nobody, really. But I come from a village that's had a curse placed on it and I need help from someone who can—"

Alec pulled a handkerchief from his pocket and blew his nose.

Madrigal huffed. "He's useless. A witch who can't even stop up his own runny nose will be no help to you."

Unless he doesn't have magic to fix himself, Gale thought.

She hadn't felt magic in this place, and only identified him as a witch by his ear. Maybe he wasn't a vessel for it anymore.

Her skin prickled with fear, like she'd just paused on a pleasant walk through the woods and seen a hungry wolf watching from the shadows. She shot a questioning look at Madrigal.

The ghost shook her head. "I know what you're thinking, but no. There's magic in him, he's simply adept at hiding it. I assume that's why your brother hasn't shown up yet. This one hasn't tainted himself with blood magic. He didn't set the curse."

Alec glanced over his shoulder, then frowned at Gale. "What are you looking at?"

"Nothing. Sorry."

Alec sat in one of the chairs and gestured toward the other. "Very well. Tell me about this curse."

Gale perched on the edge of the chair, unwrapped her forearm, and held it out to him. The rash had turned a deeper red since she'd last looked at it and had crept up to the edge of the bandage, reaching almost to her wrist. At its centre, it had eaten deep, leaving the flesh bloodless and raw. Not dead yet, but dying. She looked away. "I've been holding it at bay with medicines, but there's only so much I can do. I need a cure I can take back to my village, something that can fight a curse and not just sickness. People have died. I thought if I found a witch who could help, we might prevent more deaths."

Alec's moustache twitched as though he might be holding back a smile, but perhaps it was only discomfort. Gale didn't want to assume the worst simply because he was a witch. Still, there was something about him she didn't like, and she wished she'd managed to find a different witch to beg for help.

"It sounds terrible." Alec drummed his fingertips against the arm of his chair and sniffled again.

"Please, mister… Alec. We're running out of time. *I'm* running out of time. I've managed to work up a salve that's slowing the progression, but I have only days before I'm too weak and feverish to do anyone any good. I came to the city looking for insight, for help, maybe for the ingredients I need to save us."

Alec sat back in his chair and crossed one ankle over the opposite knee. If Gale's pleas had any effect on him, he hid them as well as he did his magic from the outside world.

"I don't know much about curses, myself," he said, "though I do have a strong interest in medicine."

"Oh?" Gale tried to sound politely interested even as she noted the redness around his nose from being wiped so often.

Alec sighed. "The sniffles, yes. This illness is going around. I infected myself and have avoided healing by magic so I could test medicines on myself before others. If you'd kindly stop judging me for that, we can move on to your problem."

"Sorry, I—" Gale paused. "You think you can help me?"

"I can offer advice. Let me think."

Madrigal paced behind his chair, eyes narrowed. She didn't seem to like him any more than Gale did but could afford to be open about it. Being invisible did have its advantages.

"The ingredients exist," Alec said, "but the problem is where to find them. And of course you'd need magic to prepare them correctly."

Gale decided not to mention she'd be doing the work herself.

"Unicorn horn is expensive, unless you steal it." Alec seemed to lose himself in thought for a moment, then nodded. "You'd need ballywally, goralsum leaves, knockburn roots. Equal parts each, then speak *irinda* over them to combine. I might be able to prepare it for you for the right price, but you'd have to fetch the ingredients yourself. Might find them in the garden the king's mages keep, but they're rather possessive of their stock."

"Garbage," Madrigal said. "Half of those don't exist, and goralsum will give you runny bowels for a month."

Gale gritted her teeth. "If you don't want to help me, just say so."

"Help you?" Alec leaned closer. "Why don't you tell me the whole story? Where are you from? Why would anyone curse your village?"

Gale felt the blood drain from her face. "I don't—"

"Bright Hollow, right?" Alec nearly spat the words out. "The only village I know of that would deserve such treatment."

A lump formed in Gale's throat, and she swallowed it back. She hadn't expected the conversation to become an attack and struggled to think of anything she could say to fix it. "I know we've done wrong, but—"

"Wrong?" Mad laughter played at the edge of Alec's voice, but his face showed only barely controlled anger. "How many witches have made their homes on the mountain for the sake of its magic only to be driven away? How many have been murdered, their homes set aflame?"

Gale looked to Madrigal, who shook her head. "He was never at my home, but others passed by over the years. Stories spread."

Alec's eyes brightened, catching the lamplight. "Yet here you are, seeking a magical cure when it suits you. Carrying magic on you. A witch's vessel?"

Gale pressed her hand over the brooch, which she wore concealed beneath her jacket. "I didn't steal it from anyone. It belongs to another witch. She's helping me, she just can't be here."

"What's her name?"

Gale didn't answer. If he knew about Madrigal's death, he probably knew her name. There weren't that many witches in Andonia, after all.

"If you'd left us alone, we'd never have harmed you," Alec said, hatred dripping from every word. "Perhaps you picked a fight with the wrong witch in the recent past and you're finally getting what you deserved. No, I won't help you. No witch in Andonia would forgive me if I did."

Gale's cheeks warmed with anger as her hope of finding help vanished. "Then you're no better than people say. Refusing to help is inhuman." Words failed her, and she ground her teeth together, trying to regain her composure. "Not that you're inhuman."

"That's what you think, though, isn't it?" Alec's moustache twitched as his lip curled in a sneer. "Monsters. Souls wasted away."

"I don't think that," Gale said, her temper carrying her words even as she tried to hold it in check. "Many do, and they wouldn't be sitting here asking polite questions. You're lucky I'm the one who found you and not—"

She stopped herself, but too late.

Alec stood. "Who? Who else is looking for me? They're with you?"

"No!" Gale stood, too, and held her hands out in a gesture of peace. "I'm looking to cure the illness. He's here about the curse itself. If you'd help me, I'm sure I could convince him you're on our side."

Alec took a long breath, glanced past Gale to his bag in the corner, and seemed to dismiss it. He went straight to the door, instead. "Cas! I need to disappear. Now. Alone."

He stepped into the alley and slammed the door behind him.

"Wait!" Gale called, and reached for the doorknob as Alec spoke a few muffled words outside and the lock clicked shut. She tried to open it, but it wouldn't budge.

Cas's voice reached her through the door. "Wait there. I'll be back by morning."

Then there was nothing.

Madrigal moved through the wall into the alley but returned quickly. "I can't follow. They're gone."

Gale tried to twist the lock again, but all she got was sore skin, a deeper ache in her arm, and a hair's breadth of movement from the mechanism. She paused, gritted her teeth, and tried again. This time the lock opened, but the alley was empty.

"What do you want to do?" Madrigal asked.

Gale stepped back inside. The alley was too dark and the city too frightening for her to think properly out there. Alec's secret rooms weren't the most welcoming place, but the building had to be reasonably secure if he was using magic to hide here.

She slumped into one of the chairs. "Made a mess of that, didn't I?"

Madrigal sat in the other chair and rested her chin on one hand. "He wouldn't have helped even if you hadn't mentioned your brother. And it's not a complete dead end. At least you have a quiet place to create your vessel, and maybe there's something useful in that bag of his."

Gale pressed her fingertips to her closed eyelids, trying to wake herself up. Even after that bit of excitement, she was dragging. It felt like the curse was consuming not only her flesh, but her spirit and her mind. "I should have handled that better. Been more honest, maybe."

"Or less," Madrigal suggested.

"I suppose. At least he has a chance to hide before Hawk finds him."

"Would you feel terrible if Hawk caught and harassed him

after the way he treated you?" Madrigal sounded genuinely curious.

"Not if he was only going to give him a stiff talking to." Gale forced herself to her feet and passed through the door to the front of the shop. Soap-covered windows let in faint evening light from outside that shone over the dust-covered surface of a wide wooden shop counter and the stack of similarly dirty crates stacked behind it. "It's what else might happen that concerns me. I don't like Alec, and he doesn't like me, but he doesn't deserve to die for a curse he didn't create. And the way Hawk was talking before he left..." Gale thought back to the headless body in the square and shuddered. "No one deserves to die for magic. It's not like folks back home think. Bad people can use it to do terrible things, but that doesn't mean everyone who uses it is bad. Or corrupted. Seems to me like some witches have fine souls."

Gale leaned against the counter. She knew she needed to keep moving, that if she slowed down for too long she might not want to start again, but it was so tempting to rest. She couldn't help thinking of the small store of *lucistra* and the ingredients to make more that she carried in her bag, and how good it would feel to have magic in her, if only for a moment.

"Your Teachings say people should die for magic," Madrigal said. Her voice barely broke the room's silence, but it drew Gale out of her thoughts.

"Cast out." Gale drew a long breath. "Though some in the past interpreted it to mean they should be cast out from life. They're clear on that from the first writings. Keeping humans far from magic is one of the reasons we separated ourselves—that and not wanting to mix with those who worship lesser gods." Her chest clenched tight. She couldn't tell whether it was with guilt, fear, or both. "But I can see how magic could be God's will to save us from this curse, too. So maybe the Teachings are..."

She couldn't say *wrong* out loud. There had to be an explanation, a different way the old words could be interpreted. That was, after all, what the Luminary and acolytes were for.

And if the message is clear? she asked herself. *If the Teachings insist Madrigal deserved what she got because she used magic to shape creation to her will and not God's?*

What then?

An icy chill spread over her shoulder as Madrigal laid a hand on it. "It's hard, I know. Keep thinking. Keep growing. Who knows, we might make a witch of you yet."

Gale chose to ignore that, though the thought called to her now in a dangerous way it hadn't before. She took her new necklace from her bag and held it in one hand, imagining what it would be like when it was filled with magic, when it might be the key to saving Bright Hollow—if she could find someone who would share the answers.

"Not a witch," she said, without any rancor. "But I'm willing to try for hero."

CHAPTER TWENTY

"Your cure's not here."

Gale heard Madrigal's words, but as she stared down at the jars of herbs she'd pulled from Alec's massive carpet bag it didn't seem possible there was no answer there.

She turned one of the jars over in her hands, reading the label marked in clear, obsessively tidy modern Andonian. "But there's so much here you didn't have in your garden."

"I know, child. Brought in from all over the world, and much of it useful for other, more mundane ailments. It seems Alec has a genuine interest in medicine after all, but we're dealing with something else entirely. Treating the symptoms alone isn't enough when we know the curse is going to fight back. We need more. Something deeper." Madrigal sat cross-legged in the shadows, looking as solid and real as Gale had ever seen her. The magic in the shop was difficult for Gale to feel even when she was inside, but Madrigal seemed more comfortable in its presence than she was with only her vessel to hold onto.

"So what do we do?"

Madrigal's smile looked forced, but Gale appreciated the effort. "We prepare for the next step, for when we do find what we need. Between what you brought from my garden and what Alec has preserved here, you have everything you need to make plenty of *lucistra*, and you'll use that to create your vessel."

Gale tried to imagine what it would be like to draw power from a vessel—magic that would not only be stronger than what she took from the potion, but more uniquely her own, ready to be drawn out whenever she needed it. "Do you really think we'll find a cure somewhere if I do this?"

"Maybe. If not, at least you'll have me to show you around the borderlands until Lord Death carries you away."

Gale gaped at her. "That's not comforting!"

"I didn't mean for it to be." Madrigal came closer, rising and stepping into the lamplight. "This is your choice. Walk forward, not knowing whether you'll succeed or not, not knowing whether you'll be forgiven or not... or give up, go home, and take comfort from your faith and your folks until the curse takes all of you."

Gale pressed the heels of her palms to her eyes to keep from crying.

It had all seemed so simple a few days ago. Find the cure, save everyone and be a real hero, live the life she wanted among the people she loved. It was solid. Good. Easy, and so clearly God's will.

Now all she had was a handful of splintered shards of intention and purpose, and nothing about it was clear. Her desires, God's will, dangerous flight and familiar cages, the comfort of certainty and a new yearning to learn the truth beyond the Teachings... None of the pieces fit together.

So focus on one piece. What do you know for sure?

The cure was the only thing she knew to be God's will and also her own. Everything else would have to wait.

The Teachings forbade what she'd already done, but enchanting an object to hold her own magic was something else entirely. Something worse. A true commitment, however temporary.

Another step off the path.

But the Luminary had implied that there were degrees of sin when she'd given Hawk leave to do what he must to break the curse. If he could murder to save Bright Hollow, surely magic would be absolved just as easily.

Excitement twisted deep in her belly, desire for a thing she had no right to want, let alone have.

Magic of my own, at least for a while.

"Are you ready?" Madrigal asked.

Gale took a deep breath and uncovered her eyes. "I am." She dug through her bag and found the carefully wrapped plants she'd brought from Madrigal's garden, then selected dried specimens from Alec's jars and slipped a few copper coins into the bag to pay for what she'd taken.

"Good enough," Madrigal said. "Go ahead." The witch sat in one of the chairs, fingers tented beneath her chin, and waited.

Gale stared at her. "I thought you'd walk me through it again. I only did it once, and there were so many other recipes we tried after that..."

Madrigal gave her a thin smile. "You'll need to be sharp if you want to learn magic, even if you're sick and exhausted. Let's see what you're made of."

Gale set her jaw, rolled up her sleeves, and got to work. Madrigal's instructions from that nearly sleepless night jumbled together in her mind, names and spells and amounts of various substances. It was there, though—the first potion she'd created under the influence of Madrigal's old magic. Simple ingredients, but how much of each?

The incardium, the iris, the bark... Crush, stir—water, I need water.

She kept glancing at Madrigal, but the witch could have been a statue carved from air for all the response she showed. No approval, no dismissive *hmph* if Gale had made a mistake, and certainly no hints. This was a test, and Gale had no intention of failing.

Minutes passed as she wracked her mind, searching for the strange word she needed to speak to bring it all together.

Belitata... No, that was to enhance the fever-reducing effects of willow bark by changing its reaction to incardium in another recipe. She remembered watching it happen when she'd tried the third version of her medicine, feeling how the word directed everything. Only a dunce could forget that.

Orichaelum... Vlaxinticat... Hurbrinari... She formed the words silently with her lips, enunciating them perfectly and remembering their effects, but none were for this recipe. Her brow furrowed, her jaw clenched until her teeth ached. Madrigal cleared her throat, and Gale ignored her.

It was a longer spell, not just one word.

And then, in a flash, it came to her.

"Hercalae voldanu re'ardiun," she said, and looked down at the mixture. Nothing happened.

Her chest tightened, and her fingers twitched with the urge to release her frustration by dumping the bowl on the floor.

Then she remembered, and she choked back a nonsensical urge to laugh at herself.

She turned and reached for her bag, pulled out what was left of her last batch of *lucistra,* and drank.

Power flowed through her, as bright and enthralling as it had been a few nights ago, but less shocking. She welcomed it, letting herself enjoy the expansion of her perceptions, the warmth, the *rightness* of it, only speaking the spell again when she felt the magic slipping away. She directed it through her fingers and into the mixture. This time the reaction was immediate, changing the muddy, muddled contents of the bowl into the thick liquid she wanted, bright as sunlight and more valuable than gold. She knew without testing it that she'd done well.

"Better than what you made before," Madrigal said. "You almost forgot to drink, didn't you?"

Gale scowled at her, though it wasn't easy to do with the echoes of magic still resonating through her. "I did this all from memory—by myself and on my first try—and all you can do is criticize what I *almost* forgot?"

Madrigal smiled, more warmly than she had since they'd met again at the cabin. "It wasn't a criticism. Seemed to me like you expected the magic to come from within you. That you might already be thinking like a witch."

Gale looked away. "I just forgot."

"In any case, that should be good enough for you to create your vessel. You'll just need more to fill it." Madrigal crouched and passed her hand through the syrup, the bowl, and the floor beneath.

"You really think I'm ready to perform an enchantment?"

"No." The witch frowned. "Not nearly. You should have been studying for years to get to this moment, learning the language of magic—not just to speak it or understand it, but to think in it. You should have been opening channels within yourself through regular exposure to power, understanding the theory of what we're doing. It's going to take a lot of power, near-perfect concentration on your part, and me in your ear the whole time. Even then, I don't know."

"But?"

"The only thing that gives me a shred of hope is that you found a way to keep in touch with magic over the years, even if you thought you were controlling your desire for it. That connection might help." Madrigal stood, drifted back a few paces, and looked her over. "My apprentice's first vessel should have been a powerful thing, capable of holding all the magic she wished to put into it, of powering spells that could call a thunderstorm or create an illusion visible to a crowd of hundreds.

Yours will be..." She shrugged. "Well, I hope it will be enough to concentrate the magic you'll need to cure a rash."

For a moment Gale ached with regret. *If we hadn't killed her, if I'd stayed with her, if I'd studied, I could hold so much magic in my hands.* She wondered what it would be like to feel that strong. What she felt when she drank a simple magical syrup would seem like a dripping faucet compared to the flood of power she'd get from a proper vessel, which would in turn be rendered insignificant by what Madrigal herself had held in her own body when she lived.

But that wasn't my path, she reminded herself. *I did what was best—what is best—for me.* If she'd stayed on as a child, Hawk would have gone home, reported both of them, and Gale would have lost everything. Her family. Her friends. Her community.

Everything but magic.

"It'll have to do," she said, the words falling dead and hollow in the nearly empty room. "I'll do my best and pray that it's enough."

Madrigal rested a hand on her arm. Gale felt nothing save for the chill but appreciated the gesture, nonetheless. "Your pretty necklace might not come to much, but it's not too late. If you did change your mind and decide to pursue this, you could destroy that vessel and create a stronger one later. And if you made the sacrifice, both you and any external vessel you created from that influx of power would..." She trailed off and sighed. "We should get started. Pour a little of the *lucistra* back into your vial for later, and the rest into that empty jar there. You'll need several more batches before we have enough to finish this."

Time became inconsequential in the back room of the shop as Gale worked, focusing on the creation of magic, taking a larger dose of the golden potion on one attempt and less on the next, asking Madrigal every question that popped into her mind about the interactions of the ingredients, what would happen if the ratios were altered, and why it all worked. There was nothing but the magic passing through her and the difficult but fascinating work in front of her. Her mind raced, her hands flew, and soon enough she had four carefully prepared batches of the magical golden syrup.

It was only when her stomach growled that she thought to look out the window at the front of the shop and saw that the sky over the city was fully dark, and when she checked her watch, it showed they were only an hour from midnight.

"When did that happen?" she asked.

"While you were having the time of your life." Madrigal smiled. "Admit it."

Gale couldn't help grinning back. "I wouldn't have minded having something new to work on, but... yeah. That was fun."

Madrigal rolled her eyes toward the ceiling. "Fun, she says."

Gale laughed. But her joy vanished when she took the garnet necklace from around her neck and set it on the table.

A dozen thoughts crowded into her mind, all speaking over each other, and every one of them a reason not to do this. Loudest among them wasn't a question of right or wrong, as she might have expected, but time. *I could do better if I practiced more first—made more medicines, played with spells, maybe tried working some small enchantment that didn't require a vessel. If I could go back to the cabin and read more books, understand what I'm doing instead of going through the motions, I could be smarter. Stronger. Make the vessel better, and my medicines—*

A searing slash of pain in her cursed forearm brought her back, reminding her of the reality of her situation. Perfection didn't matter. *Better* didn't matter. Only *done* was important now.

If it worked, none of what she did here would matter in a few days. It would all be over. No more messing with magic. No more doubts. She'd be back home, in the arms of her family and community, living according to the Teachings and God's will, playing her small part in the life of Bright Hollow.

The thought didn't make her as happy as she wanted it to.

She slathered a layer of salve over the rash and re-wrapped it to keep it from distracting her, then ate a pear from her bag to ease the ache in her empty stomach.

"Anything else you can do to put this off?" Madrigal asked, not unkindly.

"I suppose not."

"Good. Take that last batch and put it in a cup—it's your best one. Then take Alec's stylus. That silver stick inlaid with gold over there."

The instrument Madrigal had indicated made Gale think of the ceremonial wands the king's mages were said to carry. She knew little about them. In Bright Hollow magic was magic, and the difference between doing it legally in service to the king or illegally for one's own purposes was blurry at best. But here, in this dark, secret place with forbidden magic in the air, knowing she could be executed for what she was about to do when those mages were well trained and held in high esteem as they did their work, it seemed like a great and strange difference, indeed.

"Why?" Gale asked, examining it carefully.

"Because it will help direct the magic more precisely, and you need all the help you can get." Madrigal paced smoothly back and forth through the table. "I'll give you the words to speak as you go along, but it's your intention that will be the key to success, more than it ever was while making a simple potion or salve. The spells will tell the magic precisely what to do and the stylus will carry the power outward, but your intention to create the vessel is what will bring it all together and create the enchantment. No pretty tool can make up for weakness there. Lose your focus and you'll lose the magic."

Gale clenched her hands into fists to keep them from shaking. *For Hawk. For Bright Hollow. Whether they like it or not.*
For all of us.

"Understood."

Madrigal tugged her fingers through her hair, pushing the

loose curls back from her face. "The first step is to enchant your pendant and prepare it for its new purpose. Focus on the stone or on the entire piece, it doesn't matter. Only be consistent in your desire to open it to magic, to amplify its power. Are you ready?"

"No." Gale's cheeks warmed. "I'd like to pray first."

Madrigal pressed her fingers to her temples, but nodded. "Make it quick."

Gale knelt and closed her eyes.

"Hear me, God," she said softly. "I beg you, in this more than anything before. If it is your will, grant me success. I know little, and can only hope I'm doing the right thing. Use me to save the sick in Bright Hollow if it be your will. If not, so be it."

She stood to find Madrigal watching with keen interest.

"What?" Gale asked. "What's so wrong about wanting to do God's will? You seem convinced that magic falls within its scope. I just want to be sure."

"I only wonder where *your* will comes into this." Madrigal spoke gently, but her voice held a vein of pure steel, sharp and strong. "Where you begin to take responsibility for your actions instead of passing the credit or blame on to an invisible power."

Gale's breath sharpened. The words hit her like a slap, but she didn't know why it should be so.

"We don't have time to argue about this," she said.

"No." Madrigal's voice came out soft and sad. "But one's will is an important question. You've been raised to give yours over to others to control. I only hope you have enough left in you to direct magic as you must." She glanced up. "The roof hasn't caved in since you prayed. Perhaps that's enough of a sign to go ahead?"

Gale tried to remember the reasoning she'd come up with earlier for doing this, but it felt hollow in the face of what she was about to do.

Forward. It's just one more step. I can still go home.

"Shall I sit or stand?"

"Stand. Always stand, if you're able. Brings the body and its energies into alignment."

Gale stood next to the table.

"Imagine it now," Madrigal said. "Look at your vessel. Imagine it filled with magic. Imagine—"

"How, though?" Gale asked. Her heart had begun to race. "Am I imagining it just sort of concentrated in there? In the middle, or through all of it? Or is it channels, like you spoke of opening in a person over time, like little tunnels through the stone?"

Madrigal swept around behind her and spoke into her ear. "Those are the questions that will distract you. It doesn't matter how you imagine it. The magic will do its work as long as you guide it by your focus and will. Take the first image that comes to you and let it develop."

Gale remembered the black marble at the curiosity shop and the universe of stars within it. Infinite light in those pinpricks but with a larger infinity of space between them that could hold more light. Limitless. Unfathomable. She focused on the garnet, imagining the same potential inside of it but with magic instead of light.

Her muscles relaxed. Her eyes focused until there was nothing but the red stone set in gold.

"Good. Now drink everything from the cup, holding that image in your mind."

Gale swallowed the sweet liquid, closing her eyes and remembering the stars as magic swept through her, far more than she'd dared to take into herself before. The world vanished, and she struggled to hold herself to reality. She lost track of her breath and her heartbeat as magic carried her beyond thought. It was good—too good. Too tempting to give herself over to it completely and let it do as it wished. Magic filled her to bursting, and she struggled to finish the cup.

"Drink all of it," Madrigal ordered. She sounded far away.

The magic battled against her, threatening to run riot as she forced her weak and inexperienced body to hold more of it.

It's mine, she reminded herself. *My magic, made in part from my will. It will do as I say.* She forced her eyes open and looked again at the garnet, which now seemed to glow with potential.

From a great distance she heard Madrigal's voice. "Press the tip of the stylus to the stone, and guide the magic through your hand and out of your body. Remember your intention as you speak the words I give you, then be silent and let the magic flow out into your enchantment."

The magic pushed against the walls of Gale's body until she felt she might burst. It was too much—too big, too overwhelming, and she finally understood what Madrigal had meant about her not being ready. A person needed to be stretched gradually before she could be prepared to hold such power.

"Hurry," she whispered, though she couldn't hear herself.

"Madalag she'halaim voldunaismi," Madrigal said, strong and clear.

Gale repeated the words and what felt like hundreds that came after. She seemed to grow smaller even as the magic pressed outward, and felt herself slipping away as Madrigal's voice and her own fell silent.

Stars. Infinite magic in a tiny stone. The image rested in her mind, sharp and perfect.

The magic brightened, setting her alight, and she gasped as it flowed out of her.

I'm doing it, she thought.

And with that, more thoughts came.

Instead of simply experiencing how incredible the magic felt, she thought about how good it was. With that came desire, and the understanding that she wanted magic for its own sake, that she could be great instead of being one more humble stone in the Path. She wanted this feeling that came with shaping the world to her own precious will instead of doing what had been handed down to her as duty. She understood it as destiny, as potential both beautiful and terrifying. In that moment she felt magic bending more fully to her intentions, entering the stone, shaping and changing it to make it ready to hold a universe of power. Her focus was perfect, balanced between experience and intention, shaped by her, carried by magic.

Desire is the key, she thought. *Intention. My will be done.*

Your will? answered a dark voice within her—not hers, but the voice of her parents, her teachers, Hawk, the Luminary and acolytes. The magic in her reared and bucked, slipping from her control as the voice divided her focus. *You stand in opposition to God, the Teachings, the Luminary, those who walked the Path before. You think you're wiser than they?* It laughed cruelly. *Corruption. You're blind to it already, drugged on power that's not yours to hold, that—*

"Stop," Gale whimpered. The voice fell silent, but it had done its work.

She doubted. Not the magic, not the spell, not even her own ability, but whether she was truly doing good. The idea lasted only a few seconds before she wrestled her attention back to her intentions, but it was enough. The magic, which had been flowing through the stylus and into the stone, exploded out from her, suddenly wild and dangerous.

The air in the shop blew around her, whipping her hair and her dress.

"Call it back!" Madrigal ordered.

"I can't!" Gale's voice came out in a thin cry. "I don't know how!"

Pressure built up inside the room until it crushed the breath from her. Gale fought to keep the magic flowing into the vessel, but there was the ache, the confusion, the awareness of—

The roof of the shop exploded upward, releasing the pressure and sending hunks of splintered wood and shingles shooting into the night. Gale looked up and found a few stars winking down at her, barely visible above the city's haze and the glow of streetlamps.

"Focus," she pleaded, begging her mind to obey. There was still magic in her. Only a little, and flowing out quickly. She thought of her parents, of Hawk, of everyone ill at home until using the vessel to save Bright Hollow became her only thought.

The last of the magic passed through the stylus and into the pendant, and Gale collapsed to the floor, shaking.

"Get up," Madrigal ordered. A chunk of wood fell from the rafters and passed through her before slamming to the floor. "Come on. We'd best finish this elsewhere."

Gale forced herself to her feet and scooped the necklace off the table. She felt no magic in it, and bit her lip to keep from crying. "It didn't work."

"It did," Madrigal said, brushing her fingers gently over the gemstone. "You lost most of its potential in that blast, and you'll want to be careful with it—the stone and the gold are more brittle than they should be, a sure sign of a sloppy enchantment. But you did something, and we'll just have to hope it's enough. You need to fill it, but this place is no longer safe. Collect the rest of that *lucistra* and get us out of here."

There was no time to think any more on what she'd done, on right or wrong, or the incredible power she'd just held within her, no matter how poorly she'd spent it in the end.

Gale was used to following directions, and now that's just what she did.

CHAPTER TWENTY-ONE

THE STREET WAS ALREADY FILLING up with curious onlookers when Gale slipped out the shop's back door.

"Hold here a while," Madrigal said as she stepped out of the alley and into the crowd. "They'll notice anyone fleeing the scene."

Gale turned to an older man of scarecrowish proportions with straw-like hair sticking out from under his nightcap to match. "What happened?"

He didn't turn to answer but kept his eyes glued on buildings now visible through the space once occupied by the shop's roof. "'Splosion of some sort," he said, shaking his head. "I heard they've been experimenting with putting in lines to carry gas to our neighbourhood like they have in the fancy parts. You suppose it's something to do with that?"

"Maybe."

Another shake of his head. "Dangerous, that's what I told my wife when I first heard. Foolish to sacrifice life and limb for a bit of light in the evening, isn't it?"

"Certainly," Gale said, but he didn't seem to be listening. That was fine by her. She'd only had half her mind on the conversa-

212

tion, and her feet itched to carry her away to some place where she could work magic in peace.

Once the crowd had grown dense enough to hide her movements, she made her way across the street to the alley Cas had led her through earlier.

"Going to hide behind a dust bin and work your magic under the soot and the stars?" Madrigal asked.

"Not hardly," Gale muttered. She reached the boxes clogging the alley and fished out the ladder the workers had left behind, leaned it against the side of the building, and made her way up. It would have been a hard climb under normal circumstances, and her legs were sore now from the seemingly endless walking she'd done over the past few days. But the thought of magic kept her from thinking about that, or about the increasing distance she was putting between herself and the hard ground below. When she reached the top, she set her bag gently over the rim that surrounded the flat roof, eased one leg over, and heaved herself up.

The building stood two floors high—not as tall as some she'd seen in the city, but the roof stood as high as any that surrounded it. Gale hoped that meant no one would be able to see her.

She turned back to Madrigal. "I'm going to hide on a roof and work my magic under the soot and stars, thank you very much."

On the street below, hoofbeats clattered over the cobblestones and shouts rang out—the cops arriving, Gale supposed, but she couldn't be bothered to look. Not when she had several jars of magic in her bag and instructions to consume as much as her vessel would hold. The thought of that much magic passing through her was enough to distract a person from anything else.

She set the jars out on the rooftop and loosened the lids, then held her vessel in her cupped hands.

"So?" she asked. "How badly did I do?"

Madrigal stood at the edge of the roof, watching the commotion below. "You released a lot of magic back there. Why? Did you lose focus?"

Gale swallowed hard. "Only a little."

"That's all it takes." The corners of Madrigal's mouth turned down as turned back toward her student. Gale braced herself for a tongue-lashing, reminding herself that it would be the worst the ghost could do to her. But then Madrigal laughed, so loud that Gale almost shushed her before she remembered no one else could hear.

"I hardly see what's so funny," she said, frowning, when the witch had calmed herself. "I messed up. Badly. I suppose I won't have a terribly efficient vessel after all that."

Madrigal wiped tears from her eyes and drifted closer to examine the necklace. "No, you won't, and it'll snap in half if you so much as drop it. I'd offer you a spell to strengthen it, but you have neither the power nor the skill required. You finished the enchantment, though, and something happened. Wouldn't be much by most witches' standards, but it'll do for your medicine." Her smile faltered. "And that's all you need it for, I suppose."

Gale scowled at the vessel. She should be glad, of course. There was no reason to have wanted success beyond the bare minimum required for curing the curse-sickness—in fact, having access to greater magic would only have been a temptation. But she'd wanted to impress Madrigal, to reveal some innate talent the witch hadn't expected or seen in her. She'd wanted it to be natural and easy and blindingly successful.

But it was as hard as Madrigal had warned her. Worse, even. And the witch's expectations were so damn high...

She hated that she cared at all.

Maybe this was God's will, she thought, *that it should only be enough for this one task.*

She released the idea. It only made anger boil up from her belly to think that God would be so miserly and controlling as to offer her only what God required and none of what she herself truly wanted.

"Then what's so funny?" she asked. "I failed. I disappointed you. I'm as useless an apprentice as you've said."

Madrigal's eyes shone. "You didn't direct it as you wanted, but you certainly got results. And the look on your face when the winds blew. And then the roof..." She pressed her lips together and took a long breath. "I shouldn't laugh."

"No, you shouldn't." But Gale had to hold back a smile as she peered over the edge of the roof, careful to stay out of sight. The top of the building across the street was gone, leaving the inside of the supposedly abandoned shop and the street in front of it a mess of wood and debris. A quick laugh escaped before she could bite it back. "I do feel terrible about Alec losing his hiding place."

"Do you?" Madrigal's eyes shone with laughter.

"Not really." She felt guilty saying it, but only a little. Alec had good reason for hating the people of Bright Hollow, but he'd also tried to loosen her bowels and send her on a deadly mission to get magical ingredients from the king's mages.

She didn't dare picture his face when he came back.

Gale cleared her throat and turned her thoughts toward more important things. "We should finish this before anyone finds me up here."

As it turned out, creating the vessel was far more difficult than filling it. Though the filling required the consumption of a great deal more magic, large doses weren't necessary. Gale took it in smaller sips, maintaining the magic within her at a gentle hum that lifted her spirits and took her mind off her physical woes. Smaller amounts, she found, were less earth-shattering but far easier to control, and she only had to speak the spell once to direct a steady flow of power through Alec's stylus and into her vessel.

Soon there was a full jar of the syrupy magic potion left and plenty buzzing through Gale's body, but no more power would flow into the garnet pendant.

"Don't force it," Madrigal told her. "That thing's fragile enough as it is."

"But it's still in me." Gale's heart fluttered in irrational panic as she was overcome by the urge to use the power for something. "What do I do?"

Madrigal sat on the roof with her knees pulled to her chest, facing Gale but looking up at the sky. "Release it. You're not going to bring the building down."

I don't want to let go, Gale thought, but she had no choice. Even as she'd asked the question, she'd felt the magic leaving her, leaking out, wasted. She wasn't a vessel, and the one she'd created could hold no more. She released a breath, long and slow, and the emptiness returned as the last of the magic left her.

She was no worse off than she'd been before, but her natural state felt dismal and bland in comparison to the sparkling heights of magic. She'd told herself before that it was no real loss, but with every dose of magic, she felt herself sinking deeper into the warm seas of its power and becoming more reluctant to return to dry land.

Magic felt natural now. Not this cold, desolate nothingness.

"Good enough," Madrigal said softly. She looked at Gale, her eyes dark and sharp. "I imagine it's hard for you to empty yourself."

Gale turned her attention to packing up the jars, setting the full one carefully in the bottom of her bag. "Of course it's hard. You must remember from your own apprenticeship, back before you became a true witch."

"It wasn't the same, though." Madrigal leaned forward. "When I was an apprentice, it was building toward something. I'd feel the ache of emptiness, the longing to take magic into myself again, but it was with the promise that it would end in something more. I knew that my hard work and self-denial were all part of the commitment I was making, and that it would lead to me becoming a vessel and having magic within me always. It's not so for you. You're tasting something you desire, I think, more than anything else in the world. Each taste is only deepening your craving, but you know it will end soon." She paused. "If that is still your plan?"

The thought filled Gale with cold dread like she hadn't felt since she'd wakened in the forest, starving and abandoned.

"It is," she said, her voice catching in her throat.

Because as badly as she wanted magic, as enthralling as the idea of becoming a witch and a vessel for magic might be, the cost was still too high.

Maybe the Teachings were wrong about witches and corruption, but there was danger here. She'd felt the change in herself already—the desire to shape the world to her will without knowing whether she deserved that power, the pull toward what would take her away from everything and everyone she'd ever loved. Magic in and of itself felt right and good in the moment, but when she thought of home and family, of sunny days spent splashing in the river and the lamplight shining in windows as she walked in the evening with no concern for her safety, her heart swelled with longing.

If becoming a witch meant being banished from home and having to live in this world of cities and strangers, crime and mistrust, how would she bear it?

She held the necklace in both hands and pressed it to her heart. It felt familiar in a way Madrigal's vessel didn't. Stronger, fresher, fuller. Magic pulsed within it, echoing her heartbeat.

"Don't get too possessive, dear," Madrigal said, her voice heavy and a little sad. "Magic belongs to no one. We might use it, direct it, even control it. We might hold a tiny portion of it for a time, but it's not ours. Those who forget that, who let their hunger to keep it for themselves outweigh their good sense and decency, will more often than not meet bad ends."

But it's mine for now, Gale thought.

She wondered whether she might be able to sneak a vessel like this back into town without anyone knowing—not a thing she'd use, of course, but just to have it, to sleep with it under her pillow and lock it away in the morning, or to wear when she worked in her own garden. *If I lived alone, if I took that plot of land outside of town and lived there...*

She could imagine it. She'd become something of an outsider, but she'd still be welcomed in the Hall and at her parents' home. She'd work with medicine, for surely the success of this venture would change the Luminary's mind on that matter, and the town would love her for it. She'd have a little magic. She'd have to hide it from Hawk, who would never forgive her if he found out, and no one else would know. And in time, perhaps...

Gale squeezed her eyes closed to hold back tears.

No witch shall live among those who hold to God's will, nor shall any who take magic for their own. They shall be cast out, lest they bring corruption to all.

The Luminary might be swayed if it were only up to her, but the Teachings were firm. If Gale cured the curse and destroyed her vessel, she might be allowed to live in Bright Hollow. She might be allowed to work with medicine.

But no more than that. When she went home, she'd lose magic. And if she pursued magic, she'd lose home.

For the first time, neither option seemed bearable.

"Come on, now," Madrigal said. "We'd best find some kind of shelter for the night."

Gale hung the pendant around her neck and slung her bag over her shoulder, then carefully descended the ladder, more mindful of the danger now that her work was done. She'd lost track of time while she was absorbed in her magic, but plenty must have passed. The crowd had dispersed, and the cops' carriage was gone.

She knew she should leave, but she couldn't help approaching the building for another look. Madrigal moved closer, passing through the window for a peek inside

The street was littered with wood and shingles and bits of brick from the chimney.

I did that, she thought. *Imagine what I could do with a little control.*

She smiled and stepped closer.

A hand closed around her upper arm, and the smile vanished. She turned, trying to pull away.

"Gale?" Hawk squinted down at her as he released her arm. "What in the world are you doing here?"

CHAPTER TWENTY-TWO

"Hawk?"

A strange numbness came over Gale's limbs as she looked at her brother—her best friend, her protector...

...pursuer of witches, hater of magic, and suddenly the person she feared more than any other. Her heart raced. Energy flooded her muscles, and all sense of exhaustion and pain left her as her body urged her to run.

I shouldn't be afraid, she reminded herself as she took in the deep colour of his cheeks and the bright shine of his eyes that reflected the flames of the streetlamp behind her. A thin film of sweat covered his brow. Fever, proof the curse was taking him just as it had so many others.

Hawk and I want the same thing—to save ourselves and our town from this curse.

And I'm not doing anything wrong. I'm not a witch. I have nothing to fear.

But that last idea, one she'd held close through her spells and enchantments thus far, felt foolish as she stood before Bright Hollow's most promising young witch hunter. He had become the monster slinking through the shadows, and she the child pulling her blankets over her head as a shield.

Madrigal stood behind Hawk, hovering behind his left shoulder, but she said nothing.

He gave Gale a tight smile and reached toward her face, brushing a finger over her cheek. He still wore his gloves. "You're bleeding."

Gale stepped back and wiped at her cheek with the sleeve of her jacket. It came away stained with rust. "I hadn't noticed. Thank you."

"You didn't answer my question. What are you doing here?"

"I heard the explosion and came to see what happened," she said, and it sounded natural enough. "Or did you mean to ask what I'm doing in Queen's Run?"

He nodded.

"Following up on my mission, as you are. I went to the witch's cabin to see what I could use from her garden and came up with some good ideas for medicines, but there weren't enough ingredients there. I thought I might have better luck finding them here. Maybe from foreign lands." She knew she was rambling, and her cheeks felt feverish under his steady, hard gaze. "I didn't expect to find you."

Hawk nodded toward the old shop, and they both watched as another chunk of the roof fell in with a dull clatter. "I tracked the witch to this area. The one we drove from the mountain."

Gale's stomach felt as though it were filled with rocks. *Alec. He's tracking Alec. Which means—*

Hawk frowned at her. "Don't suppose you saw anyone suspicious?"

A lump formed in Gale's throat, and she swallowed it back. "No, but as I said, I only came after the explosion. I suppose anyone who was inside is either dead or long gone by now."

"Hmm." Hawk took a few uneven steps toward the building, leaning heavy on his left leg.

Gale followed in spite of her fear. "You're sick, Hawk."

"It's not as bad as it looks." He turned back to her and frowned, carving a pair of deep lines between his eyebrows. "You're faring better than I am. And you seem different somehow."

Gale dug into her bag and pulled out a jar of the salve she'd made back at the cabin. "Here, give this a try. It won't cure anything, but it will slow the progression of—what?"

He was looking down at her hand with his lip curled like she was holding out a poisonous snake instead of medicine. "I don't want it."

Gale unwrapped her bandages. The rash had grown worse, but not by much. "Look. Mine was nearly as bad as yours when you left town. Compare them now. The medicine works."

"There's magic in it, isn'er?" He gritted his teeth. "*Isn't there?*" Before Gale could answer he snatched the little glass jar from her hand and clenched it in his own. "No, not in this." He handed it back, nearly dropping it in the process, and Gale slipped the jar back into her bag. "But I feel it. Here. With you."

Gale's fingers twitched as she resisted the instinctive urge to guard her vessel, which lay against her skin beneath her blouse.

"Give him mine," Madrigal whispered. "Yours is stronger. I can hold onto it just as well, and I might be able to use your personal magic to find my way back from the borderlands as I do my own."

That *might* made Gale's stomach drop, but she reached under her jacket and removed the brooch. "Is this what you feel?"

Hawk took it and grimaced. "Must be. Where did you get it?"

"At the cabin. I thought it might be worth something."

Hawk closed his fingers around the brooch, thought for a moment, then pocketed it. Gale stiffened, resisting the urge to grab it back, to hit him, to scream at him to give it to her.

His eyes never left hers. "Coldstream's barn smells less of

horse shit than your words do. You've used it, haven't you? To make that med'cine?"

It was faint yet, but he was slurring his words.

"What? No, I swear." It wasn't technically a lie. She hadn't used that particular magic to do it. "I couldn't use a witch's vessel if I wanted to. It's protected."

The feverish glint in Hawk's eyes sharpened, and Gale understood for the first time what it was to be not under his protection but to be his prey. "You know an awful lot about it, don't you, little bird?"

"I—" Gale wanted to look to Madrigal, to beg her to help, but there was nothing she could do. Gale squared her shoulders and made herself look straight into his eyes. "I found books at the cabin. Some about witches, some about magic, but also some about more benign topics that I'm using to make medicines. I had to read through the... the badness to get to what I could use."

"Is that so?"

"Yes."

"That's good. For a moment there I had this mad idea that I'd been a fool to track a witch from outside Bright Hollow." Hawk held up his hand, showing the glove stretched and misshapen by the bandages beneath it. "I wondered whether this might not be a curse at all but corruption brought on by a secret witch living in our own town."

Gale opened her mouth to answer, but only got out a squeak as Hawk grabbed on to her with his good hand, harder than he had before, his fingers digging into the flesh of her upper arm. He looked her over again, then pulled her closer, leaning down so his face was in line with hers. "This is my fault. I should never have protected your secrets after the witch corrupted you."

Gale struggled against him, but his grip only tightened.

"I should have told the Luminary exactly what you'd done as soon as we made it home after I killed that witch. You still would have been a hero, but we could have protected you better from your dark urges." His glare turned to something more like sadness, but the knife-sharp edge never left his gaze. "I've seen it, you know. Your fascination. The way you're drawn to it when you should be as repulsed as I am."

He sounded like his mind was unravelling. "You already told me that," Gale whispered.

"That's why I warned the Luminary," Hawk went on, as though he hadn't heard her. "But I was too late."

Beneath the streetlamps, Hawk's eyes shone too bright—not just with fever, Gale thought, but with something worse. True delirium came late in the curse's progress, but that didn't mean it couldn't shake the foundations of reason long before that.

"Hawk, please. You're hurting me."

He looked down, surprised, and loosened his grip. Not enough for her to pull away, but it was something.

"Think reasonably," she said, keeping her voice as calm as she could. "You know this is a curse, not any other kind of corruption or disease. The Luminary wouldn't have let you come on this hunt if she thought otherwise." She waited until she had his full attention, his eyes locked on hers, before she continued. "We're fighting on the same side."

Hawk closed his eyes, shook his head. "Do you know how I was tracking that witch from the mountain?"

"No."

"No. You've only been exposed to it unaltered, or through her. Or..." He sighed. "A witch's magic has its own signature. You can feel it, and you can learn to sense the distinction. And this?" He patted the pocket Madrigal's vessel had disappeared into. "This isn't all I feel here. You reek of it. Not of wild magic, but something that's more *you*."

Gale pulled again, twisting her arm. This time, he let her go.

"I've done nothing but what I believe to be God's will," she said, backing away as she spoke.

"Then magic has already corrupted your thinking," Hawk

said. He didn't reach for her again but matched her step for slow, cautious step, keeping the distance between them steady as she crossed the empty street. "The Teachings are clear."

"The Teachings?" The cold fear that had filled her eased as his words struck home, leaving her better able to think. "The Teachings are good, Hawk, but they are not God. What if magic is the only thing that can save those who are already ill? Do the Teachings forbidding it mean it's God's will for us to die?"

"God will save us if we're obedient." There was no doubt or hesitation in his words, even as his ankle turned beneath him and he stumbled. "You can repent. Come home with me now. Leave this mad quest to find a medicine, leave it to me to cut the curse off at its root. Face what your sins have done, to yourself and to all of us. Make a new start. God will forgive you if you're strong enough to turn away from magic now, and God will provide us with a cure that doesn't corrupt your precious soul."

Gale froze, and the world around her fell silent.

She imagined repenting, turning her back on everything she'd learned in the past few days. Condemning Madrigal again. Losing magic forever, letting herself be judged by those who could never understand.

Iron bars closed around her heart, and it pounded in her chest like one of the nightingales Madrigal had told her about, the ones that broke themselves in their desperate attempts to obey the call of their tiny destinies.

Suddenly the Path and all of Bright Hollow's ways looked more like a cage than they ever had when she'd lived within them.

She looked to Madrigal, silently pleading for the right answer, but Madrigal shook her head. "This isn't my decision, girl. Do what you will."

"Tell me you'll do it," Hawk said, his voice little more than a gentle, pleading whisper. "Go home tonight. I'll kill the witches—

first the one I'm tracking, and then any other who harms us with their presence."

"Only one has harmed us," Gale said. Her voice trembled. "You would kill innocent people for the sake of magic?"

"None are innocent," Hawk said, speaking with conviction that shook Gale to her bones. "They are the curse, and we're being punished for tolerating them for too long. You don't have to fall with them, little bird. Once you're cleansed of your corruption, the town will be stronger. God will save those who have fallen ill."

"No."

His lips tightened, his brow furrowed. He stepped forward and stumbled again, and before Gale could think to do otherwise, she reached out to catch him.

They'd always caught each other when they fell.

Hawk grabbed onto her to pull himself up, then stood straighter than he had before, his good hand gripping her cursed forearm tight, pulling at the injured flesh. Gale bit her lip to keep from crying out. "One way or another, you're coming home."

"And if I won't repent?"

"You will." Hawk's eyes shone—not only with fever, but with tears. "You must."

Terror pulsed through Gale in cold waves. "Or what?"

He didn't answer, and that was all the answer she needed.

He'd kill me for my sins. He might never forgive himself, but he'd do it for the good of the town.

The ghosts of old lessons rose in her mind, insisting he was right. She'd played with fire, and the whole town was burning. *Sin. Badness. Stepped off the Path. Repent.*

She pressed a hand against her vessel, and a hint of its magic seeped through her muscle and bone. It grounded her, reminding her of what she'd found by straying into the dark and wild woods, of what she'd lose if she gave up now. And she knew what she wanted—what she needed—to do.

I've hidden myself for so long. This can't be the end, just when I'm uncovering the truth.

"Madrigal, I've decided. Help me." The words came out as a soft squeak, but Hawk heard. He gripped her by both arms and shook her so hard her teeth clacked painfully together.

"What? Who—the witch is dead, Gale." He looked around, scanning the shadows. "Who are you talking to?"

"You need to knock him out before he's got you bound and slung over the back of a horse," Madrigal said. "Can you draw on your vessel?"

"I think so."

Hawk shook her, and his eyes widened in what looked an awful lot like fear. "Shut up. Shut up."

Never a copper around when you need one, Gale thought, and didn't know whether to laugh or scream.

"You're going to knock him out with a spell," Madrigal said, louder now. Hawk might feel magic, but he obviously couldn't see or hear her. "Focus your intention on that—on blackness overcoming his mind, on the nothingness that will be within him."

Gale nodded and did as she was told, holding eye contact with Hawk. She felt the magic within her vessel moving, expanding, entering her body through the place where it rested above her heart.

"No!" Hawk yelled, and pushed her away.

At the same moment, Madrigal gave her the spell.

The words flowed from Gale's mouth as though she'd practiced them a thousand times. There was no room for thought, so there was no room for fear or doubt.

"Alehia aldomor ic'lieni dorsuma," she said, strong and sure. The magic didn't pass through her smoothly as it had when she'd made her potions or enchanted her vessel, but blasted out, sending her reeling into the side of the abandoned shop. A sharp pain shot down her arm as she struck her shoulder on the brick.

Hawk stumbled back in the opposite direction, spun, and collapsed face-first on the ground.

Gale darted towards him, but Madrigal drifted in front of her. There was no physical presence to stop her, but Gale paused. "I can't tell whether he's breathing. I have to make sure he's not dead."

Madrigal caught her gaze and held it. "You're not good enough or strong enough to kill anyone, girl, or even to do a good job with the spell I gave you. Look."

Hawk groaned and tried to push himself up, but collapsed back to the ground.

It was enough. Gale turned on her heel and hurried into the darkness, searching for a crowd to lose herself in, trying not to think too hard about why she felt safer among Godless strangers than she did with her own family.

CHAPTER TWENTY-THREE

GALE HURRIED THROUGH THE CITY, the buildings dark and the streets a blur beneath mist-haloed streetlamps, her old boots tapping softly over the ground beneath her feet as she turned left, right, left again, weaving through alleys and crossing streets until she believed Hawk might not be able to follow.

Her steps slowed, and soon her pounding heart did as well. Madrigal slowed with her but kept glancing behind.

"Sorry about your vessel," Gale said.

"Don't worry yourself." Madrigal floated with her fists clenched at her sides, and a flush had come into her cheeks. It couldn't be easy, seeing something of such deep, personal meaning stuffed into the pocket of the boy who had killed her.

But Gale didn't ask. What was done was done.

"You did well back there," Madrigal said a few blocks later.

Gale wrinkled her nose at her. "Not well enough to keep him down for long."

"No. But for a first attempt it was... respectable. Your focus is improving."

"Panic helps with that, I suppose." Her voice came out dull and flat. Now that her desperate flight had slowed, she noticed the way her pulse pounded painfully behind her eyes, how the night felt colder than it should.

Even with Madrigal's salve her exertion was driving the illness onward.

Madrigal looked like she wanted to say more, and Gale was glad she didn't. It would probably be some observation about the choice she'd made to step further from the Path, to use magic to escape instead of returning home to repent.

Gale wasn't ready to talk about that yet, or to think about what it would mean the next time she saw Hawk. Focusing on the immediate future seemed less fearsome by comparison.

She kept moving, her head down and her hood up, shoulders hunched like the few other women she saw walking about so late at night. They'd returned to the outskirts of the factory district near the river. Few of the big buildings seemed active now, but there were plenty of people out enjoying the pubs. Gale shrank into the shadows around the inset door of a general-goods store as a group of men approached singing a drunken song. Their voices were terrible, the words slurred, but she caught some of it.

"With her heart stole away, the night darkened the day, and the knights and the heroes did faaaaall..." The fellow singing collapsed dramatically against the larger one next to him, who shoved him aside with a muttered curse and a lopsided grin.

They passed Gale by, leaving the street nearly empty.

"What are you thinking?" Madrigal asked.

Gale pushed her hair back from her face and pulled her hands into the sleeves of her jacket to warm them.

"I'm thinking I have no safe place to go in this city," she said, speaking softly, knowing that anyone who heard her mumbles would assume she, too, had been into the pub on the corner and had a bit too much to drink—or whatever else was on offer in there. "I'm thinking that Hawk is a good hunter, that it's going to be hard for anyone to hide from someone like him for long."

"Not only for you."

"Right." She walked on, willing her mind to focus on anything other than her own safety as she turned down a street that looked like it might lead deeper into the factory district. "If Hawk thinks he won't catch me, he'll keep going after Alec."

Madrigal floated in front of her, moving backward, passing through a streetlamp that flickered at her touch. "Not your problem. You warned him."

"I did, before I realized Alec is the witch Hawk and the others drove from the mountain. If I'd known, I would have been more careful questioning him."

"We know he didn't create the curse," Madrigal said, speaking gently. "He can't have."

"But mightn't he have hired someone to do it?"

"I suppose. Blood witches are rare as basilisk's teeth and a thing like that wouldn't come cheap even if he found one, but… well, maybe."

Gale pulled a handkerchief from her pocket and wiped the sweat from her brow. "I bet he knows more about the cure than he was willing to let on. If Hawk kills Alec before I find a way to get answers from him, he'll kill our only connection to information about the curse. Alec knows more than I realized. He could end this thing."

"He doesn't want to," Madrigal said, her voice gentle. "He made that very clear."

"No. But he's a person, not a monster. I handled things badly, but surely there's a way to make him see reason."

A deep sense of exhaustion stole over Gale's mind and body. Every sheltered doorway she passed looked like an inviting place to sleep, and she wished Olivier or Basim would appear to offer her company and protection for another night.

She forced her feet to keep moving and ignored the ache in their soles.

"We need to find Alec before Hawk does," she said. "I could kick myself. I had him right there and I chased him off."

"You didn't know who he was."

"No. But Hawk did. If we'd been working together—"

Madrigal chuckled. "How would that have worked? Do you think you'd be here now with a full vessel, hunting for the magic that will cure you, if you'd had your brother breathing down your neck every step of the way?"

Gale's shoulders slumped. Her steps dragged. *God, grant me strength.*

She didn't add *if it be your will.* At that moment, she didn't particularly care.

It wasn't God who answered, but magic. The pendant warmed against her chest, releasing magic that she accepted without thought, letting it awaken and soothe her.

"Careful," Madrigal said, though she didn't sound displeased. "Don't waste it."

Gale hardly thought it a waste. Her thoughts sharpened, and the answer became clear.

"There's only one person in the city who knows where Alec has gone. We should go back to the shop. Or—" Gale stopped and turned to Madrigal, then waited for a young couple to pass by before she spoke. "That note you found with Jes's name on it— wasn't that about a meeting?"

"It was. Two in the morning at the Grimy Gryphon. We passed it earlier today."

"Good. We'll check in there on our way to the shop. They're sure to be at one place or the other."

THE GRIMY GRYPHON stood on the corner of Fairfax Street and... something. That portion of the sign had been knocked down or forcibly removed at some point. The fact that there were street signs at all meant they had left the factories and tenements behind. Gale supposed that meant this would be what Cas had called a safer neighbourhood, but she wasn't feeling much better about the situation. In spite of the quiet street outside and the warm glow of lamplight that shone out from coloured glass windows, Gale stood frozen in place outside.

The door opened and a pair of gentlemen in fine wool coats stepped out, laughing together, one leaning on the other for support. He tipped his hat to her as they passed, but Gale barely noticed. She was focused more on the world she glimpsed beyond the door before it swung closed—the light, the music, the chatter of more voices than she'd expected this late at night.

"We could try the shop first," she said.

Madrigal moved forward, the light from the windows shining through her. "Come on, it'll be fine. You're not scared, are you?"

"Not scared," Gale said, dropping her voice in case anyone might be approaching. "But I've never been in a pub, and I don't know what to expect. The Teachings call everything about this vile and unworthy. I shouldn't be here."

Madrigal burst out laughing. "Is it worse than what you've done in the past few hours?"

Gale bit back a bitter laugh of her own. "Good point, I suppose. But I'm not dressed for this. What do I do? How do I—" She sighed.

It was like magic, and she knew it even as she spoke her objections. Doing the thing right would be wonderful. Being comfortable and capable would be amazing.

But getting it done was what would keep her alive.

Madrigal's eyes wrinkled at the corners as she smiled. "Come on, then. I haven't been to any place this fun in far too long."

Gale pushed the door open and stepped inside. The pub wasn't what she'd been led to expect by the warnings of her elders at home. Though the place smelled of ale and stronger things and the tables looked a bit sticky, it didn't seem *bad*. No one was wildly drunk and shouting, no one was cursing God or openly committing a crime. It was just full of people. Regular folks, if ones that seemed a bit looser somehow than the ones she knew at home. Some sat in booths at the sides of the room or stood at tall tables in the centre, in quiet conversation or raucous laughter. A few danced to the music played by a fiddler, and they kept going even after they got dirty looks from the people they bumped into. A fellow in the corner nursed a bloody nose but didn't seem upset about it. One woman at the bar wept quietly into a massive white handkerchief, and the fellow next to her rested with his eyes closed and his head on his arms, drooling onto his sleeves.

Is this what we're afraid of?

But there was no time to stand and take it all in. She needed to find Cas to ask where he'd hidden Alec. And besides that, people were already beginning to notice the strange, shabbily dressed girl lingering in the doorway.

Gale moved toward the bar, squeezing between tightly packed tables of seated patrons she tried not to knock into with her bag, scanning faces as she went. Not one was familiar to her. Madrigal went ahead of her, then motioned for Gale, waving one arm above her head.

"Over here—booth in the back."

Gale inched closer.

The back of the pub was more shadowed, less inviting. Better for dark dealings, maybe or—she caught sight of a couple kissing in a booth and looked away.

Jes and Cas sat on one side of a booth, facing an older man with heavy jowls and a jaw covered in a salty sprinkling of white, bristly stubble. Jes might have seen Gale from where she sat— both seats had a direct view of the door—but she was intensely focused on her conversation. Cas turned slowly to scan the room, and Gale put her back to them.

"They're busy," she murmured.

"So interrupt them."

Gale glanced back. The conversation behind her seemed to be

getting more intense. The older fellow glared and knocked his knuckles against the table. Jes shook her head, and the other fellow sneered back at her.

The barkeeper approached Gale, a wary smile on his broad, moustached face. "Get you something?" He looked her over, and Gale became acutely aware of what a state she must be in after the incident at the shop and the long run following her escape from Hawk.

"I, um... water?"

He nodded to a patron who was signalling for him at the other end of the gleaming wooden counter, then turned back to Gale. "This establishment is for paying patrons, not beggars looking for a gentleman to buy them a drink."

"I know, I'm waiting for someone."

"Sure you are. I'll give you one minute to warm your bones and leave gracefully before I throw you out myself. If you bother anyone, I'll have you arrested. Understood?"

Gale nodded, and he went back to work, though he watched her as he poured the next drink.

"Rude," Madrigal huffed.

"Can you distract him?" Gale asked. "Give me a chance to get closer to them?"

Madrigal vanished, leaving Gale feeling alone in the crowd.

Time passed too quickly, and with each moment the glares from the bartender grew more intense.

Then the drunk at the bar groaned. His head rolled off his arms, and his breath hitched.

"Don wannit," he mumbled. He pushed suddenly against the bar, toppling backwards to the floor.

The music stopped, and someone laughed.

The barkeeper rolled his eyes. "Jimmy, give me a hand with—"

He didn't finish his request. The drunk was on his feet, eyes wide and unseeing, arms sweeping the air in front of him like he was trying to grab at something. He took a step forward, then another, sending a table crashing to the floor and several people scrambling out of his path.

They moved faster when he pulled a knife from his pocket and started slashing at anything that moved in front of him.

Gale lunged out of his way and looked to the table in the back. Jes, Cas, and the other fellow were already on their feet, hats and bags in hand. The drunk came toward her, moving with the crowd that pressed toward the front door, pulling Gale along with it.

She only caught one more glimpse of Jes as she headed through a swinging door in the back.

Gale huddled against the bar and let the crowd move past her. The drunk fellow screamed and dropped to the floor, as dead to the world as he'd been before the episode started, and the barkeeper ran to him. As soon as the crowd thinned, Gale followed Jes, pushing through the door into a little kitchen. There was no one there.

Madrigal appeared beside her.

"What was that?" Gale asked.

"A distraction." Madrigal looked pale—not just from the light passing through her, but from the lack of the usual rosiness in her cheeks. "I only hoped to give him a nightmare, and to give the barkeep something to focus on. I'm used to dealing with sleepers, though, not intoxicated folks. His dream was... sticky."

Gale didn't ask for more explanation as she wound her way past a wide table covered in scraps of bread and meat, heading for the door at the other side of the room. "I guess it worked, anyway."

She pushed through the door and into an alley so dark she couldn't see two paces in front of her. But when she looked to her left, she spotted two silhouettes outlined against the lamp-light at its end, hurrying away from her.

"Wait!" she called, and ran to catch them.

Jes glanced back, then said a few words to Cas before they stopped.

"I need to talk to you," Gale said as she caught up, still catching her breath.

Jes and Cas exchanged a look, and Jes folded her arms over her chest. It was impossible to see the strange colours of her eyes in the dim light, but Gale caught their steely sharpness as they looked first at her, then at the empty alley behind her. "You again. Are you alone this time?"

Gale turned to Cas.

He shrugged. "No secrets among thiev—er, business associates. I told her about your ghost."

Jes raised her chin and looked past each of Gale's shoulders. "Is it here?"

Gale frowned. "You believe me?"

"I believe it explains how you knew my name, and maybe how you figured out that box. Right now, I'm more concerned with what you're doing here."

"I need help again. I have to find Alec. I think he knows more than he let on about the curse on my town, and he might know how to cure the illness."

Cas frowned. "He said he was in danger. That your brother was hunting him."

"He is, and he's closer than I thought. That's why I need to find Alec first. I know he's a witch. More to the point, so does Hawk."

She thought Jes and Cas would exchange a glance as they had earlier, but it seemed it was unnecessary now. Both shook their heads, but only Jes spoke. "Absolutely not."

"Why? You helped before."

Jes held up one index finger. "First of all, I've extended you enough favours. You figuring out an enchanted music box is only worth so much."

"But I could—"

A second finger joined the first. "Second, and more important, I don't betray the confidence of my employees and associates. And Alec has no desire to see or speak to you again."

"But it's important," Gale said, hating how close her voice sounded to a whine. "People are dying."

"And Alec could die if you're not who and what you say you are," Cas said. He, at least, looked somewhat apologetic. "You weren't entirely honest with us before. Alec is a valuable asset, and... well, you've seen for yourself how hard it is to find a real witch in this town. Losing him isn't a risk Jes is going to take, even if Alec would agree to meet with you again. Which he won't."

Gale looked from one to the other. Cas seemed like the easier one to reason with, but Jes was quite obviously in charge of whatever racket they had going. "There's no way I can persuade you?" she asked her.

The shopkeeper's expression softened. "No. I understand this is important to you, but I can't tell you anything. If it's any consolation, I'd protect you in the same way if you worked for me."

Gale let out a huff of breath. "Under other circumstances I suppose that would be very comforting."

Jes smiled wryly. "Sorry you came all this way for nothing."

Gale swallowed back the bitterness that rose in her throat. It figured these people would turn out to have morals when she needed them not to.

"I meant what I said before, though," Jes said. "If you're ever looking for work, come back. I might have something for the pair of you."

Madrigal scoffed under her breath. "Over my quite literal dead body," she said, louder than was necessary.

"Very kind of you," Gale said. Madrigal looked like she wanted to pinch her. "I'll keep that in mind if I survive."

Jes looked like she wanted to say something else, but didn't. She took Cas's arm and they walked away, heads down, looking for all the world like a regular couple out for a little midnight stroll.

"What now?" Gale asked. "There's no one else who knows where he went."

"No one, no. But nothing?" Madrigal smiled. "I think not. Perhaps it's time to try what witches always try when people fail us."

The words *I'm not a witch* came to the tip of Gale's tongue, but she let them die there. They'd grown stale and pointless.

"Magic?" she asked, and a wave of irritation made her skin prickle. "I could track him with magic? Why didn't you tell me this before?"

Her tone didn't seem to bother Madrigal. "You're still stuck in old ways of thinking and doing things. How will you learn to rely on magic if you don't come to it yourself?"

Gale pressed her fingertips to her pounding temples. "At another time I'm sure I'd appreciate the lesson," she said, biting back harsher words. "But I'm dying. I don't have time to learn the right way."

"Very well. Come on. We'll need a quiet place to work."

Gale headed down the street, letting her mind focus on magic, on what might be possible, on learning something new.

Instead of the fear and uncertainty that had once filled her at the idea, excitement kindled like a flame in her chest. She needed to do this. But more than that she wanted to.

CHAPTER TWENTY-FOUR

"My question is—"

"Will there be enough?" Madrigal's eyes narrowed with her smile. "That does seem to be a concern for you, doesn't it?"

They'd followed behind Jes and Cas until the pair vanished into the darkness, then kept on until they reached the park across the street from the shop. It wasn't a safe place, or sheltered, but the park was at least quiet, and the bushes and trees made for a more comforting and familiar setting than anything else the city could provide. And even if Gale didn't particularly trust Jes, her shop across the street had become a landmark in the journey—not a home base, but a place to map everything else from. And when a light appeared in the window upstairs, it made her feel less alone.

Gale lifted her vessel in one hand. The pendant hadn't taken on any extra physical weight when she'd enchanted and filled it, but it felt more significant than it had before.

"Of course it's a concern," she said, and went on before Madrigal could respond. "I'm limited. I have one jar of *lucistra* I can use to refill the vessel when it's emptied, and I don't have the means to make more."

"Fine, you know what you lack. What do you have?"

Gale took a long breath. The air was cleaner here than it had been near the factories, but even the trees and budding flowers couldn't hide the stink of the city. "My vessel might be disappointing to you, but it still gives me access to exponentially more magic now than I had when I was only drinking your potion."

Madrigal drifted beside her as Gale walked through the park. It was dark and felt dangerous, but Gale remembered the spell she'd used against Hawk and held it on the tip of her tongue. The police would take any mugger's side if it came out that she'd used magic against him, but she'd be gone long before they woke to tattle on her.

The knowledge made her feel powerful. Competent. It was strange to imagine handling such things on her own when those who walked the Path insisted that weakness was a blessing because relying on others was God's will.

"A good word," Madrigal said, "exponential. You've learned maths?"

"Of course. Mathematics are proof of the constancy God placed in this world, a thing to lean on when variability brings confusion or doubt, or so my teacher said. I never cared for equations, myself, but I have learned a few things while I was busy not studying magic."

Madrigal laughed softly. "I suppose you have. Not an entirely wasted childhood, then. In any case, you are correct. If we were to place a number on the magic you put into the vessel—an impossibility, for magic can't be measured so strictly—you would find that what you hold now in your hand is many times greater than that. You got that much right."

Gale looked down at the red stone in the pendant and wished again that she'd had time to learn how it all worked, that she'd really understood what she'd been doing when she spoke the enchantment. It was a beautiful art, really—not just creating music boxes or can't-miss marbles for children, but a chance to make useful things that only became more beautiful the more deeply one understood their magical workings. The music box she'd explained to Jes looked like a pretty parlour trick on the surface, but she thought that if she could really understand it, she'd see something far lovelier.

A person could create miracles if only she had the creativity, depth of understanding, and raw power required.

Astonishing.

"To answer your question," Madrigal said, "yes. You have enough, as long as you focus and use it well. If you can do that and manage not to blow anything else up with wasted magic, we should be able to find Alec before your talented brother picks up his scent."

"Without using all of it?" She felt silly asking again, but the thought of losing magic chilled her to her darkest depths.

"You'll likely lose most of it, but you'll need to keep a little if you want me to stay with you. But remember, the vessel can be refilled." Madrigal stopped in front of her and looked into her eyes. "I know it's frightening to have power that can be lost so easily. If your vessel were destroyed, all would be lost. I remember how frightening it is, and how tempting it can be to simply hold on to what you have instead of taking the risk of using it."

"But?"

Madrigal shrugged. "But what good is magic to you if you're dead because you refused to use it up?"

Gale gave her a wry smile. "I see your point."

She sat in the shelter of a wooden gazebo, legs crossed beneath her skirt, her bag set on the ground beside her and Alec's silver stylus in her left hand. Madrigal spoke the instructions— intention and spell—and Gale's brow furrowed.

"That's all there is to it?"

"It's more than it sounds." Madrigal moved in circles around her. "You don't know Alec well, and he's clearly adept at hiding his magic. That will make it more difficult, but I'll work a variation on a seeking spell my mentor passed down to me. You must promise never to repeat it to another. In the wrong hands, a spell that could direct someone toward witches would be a dangerous weapon."

"I promise."

"Good." Madrigal still appeared unsettled, but she went on. "Focus on what you do know—not about him, but *of* him. His presence, his being."

Gale thought of Alec. His appearance first, then the tremble in his voice when he spoke of Bright Hollow, the rage he'd barely hidden, his bearing and mannerisms. She hadn't felt his magic, but every person had a particular energy and a certain way of being. It would have to be enough.

"The better your focus is," Madrigal said, "the less magic it will take to get the spell started—and more importantly, to maintain it. You need to hold onto your focus on this spell until it's served its purpose. You're not experienced enough with it to do otherwise."

"Understood."

As long as I don't doubt, as long as I shut out the voices...

An easy thing to think, but there was no denying what she was really doing. There was a chance Hawk was right, that magic was corrupting her into thinking such things, that she'd walk into the woods, get lost, and not find her way back to the Path.

Enough. Either do it or don't. Half-measures will be what kill you.

She closed her eyes and took three long, deep breaths—enough to slow her racing heart. Her arm throbbed with sharp pain that trailed toward her shoulder, but she told herself it was good that she still felt something and ignored it. She pushed thoughts of Hawk from her mind, along with memories of how she'd managed to at least partially fail at every difficult spell she'd tried so far.

Nearly every one, she reminded herself, and relaxed. *When I attacked Hawk, it worked as well as I intended it to. No doubts, just intention and action.*

She reached for that again—not calm quiet, but intense focus. She drew on her vessel, letting its magic flow until its golden warmth filled her and she felt that if she took in any more, she might once again lose control. It felt right. Natural. Good.

Then she spoke the words.

"Saehaelthan Alec'dru homilcorpu," she whispered, directing her intention toward the stylus and then out into the world. "Show me," she added in the common tongue. It wasn't part of Madrigal's instructions, but it felt right. The spell was formed by the language of magic, but this, her intention, should come in the language of her thoughts and speech.

Magic left her in a steady stream, flowing through the stylus. It felt directionless, wasteful. But when she opened her eyes she found a pale green glow to the east of the gazebo, hazy and indistinct but clear enough to offer direction. She gasped, and Madrigal laughed.

"Can you see something, girl? Have you done it?"

She didn't answer, afraid that doing so would break the spell. Magic continued to flow through her as she walked, eyes forward, focused on following the light. She was barely aware of her feet on the ground and felt as though she might be floating like a ghost. Madrigal hung back, offering no distraction.

Gale followed the light down strange streets and around long lines of buildings until she reached an unfamiliar part of the city —not the factories, not the parks and the shops, but a nicer neighbourhood with red-brick houses and mature oak trees lining its streets.

The light grew more focused as she walked. What had been diffuse enough that it could almost have come from her imagination became something more like dim lamplight, though still in that strange green and without any obvious source. It led her past the houses to a tall iron fence topped with decorative spikes.

Gale saw the fence as she'd seen the houses, as she'd vaguely noticed the few carriages on the streets—passing by them, but not really taking note of them until this obstacle, which demanded her attention. Even then, the light was all she thought of. There was no strategy, no thought of how this effort was depleting her vessel. Only the knowledge of what her body could do and her desire to reach the source of the light.

She tossed her jacket over the iron spikes to dull them and jumped to grasp one in each hand, grunting as she struggled to pull herself to the top, boots scrambling against the thin bars. The spikes poked into the flesh of her belly as she hauled herself over, then caught on the front of her blouse, tearing it near the hem. But then she was over, dropping to the ground, continuing on her way, the fence forgotten.

Then she stopped. The source of the light was clear, beaming up from between boards covering what looked like an abandoned well.

And with that thought, the light vanished, and Gale's stomach dropped.

She turned to Madrigal, panic gripping her. "What happened? I swear I was focusing."

Madrigal seemed unconcerned. "The spell has brought you as far as it can. You did it, and far better than I'd have expected given past performance. What's changed?"

Gale sensed that the witch knew the answer, that the question was for the student's benefit rather than her own. She'd never liked those questions in school, but gave this one some thought. "I focused better."

"And?"

She shrugged. "And I believed I could do it."

Madrigal's brow creased, though her lips still smiled. "Come on. This is important. If you want to finish your noble quest, you need to be able to repeat this kind of performance when it comes time to create your medicine."

The answer was clear. Gale just didn't want to say it.

"I committed to it. Not to leaving the Path forever, but to exploring away from it without looking over my shoulder every few moments to make sure I could get back. Without listening to those who would call me home." She swallowed the lump in her throat. "I'm a little scared to look back now."

"Then don't. Stay committed to saving your people. There'll be time to sort the rest out later." Madrigal gestured to the well. "I'd offer to help with those boards, but I don't think I can manage much."

But Gale couldn't help searching her heart, imagining her way home. The Path was still there, brightly lit, wide and welcoming, with all her friends and family waiting for her, if only she'd give up the darkness of the forest.

But it was strange now. Like looking in from the outside.

She wrapped her fingers around her depleted vessel, feeling its remaining magic without drawing on it, and turned her attention back to the real world.

Without another word she worked her fingers beneath the planks that covered the well, slid them aside, and climbed down a half-rotted wood ladder into the darkness.

CHAPTER TWENTY-FIVE

THE SMELL of leaf rot and damp stone hit Gale's nose at the same moment her boots hit the thin layer of water at the bottom of the well's shaft.

"Are you here?" she asked, keeping her voice low. It was black as tar at the bottom of the well, and even Madrigal was invisible.

"I am." Madrigal, too, spoke softly. The fact that Alec hadn't seen or heard her before didn't mean he couldn't with the right spell, and his defenses would be up now. There was no sign of light or life at the bottom of the well. He was clearly protecting himself from all magic, or perhaps from those who might wish to hunt him.

The air was as cold below as the night had been above, but wetter and heavier. A part of Gale almost hoped the magic had been wrong, that no one was actually trying to hide in such a place.

"There's a tunnel here," Madrigal said. She moved forward. It was too dark for Gale to see anything but her soft glow, and she stumbled as her foot hit something hard beneath the surface of the water. Her movements startled some creature that leapt away and landed in the water behind her with a soft *plop*.

"Watch your step," Madrigal whispered.

"Gee, thanks."

Gale ran her fingers around the entrance to the tunnel, which was made of stone blocks set in a circle and would be large enough to walk through hunched over. An old section of the sewers, perhaps, or for carrying water when the well had held something other than mud and toads. She hoisted herself into the passage and felt her way along the wall, stepping cautiously over branches and other litter that seemed determined to trip her up again. The passage's floor was dry, but water from the well squelched in her boots, freezing her toes.

"There's life ahead," Madrigal said.

"How can you tell?"

"The dead know."

Sure enough, as Gale picked her way over puddles and patches of slimy twigs that had collected in the passage when it had been useful, she detected a faint yellow light—barely noticeable at first, until she rounded a curve and it became clear, shining from a space to the left of the tunnel.

Madrigal drifted ahead, and Gale waited. There was only so far the ghost could go now that Gale had less magic for her to anchor herself to, but there was no denying the usefulness of her silent, invisible companion.

"Come, girl. Quickly."

Gale hurried ahead, less concerned now about making noise. She reached a small room, barely more than an alcove off the main passage. A small lamp rested on the floor, offering a hint of light but not nearly enough warmth to make any difference, and Alec lay next to it wrapped in a thick wool blanket. He pushed himself up on one arm and held the other hand out in front of him in a warding gesture.

"You," he whispered. He didn't seem to have the energy to put much force behind it, but his expression made his irritation clear. "I felt you coming."

"Yet you didn't run. Aren't you afraid?"

"Should I be?"

"No."

He sighed and lowered his hand, then sat up. He still wore his fine suit under the blanket. "What do you want? I think I was quite clear about not wishing to help you."

"I know." Gale crouched with her back against the wall. "We got off to a bad start back there. When you tried to send me on a wild chase for a cure that didn't exist, I was angry. It would have killed me, you know. Wasting that much time. Even if the mages didn't." She spoke as calmly as she could manage. Facts, not accusations. Much as she wanted to grab him, shake him, demand that he tell her who had set the curse and how to reverse it, she held back. Anger would only harden him again. Better to go slowly, feeling out each step as she had in the dark passage. "I think you know more about Bright Hollow than you let on."

Alec looked down at his hands. "I omitted information."

"You had something to do with the curse."

Alec pulled the blanket tight around his shoulders and sank against the wall. "Who told?"

"My brother. He was closer on your tail than I suspected when I warned you away. He told me you're the witch he and the others ordered to leave last year."

Alec snorted. "Ordered to leave... that's one way of putting it." His gaze sharpened, giving his angular features a rat-like look. "I wasn't harming anyone by being there."

Gale said nothing.

"I was occupying space on the mountain, nowhere near your town. Foraging, hunting a little, working with the magic of the land."

"Did you know about Bright Hollow before you made a home on the mountain?"

He waved one hand dismissively through the air. "Everyone does. Your people are legendary among witches. Not all take you seriously as a threat, but we're universally glad you've decided to keep to yourselves. I thought you might continue to do so as long as I stayed away from your village."

Gale fought the urge to correct his use of *you* and *your* when it didn't fit her anymore. It turned her stomach now to think she was one of those people who had chased him away, but she was. Or had been a few days ago, and guilty of far worse when she had helped Hawk kill Madrigal.

There was so much good in Bright Hollow that she longed to return to even as she wished to reject the bad.

And if I can't have one without the other? she wondered. *If being a part of Bright Hollow means being a part of everything it stands for?*

"I was wrong about that," Alec continued, interrupting her thoughts. "They found me. There were no charges of disturbance, no explanations. Only threats. They entered my humble cabin, smashed my potions, and threw my equipment about, screaming all the while about corruption and sin and God's will." Alec cleared his throat. "Then they set my notes on fire, and the walls with them. They didn't say they'd do the same to me if they ever laid eyes on me again, but..."

"But the implication was clear."

He looked up, eyes shining. "I've never been so afraid in my life. Never felt such a loss of control. There were things I wanted to say, spells I wanted to speak, but I knew anything I did would only aggravate them further. There were six of them, one of me. So I watched as they destroyed my work and my life. And then I left. What else was I to do?"

"What else, indeed?" Gale sank the rest of the way to the floor, arms wrapped around her knees. "So you were afraid... and then angry."

Alec glared, though not exactly at her. "Angry even in my fear, and increasingly so as time passed. The sharpness of it eased, but not the burn. That only grew deeper and made itself a home within me. Rage became hatred. Can you blame me?"

"For anger at those who hurt you? No. But for taking it out on the rest of the town?" She let the question hang in the air.

"The rest of the town," he scoffed. "The town that birthed those monsters. No, I have no regrets. Perhaps none of you chose to be born into the teachings that led to what those men did to me, but you've all embraced them, haven't you? If you disagreed with them, you'd walk away. And if you don't disagree with harming folks, what good is your God to anyone?"

Again, she wanted to object, to say that perhaps one could stay in the hopes of making things better, but she didn't. He was right. A deep, piercing ache spread outward from her heart.

I did that to him. Not with my body or my mind, but with my silence.

She glanced at Madrigal, but the ghost had turned her face away.

Gale's cheeks burned with shame.

"I didn't ask to be born into it," she said softly. "I don't know how I could have known to question any of it. I knew no other truth, no other way of being. But I'm sorry I was afraid to ask questions. I'm sorry I didn't trust the truth enough to let doubt take root, especially after I met a witch who tried to show me how wrong we are." She spoke as much to Madrigal as to Alec.

Alec nodded. "That's how they hold you, isn't it? The fear. The threat of corruption, of God turning God's eyes away from you. I'm correct in that? That your God is not he or she or it, but—"

"But only God, yes." She drew a deep breath and let it out in a long sigh. This repugnant enemy was taking more care with her beliefs than anyone in Bright Hollow had ever taken with his, and it only twisted the knife deeper. "It doesn't help, I'm sure, for me to say I'm sorry for what happened to you, or to say I'm trying to do better now. I'm learning that magic isn't what we think, that witches aren't bad or corrupted or monstrous. It's hard. Terrifying. But I'm trying."

"Are you?"

"I am. It's frightening to think the Teachings could be wrong, and even more so to think of what could happen if I'm wrong for questioning them." She shivered, imagining a corrupted soul and separation from God.

"I suppose it's a start," Alec said.

Gale reached into her bag and took out the bread and cheese she'd bought earlier, offering them to him. "Here. You'll need these if you have to stay down here much longer."

He accepted the food with a nod of thanks.

She looked around their dank, filthy surroundings. "This was the best Cas could do for you?"

Alec chuckled ruefully. "No. He got me to what he believed was a safe place, and maybe he was right, but I couldn't rest as long as even he knew where to find me. Much good it did me, eh?"

"I had to use magic to get here. My brother won't be able to do the same."

Alec took a bite of bread, then put the rest in his bag and stood. "He can feel it, though?"

"He can."

"Then I'll have to keep moving. Mine is well hidden, but he could have followed yours." He folded his blanket, slung it over his bag, and walked down the tunnel, away from the well.

"Go, girl," Madrigal said, shooing her with her arms. "Don't lose him now."

Gale hurried along behind him, taking quick steps to keep up with his longer strides, following the light of his lantern.

"About the curse," she said as they went, following a twisting path through what had opened into an underground maze of tunnels, pausing only for Alec to make some sort of calculation as to which way they should go. "It has to stop. So many have suffered and died already. I understand your anger, your need for revenge. But—"

Alec stopped short, and Gale bumped into him before taking a quick step back.

"I owe your people nothing, you understand that?" He glared down at her. "If you've warned me of danger, it's only danger brought about by the people I cursed with good reason. This isn't motivation for me to save any of them."

He'd said *them* this time, not *you*. She took that as progress.

"I've been affected as well," she reminded him as he pulled open an iron gate. The squeal of its hinges set her teeth on edge. Alec passed through, and Gale followed.

"You're working with magic," he said, and motioned for her to close the gate behind her. "If you find someone to teach you quickly enough and become a true witch, the process of becoming will knock the curse clean out of you."

Gale glanced back at Madrigal, who nodded. "Sounds right. You could be cursed again, but it would work this once."

There was no point asking why Madrigal hadn't mentioned it before. It was Gale's own fault—she'd made it clear enough that becoming a witch wasn't an option for her. And besides that, it would do no good to anyone but herself.

"Even if I did," she said, "and I'm not going to—but if I did, how would I save everyone else?"

Alec said nothing and walked away. Gale grabbed his arm, forcing him to face her. "If I can overcome the fear that led me to cling to wrong thinking, there has to be hope for others. There has to be a chance of opening people's eyes."

"A few, maybe. Let go, please, you're wrinkling my jacket."

Gale released his arm but stuck close beside him, her fists clenched and shoved deep in her pockets.

The heaviness in the air had lifted as they walked, and a fresh breeze now played over Gale's cheeks. There was no light ahead, but the darkness beyond the lamp's light changed, becoming less oppressive. Soon they had to crouch to pass through a narrowing of the tunnel that opened into the night air of the countryside.

Gale looked over her shoulder as they stepped out and saw an orchard and a farm on the hill above the tunnel, and beyond them the lights of the city. A nearly full moon hung overhead, bathing the land in its cool light.

Alec looked around, then put out the lamp. "This is where we part ways."

Gale held his arm again. "Please, Alec. You've hurt them. You've made your point. You've shown them just how dangerous magic can be." She paused. "Was that your intention? To corrupt their flesh as they believe magic corrupts the spirit? To reinforce everything they believe about you?"

Alec let out his breath in a quick huff. "I was doing nothing wrong when your people attacked me. It shouldn't be my job to repay their cruelty with mercy or to leave their transgressions unpunished. How, then, will anything change?"

"You're right." Gale gritted her teeth to brace herself against the riot within her. "I don't know whether most of them will ever change. I guess they won't. But is this what you want? To have so much blood on your hands? People are losing their limbs, their minds, and their lives. Children are dying. Babies. People who have never had a chance to know better but who might open their minds if I can show them magic is within the scope of God's will."

Alec scrubbed at his lightly stubbled cheek with one hand. "I didn't mean for it to go this far when I made my request. I said I wanted Bright Hollow to be punished, but I didn't know how it would be done." He stepped toward the orchard, away from the farm buildings. "Walk with me a little farther."

Gale fell into step beside him, and Madrigal floated along with them. Gale tried not to let herself hope, but if he was willing to listen, to explain, maybe to see reason...

"I told you I was angry," Alec said, "and that's true. I wanted revenge. No—I wanted justice. I wanted the people of Bright Hollow to pay for what they'd done to witches over the years, for the lies their ancestors spread through Andonia before they had the decency to remove themselves from society, for all of it. But I didn't have the means to do anything significant on my own. I could have done some poisoning here and there, of course, or cast spells to ruin crops, but it all would have required that I stay in the area, and I'm not a strong enough witch yet to do anything that would have satisfied me. I wanted a true curse, but I wasn't willing to learn or use blood magic."

"So you found someone to do it for you?"

"Of course."

"Who?"

He shrugged. "I have no idea. No witch or mage is foolish enough to openly associate themselves with blood magic. To find someone capable of it is nearly impossible, and it requires going through intermediaries and past security checks. And none of it comes cheap. There's the cost for the curse, which is more than enough to deter someone who's not entirely serious, but there are also bribes along the way. This is why I don't have the funds necessary to leave the city and make myself disappear now. But yes, in the end I did find someone. Or rather, in the end they found me through intermediaries. I explained the situation and gave an idea of what I wanted, they enchanted a curse into a set of stones that I was to throw into every well in Bright Hollow, and that was the end of our interaction. They—the enchanter, whoever they are—wanted to keep their hands clean, you see. Merely created an item in exchange for money. I was the one who chose to place the stones and set the curse in motion."

"So it is the water, then." Hope welled in her chest. "If we found the stones and removed them—"

Alec cast her a pitying look. "They only carried the curse. It's in those wells forever."

Madrigal nodded. "He's telling the truth. No self-respecting witch in that line of work would make it so easy to avert the results."

"But if they dug new wells, it would solve the problem?" Gale asked.

"I suppose. No one intended for the entire mountainside to be poisoned, only those who drank from the wells." Alec raised an eyebrow as he looked down at her. "I assumed you'd all figure that much out once you realized it was a curse and not God's wrath coming down on you. But by then the damage would be done, and I'd be satisfied."

The urge to race home to share the news was nearly overwhelming, but Gale forced herself to fight it. Alec was right. They had figured it out, or at least suspected, so there would be no more new cases. Her place was here, seeking the cure for those who had already fallen ill.

"So you didn't know what the effect would be when you cast those stones and cursed the townsfolk?"

Alec's steps slowed. "I requested corruption. Beyond that I cared little how they suffered."

"The blood witch certainly delivered." Gale's chest ached as the unspoken conclusion to Alec's story became clear. "There's no way of finding out who created the curse?"

Alec raised an eyebrow. "What, so you can kill him and end it? Or her, perhaps. I attribute masculine traits to blood magic, but I really don't know who this person is."

"So I can find answers. A treatment. A cure. Or beg this person to end what they started."

"I'm afraid I have no answer to give." Alec paused and looked at her, eyes narrowed with keen interest. "I can't say I'd change anything if I had it to do over. Your people deserve no less than to be removed from this world before they can do more harm. But at the same time, I am sorry it's affecting you now that you're trying to understand better." He rubbed his chin. "Though tell me, changed one, would you have been so open to exploring the positive side of magic if you hadn't been pushed to it by the curse I laid at your doorstep?"

"I don't know. I was always drawn to it, but I..." Gale's shoulders slumped. "I thought that was my scar. My sin. I might have spent the rest of my life trying to hide from it if not for this."

"But you're leaving the Path now?" Alec's voice became deeper, his tone more urgent, and in that moment, Gale thought he might have more power in him than he let on as she caught a hint of his magic on the air. "Or you're at least considering the idea that persecuting witches might not truly be God's will, if such a thing exists at all?"

"All I know is that I've changed." The words caught in Gale's throat. "I've seen too much that was kept from me all my life, and I've begun to understand a little of it. I don't have answers. But I am asking questions, and I know that for me nothing will go back to the way it was. I want to help others see what I see."

"Then that's something." Alec rubbed his chin again, then gave each side of his moustache a quick twist. "I suppose what's done is enough. I don't know what ingredients will cure you or anyone else. I wasn't being entirely facetious when I said you'd find answers with the king's mages in Embercliffe, though. They might not use their knowledge to help commoners, but that doesn't mean they don't have it. They've been allowed to research and test magic for hundreds of years, to grow plants that would be illegal otherwise in a country where those in power are so afraid of the common folk grabbing some for themselves. Their garden is the only place you have any hope of finding a cure. They'll have plants growing there you won't find elsewhere in Andonia or on any ship in any port."

"But they won't help," Gale said. "And if they knew I was using magic, they'd kill me. And even if they wouldn't, I don't know how I'd get there in time."

"Time, yes." Alec cast a glance back toward the city. "I said I have no money left to flee Queen's Run, but it seems I have no choice now. Go speak to Jes again. I won't be working for her anymore, at least not for a while. Perhaps if you offered your limited skills, she'd arrange transport."

"And then?"

Alec shrugged one shoulder. "I'm sorry I can't help more. And though I'm not sorry for what I've done, I do wish you well in finding a cure. Go to Embercliffe, find a way into the mages' garden, and—"

Something whistled through the air, lower and quieter than any bird's call, cutting off Alec's voice as his breath caught in his throat. Gale was about to ask him to go on when she noticed how pale his face had become, the shock in his widened eyes.

He opened his jacket and revealed the bloodied tip of an arrow protruding from his chest. Before Gale could say anything, he collapsed.

Gale crouched to catch Alec beneath the shoulders before his head could hit the ground, but her attention wasn't on him. It was on the orchard that surrounded them and what might be hiding in the shadows.

Nothing moved but the breeze in the branches. The only breath was Gale's own.

She set Alec on the ground and rolled him onto his back.

"He's dead," Madrigal said. "Lord Death will come soon."

Gale glanced around frantically, trying to catch a glimpse of a new ghost. Her heart slammed in her chest. There was nothing. Even Madrigal was invisible.

Something moved in the darkness. Gale didn't stop to be sure it was Hawk, and she had no thought this time of reasoning with him. He'd killed Alec without hesitation, without questioning. He'd likely heard Alec trying to help, and it hadn't mattered.

For the second time that night, she ran from her brother.

CHAPTER TWENTY-SIX

GALE FORCED her body to carry her away from the orchard, past a farm, and through a field of cattle. Chills came over her even as she burned from the exertion, and panic clawed at her as she realized the fever was sneaking up on her, threatening to settle in until her dying breath. Still she forced herself on, putting as much space between her and Hawk as she could manage.

It was only when she slowed, when her legs shook too hard to run, when she made it back into the city, that she realized Madrigal was gone.

"Madrigal?" she whispered. A tight stitch had formed in her side, one she'd ignored until she'd reached the relative safety of the streetlamps and roads that seemed busy even at this ridiculous hour. She rubbed the skin beneath her jacket, pressing hard against her ribs to loosen the pain.

There was no answer.

Gale ignored the pounding of her heart and tried to force her mind to reason.

She said the dead go to the in-between place. She must be there with Alec.

Alec. She closed her eyes and saw his, wide and shocked, the life gone from them before she'd set him on the ground.

Hawk had always been a good hunter.

A sob caught in her throat. Alec had been an enemy. The source of their trouble. But it wasn't as black and white as those at home imagined it, the corrupted witch cursing the virtuous townsfolk. They'd been his monsters as much as he was theirs.

And he'd been her last lead, the only living witch she knew in Andonia.

She made her way through the city, not sure of where she was going, only that it would be easier to lose herself in crowds if she could find any at this hour.

As she passed a clockmaker's shop, a dozen clocks chimed or chirped in short, discordant song, marking five o'clock in the morning.

It seemed impossible that so much should have happened in such a small slice of a night.

Gale wrapped her fingers around her vessel and rubbed her thumb over the red stone. There was still a little magic in there, humming and throbbing. Enough for Madrigal to anchor herself when she came back.

And she would come back. She had to. Without her, Queen's Run was a darker and far more frightening place than it had been. Even when Gale had stood up to Hawk it hadn't seemed so grim and dangerous because she'd had an experienced guide.

A friend.

And now, walking alone, she jumped at every clatter in a dark alley, shrank away from the gaze of every gentleman and rogue she passed.

She said Lord Death was coming. What if he decided to take her now that she's passed on her wisdom to me? What if she can't find my vessel like she could her own and she's trapped in the borderlands? What if—

A pale presence materialized beside her, and Gale let out a

laughing gasp. Her arms twitched with the urge to hug the witch, but of course it would do no good to try. She shoved her hands deep in her pockets instead.

"Miss me?" Madrigal asked, arching an eyebrow.

"Not at all." Gale grinned, feeling a bit unhinged in her relief and not caring at all who might hear her. "I mean, I may have been a little concerned, but miss you? Worry that you weren't coming back? Hardly."

Madrigal chuckled. "Glad to see you're all right, too."

"For now." Her empty stomach ached, her legs trembled with exhaustion, and she didn't dare let magic come into her when there was so little of it left. But she was alive, and no longer alone.

Madrigal walked beside her. "Drop your voice, now, lots of folks about up ahead. Where are we going?"

Gale looked around, surprised to find herself in familiar surroundings. "I hadn't thought about anything except getting away and hiding." Her stomach sank. "But it looks like we're headed back to the shop."

Madrigal moved in front of her and floated along backward. Her arm brushed against a middle-aged woman dressed in ragged work clothes who stopped and shivered as the ghost passed. "I can't say I care for that shopkeeper."

"But?"

The witch shrugged. "It's not an unreasonable destination if she might help you get to Embercliffe."

They went on in silence until they'd left the square and its pubs behind them. "What happened when you left me? Is Alec all right?"

"For a dead man who hadn't intended to end the night in that state, I suppose he's fine. He was confused, quite disoriented. Normal for the newly dead. Not much good for conversation."

Gale frowned. "Not ideal, but at least he has unfinished business. If he's sticking around for a while, maybe he'll have something to tell us once he's calmed down a bit."

"He's gone. Lord Death took him through the veil." Madrigal sounded hollow.

Gale's steps slowed. "But I thought—"

"I don't know why he was able to leave his earthly concerns behind any more than I know why Lord Death once again left me here without a word."

"I'm sorry," Gale said. "For you being left behind, but more for how glad I am that you're still here."

"It doesn't matter."

It clearly did, but Gale couldn't think of anything to say that would make it better.

They reached Deermont Street and the curiosity shop. Gale glanced up and found a dim light in the upstairs window, but wasn't ready to knock at the door.

Still, a light appeared at the back of the shop and bobbed toward the door.

"Is Embercliffe really our only option?" Gale asked, suddenly sure she didn't want to face Jes at this hour.

"I don't know. We could try to find another witch here who might have better connections to foreign merchants than Alec had. But he was well schooled in medicine. He seemed sincere enough when he said your answers would be there."

"And what are the odds of us finding another witch here?"

Madrigal frowned. "In the time you have left?"

The question was its own answer, and Gale left it hanging.

The lock thudded dully, and the shop door swung open, its bell chiming cheerfully. Jes glared out at Gale. She was dressed, but her hair hung over her shoulders in loose waves and dark circles shaded the skin beneath her eyes.

Gale offered the friendliest smile she could muster. "You're awake! How fortuitous."

Jes pulled a watch from the pocket of the dressing gown she

wore over her wool skirt and white cotton blouse, checked it, and shook her head. "It's not good fortune. I decided there was no point hoping for sleep while you were still skulking around my city, and I had a feeling you'd be back to bother me again. I've been watching from the window, though I'd prefer to be in bed."

The words were unkind, the shopkeeper's voice as husky and hard as ever, but when Gale looked into her mismatched eyes, she caught a spark of interest that Jes couldn't quite hide—or wasn't trying to.

"I need your help," Gale said.

"A shocking turn of events." Jes yawned. "Do tell me more." She stepped aside and held the door open so Gale could enter, then locked it behind her.

"I need to get to Embercliffe. As soon as possible." She decided not to mention Alec's death in case it might make Jes less likely to help. It felt like a lie, but with fever threatening and her arm being eaten away, honesty was becoming less of a priority.

She hated the curse for that, too.

Jes's eyebrows crept upward. "Is that so? Cas just set off for a trip to that very city. You might catch him if you hurry."

"How—" Gale began, then sighed. "You'll want something in return, of course."

"Of course. Something you can deliver on now," Jes said, her gaze falling from Gale's face to the amethyst on her finger. "You're not looking so good. I'd hate to lose out on my payment if you die before you make it back."

Gale's clenched her teeth until her jaw hurt, and used the pain to keep herself from snapping back as she wished. "Perhaps this is a decision Cas could make for himself. If you'd be so kind as to tell me where he's gone, I'll work out payment with him."

"I see." Jes rubbed a hand down her face. "You know Cas to be kind, and you think that makes him soft."

"I don't know about that. I do think he's a rational person, though, who might ask for less because he sees that it's costing him nothing to let me tag along in his carriage."

Jes's lips curled into a little smile. "I ask for payment because I know you have something to offer. A lot to offer, in fact, if I could persuade you to stay and work for me. But circumstances require that you leave, so I ask for something of measurable, if not equal value." She stepped closer. "Do you see potential in yourself, young witch?"

"I'm not—"

"No. But you could be. You could be many things, I think, but here you are begging for help and offering nothing in return, relying on... what? Pity? A belief that the world and its people are inherently good and helpful?" Jes shook her head. "Maybe that worked for you when you were a sweet little girl in a sheltered village, but you're in the real world now. It's a hard place, and anyone who offers you something for nothing is likely out to get everything."

Gale scowled at her. "So you're the only sort I can trust, then? The kind who makes it clear she's out to take whatever I've got?"

"Calm yourself," Madrigal murmured. "When a wolf shows you its teeth, you'd best respect them."

But Jes seemed unperturbed. If anything, her smile broadened and her shoulders relaxed. "I'm offering you something of value. Free advice, if you'll listen. Call it an investment on my part."

Gale leaned back against the doorjamb, too tired to fight. "Go on, then."

"Forget pity. Forget goodness. Recognize that you have much to offer, and start using your skills and your brain to get what you want. It's the only way to make it in this world. Pay your debts, don't owe favours. Those who hold your marker hold your freedom."

Gale folded her arms across her chest. "I think people are better than that."

"Some are. But you won't know which ones until it's too late.

So here we are—you need help, and I'm not willing to have you in my debt if you might die tomorrow." Jes tilted her head to one side. "Be glad of that. There are plenty who do owe me."

Gale stood frozen, unsure of what to do. In the silence of the shop, Jes's pocket watch ticked audibly. Cas would be gone soon and it would be too late.

She turned to Madrigal, not caring whether Jes thought her mad. "The mages definitely have the means to help?"

Jes's eyes widened in surprise, but she didn't comment.

"The means if not the willingness," Madrigal said.

Gale stripped the ring from her finger and tossed it toward Jes, who snatched it out of the air and pocketed it without pausing to admire her new treasure.

Gale's finger felt lighter without it. Naked.

Jes stalked back to the desk at the rear of the shop and dashed off a quick note that she sealed in an envelope and handed to Gale.

"He's not taking a carriage, but the train," she said. "It'll be in Embercliffe this evening."

Gale thought back to the map in her bag that Basim had given her, showing Queen's Run near the western mountains and Embercliffe by the ocean in the east. "That's impossible."

"Is it?" Jes smiled. "Can you get yourself to Fortenbal Station?"

Gale turned to Madrigal, who nodded.

Gale nodded, too, and pocketed the note.

"Better hurry, then," Jes said, and stepped around her to unlock the door.

Gale didn't need to be told twice.

CHAPTER TWENTY-SEVEN

Fortenbal Station rose high above the street, its glass-panelled roof glinting in the orange pre-sunrise light from the east. A palace of travel and adventure, the building was closed off to all but the wealthiest and most important travellers to and from Embercliffe and other distant cities. Gale's lungs burned and her legs ached as she stopped across the street to look the building over—and to wonder how she'd get in.

She'd expected crowds of travellers she might blend in with as she made her way through the wide arches that opened onto the street, but with the exception of a few passing carriages and a baby wailing somewhere down a side street, all seemed quiet.

"They must've boarded already," Madrigal said, scouting ahead as far as she could to assess the situation. "Hurry."

Gale forced her poor mortal legs into motion again, this time at a quick walk, and wished that, just for a few minutes, she could be free from the weight of her cumbersome physical form. Madrigal had kept pace with her the whole way and was neither winded nor sweating nor the least bit dishevelled.

Not worth the trade, Gale reminded herself, and raked her fingers through her hair. She caught her reflection in a window and grimaced. It looked as though she'd already been riding the train, standing on its roof.

She shoved the mess of her hair into the back of her collar, tucked her blouse into her skirt, and buttoned her jacket.

It was no use, really. Madrigal had explained about the train on the way. Fortenbal Station wasn't built for regular trains—the chugging, groaning things that were meant to carry passengers and heavy cargo at a somewhat quicker pace than could be achieved by carts and horses. This station was only for the train known as The Dragon, a sleek and magically fast machine made to carry the wealthiest and most important folks to and from the king's city.

No one who had reason to enter this station would wander in looking like a drowned alley cat.

Gale turned to Madrigal. "Magic?"

Madrigal arched an eyebrow. "Did you fill your vessel when I wasn't looking?"

"No, but I still have some of the potion I didn't use last time."

Madrigal shook her head. "Not enough, and you're nowhere near ready for illusions. Best get on with it as you are."

But it would be possible, Gale thought, and shivered. *What a marvelous skill to have.*

She thought she'd prefer to study enchantments or potions, but focusing on those areas wouldn't mean she couldn't also study illusions and...

She caught herself, gave her head a shake, and forced her breathing to slow as she entered the building, following Madrigal's lead.

She'd have liked time to take everything in—the posters advertising theatre productions and local shops, the ornate metalwork atop the four-faced clock that hung from girders beneath the glass roof, the flowers growing in planters beside wooden benches that faced the tracks. All she caught was a glimpse of it all as she hurried on.

But her steps slowed as she passed through another brick archway and stood on the platform, then stopped entirely. The train sat before her on its tracks, and nothing Madrigal had told her as they rushed toward the station had prepared her for the sheer size and magnificence of it.

The black engine, its nose dipped toward the tracks and sweeping up and back toward the windowed compartment behind, did remind Gale of the head of a mighty dragon, complete with wisps of smoke rising from a series of openings along its sides. The beast's body, made of five cars as black as its head, lay in a straight line here in the station, but Gale could easily imagine it winding over the tracks through the country-side, slithering and serpentine, as true a dragon as anyone now living in Andonia would ever see.

"God have mercy," Gale whispered, half actual prayer and half thoughtless expression of awe.

Madrigal sniffed. "It's not bad."

The platform was quiet, but not completely empty of people. Several porters in crisp green uniforms with gold trim were loading the last few pieces of luggage into the rear carriage of the train as the last few passengers ascended wrought iron steps into their cars. Every one of them wore a fine dress or a perfectly tailored suit, nicer than anything folks wore at home even to weddings or dances.

Act like you belong, Gale decided, watching as the last passenger, a portly man with white whiskers sprouting like weeds from his ears and beneath his nose, climbed the steps.

A hand came down on her shoulder, startling her out of her wide-eyed stare.

"You can't be here, miss," said a gentle voice. Gale turned to find one of the porters holding her. He couldn't be much older than she was, and though he appeared to be making a valiant effort toward growing a proper moustache, the patchy hair on his upper lip was clearly reluctant to become so. "If you're looking for somewhere to sleep—"

Gale shook his hand off. "I'm not destitute," she said, as haughtily as she could. "I'm only in a hurry. I'm supposed to be on this train."

She considered saying she'd been robbed and decided against it. That might encourage this fellow to call the police on her behalf, and that was the last thing she wanted.

The porter looked her up and down, taking in her dirty dress and mussed hair. "Where's your luggage?"

"My travelling companion has it."

"Don't give his name," Madrigal said. "It's anyone's guess what he might be calling himself today."

"May I see your ticket?" the porter asked, polite but with a suspicious edge to his question.

"I—" Gale glanced around and spotted a ticket office shaped like a wooden hut some distance down the platform. "He might have left it for me, I'm not sure."

"Tickets have all been claimed, miss." The porter clearly didn't believe her, but he did at least sound as though he was sorry about it.

Tears prickled at the backs of Gale's eyes. She considered releasing them, hoping for pity and good-hearted assistance. But as much as she'd hated Jes's advice, she knew in her heart it wasn't wrong.

She straightened her shoulders and lifted her chin. "My companion will be most displeased if he learns his assistant was left behind because you wouldn't allow her the simple courtesy of announcing her arrival. You will allow me onto the train to find him, and we will sort this out."

A sharp whistle blew, piercing the air inside the station. The porter wiped sweat from his brow with the cuff of his jacket. "I could get in trouble for letting you set foot on there if you're not who you say you are."

Gale set her jaw and glared back at him, ignoring the guilt that squeezed her heart. The girl her mother had raised would never have manipulated an innocent porter like this, no matter how good her cause.

But I'm raising myself now, and I'm not who I was.

She leaned in closer. "That trouble is nothing compared to what will happen if you don't."

Madrigal smiled.

The porter, looking paler than he had when Gale had first turned to him, sighed. "This way, then, and step quick. If we can't find him, you'll have to leave the station." He held up a hand to signal to another uniformed fellow who was hanging out of a window at the engine. The train hissed as though displeased, but it didn't move as they ascended the steps.

Gale's stomach twisted into knots, but she held her head high and tried to act as though this wasn't the first train she'd ever seen. She pretended not to be at all surprised when she stepped into the first car and found it not dark, as the black exterior of the train suggested, but well lit by big windows along both sides of the car that had been invisible from outside. The walls between the windows were covered in emerald silk damask, and the carpet beneath her feet was the soft grey of a clouded summer sky. Folks sat in chairs upholstered in green velvet around dark wooden tables, and a fine haze of cigar smoke hung in the air. Servers were already handing out drinks. Gale scanned their faces and shook her head. No Cas.

Madrigal moved ahead as far as she could and waited.

The porter led her through a set of doorways, across the gap between cars, and into another large room. Gale had barely taken in the smaller tables with white tablecloths, breakfast being served, when Cas rose from a chair at the far end of the car and came toward them. If he was surprised to see her again, he didn't show it.

"I didn't think you'd make it," he said, sounding a little disappointed in her. He turned to the porter. "Thank you for bringing my—"

"Assistant," Gale mouthed.

"My sister to me."

The porter frowned. "She said she was your assistant."

"She's both." Cas patted his pockets. "I've got her ticket here somewhere." He sighed. "I suppose I've left it in my checked luggage."

The train whistled again, and the porter glanced over his shoulder. "You're responsible for her, then?"

"Absolutely. Here. For your trouble." A few coins appeared in Cas's hand as though by magic, and he handed them to the porter.

"No trouble at all, sir." The porter gave Gale one last curious glance and hurried off the train. A moment later it lurched into motion, jerking slightly as the attachments between cars tightened, then rumbling over the tracks as the station disappeared and the city took its place outside the windows. Gale's heart squeezed tight as she stumbled and caught herself on a nearby chair, then continued to pound even as she righted herself. Cas, far more sure-footed than Gale, led her back to his table.

No one else seemed at all awed or concerned, so Gale tried to mimic their placid expressions as the station and the city outside flashed by at a higher speed than Gale had ever moved before.

"Do you like eggs?" Cas asked as he sat again. "They'll bring whatever you want." He glanced around and lowered his voice. "Is your companion with us?"

Gale took the other chair and nodded toward Madrigal, who was looking over Cas's shoulder with something like approval. "She's right behind you."

Cas's mouth twitched as though he was holding back a grimace. "Excellent. Excuse me?" He motioned for a server in a white uniform to come closer, then looked expectantly at Gale.

"I'll have whatever he's having. Please."

The server, a middle-aged woman with a thin frame and iron-grey hair, nodded. "Another teacup?"

"Yes, thank you." Then, to Cas, she added, "Please, go ahead. Before your food gets cold."

He lifted the silver dome from his plate, revealing a mountain of golden scrambled eggs topped with delicate greens, plus a pile of bacon and four slices of toast. "Help yourself."

Gale snatched a slice of toast and slathered it with butter and strawberry preserves, not caring whether anyone might be staring, and tore off a big bite. "Thanks," she muttered, her mouth full. "For all of this."

Cas smiled. "I assume you found me because Jes told you where I was. But that doesn't explain why you're here."

The second plate of food arrived. Gale handed Cas the envelope Jes had sent and let him read while she tucked into her meal. He scanned it in a few seconds, nodded, and slipped it into his pocket.

"Tell me everything," he said. "Keep your voice down and act like we're catching up on something pleasant. Or boring."

Gale told him quickly what had happened since she'd seen him such a short time ago—confronting Hawk, Alec's death, and the information he'd passed on before he crossed over. She spoke quietly, especially when the subjects of magic or ghosts came up, and around mouthfuls of food. Cas's expression remained even and calm throughout, though he flinched when she explained how Alec had died.

"So you just need to get to Embercliffe?"

Gale touched her empty ring finger and forced a smile around a bite of toast. "That's what I paid for. Small price if I can save Bright Hollow, right?"

It wasn't true. The loss hurt. Losing the ring felt like losing her connection to home and family—one she needed more with every step she took into the wilds. But it would be worth it in the end.

The lamps on the wall flashed red three times. No one seemed troubled by it.

Cas glanced out the window, where the city had thinned and rolling fields came into view. "Hold on a moment. The transition isn't always smooth."

Gale was about to ask what he meant when the train car jolted and her stomach lurched. The view outside the windows shifted as the train lifted slightly, then clunked back down onto the tracks.

"They're casting now," Cas said, as though that explained everything.

"Excuse me?"

"This train doesn't run on set tracks. The mages cast them ahead and pull them up behind. Much more efficient—no permanent tracks to maintain outside the city like others have, and we can go around obstacles if they come. We've just left the permanent tracks in Queen's Run and moved onto our own."

Gale leaned over to press her face against the window but couldn't see anything ahead except the countryside.

"So this train could go anywhere?"

"No, but close enough with the right mages and reasonably level ground."

Madrigal grumbled something under her breath and scowled out the window. The early morning sunlight made her almost invisible.

Cas poured each of them a second cup of tea and drank his quickly. "Take your time here, finish your meal. Order more if you'd like."

"Where are you going?"

He stood and slipped his jacket on. "If you're going to step off the train in Embercliffe, you'd best look like you belong there. There's bound to be a lady on the train who has a spare dress with her and will part with it for the right price."

"I don't have much money," Gale said. "Or another ring."

"I know." Cas's expression took on a pinched look, but only for a moment. "We'll work it out later."

Madrigal settled into his seat as soon as he was gone. "Not a bad sort, is he?"

"Hmm," Gale said—a noise she hoped would be mistaken for satisfaction with her meal as she used a piece of toast to scrape the last few scraps of egg off her plate. The food sat heavy in her stomach, but she wanted to finish every bite.

Madrigal glanced around the car, which by now was slowly emptying as people made their way farther back or forward in the train. "No one is listening."

"They'll notice if I'm talking to myself," Gale said, trying not to move her lips. She turned to the window again and watched the scenery whipping by, slouching against the back of the chair. The meal had helped, but she still felt ill and weak. If the mages wouldn't heal her, she'd fall into fever and delirium soon enough.

The mages will help, she told herself. *They have to.*

The ride was smoother now that the train was moving faster, giving the impression that she was sitting still while a village with its fields of cows passed at dizzying speed. She leaned back and sipped her tea, resting one hand on her full belly, fighting the urge to close her eyes and sleep.

Madrigal smiled, but the skin between her brows remained creased. "No wonder the wealthy folk travel this way, eh?"

"It's incredible." Gale checked to make sure no one was listening, but kept her voice quiet. "I'd better be careful not to get used to it."

Cas entered a few minutes later and motioned for Gale to follow him. They crossed between cars, and Gale tried her best not to look down at the tracks rushing beneath them. The next car had a narrow corridor down the right side with windows on the right and doors on the left.

"Sleeping cabins," Cas explained. "Mine's in the next car."

Gale followed close behind as they passed through the corridor. "The mages who cast the tracks... that's all they do?"

Cas glanced back at her. "That and keeping the train running smoothly, preparing the ground ahead if we need to go off-course. Hard work, but it's what they've trained for. Why?"

She shrugged. "I just hadn't considered how boring a life of legal magic could be."

"Incredible power," Madrigal said behind her. "But for what?"

"They certainly don't all love it," Cas said. "They hold great power without fearing for their lives, but it comes at a high cost."

"Indeed," Madrigal said. "What good is power if you don't get to choose how you use it?"

They reached Cas's cabin, a small room with a wide, plush bench and a little, round table. The curtains had been drawn and the lamps lit, and a grey dress hung in the corner.

Gale looked around. "Where's the bed?"

Cas nodded at the bench. "That's it, if you have the servants come in to make it up for you. There are better cabins, but they seemed excessive for daytime travel."

"And none of the rest of it does?" Gale asked, offering a smile. It was funny, but she didn't have the energy to laugh at the ridiculousness of it all. "Most people have to make the journey over the course of days in a carriage or a wagon or on horseback. We're practically flying in the lap of luxury."

"It is a bit much, I suppose. But moving quickly works for your needs." Cas glanced at the bandages protruding from beneath her sleeve. "How's that doing? You don't look well."

She frowned. "I didn't tell you about the curse."

"Alec was paid for more than just analysis of enchanted objects."

"Of course." She found she didn't really mind that he knew about her situation. "It's better. Thanks for asking."

In truth, the pain was growing deeper around the edges of the wound, but when she touched the centre, it had gone numb. She desperately craved the sleep that might allow her body to recover, or at least slow the curse's progress for a time.

"Shall I leave you to change, then?"

"Please. And would you have them bring more tea? And fresh bandages, if they have any."

Cas chuckled. "See? You're already getting used to a life of luxury."

He stepped out and closed the pocket door behind him, and Gale shed her dirty clothes, leaving the jacket, blouse, skirt, socks, and undergarments folded on the floor. The air was warm, but she shivered as she stood naked, wearing nothing but the vessel around her neck and the bandage on her wrist. She stared down at her forearm.

"You'd better check it," Madrigal said, settling herself on the floor in the corner. "You still have some ointment?"

"A little. Let me dress first."

Madrigal nodded. "I'll leave you for a while, if it's all the same to you. You seem safe enough here, but your vessel needs filling and I'm exhausted from trying to anchor myself to what's there. I'll retire to the borderlands, then find you at the other end. Call if you need me. I'll do my best to come."

She vanished completely, leaving Gale alone in the gently swaying train car.

It seemed a shame to put on such a fine dress over dirty skin and hair, but there was nothing to be done about that. Either Cas or the woman he'd got the clothing from, had thought of everything, from underclothes to stockings to the full-skirted dove grey dress with cap sleeves and a wide sash, to the matching jacket cut to hug her waist. It felt as though the jacket's lining might be stuffed with a thin layer of feathers, protection against the chill of Embercliffe's ocean breezes. The only thing he hadn't managed to get was shoes, so Gale would wear her old boots. They'd hardly show under the long skirt, anyway.

At least he'd thought to find a hairbrush.

She'd just finished lacing the bodice of the dress—which exposed more of her upper chest than she was used to but otherwise fit well enough—and slipped her vessel beneath its neckline when Cas knocked.

"Come in."

He carried a bowl of steaming water and a roll of bandages that he set on the table. "It fits you—that's good. I'm not always a good judge of these things."

"Really? You don't strike me as a man who misses much."

Cas removed his jacket and sat on the bench, his hands dangling between his knees, fingers moving, teasing the air. They never seemed to be quite still. "I'm learning to observe. I have a long way to go."

"Jes is teaching you, I suppose?" Gale turned her back to him and gave her face a quick wash. Then she unwrapped her bandage, wincing as the fabric pulled away a layer of the skin beneath, leaving the wound covered in fresh, sharp pain. The rash had gone deep, eating away the muscle nearly down to the bone, sending purplish-red tendrils creeping up toward her shoulder, marking where it would attack next. She washed the wound, took the ointment from her bag and applied a layer, then re-wrapped the whole mess before looking at it could make her lose her breakfast.

The salve had done what it could, but she had days now before was too weak and addle-brained to go on.

"You don't like Jes much, do you?" Cas asked.

Gale touched her bare ring finger again and turned to him. "Not really. What amazes me is that you do."

Cas leaned back against the cushions. "Of course I do. I mean, she's hard as stone and often as cold. She's sly and cautious and frequently mean, if that's what it takes to get the job done."

"But?"

A gold coin appeared in Cas's hand, just as suddenly as the others had earlier, and he made it dance over the backs of his fingers. "It's not my place to tell her life story, but I will tell you that Jes had to fight for everything she has. She comes from a world that's nothing like the one you grew up in—she's had to rely on her wits and strength to survive. Jes would say a person hasn't really lived if life hasn't hardened them up a bit."

"And you? You seem kind enough for all that."

He looked up to meet Gale's eyes. "I grew up sheltered, like you did."

"I doubt it was very much like my upbringing," Gale said, sitting at the opposite end of the bench and pulling her feet up beneath her skirt. "Only Bright Hollow is Bright Hollow."

"In the details, sure. My point is that I grew up in an environment that was safe but stifling, one I eventually wanted to be free of, but I doubt I would have made it out on my own. Jes has been a good, if not patient, teacher of things I needed to learn."

Gale narrowed her eyes. "How much did that cost you?"

"Almost my life, once, but that's another story." He made the coin disappear and sat up. A second later a knock came at the door, and he stood to receive a tray of tea and flat biscuits. Gale passed the bowl of dirty water and bandages out, and the servant girl accepted it without question.

"There's a lot to Jes you don't know. Things she lets very few people see." Cas poured the tea and crunched down on a biscuit. "She makes me laugh, and I try to do the same for her—she has a wonderful laugh. She's clever, but also more compassionate than you'd believe. Not weak, you understand, but she's loyal and capable, and the best ally a person could wish for in hard times."

Gale cradled the warm teacup in her hands and leaned back against the wall. "So that's all she is to you? Your boss, your ally, your teacher?"

Cas's lips twitched. "That's also not for me to tell. And I hope you'll promise never to repeat to her what I've said here. She'd call me a sentimental fool and probably demote me for it."

But the look in his eyes told Gale all she needed to know.

She swallowed back a lump that filled her throat. *It would be lovely to have someone look that way when they spoke of me,* she thought. For the first time since the beginning of the plague she thought of her old dream—the house in the woods, the healing garden, a mysterious visitor from outside of town. It seemed childish now to imagine such things, but her chest still tightened at the thought.

Cas watched her closely. "You must be tired," he said. "I'm going to go down to the lounge car, if you don't mind. There's a gentleman I've been meaning to speak to, and I can't imagine him straying far from the card table. Shall I call for someone to make up the bunk?"

"No, thank you. It's fine as it is."

He stood and touched a toe to the drawer beneath the bed. "Blankets should be in there. I'll wake you before our arrival."

Gale nodded. But after he left, she didn't lie down. Instead, she drew the last jar of *lucistra* from her bag and set to work refilling her vessel. She'd need Madrigal with her every step of the way once she reached Embercliffe, and perhaps as much magic as she could muster.

Sleep would have to wait its turn.

CHAPTER TWENTY-EIGHT

THE TRAIN HUFFED IMPATIENTLY AS the passengers disembarked into a station illuminated by gas lamps already lit against the coming evening. Gale descended the steps carefully, assisted by a uniformed young man who reminded her of the one she'd spoken to back in Queen's Run except that this one wished the lady a pleasant evening instead of questioning her presence.

Clothing really did make all the difference. Her old things were packed in a leather suitcase Cas had acquired. Gale had placed her old knapsack inside it and carried it in her right hand. It felt heavier than it should have, and her feet dragged over the polished stone floor. Sleep had restored her a little, but her muscles felt weaker than ever, and she'd wakened trembling with chills even in the warmth of the train car.

Cas descended behind her carrying a black valise in one hand and checking his pocket watch with the other.

"Do you need to hurry off?" Gale asked.

Cas slipped the watch back into his pocket and looked past her, toward the doors. "Not at all. Do you need anything else before we part ways?"

Liar, Gale thought, but appreciated his courtesy.

In truth, she'd have liked to ask for an escort through this strange city, but didn't feel she had any right to interfere with his business. "If you could point me in the direction of the Hall of Mages, I'd appreciate it."

"Right this way."

Cas took her arm, and they passed through the station. She was glad to have him. His confident steps seemed to cut through the crowds, and in no time they had passed by gilded benches and through the heady perfume of roses that climbed the walls toward a peaked glass ceiling much like the one they'd left behind that morning. The sky at its edges was orange, deepening to cloudless purple toward the east. They passed through open glass doors, and Gale pulled her new jacket tighter around her. It was colder here than it had been in Queen's Run, and a light dusting of flurries floated down from the sky.

The city itself was entirely unlike the one she'd just left. Queen's Run wore its age like a badge of honour, with buildings hundreds of years old butting up against new construction on one end and the ruins of a nearly forgotten pre-human world on the other. The streets, at least in the areas Gale had visited, were often dirty, always noisy, and alive with people from every imaginable walk of life. Embercliffe was an old city, but it looked like the set of a stage play. Clean. Well kept. The architecture ranged from curved Kardavi rooflines to white plaster buildings with slate shingles to brick buildings set in rows like the ones in Queen's Run, but everything was immaculate. As a white carriage went by, one of the horses left a steaming offering on the stones of the street. Moments later a young man with a shovel and cart came by to clean it up.

No drunks lying in gutters here.

They stopped near the flower cart, where faint perfume touched the frigid air. Gale's fingers twitched nervously, and she resisted the urge to reach for the comfort of her vessel. Madrigal appeared beside her, eagerly taking in the city as Gale had moments before.

"I've heard the mages aren't exactly open to helping anyone other than the king, but I have to try," Gale said. "At least I won't be alone."

"You will be, though," Madrigal said.

"What?" Gale turned to her, and her stomach sank as Madrigal shook her head and Gale realized the obvious problem. "Oh. My vessel."

"I—" Cas began, then stopped himself, seeming to realize she wasn't speaking to him.

Madrigal drifted closer to Cas, making it appear to anyone looking on that Gale's focus was on him. "Such a small portion of magic might go unnoticed on its own, but they'll feel the personal signature of what's in your vessel if you get within arm's reach of any mage. If you show up as a commoner, the worst that will happen is they'll refuse you and send you on your way. Come with magic in hand and I guarantee you'd find yourself in an unpleasant meeting with one of their enchanted axes. They say the mages' weapons cut through bone like it's butter. Makes for a less painful death, I suppose, but what they'd do to you with it beforehand…" Madrigal closed her eyes and shook her head. "And I can't accompany you without that vessel."

"But surely there's magic there you could anchor yourself to," Gale said, trying not to let her panic come through in her voice, which she kept as quiet as she could.

"Only if you got me there, first," Madrigal said.

"Right." Gale sighed. "Why didn't you mention sooner that I'd be going alone?"

Madrigal watched as a flock of white pigeons crossed the sky. "You needed to make this journey if you want any chance of finding your cure. I didn't think you'd come if you realized you'd have to face the mages alone."

Gale's throat tightened. The fact that she didn't have the

energy to cry seemed like a small mercy. "At least if I'd given up in Queen's Run I could have died at home."

Cas's brow creased, but he didn't interrupt. He did check his watch again, though.

"Sorry," Gale said, speaking to him. "You need to go. Which way am I headed?"

Cas nodded past Gale's shoulder, to the left of the train station. "Do you see the palace?"

Gale turned. "It's hard to miss."

The buildings before them blocked her view of the lower parts of the structure, but in the distance, the palace towered over all of them.

It was as she'd always imagined it, yet far grander than anything she'd seen in drawings—a towering conglomeration of pale-grey towers topped with gold that glowed as though molten in the sunset. It would be hard to lose her way with that to navigate by.

"The Hall of Mages is just south of the palace," Cas said. "Big stone building. Boxy, set back from the road behind trees. Sort of frightening, if memory serves. You can't miss it."

"Right." Gale took a deep breath. "Will you be around later?"

"I'll be in town for a few days. Find me at the Crooked Cod on Arabelle Boulevard when you're finished with the mages."

"Good." Gale steeled herself and slipped the necklace from around her neck, squeezed it as tight as she could with her weakened fingers, and handed it to him. She hadn't been drawing magic from the vessel since she filled it, but the loss of its presence left her with a deep ache in her chest. "Would you hold on to my things for me? Just be careful. The necklace is more fragile than it looks."

"Of course." Cas lifted it from her hand with practiced ease and made it disappear into his pocket, then accepted her suitcase when she handed it over. "I'll see you soon. Ask for Angus Donovan at the desk, and the innkeeper will call me down." He touched the outside of his pocket. "Does your friend come along with this?"

"Tell him I'll bide in the borderlands," Madrigal huffed. "Take care, Gale. I'll want to be seeing you soon." And she vanished.

Panic fluttered in Gale's chest as she prepared herself to wander alone through a strange city, sick and weak, to approach the only people who frightened her more than the criminals and sinners she'd expected to find on every corner outside of Bright Hollow.

Don't show fear, she reminded herself. *Not even in front of those who seem like friends.*

"She's gone for now," Gale assured Cas.

"That's a relief. Good luck."

He didn't have to tell her again that she'd need it.

Gale turned away and headed toward the palace's distant spires, feeling more alone than she had since she'd found Madrigal at the cabin, praying she was ready for whatever came next.

IT WAS strange to walk without Madrigal, and hard for Gale to remember not to speak aloud to herself. Embercliffe wasn't like Queen's Run. A young woman walking alone and muttering to herself wouldn't be disregarded as drunk or suffering from mental exhaustion from long hours in a mill, but would stand out among the quiet, refined sorts who walked the cobblestone streets.

Lords and ladies, she supposed, or at least some of them would be. Gale certainly couldn't tell the difference between rich and noble. It was just a sea of warm coats in bright fabrics, skirts with gathered hems and puffed-out backsides, and top hats taller than seemed necessary or pleasing.

She tried to blend in, peering occasionally through the

window of a chocolate shop or haberdasher's as though she had any extra money to waste. She kept silent, but the conversation with herself never ceased as she tried to force her exhausted mind to settle on a plan. Her skull felt like it had grown cobwebs inside, and it took longer than usual to make ideas fit together.

It wouldn't do to tell the mages what she'd been up to. They might be merciful if she admitted she'd consulted a witch for a cure, but there was no way to be sure. Best if she didn't mention it at all. No, she'd do all she could to be a regular citizen sent to the mages for help.

And then all that was left was the truth. Mostly.

As it turned out, the lower portion of the palace was no more visible from the street than it had been from a distance thanks to high stone walls that blocked any sort of view. Even the golden gates had fogged glass panels set into them that gave the impression of transparency but left curious passers-by with nothing more than a vague impression that there was something beyond. But the size of the building was clearer up close, and the clean grey stone of its towers even more impressive. They stood stark against the darkening sky, flying the king's blue banners in salt-scented wind that whipped up from the sea beyond Embercliffe's famously steep coastline.

South, she reminded herself. She turned, navigating by the vanishing sunset, and forced her steps forward. The wall surrounding the palace sat close to the road, and Gale reached out and traced her fingers along it as she walked, grounding herself.

God, let me make it through this, she prayed. *If there's help for us among the mages, let me find it.* The only answer was the wind passing over the wall and the clopping hooves and clattering wheels of a passing carriage.

The wall ended, and a tall iron fence took its place, black as pitch with gleaming spikes at the top. A dark patch of forest pressed against it, denser and somehow wilder than anything she'd seen on the side of the mountain, like it had been transplanted here from somewhere common humans should fear to tread. Gale tried the gate, and it swung open.

Something rustled in a patch of bushes to her left as she stepped onto the overgrown dirt path leading deeper into the shadows. Images of wild beasts waiting to tear her limbs from her body and feast on her flesh passed through her mind, strong enough for her to wonder whether they might be caused by an enchantment made to turn curious folks away.

Being torn apart is the least of your worries, she reminded herself, *and at least it would be a quicker and less painful death than the one you'll face if you don't keep going.*

She pressed on, following the path through a forest that seemed larger than it should have been.

The sound of the ocean's waves reached her, crashing from somewhere beyond the woods and far below. And then, set with its back against the cliffs as though daring the land to send it crashing into the thundering ocean, she found the Hall of Mages.

It was everything the palace was not—squat as a toad, built from blocks of dark stone that seemed to have grown from the ground, like they had been there since before humans had claimed this land. An aura of magic, faint but undeniable, hung around it like rich perfume. Gale combed her fingers through her hair and wiped the sweat from her brow as she stepped up to the only visible door, one made from black wood with strange and troubling creatures carved into its surface. A thick, rough length of rope hung beside the door, and she gave it a hard tug.

No sound followed from within the building. And as she waited, Gale realized none reached her from the street, either. It was as though she'd left that world behind her completely.

She was about to ring again when the door swung open, revealing a shadowy room beyond. The pale face of a tall, young man seemed to float in the darkness until Gale's eyes adjusted and she found the rest of him dressed in black trousers and a black shirt with a high collar.

He looked down his nose at her, and suddenly Gale knew what it must feel like to be a bug that someone found stuck to the bottom of his shoe. "Yes?"

Gale smoothed her skirt and tried to calm the trembling of her hands. "I've come to speak to the mages. My town has had a curse placed on it. We didn't know who else to turn to."

Something moved in the shadows behind him, but the doorman didn't seem to notice. If he did, he wasn't bothered by it.

"The mages work for the king and the king alone," he said.

"I know, but if I could just speak to one of them, I think—"

She realized her mistake as soon as she'd spoken. The young man's upper lip twisted into an ugly sneer as he glared at her. "*I am one of the mages.*"

"I'm terribly sorry," Gale said, and didn't know how to go on. If she said, "I thought they'd have someone unimportant at the door," it would insult his position. If she said, "You didn't feel powerful to me," it would be worse.

"I speak for all of us," he went on, his tone so condescending that Gale's teeth ground together. "The rules are inviolable. We do not deal with the common folk. Our energies are needed elsewhere." He reached for the door and began to close it. "Take your problem to the king tomorrow."

"No!" Without thinking, Gale shoved her shoulder against the door, jamming it with her body. "Who knows how long it would take to get an audience? Everyone could be dead by then." She pushed her jacket sleeve up and tore off the bandages, holding her cursed arm out to the young mage through the opening in the door. He took a step back, and the door opened enough for her to almost step inside. As her eyes adjusted to the darkness Gale caught sight of another door just beyond this small chamber, and that shape again—another person, this one dressed in dark robes like the mage who had performed the execution in Queen's Run, a hood pulled up to shadow their face.

Gale resisted the urge to flee.

"Look," she said, addressing the young mage. She pushed her arm toward him again, forcing him to look at the dying, oozing flesh. "This is only the beginning. Pain follows. Madness. Death. It takes the old, the young, the sick, the healthy."

With each word, the young mage stepped back, leaving the door to swing open wider.

"We—our rules," he stammered. "Procedures." He raised a hand in a warding gesture. Magic crackled through the air, and Gale flinched.

The robed figure stepped forward, revealing itself to be a stooped old man with a deeply lined face and features like carved teakwood. He kept his eyes closed, and the lids appeared sunken.

Empty.

Gale shuddered.

"Relax, Arthur," he said, lowering the younger mage's arm with one hand. "She told you it's a curse. If she's right, it's not catching. If she's wrong..." He shrugged. "Well, we'll find some way to fix you up before all that madness comes for you. Go on. Make a prophylactic tea if it helps you feel better. I'll handle this."

Arthur narrowed his eyes. "If by *handle* you mean you'll make her leave, I can do that myself."

The older mage frowned. "I'm not going to violate the rules, Artie. But it sounds like this woman has travelled a long way to ask for our help. I can't cure her, but there's no reason I can't offer her a glass of water before we send her on her way."

Arthur's already thin lips tightened. "She's not a threat?"

The mage's smile deepened the wrinkles on his face. "Would she have made it to our door with malice in her heart? Would I let her in now if I saw trouble coming?"

Arthur sighed. "Let a glass of water be all it is, then. I'll check to see that she's gone when I return."

With that, he opened the other door, letting a warm flood of lamplight into the little chamber, and left them.

"Be a dear and swing that door closed," the old mage said. "No need to let a draught in. Gods forbid we ruffle Artie's feathers any more than you already have."

Gale stepped the rest of the way inside and closed the heavy exterior door behind her. The old man sounded kind enough, and she found herself warming to him in spite of his fearsome clothing and her knowledge of the danger.

The old man lowered his hood, revealing a head covered in wisps of white hair like a chick's first down. "Come, please." Gale followed him into a stone-walled corridor with lamps glowing in sconces. Closed doors lined a hallway that seemed to go on forever, though the mage stopped at one of the first on the left. The feeling of magic in the place was stronger than it had been outside, and though it seemed to be coming from behind the doors, Gale supposed that after all this time, the bricks themselves must be infused with it.

The old mage pushed the door open, revealing a pleasant little sitting room. A pair of lamps blazed to life, illuminating two leather armchairs, a table between them with a pitcher and two cups on it, and stone walls with no windows. The thick rug on the floor sank beneath Gale's feet, and she wished she could curl up on it like a dog to sleep.

"What's your name, then?"

"Nightingale, sir. My friends call me Gale."

"And I'm Sabbatus. My friends call me Sabbatus. Come now. Sit. Rest your feet."

Gale did as he asked, jumping only a little as the door swung closed on its own. There was no handle on either side. No way out until the mage decided to let her go.

She examined him more closely in the brighter light. Old, but it was hard to say how old. And she was sure now that his eyes weren't simply closed. They were missing.

"My sacrifice," he said, and reached over to pour two cups of water from the pitcher. "You know anything about that?"

"A little," she admitted. "I thought people who did that only took one... whatever."

He smiled and raised his cup. "Great sacrifice and great pain often lead to great potential. I lost much, and I gained more. But that's not for a nice girl like you to think about, is it?"

Gale shifted uncomfortably. "No. Sir." She took a sip of water and found it cool, clean, and sweeter than any she'd tasted even from the best wells in Bright Hollow. "Thank you for inviting me in."

"I'm sorry I can't do more." Sabbatus leaned forward. "You're from the mountains. A different sort of town. Followers of the Path." He raised his eyebrows. "Don't usually accept help from the king, eh? And certainly not from mages."

Gale's mouth went dry. "How—" she began, and stopped. Of course his gift would be vision of some sort—his sacrifice had been his intention. If he could see all that, surely he saw more, and more dangerous, things. But he hadn't called for help, and she wasn't in a dungeon yet.

"We're desperate," she said. If she was to be arrested and beheaded, she'd at least do her job first. "The cures we can make for ourselves can barely hold back the sickness. We narrowed the curse down to a water source and closed our wells, but those affected are still dying. I hoped that maybe, if you made a cure..."

Sabbatus smiled warmly. There was no hint of artifice in it, no threat. Gale knew she shouldn't trust him, but it was hard not to. "And your leader would accept magical assistance? For that's what it would be. No common cure from uncommon botanicals will help you, and no good will or fervent prayer will defeat a curse."

"I don't know. I believe the curse is against God's will, and we should use whatever means we can to be rid of it. I hope the Luminary will see things the same way."

"Hmm."

For a moment, Gale felt as though she were being watched—not by human eyes, but by something greater. She shivered, and the feeling passed.

Sabbatus leaned back in his chair. "Arthur was correct, of course. We work for the king and no one else."

"I'd heard as much." Gale swallowed back the thickness in her throat. "I had to try."

"It's really a shame. We could help you." He went on before Gale could respond. "That rash on your arm comes from the darkest magic. Did you know we have herbs and botanicals in our walled garden that are illegal to grow anywhere else in Andonia?"

"I'd heard," Gale said. "That's why I came."

Sabbatus nodded. "Too powerful to have them in the hands of those who might use them for the wrong purposes, you see." He scratched at his chin thoughtfully. "I'm not wholly schooled in medicines and curses myself, but I've had a few years to poke around a bit at everything. This would be simple enough, if you knew what you were doing. A bit of ramhorn, roots from a common rose—not that the ones in our garden are entirely common, of course—and a bit of what they call githarmus. You know that one?"

"No," Gale said, a little irritated that he'd wave this knowledge in her face when he couldn't offer to hand it over. Then something in her went still and her thoughts quieted.

He's giving me the answer.

"Pretty flower, or so I'm told. Big white blossoms on thick stalks. Smells like rotting meat soaked in honey, though. You'd have to mix it all in the moon fountain in the courtyard to get the proper effect, and do it under the full moon for any chance at knocking out a curse. But if you did, a common reaction spell like *arnithip rounduul carlatian* would do it." He gave his head a quick shake and seemed to come back to himself. "Listen to me, theorizing and rambling on about what must sound like nonsense to a good citizen like you who knows nothing of magic. Don't mind me."

"I don't mind at all," Gale said. She repeated the words silently to herself, trying to sear them into her memory. *Arnithip rounduul carlatian. Arnithip rounduul carlatian.* "You couldn't just sneak back there and prepare a little as a sample, I suppose?"

Sabbatus's smile faded. "I wish I could. But my eyes aren't the only thing I sacrificed when I became the king's mage. My hands are tied." He heaved himself to his feet and rubbed his lower back. "Come on, then. You'd best be on your way before Arthur comes back. I don't know why he thinks we have a receiving room if not to receive visitors."

"Right." Gale stumbled as she got to her feet, and Sabbatus caught her by the arm. Magic hung in the air around him, unguarded. Gale felt something inside her leaning into it, drawing comfort. "Thank you. For the welcome. And the water. I'm glad I found you and not just Arthur."

Sabbatus smiled and patted her on her arm. "A lucky coincidence, indeed. I only wish more could come of it. You've travelled such a long way."

Gale frowned. It wasn't a coincidence. He'd been waiting for her, she was sure of it. The only question was why, if not to see through her lies and arrest her.

A trick, perhaps, to tempt her to try her luck again on the enchanted path, this time with criminal intentions. Sabbatus had hinted the journey would be far more dangerous to an enemy.

Or a temptation to make her reveal her knowledge of magic.

Gale followed him back to the entryway, where a few candles now burned on the walls. As she turned, she caught sight of a painting she'd missed when they'd walked in—a portrait of the royal family done in oils, captured in lifelike detail. She almost passed by without a second look, then paused.

"This prince," she said, and leaned in to examine the figure more closely, assessing the dark hair the artist hadn't tried to tame, square jaw with a scar on his chin, mischievous eyes, and hands that even in the painting seemed like they wanted to be fiddling with something. "He looks familiar to me."

"Eh?" Sabbatus shuffled toward the painting. "Oh, yes. That'd be Prince Balthazar Caspar… eh, they all have so many names, I can never remember the whole thing. Broke the queen's heart when he left a year or so ago, but I wasn't surprised."

"No?" Gale tried to sound casually interested, not as though she'd just seen a teenaged version of Cas staring at her from the painting.

He did say he had a sheltered childhood.

"He used to take an interest in magic. Nothing unseemly, and he never had any kind of skill for it, but some of us older folks let him poke around the Hall and our library a little. Nice enough child, if a bit willful and loud. Then he found other interests and left us."

Gale arched an eyebrow. "Just like that?"

Sabbatus's lips twitched. "I suppose it's not sharing royal secrets if he's left his title behind, is it? He was asked not to return to the Hall of Mages after he found a recipe for curing constipation and baked it into a special treat for Reginald—you wouldn't know him, one of the more experienced mages. Sneaked in and left it on his breakfast tray. Those two were never on the best terms."

"I see." Gale looked closer at the portrait, examining the handsome, fair-haired king and the beautiful queen with her copper skin and dark, laughing eyes, then passing quickly over their sons before she turned back to Sabbatus. "Why weren't you surprised when he left?"

"Some people are destined for greater things than a life of luxury in Embercliffe." Even without eyes Sabbatus seemed to be looking deep into Gale's, searching. "Come, now."

Sabbatus opened the door and Gale stepped out into the

freshly fallen night. "I hope you get what you need," he said. Gale thanked him, and he closed the door behind her.

Not, *I hope you find someone to help you,* she noticed, but, *I hope you get what you need.*

Jes was right. A person couldn't always expect someone else to solve her problems, but whatever Sabbatus had seen in her had prompted him to give her what she needed to solve them herself.

At least, mostly.

Gale walked as quickly as she could manage into the night and headed for the Crooked Codfish with plans churning in her mind.

CHAPTER TWENTY-NINE

GALE WAS WAITING at the polished mahogany desk near the entrance to the Crooked Codfish when Cas came down the wide, carpeted staircase. He nodded to the clerk, who disappeared into the next room.

"A sheltered life indeed, Prince Balthazar Caspar—something."

Cas's lips moved, though not quite into a smile. "Close enough. Have you eaten since the train?"

"No."

"Then please, join me. I suppose we have more to discuss than the return of your necklace."

Gale hesitated and calculated how much money she had left as she looked around the room with its fine desk, marble fireplace, and window dressings made from swaths of luxurious white fabric. "I don't think I can pay to eat here."

"Or sleep here, I know." Cas slipped two fingers into his pocket and pulled out Jes's letter, just far enough for her to see before he hid it again. "But I have my orders."

Gale wondered what Madrigal would have to say about that. Nothing good, certainly.

They left the entrance with its dark wooden fixtures and striped green-and-rose wallpaper behind and followed the clerk into a dining room. Round tables topped with silk tablecloths had been set for supper, and most of them were occupied. Heavy velvet curtains at the windows had been drawn against the night, and a fire blazed in the fireplace at the far end of the room.

Cas led the way to a table with a discreet *reserved* sign on top and sat. The clerk appeared, whisked the sign away, and stood looking expectantly at Gale.

"Your jacket," Cas murmured.

"Oh." She slipped it off, hating to lose its comfort but knowing the room would be too warm with it on. The men had all removed theirs, and none of the ladies were wearing coats—bare arms and shoulders seemed to be the order of the evening, and she'd look out of place if she kept hers covered.

She did her best to hide her clumsily re-bandaged arm between herself and the wall, then glanced around the room again. "When you said 'The Crooked Codfish,' I expected something a little less upscale."

A server in white appeared and poured two glasses of wine and two of water without being asked, flashing Gale a curious look before averting his eyes. Cas took a sip of wine and set the glass down. "It amuses wealthy folk to give places names that sound casual and rough. There is a proper-ish pub room in the back, but it's not what you'd find in Queen's Run."

"Fewer teeth on the floor, I suppose?"

"Among other things." He looked around. "Embercliffe's inns tend to have less personality than those back home, but I do prefer the bedrooms here. Don't tell Jes I said so."

"Is Queen's Run really home?"

He sipped his wine again. "It is. For now, at least." The meal arrived—roast beef, pink in the centre, with thick gravy, mashed turnip, and roasted carrots, all of it smelling like plated perfection. Gale tried to remember the last time she'd had a proper sit-down supper like this. Before the curse, certainly, and though her mother's roast might have been made with more love, it had never looked this appetizing. "But you're not here to talk about my past."

"No." Gale looked behind and around, but no one seemed to be listening. Still, she lowered her voice as she explained how her visit had gone. Cas didn't interrupt even when she paused to sip water that wasn't nearly as good as what Sabbatus had offered.

It wasn't a long story, and half the food was still on her plate when she finished. She was tempted to shovel it down, but her stomach didn't feel like it would receive such an onslaught with good grace.

"I know the ingredients I need," she said, "and the spell I should use. It needs to happen in the mages' garden tomorrow night. Madrigal probably knows the rest." She looked around. "I assume you don't have my necklace on you, or she'd be here."

"It's in the owner's safe. I didn't feel right carrying it to my own meeting."

Because it might have been stolen, she wondered, *or because you didn't want Madrigal eavesdropping?*

But that was a question that would, at best, go unanswered, and at worst irritate him and end the conversation. It was too soon for that.

"I'll need it and her. Sabbatus gave me everything I need to do it myself. Except for access to any of it, of course." She glanced around again and leaned in closer.

"Don't," Cas said. "The more secretive you look, the more folks will think you're saying something worth listening to."

She sat up straight, hands on her lap, but kept her voice low. "I suspect you could get me in given what I know of your past. My concern is that it might be a trap. If Sabbatus saw enough in me to know I'm capable of creating the medicine myself, he must know I'm working magic illegally. He might even know about Madrigal. I don't know what he can see."

"Maybe." Cas finished his food, taking smaller bites than she had, as well-mannered as anyone in the place. He seemed deep in thought. "I can't think why he'd trap you that way, though, when they could have arrested you there and then."

"Without proof?"

Cas laughed under his breath. "You think they'd be worried about your family coming for you if you disappeared?"

A chill ran up Gale's spine. "What else? I need more reason than that to trust him before I walk back in and take what's not mine."

"What was it you said he told you about sacrifices?"

"That his eyes weren't the only thing he lost when he took his position."

Cas nodded. "I never spent much time with old Sabbatus. He'd been set aside as a bit of a relic even when I was visiting the mages, and I doubt that's changed. How did that other fellow seem with him?"

Gale thought back to meeting Arthur and Sabbatus. "Respectful enough. He seemed to think Sabbatus would know if I were a threat. But dismissive. Not respectful as I'd have expected an elder mage to be treated."

"Sounds like how I remember it. I liked him from what I knew, though, and we spoke a few times. He seemed frustrated. So much power and wisdom, but there was little he could do with either within the confines of his assigned work and his position within the order of mages."

"He gained magic but lost the freedom to decide how to use it," Gale said. "So you think him helping me is what? A strike back at those above him? At the rules themselves?"

"No, there has to be more to it than that. You said it was like he was waiting for you?"

"Seems awfully convenient otherwise, doesn't it?"

"It does." Cas frowned at his plate. "I don't like it. If it were any other mage, I'd tell you it wasn't worth the risk, but with him I just don't know. What does your gut tell you?"

Gale pushed the rest of the food around on her plate. Her appetite had vanished. She hoped it was because of the conversation and not a sign of her illness progressing. "I don't know. I'm used to people telling me the answers. Back home, I'd go to the Luminary or the acolytes for advice. If they weren't sure, they'd consult the Teachings and previous interpretations. Whatever they told me would be right. I wouldn't have to worry about being wrong."

"But they're not here."

"No. If they were, they'd tell me to stay away from that garden, that the law doesn't matter, the mages' souls are as corrupted as any witch's." Gale set her fork down and took a deep breath. The answer was there, felt more than thought. All that was left was to speak it aloud. "But I've been making my own decisions since I left home. This is my journey, not theirs, and my thinking on witches has changed. If Madrigal was good—*is* good —then Sabbatus might also be. He's using me for his own purposes. I don't like not knowing what they are, but maybe it doesn't matter as long as we both get what we want."

Cas didn't answer.

Gale's head ached. It was too many maybes, too many unknowns. But then, the other option was to quit. "I'll run things by Madrigal," she said. "If she thinks the cure sounds like it might work, I suppose it's worth the risk."

Cas caught the eye of their server and nodded, then turned back to Gale. "Then I suppose you know what you want to do."

"But how do I get in? Boost myself over the garden wall?"

"You could, actually."

The server cleared their dishes, and another set down tea and a plate of little dessert cakes drizzled with pastel icings. Gale waited for the server to leave, then poured the tea while Cas spoke.

"The trouble with that route, as I learned early on, is that there's always a mage on guard who's alerted if anyone enters that way. Or, incidentally, through the front door. Or the kitchen door. Or the windows."

Gale smiled at the thought of a determined young Cas repeatedly entering and being tossed out of the Hall of Mages. "How did you poison Reginald, then?"

He flashed her a false wounded look. "It wasn't poison. It was a remedy. For an ailment he didn't have, and with rather explosive results, but—" He hid a smile behind his napkin. "There's another way, forgotten by everyone but the oldest mages, the king himself, and children who practice picking every lock they come across, even if it's on a box in the library that holds a dead man's letters. It's a long story involving a king of Andonia and one of the mages. Nothing you'd find in the history books, but—"

"I'd like to hear it some day," Gale said, trying to hurry him along without being rude. "You're saying there is a way in?"

"I think so. I was never brave enough to try it, myself. I knew where the entrance was, but not what I'd find beyond it. Didn't want to get lost in the dark."

"But I should risk it?"

Cas shrugged. "You found Alec, so I assume you'd find your way through this. Unless you want to look for an easier way."

Gale looked over the assortment of little cakes that would have tempted her on better days. Now she didn't think she could swallow a bite, and never would again if she waited for another chance at a cure.

"So then, will you get me into the palace?"

He thought for a moment, frowning. "I suppose I could, but that's all I can offer. Jes charges more than you can afford for work that puts her people in danger."

Gale held back a groan. "Is this where we negotiate?"

"I doubt it." Cas sipped his tea and nodded to a fellow who addressed him as Angus on his way out the door. He cocked his head to one side and regarded her with new interest. "You gave up your mother's ring. You have very little left to bargain with."

Gale sighed and slouched back in her chair. "That's where you're wrong. I have nothing left to bargain with."

"We wouldn't be speaking if I thought that were true. I'll do it for a promise of a favour."

Gale drummed her fingers against the table and thought it over. Cas wouldn't ask for anything too terrible, but she hesitated. "Jes told me that was a bad sort of deal to make."

"Desperate times, and all that. One favour, owed to Jes."

Gale scowled. "You're the one helping me, not her."

"These are my terms. Take them or leave them." Cas leaned back in his chair, relaxed, apparently not caring either way. "You get out of there, you do what you need to do for yourself and your people, and then you return to the shop. I suspect that with Alec gone, Jes will need a new appraiser at the very least, but I can't say for sure what she'll ask of you."

"And if I don't make it out of the Hall of Mages alive? Or if I decide to stay in Bright Hollow after I deliver the cure?"

Cas's eyes narrowed in a shrewd look that reminded Gale too much of his boss. "If you don't make it out, we'll call it even. If you decide to renounce your magic, which I assume would be the price of returning home..." He popped a cake into his mouth and chewed slowly. "Then I'll have been wrong about you. So will Jes. I'm willing to bet on those odds."

Gale's face warmed, and she looked down at her hands folded in her lap—one arm bandaged, one healthy. *I am going home*, she thought, but without the conviction she'd once felt.

She looked up at him. "Deal."

Be it on him if she escaped Jes's favour.

Cas wiped his hands on his napkin and stood. "Let's get your magic back, then. And your mentor. Gods know you'll need them."

CHAPTER THIRTY

THE STREETS WERE BUSIER LATE the next afternoon, and Gale had to dodge past people who seemed to naturally move out of the way for her formerly royal companion.

Madrigal simply walked through them.

"They won't sense the magic in my vessel when I enter the Hall?"

Cas strode across one of the cobblestone streets near the palace, apparently without looking for carriage traffic, and Gale followed.

"Perhaps not right away," Madrigal said. "If you're caught, or if they get close to you, they'll feel it. Stay out of their way and you might make it out undetected."

Gale's stomach clenched. Cas had procured a room for her at The Crooked Codfish and she'd fallen asleep in a comfortable bed, her heart full of hope. In the light of day, though, those happy ideas of success had evaporated, and the warm certainty she'd felt was replaced by cold, hard fear.

It was only worse now. As they passed through the busy streets and through throngs of people about their business on a fine, clear afternoon, Gale felt separate from all of it—distant and alone even as she stepped aside to avoid a small child tottering up the street and returned a nodded greeting from a silver-haired lady in a feathered hat.

Gale wore the same grey dress she'd had on the day before, but with the addition of her vessel tucked safely against her chest beneath layers of fabric. She carried her old knapsack, which held a knife, Alec's stylus, fresh bandages, and a few jars to hold the medicine she hoped would soon make the bandages unnecessary. She'd slept with the necklace on and decided she'd continue to do so until she returned home and had to destroy it.

And won't that put a crimp in Jes's plans for me, she thought with satisfaction that held off a little of the despair that came with the prospect of losing her magic forever.

"Stop fretting, girl," Madrigal said. She walked beside Gale, her presence strong thanks to the freshly refilled vessel. "It'll be what it'll be. At this point, what have you got to lose?" She took a longer look at Gale. "How are you feeling?"

Gale wished the ghost had kept needling her about her impending death. Actual concern made the whole thing seem more real.

"Fine," she lied. In truth, the world seemed to shiver at the edges of her vision, and it had taken her more than an hour after her noontime bath to dress and make herself look anything like presentable. She hadn't been able to hide the dark hollows beneath her eyes, but at least a fine dress and clean hair tied back in a thick, coiled braid made her look more tragic than terrifying.

Madrigal didn't look like she believed her, but she didn't press the question.

The palace gates stood open today. Beyond them, the palace rose like something from a child's bedtime story, pale and shining and perfect. A line of people, some well-dressed and others clearly more common, trailed back from its open doors almost to the street.

"Open court," Cas explained as they passed through the gates.

"Once a month, my father allows supplicants to bring their troubles before him directly—if they're willing to make the trip and wait in line."

Gale did a quick head count of those closest to her and estimated from there. "He can't see hundreds in a day. What happens to those who haven't been heard when the court closes?"

Cas smiled grimly. "There's always next month. Or local channels, going through the nobles and hoping the message gets through."

"That's a terrible system."

"It's more than his parents did. Anyway, we're not standing in line."

Gale cast a glance back at the folks waiting to enter as Cas led her away, around the side of the building. A few watched them go, obviously curious, and some seemed to consider following them in case there was another way in that hadn't been advertised. They stayed, though, unwilling to lose their place in line even if there was no hope of them getting in that day.

"You're sure this is all right?" Gale asked, hurrying to keep up with Cas's long strides. "I mean, you're not royal anymore, are you?"

"I am not. But I do occasionally have business here, and visits with my brothers aren't strictly forbidden." He patted the pocket of his suit jacket, which bulged slightly. "I have a birthday gift for my nieces in case anyone asks why I'm here."

"And what's my excuse?"

"You don't have one." Cas's steps slowed. "I'm trusting you not to cause anyone any harm, or to stir up any more trouble than necessary. If things go wrong and anyone finds out I let you in, it won't go well for either of us."

"I'll be careful. In and out, quiet as a mouse."

Cas looked a little pale, but nodded and continued on.

The grounds were a sumptuous green even in early spring and despite the constant chill of salty wind sweeping up from the ocean beyond the palace. Cas and Gale crossed neatly trimmed lawns and passed gardens of flowers that had no business blooming in such conditions, heading toward the south side of the palace.

"Hypocrites," Madrigal muttered. "The common folk can't use magic to keep crops growing through winter, but so long as it's the king's blessed, well-trained mages doing the work for the pleasure of visiting nobles..."

Gale repeated the notion to Cas, carefully reworded to avoid as much offense as possible, and he nodded. "Our kings and queens have had good reason for not wanting magic in the hands of those they can't control—look at the situation in your town if you need an idea of what the consequences could be. But your friend is right. This magic could help many more people if only they helped these few a little less."

Gale's brow furrowed. "Maybe you shouldn't have left the royal family, if that's the sort of thinking you brought to the table."

Cas grinned at her over his shoulder and brushed aside hair that the wind had whipped into his face. "Of course. I could've been a brilliant king if only I had the drive, the focus, and the willingness to kill off more than half a dozen family members who stood in my way."

Gale smiled back. "Small price to pay."

As they walked, they passed guards, each dressed in a blue coat that matched the palace's banners, darker pants, and shining boots that reached their knees. Swords hung at their sides, sheathed but present, and ice formed in Gale's stomach at the sight of them.

Cas progressed through the grounds without obstacle, but Gale imagined what it would be like for anyone else who tried to follow them. Drawn swords, threats, arrest... maybe worse. Even if an outsider knew about the passage to the Hall of Mages, it would be impossible to get into the palace to use it.

They turned the corner, walked farther across the thick green lawn, and passed through a gate set into a low wooden wall at the side of the palace. The carefully tended grasses and gardens disappeared, leaving something that more resembled a tidy barnyard set between the palace and the stone wall bordering the mages' forest. Any view of the cliffs and the ocean at the far end was blocked by another high wall that cut the wind significantly, sheltering the people and animals within the dirt-floored yard. Wooden shelters covered pens for the chickens that scattered before them, cackling derisively. Madrigal floated higher here, keeping her ghostly toes out of the dust. They followed the pale stone wall of the palace, as clean here beside the dirt and muck as everywhere else, and entered through the kitchen door.

Nearly a dozen servants, most of them women, bustled about a kitchen that seemed larger than any building in Bright Hollow. Steam from pots bubbling on the big iron stoves thickened the air, which held the mouth-watering scents of a variety of roasting meats and baking sweets. Piles of carrots, potatoes, and other vegetables waited on a long wooden table to be cut and cooked, and a wire rack by one wall was covered in round loaves of golden bread.

The king would be hungry at the end of a day like this, no doubt. Or maybe the wealthiest folks in Andonia always feasted like this. Gale had never considered Bright Hollow a poor place, but she'd only seen food like this set out for weddings and festivals.

Cas only stopped when they reached a wooden door set into the stone wall and found an older woman standing next to it, a steaming pie held in each hand, frowning at them. Her body was as narrow as one of the fenceposts outside, her features as sharp as the guards' swords.

Cas winked, held a finger to his lips, and smiled. The cook rolled her eyes and turned away.

Into a hallway next, Cas looking both ways before they went farther.

"She won't tattle on you?" Gale asked, feeling childish for phrasing it so—but then, Cas had seemed like a mischievous child up to harmless trouble when he'd hushed the cook.

"Not unless something goes terribly wrong and they trace it back to you. Mareen knows me. Or knew me, anyway."

Madrigal grumbled something under her breath, but when Gale turned back to her, she only shook her head.

Cas led the way down the silent corridor of stone walls, brighter and newer-feeling than the ones in the Hall of Mages, with a decorative carpet in shades of blue and grey running along the floor beneath them. Then he stopped and turned to Gale.

"There are only a handful of people who know about this passage. If anyone else ever uses it to get to the mages…"

"I understand." Gale's stomach turned at the thought of what would happen to her, whether it was her fault or not, if the secret got out. "I swear I'll forget it as soon as I'm done with it."

"Good. And make sure you leave over the wall when you're finished in the garden. You won't make it if you try to come back this way without me." He handed her a folded sheet of paper from his pocket. "This is a map of the Hall—enough to get you to the garden, I hope, if you can get yourself that far. Drawn from memory, but I noted as much as I could, as I'm not sure where this passage will come out. Destroy it as soon as you can."

Gale took the map and looked it over. The hall did look larger than it had from the outside, with a wing for bedrooms, an armoury not far from the front door, the garden, a library, a massive kitchen, and other rooms marked only with question marks. "Thanks."

Cas sighed. "I'm trusting you more than I should."

"Then why not blindfold me until we get to the passage?"

"I considered it," he said, sounding grim. "Wouldn't do much good when you have an invisible spy observing every step, though."

Gale looked to Madrigal and wondered whether it might be the ghost and not Gale herself that had Jes so interested in gaining a favour.

Even without a blindfold, Gale couldn't keep track of where they were going. The palace was a maze inside, and as she followed Cas, she got the impression he was doing his best to get her lost in it.

They entered a grand dining hall. The shining mahogany table could have seated dozens of people beneath the gold-and-glass chandeliers that hung from the soaring ceiling. Though it was set for a feast, with water and wine goblets at each place, candlesticks and greenery set out along its length, the room was empty.

Cas hurried along, sticking to the nearest wall, and Gale followed close behind. Then it was up stairs and down, pausing to hide behind corners when there were people ahead, avoiding guards and servants and nobles alike, crossing a balcony where the wind whipped Gale's hair and skirt mercilessly, then passing through a series of nearly identical hallways, all floored in warm wood and lit by sweet-smelling candles on the walls.

The next door Cas tried was locked. He cursed under his breath, then reached inside his jacket and produced a leather pouch from which he pulled a few long, slender pieces of bent metal. A few seconds later, the door was open.

"I warned him this was too easy before I left for good," Cas muttered.

"Good thing he didn't listen," Madrigal said.

Footsteps approached from around the corner at the end of the corridor. Cas's eyes narrowed and he pushed Gale through the door, following close behind before closing it gently and locking it behind him.

The windowless room beyond the door was something like a

small study. Not the king's primary office, surely, but a pleasant space with a dark and clean fireplace, a pair of cozy chairs, and shelves full of books. A waist-high case made of wood and glass stood to the right of where they'd entered, set a little out from the panelled wall, displaying a golden sword with jewels set into its hilt.

"What is this?" Gale asked, referring to both the sword and the room itself.

Cas didn't answer, but held up a hand for silence. Out in the hallway, the footsteps stopped outside the door. The handle rattled, but the lock held.

"Balthazar?" The voice was deep, strong. Not angry, but Cas gritted his teeth. "Does your mother know you're here?"

Cas darted around the display case. The space behind wasn't huge, but it was enough for him to crouch, run his fingers over the wall, and pop open a hidden door so low that Gale had to crawl to enter when Cas shooed her through.

"Don't turn back for anything," he said. "Bad enough that I'm in here. If they find I've brought a stranger, it'll be worse. And as for you—"

A key turned in the lock. Cas closed the door behind Gale. It clicked shut, leaving her in darkness. Muffled voices followed, Cas and someone else, but Gale couldn't make out what they were saying. And then they were gone.

"I should…" Gale whispered, but wasn't sure how to finish.

"What?" Madrigal asked, her voice loud and cutting in the darkness. "Go after him? Defend him? How do you think his warning was going to end—*And as for you, they'll throw you a party?* They'll cut off your head. Let the boy handle his own business. He knew the risks in bringing you here, and I'd wager he'll talk himself out of this in one piece as long as you don't show your face."

Gale sat for a few more moments, listening to her heart beating in her ears and hoping Cas would return. He didn't.

"*Alhaedren glosphaxe* will be the spell you want to use to light your way," Madrigal said.

"And then?"

"Then we'll see what you can do with the tools I've already given you."

Gale focused on her vessel and let the magic flow through her, feeling as though she'd done it a thousand times before. It wasn't like the first sip or the creation of her vessel, with magic lifting and overwhelming her. This was controlled and bearable, a slow draw rather than a crashing wave, though it still made her feel brighter, stronger, sharper, and more connected to the world.

The sickness was still in her, but it felt more distant than it had a moment ago.

"*Alhaedren glosphaxe,*" she whispered, turning the sounds in her mouth and letting them settle into her soul. The magic moved through her and her surroundings grew brighter—not like lamplight with a definable source, but faint, diffuse illumination that showed a passage high enough to stand and walk in, its corners heavily decorated with cobwebs, that vanished into inky blackness ahead.

"Not bad," Madrigal said. "With practice you'll get more brightness and use less power to do it."

There was a time, Gale realized, when she would have taken that as criticism and been stung by it, wishing for praise over her efforts and meagre results. Now she found she was only eager to try again and do better.

She peered into the darkness. "I hope this isn't as much of a maze as Cas seemed to think it was."

That hope was dashed not twenty paces down, when the path branched left and right with no indication of which to take. Gale chose left.

After thirty paces she stepped on a loose stone that gave way beneath her. She darted back, heart pounding, landing on solid footing as a dark chasm opened in the floor. She sent the light down, revealing a drop to rusted metal spikes waiting to welcome anyone who cared to throw themselves on them.

She waited for her heart to stop pounding before she turned back to find Madrigal staring at her, pale and speechless.

"Other way, I guess," Gale said, aiming for confidence but not managing to keep the tremor out of her voice. She returned to the fork in the path and took the right-hand passage, which led down a steep staircase. At the bottom, she found not two, but three dank and dark paths to choose from.

"Could you scout ahead?" she asked.

"I could, a little. Wouldn't have seen that last trap until you put your weight on it, though." Madrigal crossed her arms and waited.

Of course, Gale thought, feeling foolish. It had taken her far too long to turn to magic before. It would cost her power to use the spell now, but it was the surest and quickest way to find her way forward.

Panic flickered like small lightning through Gale's guts as she tore through her memories. The jumble of unfamiliar phrases made her wish for the years she'd lost when she should have been studying the language of magic. It would make remembering spells so much easier if she understood what they meant.

But then, there it was, lying with the memory of searching for Alec. It would need to be adjusted for her new target, but it would do. She focused on the old mage, on how strange she'd felt with his non-existent eyes piercing her soul.

"Saehaelthan Sabbatus'dru homilcorpu."

Green light appeared down the passage straight ahead, and Gale released her illumination spell so as not to interfere with it.

They set off, following Gale's magic, to find the Hall of Mages.

CHAPTER THIRTY-ONE

EVEN WITH MAGIC'S AID, the journey took longer than should
have been possible. If the king had some secret shortcut, Gale's
magic didn't know about it, and with every step that didn't end at
the Hall of Mages, Gale's concern that the mages had protected
themselves against her spell deepened. The sun would be setting
at any moment, and she couldn't afford to be lost and miss the
full moon.

"We should go back," she whispered as they descended the
third spiral staircase she'd encountered, which looked suspiciously like the first.

"And do what?" Madrigal asked. "How will you sneak back
through the palace without Cas? How will you get into the
garden before the full moon disappears for another month?"

Gale crouched and rested her head in her hands, keeping half
her mind on maintaining her spell. "There's magic in these
passages."

"Of course there is." Madrigal sat next to her. "You thought
the mages would be satisfied with secret doors? If anyone
followed the king this way, they'd want pursuers to be just as
confused as you are right now."

Gale looked at the light ahead, which seemed to be shining from the bottom of the staircase. It was stronger than it had been when they began, and when she'd first seen these stairs.

"We are making progress." She stood slowly, bracing herself against the wall. "It's an illusion. A trick. Something."

The walls wavered in front of her. Not magic, but the fever gripping her tighter. A hard shudder wracked her body, awakening a deep ache in her bones she'd been trying to ignore.

"Then let's go."

Every step down jostled her, and by the time they reached the bottom, her head pounded. She wished she'd brought water along. Her mouth felt like someone had stuffed it with cotton.

Then, after more twisting and turning, the passage ended in a flat door with a simple catch on Gale's side to open it.

She paused. "What do I say to make the tracking stop? I don't need to find Sabbatus, and I'd rather save what magic I can."

"Good," Madrigal said. She, too, whispered, perhaps fearing the mages could hear a ghost. "Just let go of it."

Gale closed her eyes, shutting out the light, and focused on keeping her magic inside her vessel. It still felt strong, more full than it had after the first time she'd used the tracking spell, but it didn't seem it could possibly be enough to kill a curse.

When she opened her eyes again, the light was gone. Gale pushed the door open, just a crack at first. When nothing happened, she opened it fully and crept into the room beyond.

They'd come to a windowless study with a cold fireplace and a pair of plush chairs, emerging from a low door behind a chest-high display case. A lamp burned on the wall, identical to the one in the room they'd left at the castle.

Gale's stomach sank. "We're back where we started."

Madrigal drifted around the room, taking everything in. "Not quite. It's convincing though, isn't it? Step around here and look."

The room was a replica of the locked room in the palace, right down to the pale stone of the fireplace and the walls lined with books. But the sword in the display case was wrong—not gold, but solid, shining black. Gale held her open palms over the glass and felt magic vibrating within.

"Is it black glass?"

"Obsidian. Volcanic stone from oceanic islands, and similar to glass when you see it down to its base construction. Shatters easily if not protected magically, but if it is, it cuts like a razor. Probably ceremonial, though."

Gale looked over the books. At first glance they could be the same as those on the king's shelves, but the gold lettering on the spines formed strange and unfamiliar shapes on many of them, and the ones she could read—*Alkemy of the Highest Order, Principles of the Seeker*—would have been most out of place in the palace or any respectable home.

"The magic is strong here," Madrigal said. Gale couldn't tell whether this pleased or irritated her. "Let me see how far I can wander, get a sense of place."

Madrigal drifted through the wall. Gale sat and waited. And waited. Then stood and paced the room. She longed to sit and rest in one of the chairs, but falling asleep was too great a risk. The sun had set. The full moon would be shining, for whatever it was worth.

If she survived, Gale decided she'd need to find out why the moon's light mattered in creating a potion. It probably made perfect sense to someone who understood magic instead of clumsily using it, but she hadn't the faintest idea.

She touched her vessel and felt out its magic again. Present, but so small. There was more in the ambience of the building than she carried with her, coming from beyond the door.

Gale pulled it open and stepped into a dimly lit room. A few candles burned on the walls. They must have been burning for a while, as no one was there to have recently lit them, but not a drop of wax had fallen from any of them. Their light illuminated a narrow room lined with heavy wooden shelves, which were covered in strange objects—mirrors, bowls and platters, and weapons from swords to maces. Most of the objects felt of magic when Gale put her hand near them.

The only objects that didn't seem to contain any were narrow glass vials near the door at the opposite end of the room. Dozens of them sat in silver racks, lined up like soldiers, each filled with a small amount of dark indigo liquid.

Gale pulled Cas's map from her bag. He'd noted "armoury?" on a room at the north end of the building. One he'd heard of but never entered, maybe. It fit better than any of the other marked rooms, and placed Gale relatively close to the garden courtyard.

She looked back to the vials and wondered what part they played in magical battle, and why the mages needed so many weapons when their business seemed to lie mostly in swift beheadings and train tracks. She touched a vial and still felt nothing.

The stopper flipped open easily, and a dizzying rush of magic flowed out from the bottle, stronger than what she'd felt from any enchanted object in the room. And that was only its ambience. *If I touched it, I wonder—*

Madrigal came back through the door and frowned at the vial. "What's that?"

"I don't know. It might just be magic, but stronger than *lucistra*."

The lines between Madrigal's eyebrows deepened as she passed her hand through the vials on the shelf. "Could be like that," she said. "But it's incredibly potent. Probably contains ingredients most witches have never heard of, let alone tested. I wouldn't try it if I were you. Might not have dared even when I was alive. We all have our limits, and there's no telling what they play with here."

Gale nodded but didn't put the vial down even after she closed it and any sense of the power within vanished, perfectly hidden within what had to be enchanted glass.

My vessel is so small and weak. The curse is so strong.

"What did you see out there?" she asked. When Madrigal looked toward the door, she tucked the vial into her sash. It vanished beneath the fabric, safe and secure.

The Teachings would say it was wrong to steal, even from people like the mages who were already doing wrong. Gale decided she'd feel terrible about it later if she had time to do so.

"The halls are clear," Madrigal said. She clenched her fists tight at her sides, but they still trembled.

"What's wrong?" Gale asked.

"I peered through keyholes, and I was vexed." Madrigal dragged her fingers over her face. She wasn't shaking with fright, Gale realized, but anger. "Popped into a few rooms. No bedchambers in this bit. But the equipment they have. The books, the knowledge, the..." She shook her head. "Don't think too badly of me if I weep when I see what miracles they've got tucked away in the garden."

"I'm sorry," Gale said. "You could have done great things in your lifetime with those resources."

"No." Madrigal flashed her a rueful smile. "I could have done the king's bidding, and no more. Your new friend Sabbatus found that out too late."

"But imagine if everyone could use them."

Madrigal shook her head. "That was decided long ago, dear Nightingale. No sense moaning about it when there's work to be done. Shall we go out?"

A wave of dizziness swirled through Gale's mind, but she made herself smile. "We shall."

Gale tried the door, expecting it to be locked, but it opened smoothly and soundlessly onto a bright corridor very much unlike the one she had seen when she came in as a guest. The stone had been covered with white clay, and bright paintings hung between cheerful glass lamps, depicting detailed scenes of country life and great battles.

Guess the drab and gloomy sorcerer image is just for outsiders.

The thought cheered her, for Sabbatus's sake. If the mages had to leave their families and lives behind to do their work here, it was nice to think they did it in comfort.

Madrigal turned her nose up at the paintings. She said nothing, though, and held a finger to her lips when Gale sent her a questioning look.

She was right, of course. No one had come to investigate when they entered, but anyone could be listening.

Gale unfolded Cas's map and followed it past several closed doors, each with a different flavour of magic vibrating behind it. She wished she'd asked Cas more questions about exactly what kind of work they did here beyond keeping the train running, how long they'd been at it, how many mages there were, but it was too late for that now.

Madrigal went ahead and motioned for Gale to wait. She did, and distracted herself from the eerie silence of the sleeping building by examining a painting depicting black-robed mages standing in a ring, arms raised, surrounding a massive white column.

Madrigal returned and nodded at the image. "They probably think they hung the sun in the sky, too," she whispered. "The garden is just ahead. Open courtyard, no door to pass through. There's a mage, though. Probably keeping watch. He's drifted off in a chair not far from the garden entrance."

"He'll wake if I pass, though."

It wasn't a question, but Madrigal nodded. "I can slip into his dreams and keep him asleep. At least, I think I can. How well do you remember what Sabbatus told you? The ingredients, the spell?"

Gale's blood seemed to pool in her feet, leaving her cold and faint. "I can't do this without you."

"You can." Madrigal rested her hands on Gale's arms, sending gooseflesh racing over her entire body. "You have a long way to go, girl, but you've got talent. More than that, you've paid attention—to me in your childhood, to the shadowy bits of the world around you even when you shouldn't have been looking so close, to your lessons since you returned to my cabin." She smiled, but Gale caught the uncertainty in her mentor's eyes even as she spoke encouragement. "Use your magic and the gifts of the garden. Use your intent and Sabbatus's words. Feel it more than you think it. Pray first, if it helps." The smile faltered. "But forget the Teachings and decide for yourself whether this gift is meant for you. If it is, your God will guide your hands and your mind, and you will save your people."

Gale's mouth went dry. "Do you really believe that?"

"I believe it matters that you do."

Tears stung the backs of Gale's eyes. Her hands trembled as she reached for her vessel and the comforting thrum of magic within it. It felt right and good. Folks back home would say that was the lie of evil, drawing her away from the Path, but...

She nodded. "I'll try. And thank you."

"Good. And if you fail, get out as quick as you can. Don't let them catch you here."

A snorting snore echoed from around the corner.

"He's waking," Madrigal said. "Give me half a minute before you move."

She didn't add, *You're on your own now*, but that was all Gale could think as she counted off the seconds in her mind.

THE GUARD, a grey-robed mage a few decades younger than Sabbatus, slept fitfully in a cane chair set off to one side of the hallway. Beyond him, the corridor opened into a moonlit garden that looked as lush and abundant as Madrigal's ever had. Gale crept forward, paused as the mage shifted and let out a low moan, and moved forward again, her back pressed to the wall opposite him.

Madrigal was gone. She was doing her work, but the mage was fighting her. She'd be occupied until the moment Gale cleared the garden wall and made her escape.

I can do this. Gale repeated the thought to herself with every silent step, but it felt wrong. She wasn't a proper apprentice. Barely a student, and with only a few days' real experience. And this was a new spell, untested, perhaps dangerous.

But there was nothing to do but go on.

Gale stepped into the moonlight and forgot about Madrigal and the guard. Even her exhaustion, aches, and the pain in her arm were swept away for a moment by the magic and potential of the plants that filled the space, which was easily as large as the palace dining room. They spilled over the edges of raised beds and trailed across the pathways between, releasing floral and herbal scents into the air in a perfectly blended perfume. They climbed the three garden walls and the building behind her. They sprouted up from between the stones under her feet, a dazzling symphony of life in a thousand varieties, all of it fighting for its place in the world.

Never—not in the woods, not in Madrigal's garden—had she felt such power and clarity. The energy in the plants screamed for her attention, and when she brushed her fingers over the leaves and petals, she felt a deep sense of their potential. She hadn't learned their names or their properties, but it felt as though her understanding could take her halfway there.

A bat flitted overhead in pursuit of a pale green moth. Otherwise, she was alone.

On a pedestal in the centre of the garden sat a bowl the size of a large wash basin, gleaming unnaturally bright in the faint moonlight—the one Sabbatus had said would be the key to her success. Gale stepped closer, her chest tight, and peered in. Water filled the bowl more than halfway, reflecting the image of a full moon shimmering beneath the surface, its power trapped in the water.

She tried to remember what Sabbatus had told her. The thoughts moved like molasses, but they came.

A bit of ramhorn, roots from a common rose, and a bit of what they call githarmus. Big white blossoms on thick stalks.

Gale left the bowl and its miniature moon and searched the garden, knife in hand. She found ramhorn easily enough, with its spiralling seed pods hiding under clouds of white fluff. Sabbatus hadn't specified which part to use, so she took a few full stalks. Her left hand was going numb, but she managed to hold the stem steady while she cut.

A single patch of red roses grew on low bushes in the back corner. One of the thorns cut her as she moved the stems aside to get at the roots, plunging her fingers deep into the rich soil to pull some up and cut them away. She ignored the blood as she tore Cas's map into tiny pieces and buried them under the bush.

Whether she succeeded or failed, its job was done.

There were several flowers that fit Sabbatus's description of githarmus, and though she got a vague sense of healing from them, it wasn't enough. But there'd been more to it. *Smells like rotting meat soaked in honey.*

She closed her eyes and caught nothing. The perfumes of the other flowers were too strong. But when she leaned in close to a flower with cupped blooms like a massive lady's slippers, she caught sickening sweetness underlaid with rot. The smell intensified as she plucked one fat flower, and she gagged.

An owl cried in the trees outside the garden, breaking her focus and the fragile flow of her thoughts. She looked down at the plants in her hands. The cursed arm trembled, and a stalk of ramhorn fell to the ground. When she bent to pick it up, her fingers wouldn't obey her command.

There's still time, she told herself. *Only hurry.*

The smell of the githarmus filled the air, so thick she tasted it.

It smelled like the clinic in Bright Hollow, like cursed flesh and death.

How many have died since I left? Have more fallen ill?

She tried to brush the questions away with the thought of those she might still save, but as she gathered up her skirt to hold the ingredients, she couldn't imagine the future at all. The world swam drunkenly around her as she dragged her feet back to the bowl at the centre of the garden.

Not yet. Please, not yet.

Despair crept over her, dark and cloying, as she set the plants out at the foot of the pedestal. Suddenly they were strangers to her, and no matter how she thought it through, she couldn't figure out what to do with them. It was too much—the danger, her inexperience, the lack of trained eyes watching over her. The fever sweat on her brow felt like a layer of ice.

It's too hard. I'm getting sicker, I can't think, I need Madrigal, I can't remember anything.

Madrigal's voice answered from memory. *Feel it more than you think it.*

But that wasn't all she'd said.

Gale closed her eyes and did the thing that came most naturally to her, the thing she'd been trained to do in good times and bad since before she'd been old enough to understand what she was doing.

Guide me, God, she thought, not daring to whisper her prayer. *Let me save my people. Let me show them how good magic can be. I haven't left the Path. I only wish to illuminate what lies beyond.*

There was no answer, no rush of inspiration and understanding. No yes, no no. There was just... nothing.

But when she let herself draw magic from her vessel, her mind went still. The doubts vanished, and her fears became insignificant. She reached for the ramhorn and remembered her lessons at Madrigal's table in the shed when she was a child—

crushing plants, releasing the juices, listening to what the magic told her.

She didn't know whether this was God or magic answering her prayer, and she decided it didn't matter.

This is my calling. God forgive me if it's wrong.

Gale stopped thinking and let her hands work, using a stone from the wall of a garden bed to crush roots and seeds against the ground, discarding parts she felt wouldn't harmonize with her intentions.

She worked as though in a trance, the mages and the garden forgotten as she drew Alec's stylus from her bag, set the ingredients in the bowl with the moon water, and stirred. Magic flowed from her vessel and through her body, filling and lifting her, and the spell came as though it had been etched on her heart.

"Arnithip rounduul carlatian," she whispered. It felt like a song in her throat, full and warm and powerful, a thing that came not from her mind or from a teacher's instructions, but from the depths of her soul.

Separate bits of plant matter melted together, filling the silver bowl with warm light. The water thickened to a heavy golden ointment that glowed as bright as the stars before darkening to a deep, forbidding purple. Gale couldn't see the moon in it anymore, but it had done its work.

Movement to her right, near the top of the wall, threatened to draw her attention away. Gale closed herself off from it, unwilling to lose even a hint of the power that flowed from her into the moon bowl.

The power from her vessel lessened as it flowed into the unfinished medicine.

Movement again. A dark shape dropped into the garden and stalked closer, stumbling and crashing through the flowers.

"Stop," Gale said. She tried to hold onto the magic and her intentions, but the magic went silent. She turned.

Hawk's hair lay in thick clumps against his face, and one arm hung useless, the shoulder slumped. Above the dark shadow of his untrimmed beard, veins of cursed flesh traced up his cheek. He came closer, half-limping, his eyes bright and his skin shining with fever, terrifying as a rabid wolf stalking through the forest.

"They know you're here," Gale added, trying to keep her trembling voice quiet. She touched a finger to the thick salve in the bowl. It didn't feel like anything, and wouldn't until her power and intention finished the job. "Go back now. Run as far and as fast as you can. I'm almost done with the cure. I'll find you when it's safe."

Hawk strode toward her as though he hadn't heard.

CHAPTER THIRTY-TWO

HAWK PAUSED as he stepped out of the shadows, sweat glinting off his brow and off the dirty hunting knife in his good hand. His breath came heavy, lifting his shoulders beneath his sweat-stained white shirt with each inhalation. Filthy bandages trailed their ends toward the ground from his cursed arm, and the stink of rotting flesh invaded the garden.

And I thought I was badly off, Gale thought.

She held out her hands and nodded to the salve in the bowl. "This is it, Hawk. This is our cure. Give me a moment to finish, and I'll test it on myself first. If it works for us, we'll know it'll work for everyone at home."

Hawk took a shuffling step closer. It was a wonder he'd made it over the wall. How much prayer had it taken for him to find that kind of strength?

The whites of his eyes showed brighter than they should have in the pale light as he took her in, focusing not on her hands but on the vessel that hung around her neck.

"You're a witch," he rasped, nodding at the medicine without taking his eyes off the necklace. "Corrupted. I knew it."

She held the pendant up to him, letting it dangle on its chain. "I'm not, I swear. This is the magic I'm using. It's not in me."

He stepped closer again, and Gale took an instinctive step away from the salve.

"There won't be magic in the medicine once it's finished," she added, though she only hoped it was as true for this cure as it had been for the one she'd made with Madrigal. "It was simply necessary for its creation. This won't corrupt anyone."

Hawk's upper lip curled, reminding Gale of the hunting dog he'd kept until he'd decided he worked better alone. "You think the Luminary will accept that? Or you, after what you've done?"

Gale dropped the pendant, and it landed heavy against her chest. Beneath it, something pained her heart as she fought against the crushing weight of Hawk's words. She'd allowed herself to think she could go home, that everything would be all right, but this was the truth of it, ugly as the curse, bare as the rage in her brother's eyes.

Bright Hollow would allow folks to live many kinds of lives, but there was no room for magic.

"Perhaps she'll see the wisdom of allowing extraordinary measures in desperate times," she said. "I've searched for other answers, Hawk. This is the only way."

Hawk coughed and spat a wad of pale phlegm into the bushes. "You think the Luminary'll see this as God's will? You as God's shree—" He gritted his teeth. "*Shield* against the curse, when the price is the corruption of your soul?" He broke into another coughing fit and doubled over with its force.

From inside the Hall, a long, howling wail sounded. Human. Angry. The mage, perhaps, fighting the dream that kept him asleep. Others would hear, if they hadn't already been alerted by Hawk's entry.

"Please, Hawk." Gale's voice trembled. "Let me finish. We'll see what God has provided through magic. Then we can get out of here. Let wiser minds than ours decide."

"The decision isn't the Lumner… Lumnimary's decision, either. Luminary, I mean." Hawk wiped his mouth on his bandaged hand and winced. Another step closer and the smell of his wounds enveloped her, like the githarmus flower without its sweetness, but deeper and deadlier. "She answers to God. And the Teachings say—"

"What?" A fire kindled in Gale's heart, filling her with a certainty she'd never felt before, burning away what she'd been taught and leaving only what she knew. "They say you should suffer like this, that we should all die rather than use magic? That we shouldn't use every weapon available to us to fight for our lives and those of the folks we love? Then the Teachings are wrong."

Hawk's eyes widened as though she'd struck him. "You'd turn your back on God so easily?"

"No." Gale swallowed hard. "I am doing God's will, Hawk, even if the Teachings would have it otherwise. If you were thinking clearly, you'd see it." Gale reached slowly into the bowl and drew out a little of the ointment on her fingertips, full of potential waiting to be set free. "There's power here, given in the world God created. You've seen how the curse affects minds. Let me finish this and heal you. The pain will end, your mind will clear, and you'll be able to think better. I swear."

His eyes narrowed. "You swear on what? Not your soul."

"On our love for each other as siblings and friends." No matter where it had led, no matter what they felt in this moment, family was still the purest thing she could think of to swear on. "You're dying, Hawk. Whatever has happened between us, I want you to live and be happy. Please believe me."

Hawk lowered his head, but his gaze didn't leave her. His hair hung in sweaty hanks over his forehead, making him look wilder than he had before, but he stepped forward calmly and quietly, unwrapping his bandage and dropping it to the ground.

His knife landed beside it with a clatter of metal against stone.

The hand beneath the bandages was barely recognizable as human. The curse had eaten deep into his flesh, leaving it raw and open, and what scraps of skin were left had taken on a deathly ashen and scaled appearance. It was impossible to see how far it had spread. Certainly his entire arm, and likely further.

It's a miracle he's still walking, she thought, and a lump filled her throat. If this was the miracle, then God was on his side in this, not hers.

Her old self would have given up then, submitted to the wisdom of the Luminary and those who had studied the Teachings.

I am not that girl. I will not be caged.

"Stay where you are," she said. "The mages will be here any moment."

She raised her hands above the bowl and drew on the power of her vessel.

Magic flowed.

Hawk darted forward and, with impossibly quick and controlled movements for someone so ill and injured, grabbed her, spun her around, and pressed his stinking, rotten hand against her upper chest, his other hand gripping her vessel. With a heavy grunt he pulled, snapping the chain. Gale cried out and lunged for the necklace, but Hawk's arms were too long, and he held her away.

Hawk snarled and shoved her. She nearly caught herself, but the backs of her legs hit the edge of a raised garden bed, and she tumbled backward into the fragrant herbs.

Hawk picked up his knife and held it high—not aimed to hurt her, with the handle facing downward over her vessel.

"No!" Gale pushed herself toward him, but it was too late.

With a pained cry, Hawk dropped to his knees and brought the knife down. The fragile stone cracked and burst from its housing. Gale drew in a hard, sharp breath and felt desperately for her magic, trying to call it to her. But though the power hung heavy in the air, left behind by centuries of mages' work, there was nothing she herself could draw on. Without magic of her own, her thoughts clouded with exhaustion.

Nothing. I have nothing.

She held back a scream.

A shout echoed from the hallway, followed by another. The guard might not have wakened, but his struggles had drawn the others.

Gale turned to run, but Hawk caught her by the back of her jacket. At that moment, the mage from the hallway stumbled in, black robes askew and hair mussed, glaring at them in rage and confusion.

Madrigal reappeared between him and Gale. "I'm sorry. I tried, I—" She caught sight of the vessel lying broken on the ground and snarled, then rushed at Hawk, scratching at his eyes and clawing at his arms. He didn't seem to feel anything.

"*Galanthaen spiranti golrouns,*" the mage intoned.

Madrigal cried out and vanished.

"What did you do?" Gale demanded, her voice breaking.

The mage, seeming more able to pull himself together now that Madrigal was gone, came closer. "A simple banishment. Something anyone dealing with spirits should learn before they get into trouble."

Gale held back a sob, but her face warmed with rage even as fear chilled her to the bone. *Temporary, it must be temporary, he couldn't—*

"What's going on here?" The mage stepped toward the bowl in the centre of the garden and waved his hand over it.

Hawk shoved Gale forward. She stumbled and fell at the mage's feet, scraping her hands on the stones of the path. "This woman is a witch accused of crimes against my hometown. I tracked her here, not realizing I was in—invaporing..." He squeezed his eyes closed. "*Invasioning* the garden of the king's mages. I apologize. I'll take her now. No more trouble."

Three more hooded figures appeared at the entrance to the garden, and the mage nodded for them to come closer. Gale searched their faces, desperately hoping, but Sabbatus wasn't among them.

"No need," the mage said. He glanced at Hawk's ruined hand. "It is within our rights to deal with illegal magic, especially when it delivers itself into our hands."

Gale tried to catch Hawk's gaze, silently pleading.

Get us out of here. Get us outside these walls and we can still make this right. Don't let them take me.

Hawk locked eyes with Gale as he spoke again. "She's yours. Do what you want with her."

Gale pushed herself up to kneel on the hard ground. "You'll die, Hawk."

"I know. But I'll go with my soul clean and my conscience clear." He crossed his arms, and for a moment seemed perfectly lucid. "I'll pray for you."

A tear slipped from Gale's eye. "I'll do the same for—"

"*Alierhi praliens,*" the mage said, barely loud enough to be heard.

Hawk stiffened and fell face-first to the ground. Gale scrambled toward him, but the mage held her back, whispering another spell. The strength drained from Gale's limbs until she was limp as a ragdoll. The mage dropped her and snapped his fingers, and the others came forward.

"Take them both to the cells," he ordered.

Gale was about to object when he waved a hand before her eyes. The visible world vanished, leaving her with only the awareness of rough hands lifting her, and the empty ache in her heart.

CHAPTER THIRTY-THREE

GALE WASN'T sure when she'd lost track of her body, or how long she'd been trapped in her mind with thoughts that tumbled like autumn leaves blown on the wind. It was only when the world began to come back to her that she realized it had been missing at all.

The first things she noticed were the smells and the sounds. Dripping water, moldering hay, damp rock. Then the hard, cold stone beneath her and behind her back—someone had propped her up in a sitting position. She assumed the sense that everything was spinning around her was only part of the mage's spell, or the fever burning through her brain.

Gale opened her eyes slowly. Her head pounded, and the light from a single lantern shining beyond rusted iron bars pierced her with fresh agony and a wave of nausea. She closed her eyes, gave it a moment, and tried again.

Only two of the walls that surrounded her were stone. The others were iron bars, separating her from another, similar cell and a small room beyond. There was a door out there, plain wood and iron set into stone, but that was no use to her if the cell was locked. There wasn't much else—a lantern that lit the space, a leaking water pump outside the cell, and a table with two pairs of boots set out beneath it. Hers and Hawk's. She wished the mages hadn't taken them, though they'd have done little to ease the cold.

They'd taken her jacket, leaving her arms almost bare save for the bandage nearly covering the right.

The only other feature in the room was an axe that hung on the wall outside her cell, just out of reach. Its metal head reflected purple in the torchlight, forbidding and strange.

Madrigal's words played through her mind. *They say the mages' weapons cut through bone like it's butter. Makes for a less painful death, I suppose, but what they'd do to you with it beforehand...*

She looked away but couldn't help feeling like the blade was watching her, waiting to strike.

Hawk lay on a pile of flattened straw in the second cell. He wasn't moving save for the steady rise and fall of his breath.

I was so close.

The cure would have worked. Even without Madrigal's voice in her ear, she knew it. She'd felt it in the reactions of the ingredients, in the way her intentions had aligned perfectly with the possibilities.

A little more magic. A little more time. I could have saved us all.

She waited for despair to come. Instead, a strange peace filled her, deep and sure as anything she'd ever felt in prayer.

Maybe it was God. Maybe it wasn't. Maybe it never had been, or always would be. For the first time, she let herself simply sink into it, content with not knowing the answers, but understanding she'd done the best she could with the pieces she'd been given.

She wiggled her fingers and her stockinged toes, willing the feeling to come back into her body, and took fresh stock of her cell.

It was small, barely wide enough to stretch out in if she'd wanted to lie down and only a little deeper front to back. Rusted chains hung from a flat slab of stone that jutted out from the wall, with manacles dangling from the ends.

Hawk grunted, then slowly opened his eyes.

Gale scuttled slowly to the opposite side of her cell and braced her back against the damp wall, pushing herself to standing. Her legs burned in protest and the world tilted around her, but she managed to stay upright.

Hawk blinked up at the ceiling. "Gale, what have you done?"

"Shut up." Gale's tongue was as heavy and slow as the rest of her muscles. From her new position she could see the top of the table and the evidence laid out there—a glass jar filled with a dark substance that had to be her unfinished salve, Hawk's hunting knife, and her broken vessel. She stretched an arm between the bars. All of it was well out of reach, and all of it except the knife was useless to her now.

The axe on the wall was close enough that it seemed to laugh at her as she pressed herself against the bars, desperate for a weapon, for magic, for anything. But aside from the weapon she felt no magic in the room at all.

"Madrigal?" she whispered, but there was no answer. Without magic in her there was no way for the witch to find her apprentice, even if she'd only been sent back to the borderlands.

The wooden door beyond the bars creaked open, and an unfamiliar mage entered. She was tall—maybe as tall as Hawk— and broad in the shoulder, with ice-blue eyes and striking features that no one would ever call pretty, but Gale was awed for a moment by her stark, raw beauty. A long braid of silver hair hung down her back, but her face was unlined.

She leaned back against the table and took one of the jars in her hands. "Care to explain this?"

Gale struggled to think clearly. "I bought that from a fellow in Queen's Run. He said it would cure our curse, but only if I charged it in your moon bowl."

The mage raised an eyebrow. "You don't say? And what was this witch's name?"

"Alec." No point protecting the dead. There was nothing the mages could do to him now, and it would serve them right if she sent them off hunting him. "I didn't get anything more than that."

"Hmm." The mage set the jar aside. "You're not a witch yourself, that much is clear. But I don't believe anyone but you made this medicine." She nodded at Hawk, who now sat with his back against the wall of his cell, glaring at her. "He broke your vessel?"

Gale didn't answer.

The mage smiled. "It doesn't matter whether you confess or not. You were caught breaking into the Hall. Even if the remnants of magic weren't clinging to you, we'd be within our rights to put both of you to death."

"I didn't do anything wrong," Hawk said. "I was chasing a witch. I was doing you a favour. I had no idea—"

The mage silenced him with a cold glare. "I'll hear your confession later, hunter. I'm sure your lies will be quite amusing." She turned to Gale again and held up the remnants of her vessel. "This medicine of yours was an ambitious attempt at magic. I don't doubt it would have worked if you'd finished the job, or that you have talent. Pity you chose to use it illegally. You could have done well here if you'd come to join us instead."

Gale gritted her teeth as she thought of the garden, the armoury, the luxurious train and the king's garden.

"Well, but not good."

The mage set the necklace down. "Meaning what?"

Gale leaned her forehead against the bars. Her head felt too large, too heavy. "I could have done well. Learned much. Gone far. But what good would I have done for anyone except the king and those closest to him? My village would have died of its curse."

The mage's lips tightened. "We are called to a higher purpose, beyond even the king's whims."

Gale laughed. "Sure."

The mage slipped Gale's broken vessel into her pocket. "I'll see you again soon," she said, addressing both of them. "I'd advise against shouting for help. No one will hear, and you'll only waste what strength you have left." She left them, closing the door tight behind her. Her key turning in the lock came like the toll of a funeral bell.

Gale eased herself to the cold stone floor. "If you'd have left me alone, I could have made it over the wall with our cure and we wouldn't be stuck in here."

The lamp's light flickered in Hawk's eyes, which shone bright with fever. "I'd have died either way, by curse if not by execution. And you might have escaped if I'd let you finish." He nodded at the axe on the wall. "At least this way I'll die knowing that you..." He cleared his throat.

Gale sucked in a hard breath. "What? Got what I deserved?" It didn't seem she should be able to feel more pain than she was already in, but it felt like she'd taken a punch to the gut.

"Knowing you'll die without the permanent corruption that would have come when you made yourself a true witch." His voice caught, and a tear trailed down one side of his nose. "And you would have. Maybe not soon, but in time."

Gale opened her mouth to object but stopped herself. He was right. She'd taken every step of this journey leaving stones scattered over the ground so she could find her way back to the Path, but the thought of following them seemed laughable.

It might as well have been a breadcrumb trail eaten up by wild birds for all the use she'd make of it now.

There was no way she could believe that God's will was for her to ignore her potential and return to her cage. The idea was ridiculous. All she wished was that she'd seen it sooner.

"You're right," she said, tears burning her eyes. Not from shame or even regret, but for what it cost to speak the words aloud. "Not about the corruption, that's entirely wrong. But I would have kept going with this. No external magic would have been enough. I've tasted freedom and known the beauty of magic. To give it up would kill me."

"Then I've saved you," Hawk said. He didn't sound happy, exactly, but there was no doubt or hesitation there.

Gale turned away. They might as well have been speaking different languages, and trying to open the eyes of the willfully blind was a waste of precious minutes. She stood again, gripped the cell's bars, and studied the objects on the table.

They'd taken her bag, but that was of little use anyway. She'd used up all the *lucistra* she'd made in Alec's shop when she refilled her vessel. She had no ingredients to make more to create a new one, or to fill it. But if she'd had some...

She gasped and patted down her sides, slipping her fingers inside the sash of her ridiculous, pocketless dress. They'd have searched those if she'd had them, just as they had the insides of her boots. But there—the hard lump of a vial that didn't have to be large, given the apparent potency of the potion within.

Even now, knowing what it contained, she felt no magic in it. The mages guarded their secrets well.

Madrigal had said it was too dangerous, likely too much for an experienced witch, never mind an apprentice who had only begun exposing herself to magic. There was no telling what was in it.

But when she opened the lid again, the power called to her.

"What's that?" Hawk asked, and she ignored him.

She smelled the potion, then placed a drop on the back of her hand. It felt like magic and nothing more. But she'd had so little experience with these things. It could be something like *lucistra*, and with even a little magic in her, she could call for Madrigal, maybe find a way to finish the cure and escape from the cell. But the risks—

"Stop," she ordered herself. She didn't need Madrigal to tell her what her options were. Risk the potion, or face certain death by that enchanted axe.

Her heart pounded as she held the vial to her lips and let a drop of liquid fall onto her tongue.

Magic filled her with breathtaking force and overflowed her body, ringing in her ears like perfect music, leaving her gasping. She fought to hold herself together, but it felt as though her mind was exploding in a thousand directions, carried off by magic to become a part of the larger world around her. Her body would be left to its fate, but what of it? She would become magic itself, she would—

The cure. My people.

The magic swirled through her body, lifting her even as she felt, somewhere distant, her body collapsing to the floor.

Hold it. Use it. Don't let it use you.

Not Madrigal's voice, but her own.

You can do this.

She fought, imagining the power drawing back into her, becoming her own. She forced her eyes open and was surprised to find her skin wasn't glowing with magic. Hawk had his back pressed against the far wall of his cell, eyes wide.

"Madrigal!" Gale called.

"What are you talking about?" Hawk asked. "The witch?"

The ghost appeared, shimmering in the waves of magic Gale couldn't keep from pouring out of her body.

"You can't hold it," Madrigal said. She spoke softly, but her voice cut through the magic as though it came from within Gale herself. "You need a new vessel."

Gale cast her gaze around the cell. Chains, manacles, decaying straw... and there in the corner, the desiccated body of a long-dead rat.

She reached out, and her arms and fingers seemed longer than they should have been, the rat's body farther away. Pressure built beneath her skin, bringing agony that washed in and out on waves of magic, healing even as it harmed, drowning out the pain of the curse. She tore the skull from the body, and the rat's skin fell to the floor, leaving clean bone.

"Fine," Madrigal said. "Make it your vessel. Do you remember—"

"I remember." She felt the magic moving in her, spilling out, lost forever.

The mages could have used every bit of this power for their purposes. Madrigal, too. I'm losing it because of what I am... and what I'm not.

A witch could hold the power she'd just consumed and keep it for later. A witch was a vessel that could be small when created but expand with use. A witch wouldn't have been powerless when her external vessel was destroyed, and magic would be her partner instead of a foe to be bested.

She could become one, here and now, with Madrigal to guide her.

And what would be lost? She forced herself to look at Hawk, who shook with terror at whatever he saw in her eyes. She'd been raised to fear magic, too, and had been wrong.

I can't go home if I do this.

Gale's heart beat like wings against the walls of a cage that had grown too small for her.

There is no loss, save for the loss of people who refuse to understand. The world is so much larger than those who hold the keys to my cage would have me believe, and the only way to see it all is to step off the path. No regrets, no looking back.

Her voice in her mind, but calm and assured in a way she'd never heard it before.

"Quickly," Madrigal said. "Create the vessel before you lose this magic. Capture as much as you can. It'll be enough to get you out of here."

Gale set the skull on the floor. "I don't want as much as a vessel can hold," she said, her voice soft but impossibly strong. "I want all of it. If I'm to become a witch, let it happen now, with this power."

"No!" Hawk beat his fists against the bars. "You'll be corrupted! Damned!" Tears streamed down his cheeks. "Please, little bird. If you ever loved me or our family or God—"

The pain rampaged through her, muddying her thoughts, and the magic leaked inexorably out, lost forever.

She waited for Madrigal to tell her she wasn't ready, that it would be years before she'd prove herself worthy of becoming a true witch.

Instead, she said, "Choose your sacrifice." The witch's voice trembled, but her expression radiated joy. "Choose your pain, and feel it as wholly as you can—what wounds you now is what makes you forever, what proves your strength."

Gale thought briefly of Alec's missing ear, of old blind Sabbatus who saw so much more than anyone with two intact eyes, but there was no question of which path she wanted to follow.

To strengthen my enchantments and create beauty in the world.

To create with my hands things beyond nature or reason.

To follow and be guided by my mentor until Lord Death calls her home.

She used the bars to pull herself to her knees, then her feet, and reached out between the bars again, stretching towards the axe on the wall.

"Help me," she said, her voice low and calm despite magic that felt like it might tear her apart.

"Brilainsi algorath nualens," Madrigal said, speaking into her ear.

Gale repeated the words, willing the weapon to come to her, picturing it lifting out of the hooks it rested on.

The axe jerked wildly, spinning upward handle-first before its heavy head pulled it to the floor with a dull clank. The magic within Gale lessened, and she shook the last few drops from the tiny vial, letting them slide over her tongue. The magic came, blindingly quick. It was like being trapped beneath a waterfall, being drowned under the force of magic, until she fought her way back to herself. Her body felt as though it might burst.

"Stop!" Hawk called. Screamed, really. He sounded terrified.

Gale didn't feel at all sorry for him. And the mage hadn't lied.

No one heard, and no one came.

She clenched her teeth and reached for the axe, but the handle was out of reach.

"Brilainsi algorath nualens," she said again, stretching her fingers as far as she could, pushing her shoulder between the bars until her joints screamed for mercy.

Magical power flowed from her, only a portion of it under her focused control. The axe moved closer until Gale caught it, slid it closer, and drew it into her cell.

Hawk threw himself against the bars that separated them. "Please don't!"

Gale focused on the symphony of magic and let it drown him out. Only her heart, beating fearfully in her chest, held her back now.

Damned you're damned you're damned last chance stop now damned better to die clean...

But it was fear speaking, not truth.

I will not return to my cage when I'm called to fly.

Her entire body shook as she stood and curled every finger on her right hand save for the first, which she pressed against the stone slab that stuck out from the wall like a narrow shelf. It meant she'd be using her weak arm to swing, but it felt right. She gripped the axe tight, calling magic to strengthen her, willing herself to take aim and strike.

She froze. Magic flowed out of her, but still she couldn't move.

It was like trying to force herself to step into a burning building, against every survival instinct that had been bred into humans since the dawn of time.

Don't think. Do it.

Become.

"The spell," she whispered.

"Covaet'arun glamons ilusanth," Madrigal said, and Gale repeated the words, forcing her focus to narrow in on the sacrifice, the pain, and the magic. "Let the power flow."

She touched the blade to the base of her finger and allowed herself one practice swing.

Gale didn't need to ask what her intention should be. It came like a prayer. *Make me a vessel of magical power. Grant me control over the physical world, the magical world, and all they encompass. Let me keep my oath to help and not harm, let my actions be guided always by truth instead of fear.*

She took a deep breath and brought the axe down hard as she spoke the spell.

Madrigal hadn't lied about the magic of the weapon. It cut clean through flesh and bone, and Gale's severed finger dropped into the filthy hay on the floor.

The pain overwhelmed every other sensation, coming bright and sharp, searing and screaming. White lights flashed in front of her eyes, and the ringing in her ears left her closed off from her surroundings.

Gale cried out and fought the darkness that threatened to overtake her.

Feel it. Be made by it.

The magic moved, all grace and raw elemental power, leaving her and re-entering through the wound, flowing in a circle that threatened to tear her open with its force. But as it passed through her, Gale felt herself expanding—not in her physical body, but in her mind and soul, in all the pathways through which magic had only flowed like water before.

The magic grew, and Gale's spirit expanded to accommodate it.

Madrigal offered more words for her to repeat, and with each one the magic slowed and sank into her. She focused on the pain, on its red anger, on her sacrifice as she came back to herself and watched the blood flowing over her hand, her wrist, her arm.

The magic became more bearable. More *her*, becoming like the blood in her veins instead of something outside of herself. But there was still too much for her to hold for much longer if she didn't want it to destroy her.

She groped for the rat's head and caged it in her remaining fingers so she wouldn't crush the delicate bone.

"Hercalae voldanu re'ardiun." The magic obeyed, flowing through her and out of her, the excess rushing to escape only to be trapped in the skull of the dead rodent, transforming it into a vessel and filling it. Her blood smeared over its surface, coating the bone.

Then it was done. An overwhelming sense of peace swept through her even as the stump of her finger screamed with pain, sending bolts of agony up her arm that she didn't dare try to ease until the magic had settled and the pain had made her as strong as it could. Her blood dripped at her side, soaking into her skirt.

The magic was now *her* magic, wild and present, lifting her and filling the world around her with potential and hidden light, and now no one could take it away.

And the curse was gone, washed away as Alec had promised. She'd never felt stronger, healthier, or more whole. When she looked down at her arm it was as though the curse had never been there at all.

She'd expected leaving the Path to be terrifying. She'd expected regret. But all she felt was joy. The magic within her felt right, like the piece of herself she'd never been allowed to know was missing.

She wanted to scream and laugh and cry, to dance and mourn and fly.

This is the truth of Nightingale Goodweather. I am a witch. I am what I was born to be.

She didn't know if it was true, but it *felt* true. For now, it was enough.

The shock of it eased, and the crashing waves receded. Her breathing and heartbeat slowed, and she turned to Madrigal, who looked on with shining eyes. "Good for you, girl. Well done. Did you carry fear with you? Did you hesitate?"

Gale smiled weakly at her. "I'm only human. But I think I brought as little as I could."

"That's all that could be asked of any witch."

Gale laughed. *That word. I've become the thing we all hate and fear.*

"Gale!" Hawk shouted. She ignored him.

She opened her fingers to examine her new vessel. The bones had fused, leaving the lower jaw in one complete piece with the rest, and had blackened to a strange, glassy shine. It gleamed like the obsidian sword in the case upstairs but was still identifiable as the lowly object it had once been.

"Well," Madrigal said, holding back a smile. "No one said it had to be pretty to be powerful. And it's good. Stronger than the last, and fuller. Do you feel it?"

Gale held it tighter. "I do."

Hawk banged on the bars, drawing Gale's attention. "Look at me, damn you! What have you done?"

Gale removed her sash and wrapped her hand in it, putting pressure on the bleeding stump of her finger. "I've become a monster, Hawk. Can't you tell?"

He stared at her through the bars, his face red and eyes leaking. "How could you?" He leaned in closer. "Tell me it was the only way. That you corrupted yourself only to save us, that it was forgivable."

Gale focused on her magic. It hummed through her, filling empty spaces she hadn't known existed.

"Think what you wish, Hawk," she said. "What's done is done. I am a witch. And I will free us, and we will bring the cure to Bright Hollow." She looked deep into his eyes, remembering the dark times they'd shared, the childish quarrels, the secrets, the love she felt for him and what she knew he'd once felt for her. Something twisted deep in her heart. Not regret, but grief. "I don't need your forgiveness or anyone else's."

Her hands trembled with pain and power as she crossed her legs and cupped her hands around the rat's skull that had become her vessel.

But it wasn't the magic stored in the skull that lifted her. It was what she held within her. This magic was her own, a part of her as much as her mind or her soul.

And even as Hawk wept in the next cell, she knew in her heart that it was good.

CHAPTER THIRTY-FOUR

"YOU'D BETTER HURRY," Madrigal said, pacing outside the cell. "Even if they didn't hear the shouting someone might have felt magic like that."

"What are my options?" Gale pressed her bleeding hand against her chest, elevating the wound and trying to ignore the agony that threatened to distract her from what came next.

"There are subtle ways to work a lock, if you know the spells. But they're advanced, and require years of—"

"We don't have years," Gale said, louder than she'd intended. "We have moments. What can you teach me in moments?"

Hawk crouched against the far wall of his cell, watching and listening. He looked pathetic and pitiable. Not a dangerous hunter, but a terrified animal.

"Brute force," Madrigal said. "You have as much power available to you now as you'll have for a very long time. Direct it well. The results won't be subtle, but they might be effective."

"*Might* be?"

Madrigal shrugged. "You're young, untested, and highly under-practiced. 'Might' is the best I can offer. But you have already blown the roof off a building. Focus on releasing the power, hard as you can. A spell will only distract you."

Gale raised her hands. The sash wrapped around the right was dark with blood, and every movement sent pain shooting up her arm. But the magic was there in her, ready to be directed, and in her vessel, waiting to replenish her. And when they left this place there would be more magic in the world ready to be taken.

She pressed her injured hand to the lock on her cell door. Fresh pain lit her flesh and cut up her arm like a bolt of lightning, but it felt right.

There was no thought. No spell. She let her desperation fill her and directed it through her hand and into the lock. Magic poured from her in an invisible flood of warmth, and Gale fought the familiar urge to hold it back for herself.

There will be more. There will always be more.

The metal heated under her palm until the scent of baking blood and scorched silk filled the air, and the door swung open.

"How do I finish the medicine?" she asked.

Madrigal paced the cell behind her. "You already spoke the spell, and the ingredients are all there. Find your way back to that place in your mind, use your magic, and finish it. There's nothing more I can tell you."

Gale glanced at Hawk. His eyes were closed, his lips moving in prayer.

Gale prayed, too. Not for salvation or a sign that this was God's will, but for the peace and focus to finish what she'd started. She opened the jar and concentrated on its unfinished contents. Though the magic within her wasn't as overwhelming now that it was a part of her, it still brought clarity and insight, and she found she could almost foresee what would happen within the jars if she only willed it.

The slow release of power hardly seemed to diminish her at all, and in moments the job was done. The dark salve turned a pale, rosy cream colour, and the magic she poured into it vanished, absorbed in the reactions.

It was finished. Acceptable, if the Luminary chose to judge it on its current state and not its origins. The only question was whether it worked.

She turned to Hawk. "Give me your arm."

"Absolutely not."

"Leave him," Madrigal said. "He's made his choice. Let the rest decide for themselves."

"I can't," Gale said, looking from the ghost to the man who had murdered her. "I am a healer, whether the Luminary wants me to be or not. I took an oath before God to heal when I could, without judgement." She crouched at the bars. Hawk glared back at her.

"Hawk. Please, try to fight the curse long enough to think rationally. No magic will touch you if you let me apply the salve. Think of Frost, how she'll mourn if you never come home. Of Fox growing up without his father." Low blows, but Gale didn't care. Not one word was a lie. "Think of what you'd want them to do if your positions were reversed. Do this for your family, for Bright Hollow. Don't let it end here for the sake of your stubbornness."

Hawk's shoulders slumped, and his head hung low. "May God forgive me," he whispered as he crawled toward the cell door. He glared up at Gale even as he thrust his hand between the bars. "If the Luminary decides this is forbidden—"

"Then tell yourself I tricked you into it," Gale said, her throat tightening. "Whatever lets you sleep peacefully. I'll need to see your whole arm."

Madrigal huffed and turned her back as Hawk slipped his shirt off, revealing a red, flaking rash that covered his arm halfway to his shoulder and poisonous looking lines veining up the side of his neck and across his chest. His hand was the worst, though. Over just a few days the curse had eaten Hawk's flesh nearly to the bone.

She took a small dollop of the salve and touched it to the dead and rotting skin on Hawk's finger, the place where it had begun for him, then spread it over the worst of the damage on his hand.

For a second or two, nothing happened. Then Hawk gritted his teeth.

"It's cold," he whispered, and his arm trembled. "Stop."

"I can't. Just wait."

It started with the dark lines that crossed Hawk's skin. They pulled back, reversing their growth, leaving white streaks on Hawk's skin to mark their regress.

Next, the dead flesh in the wound vanished as though absorbed into the salve. Hawk bared his teeth and wrapped his fingers around one of the bars, squeezing tighter than he could have moments before, breathing through the discomfort. The flesh, still raw and exposed, turned a healthy red, oozing blood.

"The curse is gone," Madrigal said. She sounded pleased, though Gale supposed it wasn't for Hawk's sake. "His body is fighting the damage, just as I said." She looked to Gale, smiling, as a translucent layer of protective skin covered the withered tissues the curse had left behind. "It's beautiful, isn't it?"

Gale watched as Hawk unclenched his hand and flexed his fingers slowly, testing their strength, then carefully pulled his shirt back on. He was far better off than he'd been, but not fully healed as Gale was.

"Does it still hurt?" Gale asked.

"No."

"What does it feel like?"

"Not like magic," Hawk said, obviously relieved. "It's warm now. Prickles. A lot, actually." He pushed himself to his feet and paced a few steps, steady as he'd ever been, and when he looked to Gale his eyes were clear and focused.

Her heart swelled until she thought it might burst out of her.

I did that. Me.

"What will you do if I let you out?" she asked.

Before Hawk could answer, the lock on the wooden door clicked and a hooded figure stepped in. Gale set the jar down and raised her hands before her, strong and steady even as the pain in her hand weakened her knees and sent waves of nauseating dizziness through her.

"Go," she whispered to Madrigal. "No sense tempting them to make your banishment permanent."

Madrigal vanished. Gale's heart pounded. She held her breath.

Sabbatus pushed his hood back, leaving his downy hair tufted and wild, and held up his hands in surrender as he took in the situation, seeing without eyes. "Well, now."

Gale didn't lower her hands. "Let us go. I'll..." She trailed off, unsure of what she could threaten. The magic she now sensed more clearly in the old man was a thing of unfathomable depth, and he'd had a lifetime to hone his skill and knowledge.

"Yes, I'm sure you will. But I'd appreciate it if you didn't." Sabbatus picked up the open jar from the floor and held it toward Gale. "Finished, eh? Ready to take back to your village."

Gale took it from him and stepped back, unwilling to trust even the one mage who had tried to help her. "You're letting me go?"

"Oh, no. That would get me into a bit of trouble, wouldn't it?" Sabbatus sounded unbothered by the idea. "I did volunteer to check on things, though. Someone else will be down soon enough, and they'll find me knocked out cold on the floor, the victim of a wily young witch and her fresh magic."

Gale snorted. "I could never best you. Not if I took you by surprise and you had both hands tied behind you."

Sabbatus smiled sadly. "Kind of you to say, and probably true. But the other mages tend to forget that old Sabbatus is still strong in magic, if a bit dusty in the attic and creaky in the base-ment, if you catch my drift."

Gale wasn't sure she understood entirely, but she nodded. "They underestimate you."

"And I'm pleased enough to let them overestimate you." His lips twitched. "It's been ever so long since I had an adventure."

Gale reached for her boots and slipped them on, but quickly gave up on the laces. Even if she hadn't had a makeshift bandage hampering her movement and every twitch of her remaining fingers hadn't sent fresh agony through her, it would take time to learn how to do these things without the one she'd lost.

Sabbatus slipped his hands into his pockets. "I'm impressed. I saw potential in you when you first came to us. There was desperation, too, but I wasn't sure it would drive you this far."

"You sound like that pleases you." Gale frowned at him. "Why are you helping me? No one does something like this for the sake of a bit of fun or to push back against the rules."

Sabbatus's smile faded. "No. I've been waiting for…" He trailed off. "A hero, I suppose. I still don't know whether you're it, but I've done what I can."

"I don't understand."

"You don't need to." He stepped past her and entered her cell to pick up the axe from the floor, then set it back on the wall without cleaning the blood from it. "I will offer you your freedom and a chance to use your new power as you see fit. What I ask in return is that you make me a promise. A day may come when you have an opportunity to finish what the mages began and the king abandoned. Swear to me, on your blood and the magic we share, that you will take that chance."

Gale stared at him, completely lost. "I still don't—"

"Promise it and leave now, or don't. These are my terms."

"Fine. I swear I will." It was far worse than owing a favour to Jes, but the odds of her ever needing to worry about it seemed slim given the wide berth she planned to give the mages in the future.

"Good." Gale couldn't read the mage's tone. "You'll want to

turn left out the door, follow the passage to the end, turn right, first left, and some old fool has carelessly left the door unlocked." He shook his head in disgust. "You'll want to mind the step when you get there."

"And the rest of my things? My jacket, my supplies?"

"Locked away upstairs, I'm afraid. I wouldn't recommend going after them." Sabbatus jerked his head toward Hawk. "What of him?"

Hawk stood and grasped the bars. His gaze locked onto Gale's, his pale eyes wide and pleading.

"I'll help you get the cure home," he said. "My mind is clear now that the curse is gone, and I see that you were right. It's not for me to decide, but the Luminary." He looked down at the bloodstained sash wrapped around her hand. "I don't see how this is God's will, but I'll see you safely home to find out."

He sounded sincere, but Gale didn't believe a word of it. Maybe it had been the curse talking when he'd said she'd be better off dead, but he'd meant every word of it.

Gale turned back to Sabbatus. "What will happen if I leave him here?"

"He'll be tried and executed. You'll be free, and your hands will be clean."

Gale looked down at her bloodied hands and choked back a laugh. "Letting someone else do it doesn't leave anyone clean, does it?"

Hawk's fingers tightened around the bars. He squeezed his eyes closed. "I want to go home," he said, his voice quiet, broken. "I want to see Frost and hold Fox and know they're all right. I won't harm you, Gale. I only want to put this behind us. Please."

There was so much more Gale wanted to demand from him, but time was too short.

Madrigal would tell her to leave him.

She moved closer to the bars, close enough that he could have grabbed her through them.

She'd be ready if he did.

She looked deep into his eyes, willing him to hear and understand. "You must promise to let me take this medicine home. Others need this as badly as you did. You won't take that from them."

Hawk looked away. "I accept that this might be the only way to see God's will done. The Teachings are clear, but…"

"But?"

"But I swear I will see you safely home."

It would have to do.

"Stand back," Gale ordered, and both Sabbatus and Hawk stepped away from the cell door. Her magic moved within her, and seconds later the inner workings of the lock melted. She barely felt the depletion and felt no need to renew her power from her new vessel.

There was an ocean of magic within her, at least for the moment.

Hawk rushed forward, and Gale raised her hands, prepared to knock him down with the spell she'd used before, but he went to the open door and looked both ways, then turned back to her. "Clear, but not for long. If we're going, it needs to be now." He grabbed his boots and slipped them on.

"I assume you can make this look convincing?" Sabbatus asked, sounding apprehensive.

"I can." Gale turned to him. "I'm sorry for this. And thank you."

"No thanks needed, young witch. Only remember your promise."

"I will."

The old mage looked toward the ceiling. "They're coming." He turned his back to her, facing the cells. "Better get on with it."

"*Alehia aldomor ic'lieni dorsuma,*" she whispered, softening the spell she'd used to blast Hawk in Queen's Run.

Sabbatus collapsed face-first onto the floor.

Gale clutched both jars of her magical cure to her chest and ran after Hawk as they bolted toward freedom.

~

THE WIND WHIPPED past the exit door, which opened onto a narrow path that cut to the right, hugging the cliffs behind and well below the Hall of Mages. A bright sunrise shone down on the ocean waves, illuminating distant ships with white sails filled by the wind. Beneath the path, the land dropped away to waves so far below that Gale couldn't hear them crashing against the rocks.

Hawk held on to the door frame, assessing the vertical drop. "Ladies first?"

"I think not." Gale prodded his lower back, and he flinched. "Move."

She didn't threaten magic. She didn't have to. He knew well enough what would happen if she knocked him out this high over sharp rocks and crashing waves.

Hawk stepped out onto the path, shuffling sideways, nimble and quick. Gale wedged the jar of salve and her new vessel awkwardly into the bodice of her dress, hoping and praying they stayed put. With her bleeding hand still pressed against her body, she stepped carefully out, pulling the door closed behind her, and held her breath as the wind whipped her skirt, threatening to send her tumbling into the sea.

Every step required careful concentration. There was no more conversation as they made their way up the shallow slope, nor as they crept through the grounds of the Hall at the top, skirting the outside of the garden wall and making their way as far from the building as they could.

The pain in her hand throbbed with every beat of her heart, demanding more attention than she could give it. She cradled it against her chest, promising herself she'd take care of it soon.

Your pain is what makes you, she told herself, remembering Madrigal's instructions. *Feel it.*

They reached the top and hurried on, clinging to the cliffs, avoiding the streets—the fewer people who saw them, especially Gale in her current gory state, the better. Hawk's sharp eyes caught every movement, his ears every noise as they hurried across dewy grass and through a fenced-in park covered by sheltering trees. Now that his health was restored, Gale had no doubt he'd be able to see them safely from the city, and she followed close behind without question. She left her vessel where it was and carried the salve in her good hand, pressing the glass jars tight against her body.

They soon came to a series of fenced yards and quaint white buildings that butted up against the water, and they made their way to a quiet street. There was no one about, but there would be soon enough, and any who saw them would certainly answer the mages' questions when they came along.

Hawk's long strides carried him quickly, and Gale had to trot to keep up.

Madrigal appeared beside her, keeping pace easily. "You freed him." Disgust dripped from every word.

It wasn't a question, but Gale nodded.

Madrigal stayed, but hung back as far as she seemed able. It was a greater distance than she'd managed when the vessels were all she'd had to cling to.

They stopped in the shadowy space between a Jatlish bakery and an inn that advertised breathtaking ocean views on the sign out front, weaving their way between packing crates and stacks of supplies. The scents of bread and sweet seasonings hung heavy in the air, and Gale's stomach groaned, reminding her of how badly her newly healed body needed a solid meal.

Hawk checked the yards at the far end of their hiding space, making sure they were truly alone, and turned to Gale. "Let me look at your hand."

"It's fine. I can handle it."

"Can you? You look like you're going to faint, and I'm not strong enough yet to carry you home."

Madrigal floated into view. "Use magic, girl. Your making is as finished as it's going to get. Ease your pain, let magic speed your healing. The wound is only harming you now."

"You might have mentioned that sooner," Gale grumbled. Hawk shot her an apprehensive look, but didn't say anything. "What's the spell?"

Madrigal considered it for a moment. "Healing natural disease or injury is far more difficult than bringing back what was lost to a curse," she said. "Try *anthu'ul galainthi* to speed things along. It'll ease the pain and might stop the bleeding, and your body will finish things from there."

"*Arthu'ul galainthi*," Gale murmured, carefully directing her intentions, imagining the natural path of healing a lopped off finger would take over time. A cool sensation flowed over the injury, like dipping her hand in fresh water. The sharpest edges of the pain dulled, leaving an ache that she supposed would be with her for quite some time. Her head cleared, and she knew without looking that the bleeding had slowed, maybe stopped.

Hawk looked around, obviously seeing nothing. "I hate to ask, but who are you talking to?"

"The ghost of our deceased hostess."

"The witch?" He paled. "When you said her name and spoke to no one in the cells, I assumed you were... I mean, I thought you'd lost your mind." His shoulders slumped. "She's been waiting for us all this time?"

"Something like that. I was lucky to find her when I went back."

Hawk snorted. "Lucky."

Gale met Hawk's gaze. "She taught me everything I used to save you. And she didn't cause the famine when we were children. She couldn't have. I don't know what did, but it wasn't her."

Hawk looked away.

Gale glared at him, but realized she wasn't truly surprised. "You knew, didn't you?"

"We should keep walking." He started away from her, but Gale grabbed his arm and hauled back until he stopped.

"Answer me."

He turned around, irritation flashing in his eyes and then vanishing. A contrite look Gale didn't trust took its place. "I suspected. But not until after we returned, I swear. Not when we... not when I killed her. And after that, I thought we were heroes either way."

Madrigal drifted away to look out over the ocean, one arm wrapped tight around her waist, the other rubbing at her throat.

"And now?"

He swallowed hard. "Now I don't know. I don't regret what I did. Even if she didn't cause the curse, she intended to corrupt you."

"You still believe magic is a great evil, even after your healing and knowing how it will save everyone else?" Gale hated the pleading tone in her voice and the desperation in her heart to make him understand.

She could make it home on her own. Walk away from him, let him stew in his wrong-headed ideas forever. *But if I can see the truth,* she thought, *there has to be hope for him, too.*

She'd tested the cure on him to prove it might work on everyone else in Bright Hollow. This was no different. If he could be made to see reason, she would allow herself to hope.

Hawk threw his hands up and glared at her. "I don't know. Does that please you? I felt certain about everything when I came after you, and now I don't."

"You seemed quite certain in those cells when you were screaming at me about damnation." Gale kept her voice low and quiet, but didn't try to pass it off as a joke. His response would tell her whether she could trust him enough to travel home together, or whether it was time to run again.

He passed a hand over his face, scraping down over the shadowy beard that had grown in since they'd left Bright Hollow. "I was terrified for you. I hope you'd care enough to scream at me, too, if you saw me putting my life or my soul in danger."

"I would," Gale said, forcing a smile. "But I'm alive, and my soul isn't in danger. It feels fine."

He nodded and leaned against the wall of the bakery, then sank down to sit on a stack of empty flour sacks. "I am sorry for what I said while the curse was affecting me. My mind wasn't right."

"You're sure it wasn't just letting you speak truly?"

Hawk glared at her. "What do you want from me? I'm trying."

"Sorry." Gale leaned against the opposite wall. "This isn't easy. The things you said were cruel and hurtful, but they weren't anything other than what we both grew up hearing."

"I know." Hawk drew one foot up onto the sacks and rested his arm on it. He seemed comfortable, and it eased Gale's nerves a little. "I never thought we'd be in this position, even after that mess when we were children." He looked at her, more closely than before. "You're still yourself, even after the change?"

"I am."

"Very well. We'll let the Luminary decide on all of it." Hawk hesitated, frowning, though not at her. "My thoughts on magic haven't changed. They can't, because the Teachings haven't changed."

"The Teachings were written by people, Hawk." Gale spoke as gently as she could. "I'm beginning to think they were just as fallible as you or I."

He gave her a warning look. "Under God's guidance. They've served us well enough."

"We can do better."

Hawk looked at her as though she'd become a stranger, or

maybe a weird insect he'd never seen before. He blinked, and the strangeness was gone. "What I want to say is that you saved my life, and if the Luminary allows the use of this medicine, you'll save many more. After that, I guess I'm willing to see what happens."

"Big of him," Madrigal muttered, turning back to them.

Gale's eyes burned with held-back tears as a tiny flame of hope kindled within her. "Do you think there's any chance folks at home will change their minds about what I am?"

"I don't know." Hawk sighed and pushed himself to his feet. "This is... it's hard, you know? But you're one of ours. You've done all of this to save us. I'm willing to hope."

Gale nodded. It had been hard enough for her, and she'd been on the inside, feeling magic and knowing its goodness intimately. She couldn't expect it to be easier for him.

"Why don't you start by convincing me on the way home?" he suggested, rubbing the back of his neck and looking oddly shy. Gale's heart seemed to clench tight within her. "We'll have plenty of time to talk. The least I can do is listen. For real, this time, and try to understand."

Madrigal watched with narrowed eyes. "Don't be a fool, girl. You've changed, but he hasn't."

But maybe he could.

Gale wished she'd thought to ask Sabbatus what would happen if she set Hawk free and not only if she left him behind. But then, it couldn't be easy to see the future clearly. Opportunities, maybe possibilities. But every choice made by every person going forward would change it.

Hawk held out a hand. "Let me carry the medicine for you."

Gale clutched the jar tighter. "I'll keep it, thank you."

"Up to you." He sounded hurt, but not angry. "Let's go, then."

Hawk pulled his knife from his belt and looked at her, quick and hard, and Gale stepped back. He pressed his lips together, then turned and picked up an empty flour sack from the stack he'd been sitting on. In a few quick motions he cut two holes in the top, forming handles, and held it out to her. "This might make them easier to carry."

"Thanks."

"Sure thing."

Gale stuffed two more sacks inside the first and cradled the medicine between them.

Hawk set out again, heading south, and Gale followed.

"I'll be leaving, then," Madrigal said, and Gale turned back. "After all I've seen you through, I won't watch this. Nor will I follow him."

"You can't go," Gale said. "I still have so much to learn."

"You certainly do." Madrigal forced a wry smile. "But you are a witch now, if not nearly the kind I'd have wished my apprentice to be before I released her into the world. Perhaps I could let go of what holds me here." She looked past Gale to Hawk's retreating form. "Even if Lord Death won't take me, I won't go with you to that horrid town. I can't."

Gale's breath hitched, but she caught it and nodded. "I appreciate everything you've done for me, more than I can say. And I'm sorry I'm giving him another chance, but this might be my last opportunity to change things—to change him, and maybe everyone else. Things could still be good. Better than I ever dreamed."

"Is that what you want?" Deep lines appeared between Madrigal's eyes. "To go back there, knowing what's in their hearts and minds?"

"It's what was in mine," Gale said. "I have to try. I wish you'd come with me, but I understand if you can't. Thank you, again, for all of this."

Madrigal glowered, but there was no heat in it. "Thank Alec and his blood-magic-working friend. You'd never have slipped free of your cage without them. I only hope you're not returning to it to be locked in again."

"You coming?" Hawk called.

"One moment!" Gale spoke over her shoulder, not wanting to look away from Madrigal. "I'll miss you."

There was more she wanted to say about regrets and wasted years and how glad she was they'd made amends, but none of it would come. If she tried to let it out she'd end up crying.

Madrigal held out her arms, and Gale stepped closer. The witch's ghostly touch didn't feel as chilly as it had before. "Be careful."

And then she was gone. The breeze seemed to blow colder, and Gale hurried to catch up with Hawk.

CHAPTER THIRTY-FIVE

Embercliffe was a larger and more complex city than Gale had imagined, and it took the entire morning for them to make their way west and out of its twisting, winding streets. It might have gone faster, but Gale couldn't resist the temptation to look into the shop windows they passed, wishing she had the coin for a new coat or some food.

Hawk had to be just as cold and just as hungry, but he barely glanced at anything except the next step he meant for them to take. For the first time since they were children, Gale was glad to be under his wing. She knew the safety he offered was probably an illusion that might shatter at any moment and cut her open with its shards, but what a beautiful lie it was.

"How will we get home?" Gale asked, then paused. "And how did you get here?"

Hawk turned to her, one eyebrow raised. "A long, uncomfortable day in the baggage car of a fast train. You?"

"A more comfortable ride in the same one." Gale took a step away, out of arm's reach. "You heard me and Alec talking? Before you—"

"I did. I heard you talking about Embercliffe and headed for the train station as soon as I lost you. Didn't realize you had fancy connections that would get you here just as quickly."

Her mouth went dry. The train didn't matter, but the rest of her conversation with Alec did. "He didn't set the curse. I mean, he put it in place, but he didn't create it. With him gone, we might never know who did."

Hawk's jaw muscles flexed tight. "He was the one with the grudge against us. I doubt whoever created it will try again. If they do, we'll be ready."

Gale didn't ask more. It would be easy to start an argument about guilt and murder and magic, but there would be time for that later.

Still, every time she looked at him, she remembered the arrow protruding from Alec's chest. No questioning. No trial. Just Hawk's certainty that he was guilty of being a witch.

They left the road behind after they crossed a high stone bridge arching over a narrow river, cutting their way across grassy meadows and toward the thick pine forest that hid the western horizon.

Gale slowed as they reached the edge of the forest. "Where are we going?"

"West. Better to avoid the roads for a while in case the mages come after us." Hawk shielded his eyes against the sun and looked back toward the city. "Rich folks like to hunt for sport, and I've heard the hunting is good in these woods. These people can afford to keep cabins. If we find one of those, we'll find food and supplies."

He spoke with the same certainty he did when he said he was going out to kill a stag or a wolf. He never seemed to be wrong about such things, and even if he was, Gale didn't worry he'd get lost.

Her stomach snarled at her again, and she followed him into the shade of the trees. As they walked, she focused on her magic instead of her body, revelling in how it moved through her. It couldn't have felt more natural if she'd been born with it. There was no sense now that it might drown her. The excess she'd taken in from the mages' potion had burned away, leaving something vast, mysterious, and peaceful that no one would ever be able to steal from her, ready to be called on when she needed it.

"So," Hawk said, after an uncomfortable stretch of silence, "why don't you start by telling me... everything?"

"You're sure you want to know?"

Hawk gave her a shaky but warm smile. "I guess I should if anything's going to get better."

Gale began with her true experiences with magic when they were children, things she'd never dared admit when she worried about his judgement. She confessed how truly she'd made herself believe what she was supposed to since their return to Bright Hollow, but how magic had always called to her. Hawk nodded as she described how desperately she'd wanted to do everything in her power to save the people of Bright Hollow and her sincere intentions for doing so without breaking their laws or endangering her soul.

And then the rest. The steps away from the light of the path as she'd hunted for their cure, finding that the forest wasn't as dark and frightening as they'd all feared, spreading her wings and knowing she'd never have been truly happy if she'd accepted the Luminary's judgement and denied herself magic.

"So you have no regrets?" Hawk asked. He sounded more curious than accusatory, which Gale considered a small victory.

"No. My heart will break if I'm cast out from Bright Hollow, but it will break for the love I'll lose and for the beautiful things the people I leave behind will never experience. It won't be from regret."

Hawk smiled sadly. "I believe you. I don't agree with you, but I thank you for explaining it to me."

The sky above was a deep, radiant blue, the sun beginning to sink over the forest before they reached its border. Though the sun eased the chill on her skin, Gale still wished she had something warmer and more practical to wear. The grey silk dress was covered in bloodstains, and with night coming, the air would grow cold. Her arms were already covered in gooseflesh.

"Here," Hawk said. "A road, but it's not well used. This will lead us to something."

Soon they reached a little log cabin tucked into a clearing surrounded by evergreens. Hawk held up a hand to stop her. Waited. Listened. Then he motioned her forward, tried the door, and found it locked.

"I could—" Gale began, but Hawk stepped back and kicked the door in before she could finish.

He looked back at her, then dropped his chin, clearly ashamed. "One more for the list of things to ask forgiveness for."

Gale followed him inside. A pair of beds sat on either side of a stone fireplace, and well-stocked shelves held everything a person would need for a hunting trip in the forest—clothing, knapsacks, jars and sacks of food, knives and bows and arrows. A pair of stag heads hung on the wall, watching them with glass eyes.

"Whoever owns this place can afford to lose a few things, I guess," she said. "This isn't the worst thing either of us has done in the past few days." Still, she thought it would be good to try to repay the owner some day. A person could only carry so much weight on her conscience.

The place was small but cozy and well appointed. Gale hurried to one of the beds, eager to crash onto the pillow.

"We can't stay," Hawk said, stopping her three paces from the bed.

"Why not?" Gale turned and found him already standing at the shelves, filling a heavy canvas bag.

"I don't know. Just a feeling."

Gale knew better than to doubt him. She grabbed a floppy leather knapsack and tied a few rolled-up blankets to the bottom, then filled the bag with potatoes, carrots, hard-tack bread, a small kettle, and a cup to drink from. Hawk handed her a metal box filled with medical supplies—not as good as what she'd have found at the clinic at home, but serviceable enough. Gale stepped outside and unwrapped her hand, gasping at the pain as the fabric pulled away from her wound.

"Doesn't look so bad," Hawk said.

Gale jumped. She hadn't heard him coming.

He wasn't entirely wrong. There was the small matter of her missing index finger, gone with barely a stump remaining—a whole and proper sacrifice. The bleeding had stopped, but the wound, raw and wet, ached badly.

"Still no regrets?" Hawk asked.

"No." Gale washed her hands and arms at the outdoor water pump, cleaning as much blood and dungeon dust off as she could with simple soap and cold water, then carefully wrapped fresh bandages around her hand to cushion and protect it, already mentally cataloguing what she might find in the forest to ease her pain.

It only took a few minutes for her to change into new clothes —men's trousers and shirt, a warm coat and a hat with rabbit-fur flaps that would keep her ears warm as she slept, woolen mittens. It was all too big, but everything was clean and dry, and with a fresh pair of socks her feet felt more comfortable than they had with only stockings in her old boots.

She left the cabin, the straps of her new bag over her shoulders. She'd cradled the jar of salve deep inside and wore her new vessel tied on a piece of heavy twine around her neck.

Hawk had taken a bow, arrows, and several knives, and by the time they stopped at sunset he'd killed a pair of fat rabbits for supper. They made camp in the shelter of a low, rocky cliff inside the forest, and Hawk went to cut wood while Gale searched for common herbs that would aid with her pain and promote further healing in Hawk's body. Surrounded by evening birdsong and the whisper of wind through branches, she felt more at peace than she had in weeks.

As she made her way back to camp, the breeze passed through a patch of aspens, making their leaves tremble and shimmer, and Gale remembered an old remedy—not one of Madrigal's, but from home. A flower folks back home called mother's aid liked to grow near aspen roots. The plant wouldn't grow its tiny white flowers until early summer, but she recognized its triangular leaves as she moved closer. They didn't have much flavour, but promoted deep sleep and were often mixed into sweet bedtime drinks for rowdy children.

A witch's intentions might make the effect stronger, even without a spell.

Gale hesitated, torn between guilt and necessity.

Hawk had apologized and seemed sincere in his desire to understand and at least consider her side of things.

He'd also killed Alec, called his own sister damned, and said she would be better off dead than corrupting her soul.

Her old self would have believed him and trusted God to make things work out for the best. Her new self decided it was better to be cautious and rude than to preserve Hawk's feelings and find out too late that she shouldn't have trusted him. She plucked a handful of leaves and returned to camp.

With the things they'd taken from the cabin and what they'd gathered from the forest, they soon had a cozy place to rest. Tin cups held water drawn from a nearby stream, and Gale set them next to the fire to brew herb mixtures while the meat cooked on makeshift spits, scenting the air with the promise of a full belly. It was the kind of camp they'd dreamed of as children, back when neither of them had the means or knowledge to enjoy such a thing on their hard journey through the forest.

"No magic, right?" Hawk asked, nodding at the cups. He tried to make it sound like a joke, but the tension in his voice betrayed him.

"No magic," Gale promised. Guilt twisted into her gut like a knife as she watched him drink. She could justify theft out of necessity, but lying would take more getting used to.

He didn't ask again, and they ate in silence.

Hawk sat with his boots off and his feet up on a low boulder, picking the bones after they'd eaten. "You must be exhausted," he said. "Or does magic make all of that better for you?"

He finished his tea and yawned.

Gale yawned, too, and leaned back against the natural stone wall, legs crossed in front of her. The herbs were easing her pain, and magic was doing its work. Her hand was still a useless, wounded lump, but at least the agony had dulled to a low throb.

"I can't remember when I've been so tired. It's been a long—" She paused. She'd meant to say a long day, but it was more than that. It was the night before in the garden, the days before that in Queen's Run and at Madrigal's cabin, and the long days and nights in the clinic caring for the sick. It was the change from fear to freedom, from shame to pure magic. She smiled. "It's been a long journey. I'm glad we're at least on the same side of it now. Aren't we?"

"I hope so." Hawk tossed the bones into the fire. "And I am truly sorry. For everything."

Gale sat up and leaned closer, eyes narrowed. "Does that mean you've changed your mind about me being damned? That you think I'm all right as I am?"

"I think we'll all be all right, thanks to you."

Not an answer, but Gale let it slide.

His words were close to being everything she'd wanted to hear since she was a child, believing she was broken when magic still called to her after their return home, and everything she hoped to hear from the Luminary, from her parents, from every-one. *You did the right thing, Gale. You are a hero.*

She allowed herself to imagine it—the Teachings reinter-preted to accept magic as part of God's will, and her the local witch living outside of town, helping and healing her people, drawing on the power of the mountain without worry of being hunted and hated for it.

Her heart ached with longing for that life.

"I can take the first watch, though," she said. "This wound is going to keep me awake for a while, anyway."

Hawk looked like he could barely keep his eyes open, but he shook his head. "I'm fine. Go to sleep."

Gale slipped into her bed—just a blanket on the ground with her bag as a pillow—and watched as Hawk fed the fire and settled himself into the spot she'd vacated next to the rock. Gale closed her eyes and waited until she heard gentle snores.

But it wasn't enough. She'd only used a few leaves of a plant to push his already exhausted mind and body into slumber, and she wasn't the kind of witch who knew how to make them do much more than their share of work. Her intentions as she'd stirred the tea had helped put him under, but that didn't mean he'd stay that way for long.

She wanted to sleep. More than that, she wanted to believe it was safe to do so, that Hawk had truly heard her and opened his mind to what she'd said. But she couldn't stop thinking about how long it would take most people to change everything they'd believed since birth.

Change could happen. She'd seen it in herself, but no one went from screaming about corruption to offering acceptance and comfort in a matter of hours, no matter how much she wished it could be so.

She dragged a few pine boughs from the surrounding trees and pulled her blanket over them to look like she was still sleeping, then checked the knapsack she'd taken from the cabin to be sure her things were still there. She took it and crept away, leaving Hawk snoring softly behind her.

The land sloped away from the campsite. Gale climbed, then found a spot where she could watch from the darkness. If Hawk tried to wake her for her turn to keep watch, she'd go back and explain everything. He'd be hurt by her caution, but he'd get over it. Maybe they'd even laugh about it some day.

Hawk jerked from his slumped position and rubbed his eyes, then checked the fire, prodding it with a long stick. He stared into the low flames for a full minute, swaying slightly as he fought the effects of Gale's brew.

Go back, she thought. *Sit down, relax, sleep.*

He reached for the bag he'd carried from the cabin and pulled the long hunting knife from it.

Gale held her breath and watched as Hawk stumbled toward her bed and stabbed it into the place where Gale should have been sleeping.

Her stomach dropped, and she clapped her hands over her mouth to hold back a cry.

She'd wanted so badly to have been wrong.

Tears threatened, but she held them back, hardening her heart to the pain that cut through her as surely as Hawk's knife would have if she'd trusted him.

Jes was right. It was a hard world, and she was better off relying on herself to get by in it. If she wanted the Luminary to know the truth, it was up to her to make sure she made it back to Bright Hollow to speak her piece. Relying on the goodwill of an enemy—even a once-loved brother—would only lead to failure.

Hawk leapt to his feet, searching for her, and collapsed onto her bed, his legs too weak to hold him up.

"Gale!" he called, his voice grating with rage. "Gale!"

She turned away and walked deeper into the dark of the woods.

CHAPTER THIRTY-SIX

BY THE TIME Gale reached the road to Bright Hollow, her new coat was filthy and torn, her boots felt worn to death, and her body ached in ways even magic wouldn't soothe without a proper spell to direct it. She'd been on the road for five days since she'd left Hawk behind. The journey should have taken longer, but she'd taken rides from a few merchants and one shockingly large family to speed her travel, paying her way with food foraged from the woods or offers to tend to bored and irritable children. The food she'd gathered for herself hadn't been nearly enough, and when she couldn't find anyone to travel with, she'd pushed herself to keep walking on the roads through the night and beneath the cover of the forest during the day, resting only when she couldn't go on.

But she'd made it. She had no doubt Hawk would be home soon, if he wasn't already there, but she'd seen no sign of him after she'd left their camp. And when the rooftops of her home-town appeared beyond the last slope in the road, nestled into the broad hollow that had sheltered the town and its people for generations, she forgot her aches, if not her worries. She paused and let herself enjoy the sight for what might be the last time—

the farms at the edge of town, the sun shining on the turbulent currents of the river, the Great Hall standing at the edge of the square. The homes, the shops, and the streets she'd walked nearly every day for more than seventeen years all looked smaller than she remembered, but more welcoming and idyllic. Her chest tightened with the exquisite ache of longing for something she feared she was about to lose forever.

Home.

But she'd been away for too long, and hesitation would only delay the inevitable. More folks would have died while she was gone, and every moment she wasted could add another to their numbers. She forced her aching legs into motion.

It was late afternoon, but the streets were quiet. Gale's stomach clenched as she marched toward the hall at the centre of town.

She considered going straight to the clinic. River would take the medicine and distribute it. If she didn't tell him it was made by magic, he wouldn't get in trouble for healing everyone. They'd all be saved, and she'd ask for forgiveness from the Luminary later.

She didn't. If the people were to be cured by magic, they'd do it knowing what they were agreeing to. And if they wouldn't...

She didn't let herself consider that possibility. Even if the Luminary gave permission, there were sure to be some who refused it. They'd accept no new interpretations of old words, unwilling to risk a stain on their souls even if it cost them their lives.

And that would be their choice.

Someone stepped out of the clinic as she walked by. She hoped for a moment that it would be River, but there was no mistaking Buttercup's wide shoulders and lumbering gait as he hurried toward her.

Gale smiled through her exhaustion.

"Gale!" Her old friend picked her up and swung her around,

then set her gently back on the ground. She held him tight, hollow with the fear that it might be for the last time.

"We didn't think you were going to make it back." He took in her filthy clothing and tangled hair, his gaze finally resting on her right hand and the healing wound where her finger had once been. Exhaustion pooled beneath his eyes in dark circles, and he looked like he'd been through as much as she had in the past week. "Looks like you almost didn't."

"It was a close thing. But I have the medicine we need. Please tell me there are still people here to be cured. Tell me Willow—"

Buttercup swallowed hard and shook his head. "She left us three days after you did. Her body failed before her mind did, which I suppose is a blessing."

Gale's throat felt thick, her heart heavy, but tears didn't come. They would, and soon, but for now she was thankful for the numbness of exhaustion.

"And the others? The Luminary?"

"It's a close thing for most of them, but we've got more than twenty still hanging on at the clinic. The Luminary is at the Hall with her acolytes caring for her. Is that your first stop?"

She nodded. "Do me a favour while I'm there?"

"Anything."

"Tell River I'm back. That the cure is coming, if the Luminary allows it to be used."

Buttercup paled. "It's magic, isn't it?"

"Not exactly." She adjusted the straps of her knapsack, which had begun to dig in terribly. "It's complicated, though. I need a ruling."

Buttercup's lips narrowed as he looked at her injured hand again. "You made it, then. With..."

"Yeah."

She could have tried to justify it, could have said it was a sacrifice she'd made for everyone else. She didn't.

Buttercup's smile was forced. "Well. Let's hope it gets to the clinic soon, and that it works. That's all I care about. My ma's sick. So's little Reed."

Gale squeezed his hand, and he didn't pull away, even knowing what she was. She loved him a little more for that. "Wish me luck."

"God be with you, Gale," he said, and went back to the clinic.

Gale continued on, keeping her injured hand in her pocket. There were few people about, and no one else stopped her or spoke to her.

She climbed the steps to the Hall's twin doors. They'd stood open on the day of her declaration and on most fine days before that for as long as she could remember. Today they were closed. She knocked, and Acolyte Hawthorn opened the door a crack. He looked like he hadn't slept in a week and could barely keep his chin up.

"No audiences," he said, then looked closer to see who it was. He looked Gale over and opened the door wider. "Nightingale? What's happened to you?"

"I have the cure. The Luminary needs to see me."

"Incredible. Give it here, please."

Gale stepped back, gripping the straps of her bag tight. "No. I deliver it, or no one does."

The acolyte frowned.

"Let her in, Hawthorn." The Luminary's voice was weak, but it carried to the door. "I've been waiting for our heroes to return."

Hawthorn opened the door further and stepped aside with a respectful nod, and Gale moved past him into the Great Hall, pulling the jar from her bag as she went.

The Luminary's bed had been moved to the centre of the room, placed beneath the opening in the ceiling so the sun illuminated the space around her. She lay beneath several blankets, frail and thin, and the smell of sickness and gathering death hung in the air despite the open roof and the bunches of flowers that had been set out in vases. The angry, seeping rash had reached her neck and sent its seeking fingers toward her eyes. Her brow was damp with fever sweat, but when Gale stepped closer, she found the older woman's eyes clear and sharp.

She's holding on by sheer will. And by a thread no thicker than a spider's web.

"Closer, child," the Luminary said. Her voice wavered, but was as warm and welcoming as Gale had ever heard it. "Were you successful?"

Gale opened the jar and held it out awkwardly. "I have the cure, Luminary. It works. Hawk was in a terrible state, but it knocked the curse out of him and I think he'll recover fully in time. There's enough for everyone, but we must hurry."

The Luminary lifted a bandaged hand and patted the bed beside her leg. Gale sat, though she feared the sharp and knowing look the Luminary cast over her.

"What has become of you, my child? You're not the girl who left us such a short time ago."

Gale looked deep into her shining eyes. "Who am I now, Luminary?"

The Luminary turned and coughed into her elbow. "A stranger to me. And to your—"

A cry rang out from the platform at the end of the hall, and Gale looked up to find her mother rushing toward her. She stood in time to brace herself for a hug that was nearly a tackle.

"My girl," she murmured, stroking Gale's hair. Gale hugged her back and let herself sink into her mother's embrace—and her approval and her love, for as long as they lasted. Her mother held her at arm's length and looked her over. "What happened? Have you seen your brother?"

"He was fine, last I saw him. He used the cure. He's healed. Where's Father?"

"Helping at the clinic." Her mother hugged her again and released her. "It's a miracle. And you did it without—" She looked down, saw Gale's injury, and stepped back, fingers pressed to her lips, eyes wide.

Gale ignored the stabbing pain in her chest and let her gaze linger on her mother for another moment before she turned back to the Luminary. "Our wells were cursed with blood magic. We won't see any new cases as long as we dig new ones, but only magic could create a cure strong enough to heal the sick. There was no other way." She stopped to clear her throat. "I only did what I had to, Your Brilliance. There's no magic in the salve, but there was in the reactions that created it. It's up to you whether that's enough to satisfy the Teachings. Whether it's God's will that the dying be saved or left to suffer."

The Luminary raised an eyebrow. "Laying it on a little thick there, Nightingale. Fewer dramatics, please. More reason."

Gale sat again, ignoring the tears in her mother's eyes. "If you—"

The doors burst open and Hawk stalked in. He looked only a little better than Gale felt, healed but still weakened and exhausted. Gale wondered how he'd managed to catch up until she heard the whinny of a horse outside the door.

Another theft, she supposed, but he'd call it justified.

"Stop," he said. "Luminary, this woman isn't one of us anymore. She's a witch, corrupted and corrupting. Her cure is—"

"We know," the Luminary said, stern and exasperated. "Sit down. It's rude to interrupt." She looked into the jar, then passed a hand over its contents. "I feel no evil powers here. We have been provided with the means to end a curse. Does the goodness of the cure justify the evil of its creation? Does the evil of the curse cancel out the forbidden origins of this miracle?"

Gale's jaw tightened, but she kept her silence. The questions weren't for her.

"Perhaps." The Luminary looked to Hawk and motioned for him to come closer. He obeyed, though he stood as far from Gale as he could. "She said you were cured by this medicine. Has it harmed you? Did it bring magic into your body?"

"No, Luminary." Hawk held out his once injured arm and rolled up his sleeve. "If I'd found the cure in a shop, I'd never have guessed where it came from."

"But we know," the Luminary said. "Very well. I would not have condoned the means by which it was created, but no one asked me." She didn't look at Gale as she spoke. "We have a cure. It would be wrong to let anyone die when they could be saved."

The Luminary dipped one finger into the jar and touched the ointment to the exposed rash on her throat. She gasped as her back arched, and her acolytes rushed forward. The Luminary held up a hand to stop them even as she bared her teeth, bracing against whatever she felt from the medicine. As they all watched, the dark circles beneath her eyes faded. The red marks on her face and neck retreated. She wiped the sweat from her brow and unwrapped the bandages from her hands, revealing flesh that healed before their eyes.

Gale's mother took another step back. "Gale," she whispered, "what have you done?"

But the Luminary smiled. "I feel the workings of the medicine," she said, "but no magic has entered my body, no dark power has touched my soul." She motioned for Hawthorn to come closer. "Take this to the clinic. Tell River it is God's will that the sick should be cured. It would be a sin to ignore such a miracle as this."

Gale waited for an objection. It was the acolytes' job, after all, to judge and question interpretations of the Teachings. But then, Hawthorn's husband and son had been in the clinic when Gale had left. He hurried out without another word.

Hawk glowered.

"You disagree with my decision?" the Luminary asked.

Hawk bowed slightly. "You know the mind of God better than

I. But tell me, Luminary—if the cure is allowed, what of the witch who created it?"

Gale lifted her chin and refused to look at him.

The Luminary sat up straighter in her bed. Another acolyte, Violet, hurried over to adjust her pillows. "A witch, yes." She looked Hawk over, her gaze sharper than ever, then lifted her gaze to the window in the ceiling. "She broke the rules, didn't she? She was to find the cure without leaving the Path. Yet here we are. Is she a hero again, or a villain like the rest of her kind?"

The question hung in the air.

"How did your quest go, then?" the Luminary asked Hawk.

"As well as it could, Your Brilliance. I located the witch who placed the curse in our wells. He's dead now, but the curse lives on."

"He didn't create it," Gale said softly. "He didn't work blood magic or curses."

"So he had someone else do it for him," the Luminary said. "He had evil intent and brought harm to us through another's power. Hawk, you are absolved of his death."

Gale bit her tongue hard and said nothing.

"As for the witch who stands before me," the Luminary said, and looked to Gale. "You made a great sacrifice to save us all. I do not doubt that you tried to find a way to create a cure without corrupting yourself. The price was high, and you paid it willingly for our sakes. So I'll make you an offer."

Gale's heart leapt. "Yes, Your Brilliance?"

"God's Teachings on magic are strict, but God is forgiving, and so am I. Renounce magic now, and I will do everything in my power to see you cleansed of its stain forever." She smiled. "There is hope for you yet, Nightingale Goodweather. If you truly repent, if you cast magic aside and confess to its evil, if you agree to observation to be sure it never overtakes you again... well, there must be a way to undo the evil you had to perform to create our cure. Return to the Path. Live by its laws and never stray again."

Gale held her breath. She couldn't answer, not with the way her thoughts rolled and crashed like a sea in a hurricane.

When she didn't answer, the Luminary went on. "Consider my offer carefully, my child. If you do not repent, you will be banished. And if you leave us with corruption in your soul, there will be no forgiveness. You will be sent away from this mountain forever and treated as any other witch if you attempt to return. Your name will no longer be spoken in our streets or our homes, and you will be erased from all public memory. The good you have done will be swallowed by the evil. Do you understand?"

Gale squeezed her eyes closed. Hot tears slipped out and burned down her cheeks.

For one sharp, piercing moment she saw the two roads she could take—one with her family and friends, serving the community she'd known and loved for so long. They'd never allow her to practice medicine now, or even grow a garden. But they'd keep her safe. If the Teachings were right about corruption, submission was the only sensible choice. Any sane person would value her eternal soul over anything the world could offer.

But only if she believed herself corrupted.

The other road led into the dark woods, away from the well-lit and well-known path trodden by so many before her. Wild beasts lurked there, and danger around every turn. But in those woods, the winds blew, and she'd be able to spread her wings to see where they carried her. For good or ill, she'd be herself, and she'd be free.

"I understand, Luminary. But I cannot accept." She couldn't bring herself to look at her mother, so she focused on the Luminary's lined and weathered face. "At every step of this journey, I've placed doing good above obeying the law and the Teachings, and I will not pretend I'm wrong to have done it. I've found my calling and learned who I'm meant to be."

The Luminary's lips turned down at the corners, but her eyes remained soft. "The Teachings won't change for you, Nightingale. The path you walk will never be God's will."

"Then so be it."

Her words hung in the air of the hall like the dust motes dancing in the still, sunlit air.

Then her mother sobbed and ran from the room.

Gale turned to Hawk, defiant, ready for him to scream at her again. He didn't. He hung his head and wiped at his eyes but wouldn't look at her.

She'd have preferred a fight. Those had always ended with them making up.

"You may go, Hawk," the Luminary said. "Spread the word and clear the streets, quickly as you can. Nightingale leaves with the knowledge she's done good here and nothing more."

Hawk spun on his heel and walked out without another word. He'd be at their parents' table tonight with Frost and Fox, and they'd begin the job of forgetting her.

The thought of her nephew growing up not knowing he had an aunt who adored him tore at Gale's heart. But she wouldn't let herself break. Not now. Not here.

She cleared her throat again. "May I return to my house to collect my things?"

"No. And you may not stop anywhere else, either." The Luminary spoke with stern conviction, but tears shone in her eyes. "Are there instructions I should pass on to River regarding the medicine?"

"No, Luminary."

After that, there was nothing else to say. Gale turned to leave.

The Luminary leaned out from her bed and caught the sleeve of her jacket. "You'll be forgotten by everyone else, Nightingale, but I'll pray for you."

Gale's spine stiffened as she gently pulled away. "Thank you. I'll pray for you, too."

She left before the Luminary could answer. It was better that way.

~

Gale passed no one as she left town and didn't see anyone peeking between their curtains or watching from the shelter of their porches. The Luminary had spoken, and they obeyed. It wasn't until she was clear of town and headed down the mountain road that she heard footsteps pounding over the packed dirt behind her. She turned, hands held up to defend herself, but it wasn't Hawk.

Buttercup bent double when he reached her, shoulders heaving, and held up a finger for her to wait until he caught his breath. "You're quick."

Gale smiled. He deserved one, no matter how little she felt like she'd ever be truly happy again. "Haven't forgotten me yet, then?"

"Eh? Oh. Was that the sentence?" He shook his head and handed over a large package wrapped in white cloth. "We hadn't heard that part at the clinic yet. Guess they'll just have to forgive me."

Gale unwrapped it and found fresh bandages, healing ointment, a loaf of fresh bread, and one of the old notebooks she'd left at the clinic while searching for a cure.

Don't cry. Not for gratitude, not for regret.

"River didn't have time to dash off a note," Buttercup said. "Took him too long to find your book. And he wanted to come to you, but—"

"But he has patients to tend to. I understand."

"Anyway, he said he always knew you were a true hero." Buttercup held out his right hand. "I'm sure he won't forget you, no matter what the Luminary says. And neither will I."

Gale shook his hand, then pulled him close. Buttercup

enfolded her in his arms. He smelled of medicine and herbs. Of the clinic, her second home.

"You're really a witch, then?" he asked after he pulled away.

"I really am. Not the scary kind, I promise."

"I believe that." He stepped back and rested his hand on her shoulder. "Take care of yourself, Gale. I hope the world outside is kind to you."

She forced herself to smile again. "I'm not sure it knows how to be kind. Not like Bright Hollow, anyway. But I'll become what I need to be to survive in it."

"Good enough." He turned on his heel and ran back through town.

Gale stuffed the package into her bag and walked away from Bright Hollow, her heart heavy but her footsteps lightened by River and Buttercup's kindness.

She let her tears flow now that there was no one to see them and mistake her grief for regret.

"It'll be all right," she told herself, though now that she was on her own with no home, no money, and no family, it felt like maybe it wouldn't be. She kicked a stone that skittered into the alder bushes at the side of the road. "Maybe this is the first step toward change in Bright Hollow, after all."

"Pssht, ridiculous," scoffed a voice at her shoulder.

Gale spun to find Madrigal beside her.

"You're back!"

"And you're not a complete fool!" Madrigal flashed a wicked smile. "Don't look so shocked. I had to see how things came out."

Gale grinned. Her wounds weren't healed and her hurts weren't anywhere near forgotten, but suddenly it felt like maybe she could face what lay ahead. "Does this mean your work with me isn't done?"

Madrigal laughed. "Hardly. Look at you—more power than you know what to do with and zero skill to back it up. Left to your own devices, you'll probably blow up a city. No, someone needs to keep an eye on you and teach you everything you missed out on all these years. A proper apprenticeship this time, starting from the beginning."

Gale laughed. It felt strange when her heart still ached, but good. "You could pass me along to some living witch who would take me on."

Madrigal turned her nose up. "I wouldn't wish an apprentice like you on my worst enemy," she said, but couldn't hold back a grin.

They went on in companionable silence, walking side by side down the road.

"Where to now?" Madrigal asked once they reached a crossroads.

Gale looked at the faded road signs. "Only place I know to go. I owe someone a favour."

Madrigal sighed. "You don't have to, promises or not. They'll be bad influences on you."

"You don't have to come," Gale said.

She turned left, toward Queen's Run. And soon enough, Madrigal followed.

CHAPTER THIRTY-SEVEN

Four Days Later

Gale followed Jes cautiously up the staircase at the side of an old brick building in an unfamiliar part of Queen's Run. The smell of fresh bread rose from the bakery on the first floor, warming the cold afternoon air.

Not the worst omen when one was introduced to a new home, if a person believed in that sort of thing.

She glanced down as they reached the tiny balcony on the third floor and waited for Jes to unlock the door. Madrigal drifted behind, followed by Cas.

Gale had been glad to see him at the shop. He'd refused to answer questions about how he'd talked his way out of the king's study, and she'd returned the favour by offering only vague answers about what had happened with the mages.

He'd seemed to find that amusing.

Jes had to give the door a shove with one shoulder to loosen the catch before it popped open. She stood aside and let Gale enter the flat ahead of her.

"What do you think?" Jes asked.

Gale took in the long, unfurnished room with its peeling striped wallpaper and cold, dark fireplace, trying to imagine it as home. Jes had agreed to show her the flat when she'd explained her situation, but hadn't yet brought up the favour Gale owed her.

The longer she went without mentioning it, the more nervous Gale became.

"It's nice," she said.

"It's a third-floor shithouse," Madrigal muttered. "Where are you to plant a garden? Or keep my books?"

Gale crossed the room to one of the twin windows that flanked the fireplace. "These face south?"

Jes nodded toward an open doorway at the end of the room. "So does the one in the kitchen. They overlook the yard, which is where you'll find your shared plumbing facilities."

"It's nothing fancy," Cas added, "but it's a place to start."

Gale entered the kitchen, which had a clean water basin and a little iron stove next to a few built-in cabinets. She chewed her lip as she thought it over. "Not much counter space, but if I brought in a table, some pots and soil... might be something. Maybe a rooftop garden, if the landlord doesn't mind." She turned back to find Jes leaning with one shoulder against the doorframe. She was dressed in a cloud-grey suit, trousers and all, but cut to fit her feminine form. The effect had left Gale breathless when they'd met at the shop, but only until she remembered the cunning behind those strange, beautiful eyes and how dangerous it would be to let a woman like Jes lead her astray.

Besides, she was taken. God help Cas.

"You'll make it into something, I'm sure," Jes said. "I've got more furniture in the back of the shop and a lead on a promising estate sale later this week, if you'd like to come. I'll lend you what I can spare."

"I'm a little short on cash," Gale said.

"A little short on a lot of things." Jes's gaze dropped to Gale's hand, which had healed further with the help of River's medicine. Madrigal had insisted that Gale could make something better from roadside herbs and magic, but it had felt wrong not to use a gift given from love.

She supposed that meant she still had a bit of hardening up to do, but didn't regret it in the slightest.

Gale leaned back against the postage stamp-sized bit of countertop and crossed her arms. "What's the deal this time, then?"

Jes pouted, just a little, but her eyes danced. "You wound me with your implied accusations, young witch."

"Here we go," Madrigal sighed.

"We made a deal," Jes said. "Or rather, you and Cas did, which works out to the same. To repay his kindness I ask that you come work for me. I need someone who can do what you do. I don't have many enchanted objects coming through to be appraised, but you can make them for me to sell in the shop."

"That's illegal."

Jes bit her lower lip, clearly amused. "You don't say? I suppose enchanting things could get you into a lot of trouble if you sold them yourself, but there's no law to say I can't sell them if I can come up with a plausible source. I'll cover your tracks."

Gale thought it over. Jes was asking for a lot of trust. But then, she'd protected Alec. There was no reason she wouldn't do the same for Gale, as long as she offered as much value as he had.

She stepped into the big, empty room and ran a finger over the narrow mantel above the fireplace, drawing loops and swirls in the dust. "I can't do enchantments yet."

"I assumed not." Jes tilted her head to one side. "Until you are able to... how are you at fortune telling?"

"By every god," Madrigal groaned.

Gale felt the same. "Not the line of magic I plan on studying."

Jes chuckled. "Fortune telling isn't about magic. It's about reading people more than it is tea leaves or crystal balls. I've been looking to expand into it as a business, and you can learn. There's good money in it if you're convincing and target the right clients."

Madrigal huffed and floated to the window.

"And I'll be paid for this? Or is it strictly room and board?"

Jes frowned. "I'm not a monster. This will be a partnership, not indentured servitude. The better your work, the better your pay. You could do very well working for me. In fact—here." She drew Gale's mother's ring from the pocket of her waistcoat and held it out to her. "I only wanted this as insurance, in case you didn't come back. You can work it off now."

Gale reached for the ring, paused, and folded her hands behind her back to keep them from reaching again. "Not yet, thank you. If you'd be so kind as to hold on to it, I'll buy it back when I have the funds. Someone once told me not to owe too many favours, and I'd like it if we stayed even on the whole getting-me-to-Embercliffe business."

She glanced at Cas, and he winked back at her.

Jes's eyes shone as she tucked the ring back into her pocket. "She can be taught," she marvelled. "This bodes well." Her boots clicked over the wooden floorboards as she crossed to the door, which Cas held open. Someone in the apartment below thumped on their ceiling, and Jes stomped back, then turned to Gale. "We'll get you some rugs, too. So, do we have a deal? I'll set you up here, rent-free as long as you're working for me and only me. I'll cover the cost out of what you bring in and pay you from what's left. Once you've paid back the expenses from your trip, of course."

"And after her own generous cut," Madrigal said, drifting around Jes. "I don't like her."

Jes caught Gale looking over her shoulder. "What does your spirit friend think? As if I couldn't guess."

"She doesn't like you."

Jes laughed. "Then she's got good sense. I'm more interested in what you think, anyway."

Gale looked around the flat again. "Let's see how things go until my debt is paid—say, three months for Cas getting me into the palace?"

Jes pursed her lips. Gale couldn't tell whether she was holding back a smile. "He took a huge risk for you. Besides, it'll take me three months just to get you in shape for fortune-telling. And far longer before you're enchanting anything worth selling."

Gale looked to Madrigal, and the ghost nodded. "We're not skipping steps anymore. Back to basics until we make you into a proper witch. Language, theory, simple spells."

Gale sighed. "Six months, then."

Jes nodded and gave Gale a critical once-over, sweeping from head to toe. "That'll do for a start. I'll consider keeping you on after that if you're any good."

Gale's jaw dropped. "I'm the one who might want to leave. You—"

But Jes was already heading out the door. "Come to the shop later this afternoon," she called back. "We'll see about getting you a bed and whatever else you need."

Cas nodded a goodbye and closed the door behind them, leaving Gale and Madrigal alone.

Gale sat in the middle of the floor and let herself imagine. It wasn't a cabin in the woods, but maybe it was time for a new dream—some carpets, fresh wallpaper, herbs simmering on the stove, candles on the window ledges, and shelves for Madrigal's books... a desk for note-taking and enchanting...a bed in the corner with plenty of quilts to burrow under with a hot cup of tea and a fire blazing in the hearth...

She smiled. Madrigal drifted down and sat beside her.

"Not where you expected to end up, is it?" she asked.

"Not at all," Gale said. She flexed her right hand—she could still feel her finger above the aching stump, as though its spirit was waiting to work magic. "It's more frightening. More exciting, too, though."

"Good," Madrigal said. "On your feet, now. You've got plenty of work to do."

Gale grinned. "I'm ready."

~The End~

AUTHOR'S NOTE

Thank you for joining me on another adventure! I hope you had as much fun as I did catching up with old friends and meeting new ones. I can't wait to show you what's next. Murder, magic, missing memories… it's going to be fun.

If you'd like to stay updated on new releases (and receive some free bonus content), visit katesparkes.com to sign up for my newsletter.

Oh, and maybe bring a flashlight along for the next book. Things might get a bit dark as we go along.

-Kate

ACKNOWLEDGMENTS

I write alone, but it takes a lot of people to help me turn a first draft into a finished book. My thanks go out to all of these people, each of whom made Curses and Crimes a better story than it would have been without them.

Thank you to Krista Walsh, Laura Fischer, Mike Lowden, Kathy Dunlavey, Trisha Poole, and Margie Scheiner (in no particular order) for the time you spent reading my drafts and the notes you offered along the way; to my editor Joshua Essoe for once again helping me make my story the best it could be; to Stefanie Saw for giving this book its beautiful cover; and to Krista Walsh AGAIN for proofreading and for talking me down every time I wanted to quit. I couldn't do this without all of you.

To my family and friends: Thank you for being there, and for making my life outside of these pages worth coming back to when the story is over.

ABOUT THE AUTHOR

Kate Sparkes lives in Newfoundland and escapes from the "real" world through reading, playing video games, and occasionally writing books. She's the author of the Bound Trilogy and the All the Queen's Knaves series (which she promises she'll finish as soon as possible). She also writes urban fantasy set in Canada under the name Tanith Frost.

www.katesparkes.com

The Bound Trilogy

Bound

Torn

Sworn

All the Queen's Knaves

Vines and Vices

Curses and Crimes

Scars and Seams (coming soon)

visit katesparkes.com for links